— tim wickenden

that *girl* in the boxcar

— BOOK 1 OF THE REISEN SERIES —

An American Historical Family Saga

SLUGADO PRESS

A CYMRU INDEPENDENT PUBLISHER

Published by Slugado Press
Fishguard, Wales

❊❊❊

AMAZON Paperback edition © 2024
ISBN: 978-1-9161048-6-0

❊❊❊

❊❊❊

For more information about
Tim Wickenden visit:
www.timwickenden.com

❊❊❊

Cover & book designed by
The Naked Designer
Images & custom fonts licensed from:
Envato Elements
Text: Garamond

❊❊❊

Slugado Press
is a Cymru Independent Publisher.

Tim Wickenden

In memory of
Mum and Dad
You did your best...

Also by
Tim Wickenden

Max Becker, German Historical Crime Thrillers:
Angel Avenger
Take Back

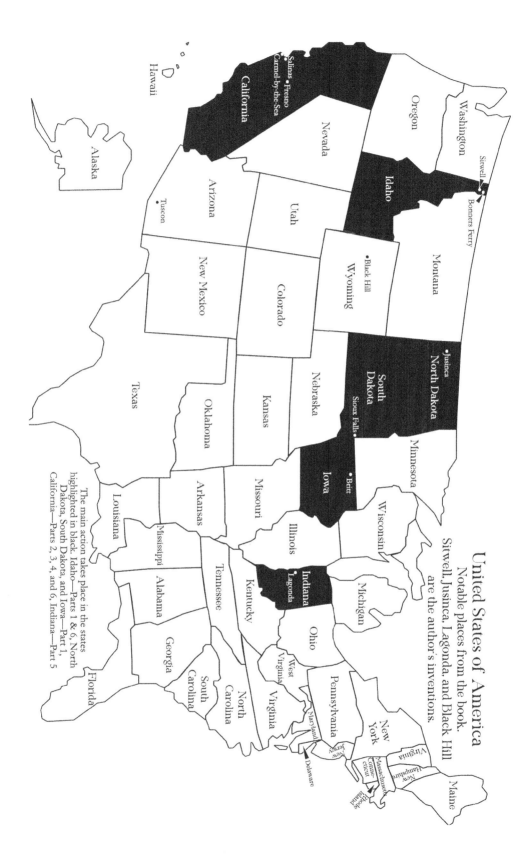

United States of America

Notable places from the book.
Sitwell, Jusinca, Lagonda, and Black Hill are the author's inventions.

The main action takes place in the states highlighted in black. Idaho—Parts 1 & 6, North Dakota, South Dakota, and Iowa—Part 1, California—Parts 2, 3, 4, and 6, Indiana—Part 5

"There is no happiness like that of being loved by your fellow creatures, and feeling that your presence is an addition to their comfort."

Charlotte Brontë

part one

— Bo Scribbler —

August 1925—Boundary County, Idaho

Some miles east of Bonners Ferry on the bank of the Kootenay river, the locos of the Big-G slow right up and make a sharp tack south, making it a fine place to catch out. I hung around lolling in the sun, and it wasn't long before that distinctive homely sound of puffing steam and clanking of hard-metal-running-smooth announced the approach of my accommodation. The long line of rust-red boxcars came creaking and groaning past about a healthy man's walking pace, and some three cars from the back was an empty, the door ajar, like an open invitation. I took pace with the iron beast, threw in my bindle and caught it on the run.

Inside it was dry with a warmth from the sun-kissed timbers. Settling back, I took out my makins and rolled a cigarette. I struck a match on the rough floor. It flared good, and that was when I observed her all hunkered down in the far corner. For a moment, I held out the lighted match to get a better look. She didn't move. Anxious blue eyes flickered in the dancing flame. I touched the match to my smoke, inhaled deep, and with a deft flick of my thumb extinguished the flame. I let my eyes find their way in the dim cabin and as they got good and accustomed, I could see well enough to make something of her. She had long, bright golden hair that looked like it needed some tending. Her grime-streaked face made her white teeth and those oh-so blue eyes stand out. I can't say as I have much experience with young people, so I found it hard to place an age on her.

I blew out a stream of fragrant smoke. 'Hey you.'

She gave me a slight nod. 'Hey,' she came back, her light, girlie voice floating above the rhythmic tack of the bogeys.

She fixed me with haunted, hungry eyes.

'Got yourself food, girlie?'

She shook her head. The tip of her tongue licked her dry lips. I reached into my bag, pulled out a wax wrap and laying it down, portioned out some rations, made up a lump, and lobbed it over. She caught it and set to devouring the simple offering. I watched and smoked. I've been that hungry plenty of times. When she was done, she looked up and wiped her mouth with the back of her hand. I held out a water bottle. She stood and approached me like a starved feral cat sure of a trap. Her eyes locked on mine. She hesitated.

'Take it. I don't bite.'

She took it a full arm's length. There wasn't a load of her, maybe a touch over five feet high and some ninety pounds. She gulped near half of it, tapped down the stopper, and offered it back.

I smiled. 'I got another; you keep it.'

She tucked it in her bindle. 'Thanks, Mister.'

'Got a name, girlie?'

She pursed her lips and looked up for a moment. 'I'm Heidi.'

'They call me Bo Scribbler.'

She tilted her head to one side, frowning a little. 'That's kinda odd for a name, Bo Scribbler. Is it like a nickname?'

'Everyone like me goes by a moniker. See, I've always liked to write stuff down: stories and poems, I guess, of a sort. I enjoy reading books too when I can get 'em. One day a long, long time ago someone called me Bo Scribbler, and it stuck.'

Her blue eyes sparkled, and she leaned forward. 'We did poems in school. I love poems.'

'Likewise.' I tapped my head. 'Got any stashed away?'

She didn't have to think much. Poems can be like that; they never leave you. 'I remember this from one I liked…' she paused. 'It goes:

> *Faster than fairies, faster than witches,*
> *Bridges and houses, hedges and ditches;*
> *And charging along like troops in a battle,*
> *All through the meadows the horses and cattle:*
> *All of the sights of the hill and the plain*
> *Fly as thick as driving rain;*

And ever again, in the wink of an eye,
Painted stations whistle by...'

She looked at me. A flush of red had colored her pale, dirt-streaked cheeks.

'I like that, real easy to picture and the words seem apt, don't they? You know who wrote it?'

She shook her head.

'Never mind, no matter. Give it me again.'

She cleared her throat like she was making a performance of it and this time she made more of it, letting the rhythm of the carriage set her tempo. I closed my eyes and let the words work my mind.

'You liked it?'

'Sure I did. You said it well, gave it justice. You like reading?'

Her eyes lit up and for the first time she grinned, showing a row of straight, white teeth. 'Yeah. We only had the bible at home, but there were story books at school, all of which I've read over several times. Miss Hannah, our teacher, read to us and sometimes she loaned me books.' She bit her lower lip, thinking. 'Can you read me something you've written?'

'Sure. That seems fair.'

I thumbed through my notebook. She had drawn up her knees, her attention focused with eyes wide.

'Okay,' I said, 'this is a poem called Hallelujah! I'm a Hobo.' I stretched out my legs, leaned back against the warm wall of the car, and began.

Not a tramp, nor a bum!
As a hobo, I roam.
My roving days unfettered,
With bindle full
And pockets light as air.
Nights below a cloak of stars,
The ground beneath my back.
My humble needs are few:
Honest toil for modest fare,
Some makins in my pouch.
A plate of hundred up,
A pile driver,
Dry shroud,

And a little oil of joy.
My dream's a hobo special,
Or a swift double-ender,
When not riding drag,
I travel by hand
Or padding-the-hoof.
And when my candle dims,
An honest life well-lived,
I'll board the spectral westbound,
To my final hobo stop
And lay me down in a patch of dirt,
In an orchard made of bones.'

I finished. Neither of us spoke. I rolled another smoke and let her mull over the words. I could see her cogitating, giving it due consideration. The kid was smart. 'You like it?'

She nodded. 'Yeah, even if it doesn't rhyme good, I like the sound of it. The words do run along nice, like you could set them to a tune, maybe. I don't know what it all means, though.'

'There's a good deal of hobo-speak in it.'

'I get it an all, just not the exact words.'

I dragged on my smoke, chuckling. 'Them words will come to you, maybe.'

'I like the orchard of bones. I get that. Is the Westbound when you die?'

'See, you catch on quick.'

For a moment, she stared at me with still eyes. Then she gave a slight nod, stood, came over and sat herself next to me. 'So, at the start, you said you were a hobo, not a tramp or a bum, right?'

'Sure, that's right.'

'So, what's the difference?'

'Well, you don't want to call a bona fide hobo, a bum, or a tramp. See us boes we travel and live by our wits, but we do so for work, what you call an itinerant worker. Many of us are skilled. Now tramps do travel but they don't work, and bums—well—they don't do neither.'

'Is writing your skill?'

'No, it's more of a diversion. I work wood pretty good but I can lend my hand to most toils. Done pretty much anything over the years, long as it's honest and pays.'

She nodded her face serious. 'Have you a piece of paper and a pencil?'

I tore out a leaf and handed her what she wanted, and she asked me to dictate my words. She had neat copperplate writing. She added the title, underlining it, and then the wrote words "by Bo Scribbler", and held it out, admiring her work. She looked at me and beamed. 'Looks good written, doesn't it?'

'That it does. Makes it real.'

She folded the paper, tucked it into the breast pocket on her dungarees and patted the place with her dirty hand twice. It seemed like an intimate act. I noticed scarring on the back of her hand, like those made by a switch, and it got me to thinking and made me sad for her.

Letting the literary moment dilute, we sat quiet for a bit. Anyone who has spent time with hoboes knows that poetry and stories are right popular. Most boes can recite memorized verses, hell I've known some to go on for fifteen, twenty minutes at a go. So Heidi getting right in with her recitation and showing an interest in hearing mine made me warm to her. I liked her. She had that honest straightness of the young, which was refreshing, but it made her vulnerable.

Heidi and I sat side-by-side as the loco of the Big-G took us blindly on our way and I realized most profoundly the strangeness of our meeting. I can't deny I had questions and, oddly, meeting her had nudged opened a faded door to my past. One long ago sealed shut. It sent a chill through me and it surprised me, almost like I knew her. I noticed she was gazing at me, those piercing blue eyes boring deep.

I smiled. 'So, what's Heidi's plan?'

She frowned. 'What do you mean?'

'Well, you got on this empty for a reason, didn't ya?'

'I walked into the yard at Bonners Ferry before the loco was pulling out and I see the door ajar. I was sick of walking, so I jumped on. I don't know where it's going and I guess I don't much care neither. I thought something might happen.' She looked at me with dancing eyes and lowered her voice. 'And I was right. It did, didn't it?'

I nodded. 'Can't fault the reasoning behind all that.'

She looked down at the floor, tracing her finger in the dust. 'I said a prayer, and you turned up.'

'You did, did ya? Well, that's real interesting, but I guess it was just chance, you think?'

She shrugged again and carried on drawing in the dust. 'I guess.' She looked at me. 'I don't have plans. I was going to ride this car until it stops and then—' she paused her doodling and looked up, frowning. 'Something will happen, I guess.'

I met her gaze. 'What if that something isn't good?'

She did not answer, just stared at me blinking and I realized that maybe fate had given me something I was unaccustomed to, a responsibility. An eerie, restless feeling sank through me. 'You want to hear my plan?'

She nodded.

'Well, every year there's this festival in a small, bo friendly town in Iowa, called Britt. It has been going on most years since the turn of the century and I go there to catch up with friends and hear the news. It's a big gathering, with a parade, and communal chow. People pay what they can afford. There's lots of talk because talk doesn't cost, but you keep your ears open and your mouth shut; you'll learn more than a lifetime in school. The highlight of the festival is they crown a hobo king and queen, you know, just for the kicks and giggles—'

'How do you become a king or queen?'

'Well, you put yourself up for it. You make a speech giving reasons it should be you. There's a panel of bo judges, and they decide on who it is by how much applause and support each candidate gets. Anyway, point is you should string along with me. It might help you find your feet. I'm meeting up with a road sister I've known a long time, and I think you'll like her.'

She frowned and made a face. 'What's a road sister?'

'It's what we call a lady hobo.'

She nodded, but looked surprised and a little unsure. She pointed at herself. 'So, I can go with you?'

I gave her a playful nudge. 'That's what I said, unless, that is, you have somewhere else to be.'

Her face lit up. 'Holy smoke. Thanks, Scribbler. That sounds like a humdinger of a plan.'

I don't know why but we both laughed out loud. Then she lay her head on my shoulder, and yawned. I could feel a weight raising from her and settling down on me, and it wasn't long before she lay down, her back to me, and shut her eyes. I wondered how long it had been since she had slept well. I placed a blanket over her and rolled up a clean shirt to make a pillow. Gently, I lifted her head and slid it under. For a bit, I watched her sleep and speculated why this smart, interesting girl had run away. I knew we had a fair bit of country to cross and hours to kill before we'd have to jump ship, so it seemed a good time to rest up. I made myself comfortable, laying my head against the car wall, the low vibrations soothing. The car rocked, and I let my head and thoughts sway until I drifted off.

2

— Heidi —

In the eight days since I'd gone on the run I hadn't got far, which wasn't much of a surprise, seeing as I'd never been further from home than my county town and I knew little about living by my wits. I guess I was still in shock, my mind foggy. Truth is, by the time I found the empty boxcar at Bonners Ferry, I was dog-tired, scared, and starving. No one was around, so I scooted inside, relieved to be off my feet and hoping the train would carry me far away. I wanted to close the door but was afraid I'd get locked in and had nothing to make light, and the thought of being alone in the dark gave me the heebie-jeebies. The train didn't move. I wondered whether it was ever going to. I sat there, brooding. Then I heard clanging, voices, and footsteps. I hunkered down in the corner. The sounds of metal rapping on metal drew closer. There was a pause, then came a loud clang on the other side of the boxcar wall behind my ear, making me jump right out of my skin. Two men passed by the open door, but they didn't look in, just breezed on by all casual like, making idle conversation the way working men do when pursuing familiar tasks. They banged on something between the next cars. The voices and clanging faded, and realizing I had been holding my breath, I let out a sigh of relief. I felt a little sick, but also a buzz of excitement. Then the train jolted twice. I could hear the distant puffing of an engine and, with lots of clanking and groaning, the car moved off. I looked to see if there was anything I could eat or use, but it was plumb empty, just dust and darkness. I tried to sleep, but hunger gnawed at me. I worried about Jeremiah and what I had left for him. A big part of me wanted to go back, but fear gave me pause.

I was at that end of the road when all I had was prayer. I closed my eyes and gave up one of those childish, desperate appeals to God, you know the type: 'Please God, help me and I won't ever ask for nothing again and will worship you forever, Amen.' I opened my eyes, muttering, 'Please, please, please.' Nothing! So, it was true; God hates sinners.

I had not discerned the train slowing up and I could feel it leaning, going round a sharp bend. Then this bag flies in through the door, followed by this figure. He whipped on in the car like a cat leaping on a fence. I was in the corner and knew he hadn't seen me. I scrunched down, my eyes following his every move. He settled himself down about halfway along the wall opposite. He took from his bag an old leather pouch and made a cigarette. He struck a match, and I saw him glance over. He had a tanned face topped by a floppy kinda felt hat. He had a stubbly face, the color of which reminded me of a mess of salt and pepper, and his hands were big and strong looking. As he held out the match, I could see his look was soft, his dark eyes twinkling in the flame. I can't explain why, but I knew he wouldn't be trouble.

I had never met a man like him before. He was interesting, gentle, and I enjoyed talking about poems with him. I'd never met a writer, either, with a notebook stuffed full of script in elegant handwriting. Then he offered to take me with him to this place I'd never heard of where we'd meet a lady friend of his. A festival for people like him with kings and queens, parades, communal food. It sounded magical and intimidating. I wondered why he would take care of me like that. But right now, I was slap-bang out of options, so I felt I had to trust him, like my life depended on it.

I was beat and, having surrendered to my predicament, exhaustion clawed at me. I'm not sure how long I had slept, but when I woke, I had a blanket over me and a rolled-up shirt as a pillow. It smelled clean but had a musky kinda scent. I glanced over and he was leaning against the boxcar wall, snoring quietly. I felt cold, so I wrapped the blanket tighter about myself and shifted a little closer to him. The car rocked, and I thought about home and Jeremiah. I thought maybe I should go back and sort it all out. But now I did not know where I was and I must confess, Scribbler, his road sister, and the festival intrigued me. I had spent my whole life in one place and, apart from between the pages of the books I read, knew nothing about the world. The least I could do was trust him. I figured if he'd wanted to harm me, he'd have done so by now. It was deciding time: stay and have an adventure or go back and—his voice broke my reverie. 'Hey, you okay, Heidi?'

I nodded. 'I little cold, maybe?'

He took off his coat and laid it on me. It was warm and comforting. It smelled of tree resin, tobacco, and that musky odor.

I said, 'Won't you be cold?'

He smiled and shook his head. 'It's not cold. Must be because you're tired and a little undernourished. We'll sort that out.' He lay his warm, rough hand on my forehead and stroked back my hair just like ma used to when I was little.

I closed my eyes. 'That feels nice.'

'Try to get back to sleep. I'll wake you when we must move.'

— § —

He nudged me awake. I guess I had slept a few more hours. 'Hey, it's time. Get your stuff.'

I sat up and rubbed my eyes. I felt stiff as a board. I stood and gathered my bag. He went over to the door and pulled it open. 'Here, come sit next to me. Dangle your feet over the side.'

We sat side-by-side, the warm breeze in our contented faces.

'Are we nearing a station?'

'Nope. We're going to jump.'

I looked at him with saucer eyes. 'We're going to jump?'

'Don't worry, not until the train slows.'

He gave me instructions. My heart was in my mouth, but I was excited: the adventure had begun.

The scenery flowed by.

'Are we still in Idaho?'

'Idaho? No, that's way behind us. We've traveled east across northern Montana. We've just entered North Dakota. We need to get off this eastbound and head south, see?'

I realized I must have slept for hours. Home felt a long ways off. The train slowed, and he told me to stand up.

'Watch what I do and then do the same, okay?'

I nodded and prayed I'd not make an ass of myself. He got on the step, holding the handrail, lobbed his bag and stepped off, facing the direction of travel. As he hit the ground, he kept on running to take the last bit of speed off. I followed suit, concentrating hard. I hesitated just a moment.

Holy smoke, we're jumping from a moving train. Come on, Heidi, you can do it, you can do it!

I made the leap of faith and when I hit the ground, ran for all I was worth and just kept from going over. It was exhilarating! By the time I had stopped, the end carriages had passed, disappearing around the sharp bend. I went and stood on the rail watching as it rumbled off and I yelled, 'Holy smoke, Scribbler, I've never jumped from a moving train!'

He came and stood by me. 'You did that like a pro. We'll make a hobo of you yet.' He handed me my bag. 'Come on. It's thisaway.'

We fell into step and followed the rail. He said, 'We call this padding-the-hoof.'

'Like in your poem.'

'That's it.'

'Where are we going?'

'A town call Jusinca. Near there is the line that heads southeast. We can get you a hot meal, a bath, and some fresh clothes. Tomorrow we'll find a ride.'

'A proper bath?'

'What other kinda bath is there?'

'What, with hot water in a tub?'

'You've never had a proper bath?'

'Uh-uh. Back home it was in the creek or standing up by the range using pots.'

He chuckled. 'You're in for a treat, girlie.'

When we got to Jusinca, no one paid us much heed. We headed for this fancy looking hotel. 'Don't get used to this but seeing as you've been a while on your own sleeping rough, I'll treat us to a night in this fine hotel. Reckon a night in a feather bed will do you good.'

I'd never slept in a hotel before or ever been in a hotel. The woman at the reception desk thought I was Scribbler's daughter; we didn't feel the need to correct her. It made me smile. I could do a lot worse than having someone like Scribbler as my pa.

The room contained a gigantic bed, an easy chair, a dresser, and two windows that looked out onto the street. Scribbler said, 'Let's go check out the bathroom.'

It was down the hall. The room was tiled-white and clean, with a bathtub big enough for two. He turned on the faucet and hot water streamed out. 'You sort yourself out, take your time and enjoy it. While you're doing that, I'll go get some clean clothes for you.' He went to the door and turned. 'Lock this behind me.'

I had been eight days in the same clothes so I didn't need asking twice to peel them off and jump in that heavenly hot water. I stepped in and wiggled my tingling toes, then gently lowered my aching body into its warm embrace. It was more than a treat; it was a revelation. I lay back, closed my eyes, and sank my head underwater, and held there for a few seconds, then opened my eyes. The tension and tiredness slipped away. I lay there for ages. Then, as the water cooled, I scrubbed and soaped days of grime off me. I got out and dried myself. I didn't want to get back into my dirty clothes, so I wrapped the towel about me, scooped them up, and made a run for the room. When I got there, Scribbler had left fresh clothes for me. Nothing fancy, dungarees, a shirt, underwear, fresh socks and a light coat. It was good to be clean and re-clothed. I teased my hair into some kinda order and stood before the mirror. A strange, gaunt, haunted girl looked back at me. She had dark circles under her eyes.

Holy smoke, Heidi, you look terrible. You gotta take better care of yourself.

I looked at her for a while, then took a deep breath and turned away.

Reckoning Scribbler had wanted to give me some privacy, I went on downstairs to look for him. He was sitting out front, enjoying a smoke. The sun was slipping away, casting long shadows along the street. He glanced at me and stood up. 'Why, there you are, shiny like a new pin. How was your bath?'

'The bees! I'm a convert. Though—' I giggled. 'Now the tub looks like I did before I got in. I tried to clean it.'

He laughed out loud. 'Don't you worry about that. Look, I need to take a bath, so take this and go across to that store and get yourself a soda. I'll meet you down here soon. We'll go eat then, okay?'

I nodded. He turned to go. I said, 'Scribbler?' He looked back at me, a glow from his hazel eyes. 'Thanks for helping me.'

He smiled, tipped his hat, and disappeared inside.

I went got myself a lemonade and came back, sat and watched the people of this quiet, tidy town go about their business. A fine-looking lady towing a young boy in hand passed by. The boy stared at me through big chocolate, brown eyes. He reminded me of Jeremiah the first time I met him. It made me feel a little homesick.

Jusinca was bigger than my hometown and had a load more stores. Back home, we only had the main general store, which was run by Mr. Garity. His daughter, Abigail, was a friend. He was a kind man. When things got real bad and I didn't have money for food, he'd sort me out. In return, I'd help in the store; he said I didn't have to, but I wanted to earn it. Abigail had everything I didn't, but it hadn't spoiled her. She was tall for her age, had gorgeous copper hair that made her delicate almond skin look like cream. When she smiled, which she did often, these cute dimples appeared on her cheeks, and her white teeth shone from under her full, red lips. I always felt kinda plain when I was next to her.

Lost in my thoughts, I did not hear him. He sat down next to me. He scrubbed up good, his face clean shaved. 'I bet you're starving. Let's go get some dinner, shall we?'

— Bo Scribbler —

We headed down the main drag, found a steak house, chose a table, and sat. She looked about her with those captivating blue eyes. 'Mmm, smells great. I've never been to a steakhouse before. I could eat a horse.'

I laughed. 'Likewise. Though, I don't think they serve horse you'll have to make do with beef.'

She giggled, her eyes dancing.

She wasn't kidding about being hungry. She could tuck it away. After she shoveled the last potato in, she sat back, wiped her mouth with the back of her hand, and took a deep breath.

I leaned forward and whispered, 'Got room for a slice of pie?'

She grinned. 'You betcha!'

It was good pie.

We paid and sauntered back to the hotel. I asked, 'You want to walk a bit or go straight to bed?'

'Let's walk, shall we?'

We headed past the hotel, ambling and taking our time. She had an inquisitive nature and stopped to look in at all the stores. A little further down, we came to a picture house.

'Holy smoke, Scribbler, they got a picture house! I've never seen a movie.'

It was closed. The notice on the front display said there was a Jackie Coogan double bill showing of "The Kid" and "Rag Man" the following day. 'Rhatz!' She said. 'It's closed and we're off tomorrow. Have they got a picture house in Britt?'

'I think they do.'

'Well, maybe I'll go there, you think?'

I nodded. 'Sure.'

In the town center, there was a square with an old tree and some benches below. We sat down and I made a cigarette. We looked at one another and she half-smiled, a faraway look in her dreamy eyes.

I lit up. 'I'm going to say this not to ride your horse, but just so you know, okay?'

'Say what?'

'If you want to go back home and you need someone to come with you and maybe help sort out the reason you left, then I can do that for you. Be happy to.'

'That's nice of you, Scribbler. I'll think about it, but right now it isn't safe.'

Her reply sent a tremor through me from almost fifty years back when I had left home.

It isn't safe. Is it safe now?

'What's her name? Your road sister that we're meeting in Britt.'

'Corbeau.'

'Her moniker, right?'

I nodded.

'How long you known her?'

'Well now, it must be nearly twenty years.'

'Is she your girlfriend or just a friend?'

It was a good question. 'It's complicated, but I'd say we're not quite one and more than the other.'

'How often do you see one another?'

'It varies. We spend a few weeks every so often. In between work or traveling.'

'Do you love her?'

The question surprised me. 'Yeah, sure, of course I do, just there are different kinds of love.' I was keen to change the subject. 'What about you, Heidi? Is there a special person?'

She nodded, her eyes flickering. 'Jeremiah Bell. We've been friends for ten years. I think I'd call him my boyfriend. I know I love him more than anyone else.'

'More than your ma?'

She looked down. 'She died when I was four.'

'Sorry. That must have been hard for ya.'

She shrugged.

An awkward silence hung between us. Eventually she said, 'I think I'm ready for that nice bed.'

When we got back to the room, I said, 'I'll be fine on the floor.'

She made a face, looking at me like a mother does an errant child. 'It's an enormous bed, Scribbler, there's room for us both. I don't mind if you don't.'

'You sure?'

'Besides, it'll make me feel safe knowing you're there.'

It was a comfortable bed. She hunkered down, said goodnight, turned on her side, and was asleep in no time. I turned over, closed my eyes, and tried to clear my mind from the maelstrom of memories and conflict. I wondered whether all my years roaming had been leading to this point, like a test. I failed the first, so maybe this was my second chance.

I must have drifted off because the next thing I heard was her shouting, sat up clawing at the air. 'He's dead—he's dead—'

'Hey, Heidi. Heidi!'

She looked at me with terror in her pupil-wide eyes. She was crying and breathing hard, like she'd been running. I said, 'It's okay, everything is okay. It's just a dream, is all.' She calmed herself. I wanted to hold her but was afraid to. I stroked her back. 'It's just a dream, is all.'

She wiped her eyes and looked at me, blinking. 'Sorry.'

She lay back down. I did too. I said, 'It's okay. We all get dreams like that sometime. You want to tell me about it?'

She shook her head. 'I'm okay.' She shuffled across and rested her head on my shoulder. Tentatively, I put my arm around her. She said, 'Thanks. I need to be held. It's been so long. Is that alright?'

'Of course. Try to get back to sleep.'

'Thanks, Scribbler.'

— § —

Light spilling around the drapes woke me. It was unlike me to sleep so late. She was curled up close to me. I slipped out of bed and went on down to the bathroom. When I came back, she was awake. She looked relieved. 'I thought you'd gone. I was worried.'

'Darn it—sorry.' I sat on the bed. 'Listen. I promise I won't go off and leave you. I'm not that kinda person. Trust me, okay?'

Her darting eyes fixed on mine, like she was reading my mind. I said, 'I don't know about you, but I'm ready for some breakfast. Get yourself fixed up and I'll meet you in the diner across the street.'

When she entered the dining room, several men looked at her in that way some men do. She had an innocent quality. It wasn't just her pretty golden hair and those eyes; she had an energy about her. It worried me because she'd always get noticed and be a magnet for depraved men. I'd have to rise to the challenge of protecting her and appraising her to the realities of the world. But I wondered, too, about what had happened to her. Maybe she knew too much already.

Whatever it was, it didn't affect her appetite. Between mouthfuls, she asked, 'What time we heading out?'

I sat back. 'Well, I've been thinking about that and seeing as we have time, what do you say to spending another night here? We can go take in that movie.'

She stopped eating, her fork hanging in the air, and beamed. 'Really?'

I smiled back. 'Sure. Life isn't all a drudge. Let's have some fun. After breakfast, we can go take a walk. The Missouri is just a mile or so south of here. I'll bet it's the biggest river you've ever seen.'

'Can you swim in it?'

'Don't see why not.'

'It would be nice to have some fun. I don't want to change your plans, though.'

'Well, that's the thing about being a hobo. I choose what I do, where I go, and when.'

We made provision for a picnic lunch and headed out to the river. We stood on the bank. She spread out her arms shouting, 'Holy smoke, it's monstrous!'

'It sure is something, isn't it? It broadens out here and if you follow it thataways, it'll take you all the way to St. Louis, where it joins the Mississippi.'

She looked at me knowingly. 'Oh, we learned about the Mississippi in school, and Miss Hannah read "Tom Sawyer" to us.'

'A fine story. Have you read "Huckleberry Finn"?'

'Uh-uh, is that good?'

'I reckon maybe even better. Opens your eyes to stuff. Maybe we can find you a copy.' We stood a while regarding the great dark river rolling by like time itself. 'I hear this is the longest river in the country.'

She grinned. 'I love this stuff. We got to swim in it, so I can say I've done it.'

'Not here, though. If we walk down a way, there's an inlet where once I camped.'

A forty-minute walk found the spot, and a perfect place to take a well-earned dip. It was hot. She dumped her bag, took off her boots and socks and went down to test the water. 'Looks great. Warmer than the Big Creek back home, a little anyways.'

It surprised me as she stripped off, like the excitement of the moment had made her forget me. She rummaged in her bag. 'Here they are.' She pulled out what looked like boys' long johns and turned to me, holding them up. 'Jeremiah's ma gave them to me. I cut the arms off and the legs above the knee so that they're better for swimming.' And when she turned to pull them on, I saw the marks on her back. It shocked me. I wanted to ask, but she was happy and excited. It wasn't the time. As she buttoned up the front, she turned to me. 'Come on, Scribbler.'

I don't swim often, but I do like it. Her youthful joyousness was infectious and as I stripped off to my underwear, I felt the years slip away. She swam like she was born to it. Powerful strokes took her swiftly out to the middle and she turned and called to me. I walked on in. The cold water was delightful on my hot skin. Once I was hip deep, I dived in and headed toward her. As soon as I got there, she jumped on my shoulders and pushed me under. She was light, so I scooped her up and threw her screaming through the air. A change came over her. She was laughing; her face a mischievous mask. She kept coming back for more and I had fun obliging her. It was, for me, a rare first. I'd never played with a kid like this before, at least not since I was a kid myself.

She was quick and swam round behind me. 'Hey, I'm going to climb up on your shoulders and dive off, hold your hands up so I can support myself.' She climbed like a monkey up a tree, diving off repeatedly. I can't remember the last time I had so much fun, and it was a powerful thing to see her so happy and I knew there was still a child there with a hope of salvation.

Time slipped by, but fatigue and the cold water drove us out. We ate our meal and lay in the sun, and she looked a long way from that girl in the boxcar I had met two days before. I said, 'Sure is a delightful spot. A man could lose himself here.'

'How old are you, Scribbler?'

I chuckled. 'Old.'

She wrinkled her nose. 'You don't look that old, and you're real strong. When I was standing on you, you felt sturdy as a tree. Back home when me and my buds play like that and I try to stand on Jeremiah's shoulders, he wobbles around like a twig in a gale. At least until I got my balance. I reckon you make a much better diving platform.'

'Well, I'm glad to know I'm good for something. Tell me more about your friends.'

'Oh, they're just regular kids from a small town. We go to school together, we lark about and—' She went quiet.

'Don't you miss them?'

She nodded. I didn't want to push things and spoil our day. She turned and propped herself up on her elbow, resting her head on her hand. She squinted in the sun and looked at me for a while. 'How come you know where everything is? Like, where to jump the train, where to walk to, where to camp?'

'I've been doing this for a long time. I come up this way most summers to work timber.' I tapped my head. 'It's all in here. Like migrating animals, they don't need a map, and neither do I. Instinct, see?'

'You been all over the country.'

'No. But I've seen plenty. Plenty good and plenty bad. Nowadays, I stick to what I know is good.'

She lay on her back, put her hands behind her head, and closed her eyes. 'I'm excited to see the movie.'

'Me too. It's been a while. I haven't seen "Rag Man", but you'll love "The Kid". It'll make you laugh, and maybe shed a tear or two.'

— Heidi —

The picture house was like nothing I'd ever dreamed of. Jam packed, we sat in rows facing a big screen and out front was a piano, a woman seated, ready to play. I had not expected the lights to dim. I sat wide-eyed, my insides fluttering. Then the lady began playing, and the screen came to life, text and images dancing before my goggling eyes, transporting me to another world, and I forgot where I was and what had happened. It was kinda like reading, but you used your imagination differently. It amazed me that even though I could not hear their speech, I could tell what was happening and the words they said. The stories were simple but poignant. Scribbler was right. I laughed and cried. Jackie Coogan played the boy in both films and I wondered how you got to be a movie star so young. He was beguiling and nice to look at. He reminded me of Jeremiah, the hair and his cheeky, cheerful face. I don't mind admitting I was a little star struck. The man who played the tramp was hilarious and heroic. He took my breath away. As we went back out to the street, I was in a daze. We walked down the main drag a while.

'Well, how was your first movie experience?'

'I can't really describe it, but it was dumbfounding. I heard you laughing during that fight scene.'

'Worth watching just for that, wasn't it?'

'The boy reminded me a little of Jeremiah. Same hair style and color, and the look. Nice-looking boy, a little young for me, but all the same, he won my heart.'

'We'll have to look out for more of his movies, won't we?'

That night, when we got into that comfy bed, I wanted to be close to him. I laid my head on his shoulder and put my arm across his chest. And like a bear protecting his cub, he put his powerful arm around me, his smell and strength comforting.

'That was a fun day! I needed that. Thanks Scribbler.'

'Yeah, I had fun too. It's been a while. Now, get some sleep. We're up at dawn.'

I kissed his cheek. It took him aback.

It took me a while to slow the tumble of thoughts writhing around my weary mind, and just as I was drifting off, a pall of dread filled me as I remembered why I was here and what had happened. I screwed my eyes shut and tried to push it from my mind. I could hear Scribbler snoring quietly. I wished I were someone else, like maybe his daughter, and we roamed the land together having fun, working and keeping things simple. Maybe that was the answer. He seemed to like me and I felt I could trust him, leastways with looking after me.

I guess I must have dropped off. He woke me as dawn dragged the dark away. A soft light trickled around the drapes. The hotel and town were quiet. I felt anxious, the fun of the day previous now long gone.

I trudge after him and with each step, home and Jeremiah seemed distant and the chance to go back, remote. It was a two-mile hike to the nearest water tower, where we waited for a ride. We found an empty and made ourselves at home. Scribbler broke out some provisions, and we ate our breakfast as the North Dakota scenery swept on by. It is vast, open country with mighty skies that never quit, and for a time we had sat in the open doorway, our legs hanging over the side, taking in the rural scenery, passing miles of wheat fields. It made me feel better with a sense of freedom, the warm air kissing my skin and buffeting my golden hair. We hopped rides, slept under the stars as we headed on through South Dakota as far as Sioux Falls, where we got off and had a near miss with some bulls—railway police—wielding batons, which was scary and thrilling. Safely away, we aimed straight east. For a time, we hoofed it along the track, setting a comfortable pace, the morning sun in our faces.

A few days on the road had quietened my troubled soul some, and I felt stronger and relished the sense of adventure. I reckoned that Tom Sawyer would have been proud of me, and I wished Jeremiah was here to share it with.

By the time we got to Britt, the sun was at our backs. The hobo jungle was bustling with a lively hubbub. Lazy smoke curled up from open fires cooking pots of mulligan, a tempting smell permeating the still air that made my mouth water. We walked on through the crowd and from time-to-time Scribbler stopped to reacquaint with folks, old buddies giving me that special, warm bo greeting, patting my cheek or ruffling my hair, and it wasn't long before my golden hair and blue eyes had earned me my hobo moniker—Straw Blue. I liked it. It made me feel like I belonged.

Scribbler said, 'I'm hoping Corbeau will be here.'

'She won't be hard to spot, not too many women here.'

'They aren't that common, kinda unusual for women to take this life, but there's a few, and she's the best. I know you'll like her.'

Soon we found a pleasant spot to make camp. We wolfed a bowl of mulligan, clay on the shuck and warm corn bread. We both stuffed ourselves good, and after resting up, we sat back and watched one of those magical sunsets. The heavens glowed coral-pink tinged with gray-edged, purple bruises and the big, blood red sun hung low in the sky like a searing coal and as it sunk into the horizon, time seemed to slow and the darkness enveloped us like a tender blanket, muffling the sounds of the camp.

Scribbler said, 'Let's go take a stroll and see what's blowing, shall we?'

As we meandered, sweet music drifted over to us and I grabbed his hand. 'Let's go hear the tunes.'

Round an enormous bonfire sat a good size group, maybe thirty. Scribbler recognized several and raised eyebrows and hands in greeting. We made ourselves comfortable. A fella was playing on a fiddle, the sounds dripping off it like ripe honey. Folks made rhythm with their feet and clapping hands. It was infectious, and it wasn't long before we joined in. During a lull, Scribbler gave a rendition of one of his poems, then told a story about a wolf cub. When he finished, he said, 'This here is Straw Blue.'

There was a chorus of, 'Hey, Straw Blue, good to know ya.'

He said, 'She got a poem she learned at school.'

There was a murmur of approval. A couple voices called, 'Well, let's hear it then, don't be shy now, girlie.'

I felt nervous, my belly turning cartwheels.

An old fella—Scribbler told me he went by Scholar Sam—said, 'It's alright, girlie, you is among friends here. We want to hear your words.'

I stood up. 'Well, alright then, I suppose so.' I paused, looked down at Scribbler. 'I remembered some more, so I'll say what I know, shall I?'

He nodded and gestured with warm, encouraging eyes. The group fell silent, a myriad faces fixed on me like ravenous wolfs. All I could hear was the pop-n-crackle from the fire and the distant hubbub of the jungle. Resolved to do my best, I took a deep breath. The firelight moved over the crowd, forming dancing shadows. I recited the words real nice, slow and rhythmic. As well as the part I told Scribbler on the train, I added the other verse. It came to me while I lay in that sublime bath.

Here is a child who clambers and scrambles,
All by himself and gathering brambles;
Here is a tramp who stands and gazes;
And there is the green for stringing the daisies!
Here is a cart run away in the road
Lumping along with man and load;
And here is a mill and there is a river:
Each a glimpse and gone for ever!

At the end I sat down quick, felt my cheeks glowing red, but had a whopping grin on my face. There was a moment's pause, then everyone clapped and hollered. Some saying stuff like, 'Well, that could have been writ for us.' Scribbler patted me gently on the back, said in my ear, 'That was mighty fine. You did real good, got yourself noticed.'

When things had quietened, Scholar Sam said, 'Now ain't them words by that Stevenson fella, you know the one gone written that Treasure Island? I most surely have heard them before, seeing as it is a poem about what you can see from a train.' He paused, rubbing his gnarly hand through his gray, bushy beard. He frowned, a thinking frown. 'In fact, I think he titled it, "Seen from a Train Window", or something like that.'

At that the fiddle struck up, and the moment vanished, swept away on the river of time, leaving only its ghost: a sweet memory.

Later, as we returned to our pitch, I said, 'I see why you like all this.'

'This?'

'This—life, I guess?'

'You're getting the rose-tinted version. Truth is, it's a hard life, and sometimes dangerous. Often you're cold, hungry, and always poor. Folks can be mean, horrible mean. There are some places you can't go, people that do, sometimes get disappeared.'

I looked at him hard, and whispered, 'But you'll be there to look out for me, right?'

He looked stunned, like I had hit him in the face with a shovel. I felt confused. He placed his hand on my shoulder and said, 'Look, it's gotten late. Get some sleep and we'll see if Corbeau is here tomorrow. We'll talk about it then.'

Sleep was elusive and nightmares stalked the moments of fitful rest, while in between I lay awake fretting about home, Jeremiah and whether he had survived, and Scribbler not wanting me cramping his style. I felt safe with him, but how long would he want me hanging on his coattails? He had his life, didn't he? With Corbeau, and the freedom to be anywhere he wanted. I struggled to make myself fit.

I woke with a start, a panicky feeling in my stomach. The sun was up. A bubble of low voices drifted on the wood-smoked-bacon-n-coffee air. I felt alone. I'd been kidding myself, hadn't I? I didn't belong here with these friendly nomads. Heidi wasn't one of them, was she? Wet tears rolled down my cheeks, tracking ticklishly down my neck, and I wished Jeremiah was here. I needed him and it was oh so stupid of me to leave him like that.

A voice said, 'Hey, what you crying about? Missing home, maybe?'

It was Scribbler. I wiped my tears away and sat up. 'It's nothing, just had a scary dream is all.'

'Alright then. You know, dreams are the mind's cobbler.'

I frowned. 'I don't get it.'

'Come have some breakfast and think about it.'

He sure had a magic way of distracting me and making me use my mind. Despite feeling blue, I still had the appetite for a good thick slice of fatty bacon and warm cornbread, which I used to mop up the salty-meaty pool of fat. It made me feel better. Scribbler said he had already had his breakfast, so he drank coffee and watched me. After a while he said, 'You thought about it?'

I stopped chewing, looked at him. 'Oh yeah, that. What was it? Dreams are the mind's cobbler, right?'

He nodded and lit a cigarette.

I dabbed at the grease with the last hunk of my cornbread, stuffed it in and thought about it. My mouth full, I said, 'So are you saying that when you are asleep, your dreams are working out problems?'

He blew out a stream of blue, fragrant smoke. 'Kinda, I guess. I think you dream what's troubling your mind and while you are sleeping, you can explore deeper than the way you can think when you are awake, see? Can you remember what you were dreaming about?'

I lied. 'Nah. All I can recall is being chased, and I was crying.'

He pushed his hat back. 'Well, I guess you are running from something, ain't ya? So, it stands to reason you're going to dream about it some.' He paused, looked at me all critical like. 'You may have noticed that us folks don't go asking much about each other's business. And I want you to know I don't care why you ran away, left home, whatever it was, but if you want to talk about things, you can tell me if you think it will help, alright?'

I nodded and strove to smile. 'Thanks Scribbler.'

A bag thudding down on the grass next to us and a mellow voice interrupted our discourse. 'Hear you've been looking for me.'

I looked up to see who'd spoken, but the sun was low behind them, putting their face in shadow. I squinted.

Scribbler jumped up. 'Corbeau!' The two of them hugged one another, kissed and held on long and tight. Breaking away, he said, 'It's good to see ya.' He stood back. 'You're looking good, girl.'

She laughed, her face lighting up. 'Charmer! You're not looking bad yourself. Bit older, maybe.'

I had stood up and hung back a little, feeling self-conscious. You know how kids do some time when a new grownup comes to the house and you aren't rightly sure what the correct etiquette is.

She looked over at me. I could see her well now. She had shiny, shoulder-length, jet-black hair kept tidy. Her skin looked too pale for someone who spends time outdoors and apart from around the eyes it was smooth. There was a rosy touch to her lips and cheeks and her brown eyes, just like Jeremiah's, were like chocolate. She smiled at me, her eyes twinkling. It made dimples on her cheeks. 'Now, you must be Straw Blue.'

I wasn't sure how she knew who I was. 'Yes, mam.'

She stuck out her hand. 'Well, please to meet ya, I'm Corbeau.' We shook. Her hands felt strong, her skin was tough, a bit like a man's but not so rough, not like Scribbler's. His hands were like hot, seasoned oak. She was about a half-foot taller than me and smelled a bit of coffee and wood smoke. She was nice to look at but not pretty in a girlie way. She dressed like a man in old but tidy clothing: a brown jacket, granddad shirt, green suspenders holding up denim pants, and on her feet a pair of stout boots. Apart from the boots, everything looked just a little oversized.

Scribbler said, 'You had breakfast? Come sit on down and give us your news.'

We all sat, Scribbler leaning on his side, stretched out, his head resting on his hand. Corbeau sat crossed-legged. She looked at us both. 'I came in real early, the sun just peaking up over the horizon.' She closed her eyes for a moment. 'Oh, I love a sunrise, don't you? I had some breakfast, and they told me you had company with this blonde-haired-blue-eyed girlie and was looking for me.' She looked at me and beamed. She had nice teeth. 'Didn't say you were so pretty, though.'

Scribbler asked, 'Been working?'

'Spent the last few months working that farm near Dodge, you know, the same one I've done the last few years. Nice family. They always try to get me to stay on permanently, but, you know, with the Santa Fe running right by—'

'—Makes your feet itch so bad it drives you crazy and you know it's time to move on.'

'You know what I'm saying.'

I had been trying to follow along, but my world had been so small they might as well have been speaking foreign. They were easy with one another and I could see the love. It made me feel outside of them, which I guess I was. I reckoned if Scribbler loved her and trusted her, then I should too. She looked at me, her chocolate eyes glowing, a warm smile, the kind a mother gives a child. I smiled back and to make headway I asked, 'How'd you become a road sister and meet Scribbler?'

5

— Corbeau —

Straw sat crossed-legged, watching me. I made a steeple with my fingers and rested my chin on them while I considered where to begin. Her mesmerizing eyes scrutinized me with an intensity that surprised.

I smiled at her. 'Alrighty, then. Well, I married young, just eighteen. Then six months later, he was dead. It broke my heart. I'd never known sorrow like it. With no reason to stay, I knew I had to get away, so I packed a few things and set my sights west. I'd never seen the ocean or a big city, so I paid Pullman to San Francisco. It was the biggest, most crowded place this small-town Wyoming girl had ever been. I didn't care for it much, but I loved the ocean. I heard about a small town some hundred miles south, called Carmel-By-The-Sea. I liked the sound of it, so I hefted my world on my back and headed there. It took four leisurely days and was when I first got that itch to travel. During those days, I walked, took rides, and for the first time slept under the stars, and knew I'd never go back home again.

With money in my pockets, I walked the area, slept on the beaches, and stretched my cash. I found Carmel most agreeable with a sweet climate, and townsfolk generous with food and a place to clean up. No one bothered me. Mostly, I kept my company and best as I could, remade my heart. When that strange, beautiful summer leaked away, I was not the same innocent girl set on a life of homemaking and childbearing. My cash was near gone and though it loathed me to leave, I reckoned the peace and charm of Carmel had done its healing work, and I had a desire to go find my place in the world.

'As winter was on the horizon and with a sense of adventure in my feet, I headed roughly east across California into Arizona. I heard folks hopped rides on freight, so I went looking and they weren't hard to find. In practically any good-size town that has a railroad running through it, you'll find a hobo jungle, and it was around the fire in one of them I first met Scribbler. He was reciting a poem that struck deep with me.' I paused and glanced at him. 'You remember it?'

'Yep, like it was yesterday.' He said, grinning.

'You say it.'

He sat up. 'Alright then, you want the whole thing or just the relevant part?'

'Just that one verse.'

> *'The heart of a lover is never at rest,*
> *With joy overwhelmed, or with sorrow oppressed:*
> *When Delia is near, all is ecstasy then,*
> *And I even forget I must lose her again:*
> *When absent, as wretched as happy before,*
> *Despairing I cry, I shall see her no more!'*

'After he finished and sat down and I asked him who wrote those words? He looked at me with his kind, dark-green eyes. He studied me hard for a moment, then he stuck out his hand and said, "They call me Bo Scribbler. An Englishman named William Cowper wrote those words." He rolled a cigarette and gave it me, then rolled another and lit them. He added, "I guess sadness has brought you to this place." He cast his hand around the twenty men gathered around the fire, he continued, "You won't find a bluer bunch than what you'll find around a jungle fire when a freight has just got in, but then it doesn't take a minute for the crack of a joke or the recall of an amusing incident to break us all out of it." I asked him where he was headed and he replied, "You're new to this, ain't ya?" And I asked him if it was that obvious to which he added, "Ah, it don't matter none. I'm headed about five hundred miles west." I told him I had just come from that way from a place called Carmel and he said he'd never heard of it and was there any work there. I told him I wasn't working, and he looked at me knowingly and said, "I know." I asked him what was in California and he told me oranges and work picking them. I said that I could do that. He thought about it and said, "I like you. It's refreshing to meet a woman. Why don't you tag along?" Well, I must admit he was good-looking and charming. I had to trust someone. It looked like a gift horse and as you've just found out, Straw, you don't look those in the mouth, do ya? We set off. He showed me the ropes and we've been friends ever since.'

Straw had hardly taken her eyes from me. 'So, what was his name, your husband?'

'David.' It had been years since last I spoke his name.

'How'd he die?'

Aside from Scribbler, no one had ever asked me that. 'He got in a stupid fight with a friend who threw a punch that knocked him over and when he fell, he hit his head and never got up again.'

She just looked at me with her intense blue eyes. 'Do you still miss him?'

'Not really, but it's kind of hard to explain.'

She looked surprised. 'But you loved him, right?'

'Sure I did, he was—' I couldn't really find the words, '—special. But it was all a long time ago, and it mattered then, but it doesn't anymore, you see?'

She frowned a little and moved her mouth about. 'I guess.' Then she asked, 'So, given time, will anything disappear?'

I smiled and lay my hand on her cheek; her skin was so soft. 'Sure, sweetheart, all you have to do is leave it behind where it belongs.' I took my hand away.

'When I was four, my ma died.' She reached into her bindle and pulled out a small packet, out of which she retrieved a lock of golden hair, saying, 'This was hers.'

'You have the same hair color.'

She nodded. 'We did. She was beautiful, but I don't remember her much, which makes me sad.'

'I'm sorry. You know, even though they aren't here anymore, people that loved us are always with us in our memories and in spirit.'

'I've been trying hard to remember things about her.' She stuck out her right hand, showing a delicate gold ring with a blue stone that matched her eyes.

'That's pretty. Suits you.'

She looked at it for a moment, like it was the first time she'd seen it. 'It was hers.'

'Best place for it now is right where it is.'

Slowly, she lowered her hand and touched the ring, thinking. She looked up. 'Do you believe in God?'

'No, not really. I believe that there is something, like fate, destiny, or call it what you will. I suppose, like a spiritual path that guides you when you got to decide important matters.'

She frowned. 'So you saying it was fate that led me on that train and fate that led Scribbler to get in the same car when I needed it?'

I shrugged. 'Maybe. Sometimes those things that happen aren't always good, like you losing your ma and me David. But then something else happens that balances it out, doesn't it?'

She pursed her red lips and nodded. 'Yeah, I get it. That seems right to me.'

I enjoyed talking with her. She was curious, open-minded, and intelligent. 'How old are you, sweetheart?'

'Almost fifteen.'

'Can't you get yourself back home?'

She looked down. Her shoulders slumping. And like she didn't want anyone else to hear, she said, 'Not safe.'

'Okay then. Just remember, you can change your mind any time, sweetheart.'

She looked up at me, her bright eyes lingering. She had one of those faces where everything just sits right. It was a nice oval shape, eyes even spaced, and her nose was just the right size. Her lips had a kiss-me quality about them and right at the bottom of her chin, it straightened out a little. It was a pleasant face, alluring, but there were thousands of others like it. I think what struck me most was her critical and intelligent manner. Her eyes watched you like they wanted to get right inside and read your soul. And that's what I found special about her. Her searching gaze and fixed expression melted into a gregarious smile. She got up and held out her hand to me. 'Let's go look around.'

— Heidi —

While **Corbeau and I toured** the festival, Scribbler went and caught up with news and old buddies. Corbeau said, 'Scribbler tell you about the crowning of a hobo king and queen?'

'He did. You ever wanted to be queen? I mean, there aren't too many women to choose from. Reckon you'd have a fine shot at it.'

'Not my style. I'm happy just as I am taking it day-by-day. I've found that keeping it simple and your head down makes for a contented life.'

'Scribbler took me to the picture house in Jusinca; it was my first time. He said you like the movies.'

'What did you see?'

'"The Kid" and—'

'Oh my, that is a magnificent movie, one of my favorites. I love Chaplin.'

'He made me laugh, that's for sure. The fight scene had me and Scribbler in stitches. Then he had me crying, too. It was so clever and like nothing I've seen. Jackie Coogan is something, isn't he?'

For a while we discussed movies and then books. She was easy to talk to and I could see we had interests in common, like swimming and taking walks. She was happy in her own company and not as a rule one for big gatherings. We found a stall selling coffee and cookies. Corbeau got us some, and we sat ourselves down.

'I asked Scribbler if you were his girlfriend.'

Her eyes widened. 'Oh, what did he say?'

'I think what he said was, you weren't quite that, but more than friends.'

'Did he now? Interesting.'

'I don't know what he meant by that. What do you say?'

She laughed, her eyes dancing and her nose wrinkling. 'You don't beat about the bush, do ya? I like you, Heidi. It's nice to talk to a girl, particularly one so direct. So, what do I say about me and Scribbler? Well, I guess I agree we're more than friends…'

'Do you love him?'

'Sure. I guess it depends what you mean by love.'

'Okay, I think what I'm asking is whether you and he, you know…'

'Are lovers? Is that what you're asking?'

I nodded. 'Is that too blunt a question?'

'No, it isn't. Let's put it this way. He is special, but I guess our love for one another is like our life: itinerant.'

I frowned. 'How do know if the person you think you love is the right person for you?'

Corbeau snickered, her eyes sparkling. 'Now that's a question, my goodness. If I had the answer to that, I'd be a wealthy woman. I guess you just kinda know if it feels right and that you want to be with that someone. It isn't compulsory, you know?'

'So, you and Scribbler love one another but you're happy keeping it open, is that right?'

Corbeau drained her coffee and wiped her mouthed with the back of her hand. 'I guess. Is there a boy you like? Is that what the questions are about?'

I shrugged. 'There's a boy—Jeremiah—he's my roll dog. We've been friends a long time and in the last few months our friendship—well, let's say, has gotten more involved.'

She grinned, and lean on her elbows, resting her head on her hands. 'Well, now I'm curious. Tell me more, like how you met.'

I popped the last chunk of cookie into my mouth and ordered my thoughts. 'It was a few days after my ma had died. Jeremiah's ma must have been worried about me because she came over with some food and fetched him along with her. I was sitting in the corner in my tatty dungarees, barefoot, playing with my rag doll. I can't really remember how I felt, but I guess I was sad and feeling lonesome. As they entered the house, I looked up. Then, Jeremiah popped out from behind his ma and when I saw his beaming, cheeky face, my heart skipped a beat and I felt real happy. I asked if he'd come to play with me. And that was that we just clicked and from then on we spent as much time together as we could.'

'What about your pa?'

I wave of nausea hit me. I looked down. 'He's— he's not a peaceful man. He likes the drink and can be violent, too. After ma died he worked and drank, mostly. I had to learn to look after myself. I managed. I had Jeremiah and my friends. I love school. My teacher, Miss Hannah, was always real nice to me.'

'Did he beat you? Is that why you ran away?'

I shrugged. I flash of that look pa had in his eyes when he came for me, stabbed at my heart. For a while, we sat in silence. I liked Corbeau, but some things are better left unsaid. If I squished it deep down in my conscience, it might just go away. I sensed she understood, and she didn't press me. She said, 'How about we go find Scribbler and have some fun?'

Like a family on carefree days out, the three of us wandered the festival enjoying the sights and sounds. I pushed aside my baggage, determined to take the good that had come my way. We made the most of it. The festival highlights took place that weekend. There was a magical parade, and the proposed kings and queens made their pitch. Their eloquence and stories fascinated me.

On Monday, once the camp had thinned out, I woke with a weight in my stomach, a gnawing sense of dread, and this dark cloud tainted all my happy thoughts of the past few days. We hadn't discussed plans for moving on and I was too afraid to ask, but more than anything, I wanted for the three of us to stay together.

We ate our breakfast each in our own world. After, Scribbler gave me two bits to go to the bathhouse, which they had set up special. I took my time, lying in the hot water right up to my chin. I loved the way it made my fingertips all wrinkly and my nose itch. I enjoyed being naked, and the feel of the water against my skin. It reminded me of the times us kids went skinny-dipping in the Big Creek, back home. It had been after one of those swims—me and Jeremiah would have been about ten-years-old—we were walking home lagging back from the others and then we were alone. He pulled me up and kissed me smack on the lips. Lingering just a heart beat long enough for my face to tingle. It startled me, my senses sparking with his hot, sweet breath, the smell of his skin, and the touch of his velvety lips. I loved the intimacy. Then he looked embarrassed. I touched my fingers to my lips and laughed and he blushed from head to toe, then said, "Come-on, Fizz, let's catch the others," and ran off. I wondered if the others had dared him do it, but then no one else had been around to see, so I guessed he'd meant it, and it made me feel kinda warm and weird inside.

I lay in the warm water thinking of home and wondered what Jeremiah had told them. I knew he would not let me down and my heart ached for him. I dried off, dressed, and made my way back to camp. As I got close, I could see Corbeau and Scribbler deep in discussion and I don't know how, but knew they were talking about me. I scooted around and crept up to hear what they were saying.

I heard Scribbler say: 'Okay then, you sure you can't take her?'

'I like her. She's smart and got a pleasant disposition but this isn't the life for her. She needs to be back in school with other kids. There must be a way we can help find somewhere.'

'Ah, I don't know. How the hell do I know what's best for anyone? Maybe I should have left her on the train. She'd have worked it out.'

'Well, you didn't, did ya? And for what it's worth, you did the right thing helping her. Tell me I'm wrong.'

He lit a cigarette. 'Yeah, alright. You're right. She's a good kid. She has those scars on her back, so I guess she's—'

I felt like a knife had been stuck in my heart. I knew the bubble would burst, those dues I owed God for my prayer and sins had to be paid.

Corbeau said, 'Look, Scribbler, it's not complicated, just take her with you.'

'What, to California?'

'Sure, she can pick oranges, can't she? You've been going to the same grower for, how many years?'

He grunted. 'About ten, I guess.'

'So you're sweet with them and they'll help. Maybe it's what she needs right now, and it will give her some money.'

'What about the Wells?' Would they take her permanently? After all, they're always asking you to stay on, so why not her?'

'They won't want us around their neck over winter. And besides, if that backfires, I may lose the chance to return.'

He sighed. 'I only want what's best for her, but I'm not sure traipsing around after this old bo is the answer.'

Acidic tears of frustration built inside my gut. I got upset. Then I got angry. Then I ran. There were lots of folk moving off and I trailed a small group and followed them out of town, heading back west. We walked along the rail track until we reached a water tower. It wasn't long to wait until a freight came along and stopped. They all hid while the loco filled up. I hid too, observing. The brakemen were about, but they didn't seem too bothered about checking for riders. Just before it set off, the whistle blew twice, the carriages lurched, the engine puffed hard and like magic, men appeared and hopped on board and in just a few moments there was nothing bar the smell of hot steam, acrid smoke and fading sounds of puffing and clanking as the loco headed west. I came out and stood on the rails looking up the track as it disappeared. I felt it vibrations under foot. I was alone. I don't know why I hadn't got on board.

It irritated me I took off with no provisions. I should have gone back, but I was too impassioned, too proud, and I didn't want to be a bother. I was going to do this on my own or die trying. Fate, right? Or is that just another way to say God's plan? While I waited, I had a look around the heavily tagged water tower. I thought I should add my moniker then at least if I died, my tag would show that I had existed. I found a sharp stone and went to it. In the custom of the other marks, I scratched:

STRAW BLUE, 8.10.1925 W

As I made my tag, a plan formed. I'd head out west to California and go find a place to pick oranges. I scouted the area and found an old can and went over to the feed hose that hung down like some ancient elephant's trunk on the water tower that had a steady drip coming from it. It took a while to sluice out the vessel and make it as clean as I could, then I filled it, drank it down and filled it again. If I carried it attentively, I reckoned I'd have enough water to keep me going.

An hour later, another loco came by and stopped. I couldn't see anyone about, so with my heart in my mouth I snuck on the deathwood and made myself as small as possible. As the train moved along at a steady clack, I felt a little better and more confident. I hadn't been with Scribbler long, but he'd taught me enough to make a start. As I traveled, I thought maybe I had been foolish going off like that. After all, hadn't he said he wanted what was best for me? I should have been more grown-up and joined in the talk, to make my case, but it didn't matter now. I had decided for them, but I felt bad about it. I just seemed to make one poor decision after another. Heidi, who left her injured best friend behind to face the music and then found two of the best, kindest grownups you could ever expect to meet, only to run off like a spoiled child. Now, as I deserved, I was alone.

After some long time traveling in the dark, we came into a city. I readied myself. It surprised me how stiff I'd become. I stretched some life back into my limbs before moving from the deathwood onto the step so that I could jump. I tried to keep hold of my water can, but it was too hard. When the train slowed right down, I faced the direction of travel and jumped, hitting the ground at a run so I wouldn't fall. I was proud of myself, felt like I'd earned my first solo badge.

I went looking for the jungle. I passed a name board with the words "Sioux Falls" on it. I'd been here before, when we had a near miss with some bulls. I was cautious, keeping to the shadows. I could smell smoke drifting on the warm breeze, and it wasn't long before that and the flickering light led me to the hobo jungle. I hung back in the shadows, watching. I hadn't had a crumb to eat since breakfast, and I was thirsty too. The smell of the mulligan and coffee set me salivating, so I plucked up courage and breezed on in and plonked myself down by the fire.

There were about twenty sitting around, some staring into the flames, others talking quiet like. As I sat down, the bubble of conversation stuttered and faded. Then I recognized Scholar Sam. He said, 'Well howdy there Straw Blue, where'd you come from?'

'Just came in from Britt.'

'Scribbler with ya?'

'Nah, I'm making my own way.'

'Well, that's mighty adventurous of you. Where's your bindle?'

I gave a nervous laugh and shrugged. 'It slipped off the deathwood.'

'Ah yeah, that can happen, though you only ever do it once, don't ya?'

I simpered; glad my story was holding up. 'I feel pretty dumb.'

Another bo said, 'Ah, don't beat yaself up, missy. We've all been there.'

Sam fished a tin bowl from his pack and walked around to where I sat. We made some room for him and he dropped next to me. 'Here, take this over to that pot and get some food inside ya.'

I didn't need asking twice.

After I'd eaten, he introduced me to the gathering and asked me to recite my poem, which I did, giving it a performance worthy of their generosity. I felt like I was making some headway and that maybe I could succeed on my own.

As the night wore on, I sat and listened to the conversation. I got asked what my plans were, and I said I was going west to pick oranges. One of the younger boes said, 'That's all the way out to California. You got any idea how far that is?'

I had to admit I'd given it no thought. I said, 'I guess it's far.'

He laughed, spat a streak of brown spittle on the dirt. 'Reckon it's over fifteen-hundred miles.'

I tried to get my head around such a big number, but I had already traveled a long ways since I got on that boxcar in Bonners Ferry. I had not the smallest idea how far, but I was sure I could get myself to California. I made inquiries, and they were happy to tell me which way to travel and what to expect. As they tripped out the names of states and towns, it sounded like a rich adventure, and I felt that itch in my feet the like of which Corbeau and Scribbler had talked about.

The night grew dark and crept toward the wee hours. I felt like I'd grown up some. I wanted so badly to tell Scribbler I'd made it this first leg. I missed him and Corbeau. Before he'd gone off to sleep, Scholar Sam had done a whip round and gathered a few things from the others and put them in an old gunny sack. He held it out his eyes twinkling. 'Here, Straw, this will get you started, but mind you keep a good hold.'

'For me?' He nodded. 'Holy smoke! Thanks, Sam, that's mighty kind of you.'

His characterful, craggy face carried a whopping grin, and he patted my cheek with his gnarly hand. 'It may look all kinda random, you know, this life. But we've got a way to do things and most of us look out for each other. Now one day you'll be able to return the favor to someone what needs it, see? And I know ya will too.' We shook hands. 'Good to meet ya again, Straw Blue. Catch you round a jungle fire sometime.'

With my mind racing, sleep was not an option, so I headed back to the rail yard to see if I could hop a ride to Rapid City. I strode out with my pockets empty and my meager needs safe in that old gunny sack. It was daunting but exhilarating and I could taste the adventure.

7

— Heidi —

Lit by just a few dim overhead lights that cast unsettling shadows, the rail yard was quiet. I walked on in and began my search. As I strolled by some boxcars, I heard this, 'Psst!' noise. Then a harsh whisper saying, 'Over here.' I turned round a few times but couldn't see anything. Then hands grabbed me, pulling me down under the carriage, and a moment later, some rail workers passed by. A whispered voice in my ear said, 'Bulls! With the festival an' all, been a lot of boes through here and they've been told to round up some, get some dues. Know what I mean?'

In the gloom, I could just make out the two young hoboes. 'Thanks.'

The darker-skinned one asked, 'You looking to ride out?'

'Yeah, Rapid City.'

The whites of his eyes glowed. 'Westies go from the far side, over that way.'

With the coast clear, I made my thanks and scooted from under the train and made off. I crossed the yard, heading under trains, keeping to the shadows, but then my luck ran out. Hugging the carriages, I got to the end and looked behind me, but when I turned round, I walked smack into a couple of bulls. The one I bumped reeked of cheap hooch, reminding me of my pa. I froze, my spine tingling. The other grabbed my arm and shone a light in my eyes, said, 'Well, looky here, we went got ourselves a little kitty-rat.'

I could smell his hot, sweaty body and malodorous breath. I swallowed, my heart pounding. 'Let me go. I ain't doing nothing, just walking home.'

His liquored-up mate said, 'No you ain't, bitch! You're a bum rat sneaking around, looking for a free ride. I can smell your type a mile off. Not commonly so pretty, though.' He licked his fleshy lips. I felt dizzy, panic rising. I struggled, but he grabbed my throat with his oily hand, choking me. His face thrust in mine, the boozy smells overpowering. He looked at me hard, his cruel, dark eyes molesting me. He said, 'Well, ain't you a tasty one? Maybe we could have a free ride on your little ass as payment.' He stuck out his wet tongue. It reminded me of a flabby, oozing slug. Then he thrust at me and licked my face. It churned my stomach. I reeled back, screwing my eyes shut, terrified.

I struggled harder. His grip tightened. I could feel pressure building behind my eyes and thought I was going to pass out. He jammed his lips on mine, his gruesome slug trying to force its way in. Summing up all my dwindling energy, I bit down on his lip and tasted a hot, metallic slick of blood. He let out a yell and released me, but as I turned to run, there was an almighty crunch and I felt like my head had exploded. I reeled and fell hard, like I was tumbling into the abyss. I felt sick. I tried to scrabble away but had no proper control of my body or grasp of what was occurring. Then one of them kicked me in the side twice, winding me. Pain shot through me like bolts of pricking fire. They lifted me like I was nothing. I hung like a rag doll and fresh blood ran like syrup down my face. A torrent of thoughts raced through my befuddled mind. So, this was the reckoning. The pay dirt. What was it? An-eye-for-an-eye. Helpless, I resigned myself to providence.

Then something happened. He dropped me. I thudded to the ground. It knocked the wind outta me. There were sounds of running and shouting. It went quiet. Gasping, I sat up all jingle-brained. I wiped my face and my hand came away sticky. I shook my head, trying to get my act together. I could hear a distant commotion but could see nothing and, realizing I was alone, made my escape. When I stood, my pins felt heavy and rubbery. My head was swimming, but I forced myself to move. I made it to the edge of the yard and pushed through into some heavy brush and fell spent to the ground. I never knew a head could hurt or bleed like it. I had a sizable bump on the back of my head, blood still oozing from a wide gash. I sat on the dirt, pulled a rag from my pocket, and even though it hurt like hell, I pressed it tight to slow the bleeding.

I must have passed out because when I came to, it was just getting light. I sat up, but my head and body screamed, so I lay back down again. I had a cotton mouth and one eye caked shut with blood. I tore apart the lids and lay still, trying to get some focus. After some minutes, little-by-little, I sat up, raised my knees and put my head between them. I had ripped pants and scuffed a knee. I was in a pitiful state. I can't explain why, but I found my crappy predicament amusing.

Well, girl, you are one dumb Dora. That's what you get from going it alone: darn fine job!

When I laughed, my ribs hurt, making me wince. I pulled up my bloodied shirt and vest and saw an enormous bruise on my side. I poked around and vile stabbing pains shot through me. Like some arthritic grandma hauling herself outta bed, I got back on my feet. With me all banged up and the rail yard hostile, I thought it best to turn tail to the jungle, but as I set off, I wondered whether my bindle might still be around. I felt this bitter wrath that I had lost it. I weighed up the balance between the fear of being caught and losing everything I owned. It seems kinda silly I even contemplated such a foolery, but then I guess I felt ashamed I'd made a mess of things and thought finding my stuff might restore some pride to my sorry ass. So, believe it or not, I went to look, and it led to what I later learned is called a case of serendipity.

— Bo Scribbler —

One thing I'd learned about Heidi was she enjoyed eating. With little time to ourselves, and as the hours flitted by, Corbeau and I caught up, and discussed how best to help Heidi, with whom we'd both grown fond. Truth is, I'd been wrestling with my conscience since the day we met. I liked her. She brought the good side outta me, and I reckoned that she'd had a rough time in her past and needed a little looking after. I realized she had opened a can of worms from my past and I didn't know exactly what I should do. Being so long on my own hadn't given me the wisdom of how to look after youngsters, but in the end, the solution had been staring us in the face.

Then came time to eat, and we realized Straw had been gone for ages. We weren't worried. We'd been here long enough for her to find her feet and I thought she'd gone exploring or maybe met up with some other kids or was being entertained by some old boes.

We split up and began asking if anyone had seen her. At last, on the western edge of town, I found a road sister who, hours earlier, had seen her heading out west. I was relieved that it looked like she was on her own, but why she had taken off was a mystery.

I tracked down Corbeau, but by the time we'd gathered up our stuff and hastened after Heidi, it was mid afternoon.

We hit the rail track and made good speed, hoping that she too had taken this route. I saw the water tower and called out to Corbeau. 'There, maybe she's up ahead.'

When we arrived, there were a few boes hanging about, none of whom had seen her. I felt desperate, wondering what had made her go off. By now it was dusk and both the light and my heart were sinking. I sensed somehow I had failed her. Then this fella came over. 'You say ya looking for Straw Blue?'

'Yeah, that's her. Why?'

'Her mark's on the tower. Here, I'll show ya.'

We went looked and sure enough there was a fresh mark with today's date and an arrow pointing west. I said, 'Well I'll be!'

Corbeau let out a low whistle. 'Well, thank goodness. Least now we know.'

It surprised me how much Straw had gotten under my skin, and it uplifted me knowing we were on the right trail. I turned to Corbeau. 'We're going to find her and make sure she never needs to run off again or so help me, God.'

It was dark before the next ride came. As we traveled, we tried to work out where she'd be going and what she would do. We knew she didn't have her bindle and the road sister who'd seen her said she was empty-handed. I clutched her stuff and hoped that I could get it back to her.

By the time the train pulled in at Sioux Falls, there was a smudge of light in the East. Hungry and dog tired, we hopped off and headed for the jungle. We reckoned that Straw would have done the same. I hoped above hope we'd find her there and I knew if she'd made it here, they would take care of her.

We smelled the wood smoke and saw the flickering light. An ancient bo sat by the fire brewing up a tin of coffee. We sat down. He didn't look up, just said, 'There's plenty if you want a cup.' We broke out our tins and he filled them, a real good pile driver, and just what we needed.

I caught his eye. 'We were supposed to meet up with a youngster here, Straw Blue. You seen her?'

He looked at us for a beat. 'Hm, I saw her, came in last night. Scholar Sam recognized her from the festival. She'd lost her bindle on the train. She ate and in return gave us a pleasing slice of verse. I don't know what happened next because I went got my head down. I guess she might still be around.'

I rolled a cigarette and gave it to him. 'Thanks for the coffee.'

We were relieved to be on the right track. As folks stirred and came to brew up and get some breakfast, we made inquiries. By the time Sam appeared, we had most of the story.

Despite his years, Sam walked easy. He saw us and came right over. 'Let me guess. You're looking for Straw, ain't ya?'

We nodded. 'You guess correct. She went and ran off for reasons that aren't clear. You speak to her?'

'Well, of course I did. She's a good tomato, spunky, and has a touch of the bearcat, too. Any gal that can say a poem like that is alright by me. Though, I thought her story of losing her stuff on the train was a load of old baloney.' He poked the fire and poured his coffee, took a swig. 'God damn, now that'll wake the dead.'

Corbeau refilled her mug and took a slug. 'We hear she's set for California and oranges—' she paused, a satisfied grin crossing her face, and she chuckled. 'Well dammit, now it makes sense.'

I frowned. 'What does?'

'You ever tell her about going west to pick oranges?'

'No, I don't recall doing so.'

'Sooo—'

The light dawned on me. 'She overheard us talking about it yesterday. Well, hells' teeth—'

'She thinks we don't want her.'

'Well, I suppose if she'd heard it all out of context, like a snippet, then yes.' I swore under my breath. 'Well, let's look at things on the bright side. We know where she's heading and maybe she'll carry on leaving her mark—' I stopped a beat, thinking. 'Hey, maybe she knew we'd follow and wanted to show us the way.'

'Well, if that's the case, why doesn't she just stop and wait for us to catch up?'

'Fair point.' I stood, gathered up my bindle and hers. 'Well, better get a wiggle on. We'll not catch up sitting around here chewing the fat, will we?'

As we left camp and headed for the rail yard, we bumped into two young boes. One was real tall and swarthy, the other regular size with a baby face, but they looked fit.

'Morning to ya, boys. You come from the rail yard?'

The taller one said, 'Yes sir, we've had quite a night dodging yard bulls.'

'We're looking for a young girl, blond hair, blue eyes.'

They looked at one another, eyebrows raised. Baby face said, 'Yeah, we saw her. She might be in some trouble.'

Corbeau scowled, her eyes burning. 'Trouble? What kinda trouble?'

The tall one related the story of hauling her under a carriage. 'She asked us where to hop a ride to Rapid City. We pointed her in the right direction and after the coast was clear, she went her way and we went ours. Anyway, a while later we heard a commotion and thought we could hear her, so we went took a peek. Two bulls had caught her and it was getting ugly. Then she bit one real hard. Must have hurt something cruel. He yowled and let her go, but before she could make a yard distance, his mate whacks her on the head with his sap. We could hear the sickening crack like the snap of a bullwhip. She went down. The one she'd injured gave her a good kicking. Then his mate picked her up. That was enough for us. We hollered at 'em and threw some stones. They dropped her and came after us. Wish we'd acted quicker.' He made a face, looked away and spat in the dirt.

Baby Face picked up the narrative. 'They were both plumb out of condition, weren't no match for us. We gave 'em a right old hunt-a-wampus, then laid low. After a bit, we came out and went back to see if we could find her. She was gone. We found her gunny sack and blood, lots of it. We looked around and saw a trail, but it was too dark and we lost track. We waited till it got light and looked again, but there were too many bulls about. There's been a shift change, and it's quieting down.'

The tall one added, 'Reckon the bulls might have gone back and taken her.' He passed over an old gunny sack. 'Here, this is her stuff.'

I took the bindle; it matched the description of the one Sam had given her. I was doing well collecting Heidi's stuff, but not so good at finding her. I said, 'Thanks, we'll go look and ask around; appreciate it.'

'You want we come and help?'

'Nah, that's alright, fellas, we got this.'

As we made our way to the yard, grave thoughts clouded my mind. It sounded like she'd come across some bulls that were corrupt. It isn't hard to get rid of someone like Straw, a kid on their own drifting, homeless.

By the time we got to the yard, it was quiet. We headed for the area the lads had last seen her. It didn't take too long to find the place. A dark stain marked the spot. There were scuffs on the ground and some torn cloth. We could see the blood trail heading off and we followed it. Every so often we'd lose it, then find another few spots, keeping us on her track. It led to some dense undergrowth and you could see where she'd pushed on in. Before I blundered in after, I called out her name. Nothing. I forced my way in and found where she had been. We were relieved and worried at the same time. I turned around, pushed back my hat, and scratched my head. 'So let's say she came here to recover a bit. Maybe she slept, or whatever. But then what?' I looked at Corbeau. 'If it were you, where would you go?'

She didn't have to think about it. 'I'd have made for the jungle, no question, wouldn't you?'

I nodded. 'Like you say, no question.' I kicked at the dirt racking my brain. 'So, if she didn't go back there, where?'

'Maybe someone other than the bulls found her. I mean, there's a powerful load of blood around. She must have looked awful. Maybe she got help.'

I hoped that was the case, but odds stacked against her and it chilled my blood to think who might have her and what they might do. I turned to Corbeau. 'I'm not losing her, you hear? We must find her. We just gotta!'

9

— Heidi —

I returned to the scene of the attack. Things looked different in the light. I could see my blood and marks in the dirt. I looked around, but my stuff was gone. I don't know whether it was dehydration or the blow to my head, but I felt like I was going to pass out and I wasn't sure I could make it back to the jungle. I heard voices, and I hid under the carriage, my heart hammering in my pain wracked chest. The sudden rush of adrenaline had deadened the pain in my head and heightened my senses. The voices drew closer. They sounded young. Then four slim, black legs, with tatty shoes, appeared and stopped.

One said, 'What's this? Is that blood? Maybe there's been a murder.'

The other replied, 'Aw man, there's plenty of it. Must have bled out.' The speaker bent down and touched the dried blood. It was a black boy, younger than me. Then he looked over and his big brown eyes widened like he'd seen a ghost. I raised my hand and attempted a smile. 'Hey.'

The boy's friend joined him and looked at me. 'Damn, you look like death, girl!'

I just stared back, my eyes wide. The two boys looked at one another, nodded, then looked back at me. 'You need help?'

Help? Oh, I needed help, and right now those beautiful boys looked to me like angels sent from heaven. I nodded.

'Can you stand?'

I shuffled out from under the carriage and they helped me up. They were a nudge taller than me. Their beautiful black skin and tight curled hair shone in the sun. 'Can you walk?'

I nodded, tried a step, and faltered. They got hold of me, firm but gentle. 'You lean on us, girl, we'll take you to Doc Moon, he'll fix ya up good.'

They knew their way around, kept out of sight, and soon we scooted through a broken fence, heading into town. I was past caring where we were going or who saw me, because I believed them boys would look after me. Enthused by their mercy mission, they gave me a running commentary, though with my canned head most of their words floated off on the mild breeze. We made off down one street, then another. We passed a few folks who stared. One or two looked real close, like to say what you boys doing with that girl now? And when that happened, one or other of them would say, 'She had an accident. We taking her to Doc Moon,' which seemed to satisfy. It seemed like a friendly place. A couple times they had to stop for me to have a moment. I felt sick, but I kept going. The boys held me up and every so often gave me a word of encouragement, you know: 'Not far now,' or, 'Doc will patch ya up, you'll be right as rain.'

At last we came to a house with a plaque on the fence: Dr. Henry Moon, MD. Nothing wrong with my eyes; I could still read and think. They opened the door, and we entered this clean, wood paneled hallway that smelled of polish. A neatly dressed lady sat behind a plain desk, attending to some paperwork. She looked up and her mouth fell agape and her eyes widened. She said, 'O lord! Whatever happened?' She stood, came over and had my angels sit me down. Then she went over to a door, knocked, and entered. A moment after, this man appeared dressed in a dark suit, nicest I'd ever seen. He took one look at me and told the boys to bring me in. They lay me on this couch real gentle, and the man gave the boys each a coin and told them to wait outside in case he needed them to run an errand. They seemed pleased and told me I'd be okay now. I thanked them and surrendered myself to the calm comfort of the doctor's consulting room. It smelled fresh, kinda heady, like rubbing alcohol. It was good to be out of the sun. The spinning in my head slowed. The man said, 'I'm Doc Moon, what shall I call you?'

'I'm Heidi, but they call me Straw Blue.'

While he looked me over, he asked, 'Who's they? Family?'

I shook my head slowly. 'Nah, my friends.'

'Where's home then?'

'Idaho, but right now I'm homeless.'

'Someone gave you a good pasting. How did you get these injuries?'

I told about my encounter with the bulls and what they had in mind for me.

It incensed him to hear that the police had assaulted me. His gentle hands were the opposite of the drunken bull's violence.

He held one finger in front of my eyes and had me follow it side-to-side. 'It was lucky Sam and Booker found you when they did.' He nodded and lowered his finger. I closed my eyes. 'That their names? When they found me, I thought they were angels.'

He chortled. 'Well, I wouldn't call them angels, but they're good boys.'

Though it made my face hurt, I grinned. 'Nice-looking boys, too.'

While we talked, he continued his exam, his questions distracting me.

The lady from the desk—Edith—came and helped get my bloodied clothing off and clean me up. She sent Sam and Booker off to rustle up some clothes. Then they got sent to the jungle with a note made out to Scholar Sam and though I did not know whether he'd still be there, I had a feeling that whoever read the note would help. I hoped with all my heart that Scribbler and Corbeau would come looking for me and I felt like a sap for leaving them.

Doc told me I needed rest and to stay put for a few days. I was in no state to argue. They made up a room and put me to bed. The doc had given me something for the pain that made me drowsy and all warm inside, and as soon as my bandaged, broken head sunk into that soft pillow, joyous sleep reached out and dragged me deep down.

— § —

When I woke, the pain had reduced to a dull ache. I blinked my dry eyes open, tried to focus and figure where I was. My head and face hurt. Everything hurt. I tried to sit up, but a searing pain shot through my side and my head screamed, so I lay back down. My desiccated mouth was not even wet enough to moisten my parched lips. I moved my head. It took a moment for my eyes to focus. A glass jug and tumbler stood on the nightstand. Real slow, I propped myself up on my elbow. A bolt of pain galloped up my body. I winced and screwed my eyes shut. I steadied myself until it faded, then reached out and poured some water. I spilled some. It took a painful while, but in the end I raised that clear water to my lips and sipped. Then a little more. It was the most beautiful thing I had ever drunk. I drank it down and placed the glass on the table except I didn't quite sit it right and it fell, smashing on the floor. I wanted to pick it up but it was beyond me.

I heard a footfall, a floorboard creaked, and the door pushed open. Edith came in. She beamed at me. 'Ah, you're awake.' She spotted the broken tumbler. 'Never mind that.'

A short while later, Doc Moon came to see me. I found out I had been asleep for over twenty hours. He checked me over and said I should stay put a few days. 'You're a tough cookie, that's for sure.' He looked a little awkward, then asked,

'I couldn't help noticing the marks on your back and hands. Is that why you ran away?'

I looked at him. He reminded me of Doc Jenner from back home, not in looks but in the manner. He cared. I said, 'Kinda. It's complicated.'

'Those marks from a belt?'

I nodded again.

'Your father?'

It felt like a betrayal, but a flicker of my eyes told him what he knew already.

'What about your mother?'

'She died long ago.'

He reached out his hand and placed it on my forehead. It was soft, like Doc Jenner's hands, cool and comforting. He said, 'I'm sorry to hear that. Kids need their mothers.'

Like a butterfly lifting away, he removed his hand. It was like he took away some of my anguish with it. 'This'll help with the pain.' He gave me some medicine. 'You've got some good people in that hobo camp. When they got the note, this man and woman came over, worried sick about you. They sat with you all night. I convinced them to go get some rest.'

My heart and hopes soared. 'Scribbler and Corbeau were here?'

'That's them. They told me you had run off because you thought you were in the way. You got that wrong.'

I closed my eyes. 'I can be so dumb.'

'If you need me to help you find a place here and get back on your feet, I'll do that.'

I frowned. 'What kinda place?'

'There's an orphanage that would help.'

I looked at him. 'Thanks, but no. I want to see Scribbler and Corbeau, please.'

'Okay, I'll send Sam and Booker. You must have dumbstruck those boys. Been hanging around all day asking after you. It'll cheer them to hear you're awake.'

He pulled back the drapes and opened the window wide. Muted sounds of the town floated in on the warm breeze. I sat propped up on those fluffy pillows and looked at the sky. I felt lightheaded and detached. He said, 'Plenty of rest and fresh air, doctor's orders,' he chuckled. 'Let nature take its course.' He took out a pocket watch, muttering something about not enough time. Then he left, closing the door behind him.

When he was gone, everything that had happened in the previous weeks came crashing down on me and I cried like I've never cried before. I sobbed so hard it made my head and chest hurt, but I didn't care 'cause the tears spilled the pain away. When I was done, I felt empty and exhausted, like I had nothing left to give. I closed my eyes and tried to figure out what I should do, but my mind was blank and, thankfully, once more, sleep took hold.

When I woke, Scribbler and Corbeau were by my bed. He held my hand. It looked tiny and pale in his, like a doll's hand. He looked pained and tired. When he saw I was awake, he smiled the warmest smile I'd ever seen, like his soul was radiating. I knew I had been so childish. I said, 'Sorry, Scribbler.'

'No. No, you've got nothing to be sorry for. We all got our wires crossed is all and we should never have talked about you without you being there. What's important is we've found you, because we're supposed to be together, see?'

Corbeau said, 'That busy little fate has been at work again. You can't escape us.'

'I don't want to be in the way.'

Scribbler frowned, a flash of sadness in his warm, green eyes. 'You aren't and you never have. We'll take care of you long as you need us.'

'You'll do that for me? You sure?'

'Never been more certain of anything. Now, you get some rest. We've found some work, and as soon as you're strong enough, we're all going west to pick them sweet smelling oranges.'

I closed my aching eyes and whispered. 'I like the sound of that. I can do that.'

He laid his hot, rough hand on my cheek, stroking it with his thumb. It felt nice. 'You ever seen the ocean?'

I shook my head.

'Well, you haven't lived until you have, so we'll fix that too. Rest now and we'll come by later.'

As the days went by, my strength returned and my body healed. They sat me in a chair in the garden. It wasn't like the plot of land back home but full of sweet-smelling late summer blooms, the buzz of insects, and the birds singing like their lives depended on it. Every day, Sam and Booker came and sat with me. They brought these special playing cards and taught me a game called *Flinch*, which we played for hours. It seemed like a lifetime since I had played with other kids, almost like I'd left my childhood behind that day and now I existed in a kinda limbo. They made me laugh, but when they had gone, I thought about Jeremiah and wished I could see him. I closed my eyes and imagined his soft lips touching mine, the smell of his skin, the way he threw his head back when he laughed. I don't think I'd ever find anyone else like him, and I wondered if I'd ever see him again. Maybe the cost to see him just one more time would be worth it. I wished I had told him I loved him.

It wasn't long before I was well enough to move on. It was hard saying goodbye. Doc Moon wouldn't take payment for my treatment. The boys gave me the card game. They told me to visit any time I was in town, and hugging them, I said I would.

Reunited with Scribbler and Corbeau, we headed off. They reckoned it would be better to give me a treat and while I had spent two weeks getting back my health, they had worked to pay passage all the way to Fresno. I'd never ridden on a train legally. Scribbler said they called it riding the cushions but that I shouldn't get used to it.

part
two

10

— Corbeau —

As the loco steamed west, Heidi sat back in her seat, her head turned to the window. It was hard to tell whether she was drinking in the arresting scenery or lost in some other world. Joe, too, sat still, his eyes closed and chin resting on his chest. Something in him had changed. I hoped a time and place might present itself for us to talk it through, but meanwhile I knew my responsibility was to stay with them, and though I could not explain why, I needed them. We needed to be together.

It had knocked me off my feet how Heidi's flight and assault had affected Scribbler. I'd never seen him cry before, and it got me thinking. He'd always had this kind of detached connection to people, like he was afraid to get too close. But she had crawled under his skin.

By the time we steamed into Fresno, she was quiet, but seemed content. It was near mid-September, the morning heat rising. We told her the harvest didn't get underway until November, but we should go down to the grove and make sure there was work for us. It was some forty miles due south and, given that we had spent the last days sitting pretty, we looked forward to stretching our legs.

Scribbler had bought Heidi a brimmed hat, and she said it made her feel like a pioneer. She was eager to get working and earn her keep and was truly excited to see the ocean.

By afternoon we'd made it to an elegant town called Kingsburg, populated mostly by Swedish Americans. The Central Pacific Railroad ran through it, and the surrounding fields cropped mainly with grapes for raisins. We bought food and filled up our water. As we strolled the bustling main drag, a store selling ice cream and sodas caught her eye.

She gazed in eyes wide. 'I've never eaten ice cream before.'

Scribbler raised his eyebrows. 'Well, that needs fixing, and I reckon our hot walk has earned us a scoop or two: my treat.'

She looked at the inviting display. 'That one, for sure. I love chocolate.'

Scribbler had vanilla and I, strawberry. We stepped out on the sidewalk, and she took a spoonful and popped it into her mouth. I watched her. She closed her eyes. A cat-got-the-cream smirk swamped her face like a painted veil. I nudged her. 'So, how is it?'

She turned to me. 'Ho-ly-smoke!'

'That good, eh?'

'I didn't expect it to be so cold. It feels so soft and luscious in my mouth, the blob melts on my hot tongue. Then, I get this rich creamy, slightly bitter chocolate taste, and after that a hit of something sweet that brings it all together.' She held up the cup and regarded it like an archaeologist finding a rare treasure. 'Where have you been all my life? This is sooo good!'

Scribbler and I laughed out loud. She licked out the cup until it was bone dry and had a smear of chocolate goo around her satisfied mouth. She wiped it off with the back of her hand and then licked the last morsels off.

Scribbler said, 'You liked that, then?'

She shrugged. 'Yeah, I guess it was okay.' She giggled. 'Only kidding! That was the bees!'

A short distance from town, we came to the Kings River and found a pleasant spot to spend the night. We stripped off to our undergarments and got straight in that cooling water. Heidi made a beeline for Scribbler and the two of them began ragging around. As she was still mending, he was careful not to be too rough. I watched them. It was real interesting. He had a natural playfulness about him I'd not seen before. He enjoyed messing about with her and she was like a whole new person: bubbling with energy and laughter. She would jump up and try to duck him, then quickly move behind, grab him around the neck and hang on as he tried to free himself. They looked like they belonged together, and it made me see him in a whole new light.

That night we lay on the bank looking at the immense, inky sky. A myriad of stars stretched like a giant sparkling hood over our heads. She raised herself up on her elbow and said, 'Can I ask you both a question?'

I replied. 'Sure, honey.'

'What are your real names?'

Scribbler gave me a look. I nodded. He sat up. 'Well now, I guess it is time you know that. I'm Joe Reisen and this here is Ella Frank.'

She let the words digest a beat. 'Joe and Ella. Yeah, I like those names. I'm Heidi Schlager. Ma and pa came from somewhere in Germany. I don't know how they ended up in Idaho. Is it okay if I call you by your proper names and you use mine? I mean, I like my moniker but well—it's hard to explain—'

'No, I get it, sweetheart. If we're together, we need to trust one another, don't we?'

Scribbler said, 'I think you Germans would call us a *Freundeskreis*—circle of friends.'

She looked at him. 'You speak German?'

'No, I just remember that from a German hobo I once met, my mind is like that, full of useless stuff. Did your ma and pa speak German to you?'

'Ma did and I remember some, but once she died, that died with her. Pa said little, leastways not stuff you'd want to repeat.'

I said, 'I like the sound of *Freundeskreis*. It's a good word for us.'

Heidi rolled over onto her front, leaned on her elbows and rested her head on her hands. 'How about we use our real names when we're together and monikers when we're in company?'

'Well now,' mused Scribbler. 'Heidi and Ella— I think even I can manage that, though it's going to take a bit of getting used to, mind.'

A night of freedom and the open road ahead seemed to give us all a boost, and the following morning, we set off upstream. I think walking alongside a body of water, or in a forest, is about the finest thing a person can do. It wasn't long before rows of fragrant citrus trees radiated off to the distance and we picked up a trail that led us to the land of Luther and Eliza Van de Berg. We strolled up the hot driveway at the top of which was a great single-story ranch made mostly of wood.

Heidi stopped and gave a little whistle. 'Holy smoke, that is one humdinger of a house, and look at that barn!'

Joe told us to have a sit in the shade while he went and looked for Luther. He headed for the barn and before he got there, this man appear from the great, darkened doorway, and seeing Joe, he hastened toward him, hand outstretched. They shook, and it was clear there was mutual respect. Joe pointed at us. Then the man waved us over.

Joe made introductions, and Luther welcomed us as he ushered us inside the barn's cool interior. Inside there were rows of machinery, these long, wide black belts, benches and hundreds of wooden crates which had a label on them with a picture of oranges and the words "Sanger Gold". Luther walked us over to the far end to a boxlike room. We entered. He took a jug from this strange-looking cupboard and poured us each a glass of juice. He handed one to Heidi. 'Here, young lady, try that.'

She took a sip. Her face lit up, glowing eyes feasting on the bright liquid. 'How'd you get it so cold?'

He pointed at the cupboard. 'This here is a Kelvinator cooling system, runs on electric. We got a bigger one in the house that can freeze the juice. Keeps it fresh for months so we can drink it all year round.'

Heidi took another long slug. 'Like the ice cream store in Kingsburg.'

'Exactly. My wife, Eliza, makes ice cream too.'

'Does she make chocolate?'

He beamed. 'Best there is and my favorite.'

'Mine too.'

She must have been thirsty because she gulped down the rest of the cool, sweet juice without taking a breath. He watched her, an enormous grin on his characterful face. 'Well, Straw Blue, what do you think of my orange juice?'

For a while she studied her glass, thinking. 'Well, sir, I can't say I've drunk a lot of orange juice, but I reckon it doesn't come any finer than this. I can honestly say it is the sweetest, tastiest drink I have ever had and is second only to Kingsburg ice cream in my preferred things to eat and drink.'

And there it was, that way she had with strangers. I reckon even if she hadn't liked the juice, she would not have told him so. He laughed out loud and laid his hand on her shoulder, and taking the glass, said, 'Oh, I like you, young lady! I'll have to get you working on my marketing. Reckon you can manage another?'

She nodded, her hungry eyes sparkling. 'Yes, please. What's marketing?'

He handed her a full glass. 'We can discuss that another time,' he said, tapping his nose.

After we'd drunk, he agreed that he'd take us on. When he discussed payment rates, Heidi's eyes near popped out.

As we headed off, she asked, 'What are we going to do until the harvest? I mean, it's weeks away.'

Joe said, 'Well, it's been quite a year and I reckon it wouldn't hurt to take a vacation. What do you all think?'

She span around, her arms splayed out. 'A vacation, holy smoke, yes! Can we go to the ocean?'

Then it came to me, like a revelation. It had never occurred to me. I stopped them. 'How about Carmel-By-The-Sea? We can ride the rails back to Fresno, pick up a freight to Salinas, then walk to the coast and follow the shoreline. It'll be perfect for us.'

Joe and Heidi looked at one another. 'Sounds like a dandy plan. What do you think, Heidi?'

'If it's by the ocean, I'm all in!'

Joe said, 'You sure you want to go back there, Ella? I mean—'

'Oh, I've got nothing but sweet memories of Carmel, besides it's been almost twenty years; it's time I went back. It is a beautiful place and I want to share it with you.'

— Heidi —

Riding the cushions was all well and dandy, but I liked the adventure of hopping rides. We found easy passage to Salinas. Ella said there was a river nearby that would take us to the coast. The vacation excited me. I'd never been on one, nor rightly knew what you did with it.

After the hot summer, the river was quite low, but we found a pleasant spot with a deep enough pool to wash off the journey's dust and relax our aching bodies. I dumped my clothes and as I lay on my back floating in the early morning sunshine, my mind unoccupied, the past crept up and caught me unawares. Since I had my run in with those bulls, I had been having even more vivid, disturbing dreams about that, and the day I left home. But this was different. It was like a waking dream and I was back in that horrific moment when my life changed forever. I sat up, gasping. A finger of foreboding ran down my spine as I recalled the bits that were vivid and struggled with the parts that were not. I screwed my eyes shut, trying to block it all from my chaotic, panicky mind, muttering. 'Go away, go away, please. I didn't mean it.' The moment passed, leaving me trembling and empty. It was going to be tough putting it to rest, and I felt that until I could, all this was just a lie.

'You okay, sweetheart?'

Ella's voice dragged me back, and I looked over, squinting my eyes in the sunlight. 'Yeah. Just get the odd, weird feeling about what happened with them bulls.'

She swam over. 'Give it time and go slow. You know, the first time I went to Carmel, my heart broken, I thought I didn't deserve to live happy anymore. I set my mind on keeping me down in the dumps. But things changed, because I made them. Experiences, events, stuff, whatever you call it, takes a little of you and molds you different and whichever way you go, you won't ever be the same again.' She beamed; her chocolate eyes glowing. 'But that doesn't mean what's coming can't be better. It'll be different, but it can be good.'

I listened. Her words made it sound so easy.

'I don't remember crying when my ma died.'

She moved closer and reached out her hand, laying it against my cheek. 'There's no rule about any of this. You'll cry about stuff when the time is right, if that's what you need. Just remember, you aren't alone, sweetheart.'

Joe appeared by the bank. 'If I can interrupt you ladies to come get some breakfast before it gets cold?'

Ella took her hand from my face. 'Come on, it will be alright, give it time. Think about all the good stuff.'

We ate, then rested for a couple of hours. I slept. When I woke, the sun was high in the sky. Joe was sitting quietly, smoking. He said, 'You were talking in your sleep.'

I sat up and rubbed my eyes, shook my head. I felt woolly. 'What was I saying?'

'You mentioned Jeremiah, and that you were trying to find him.'

'Oh. I must have been dreaming about him.'

Joe grinned with mischievous eyes. 'A pleasant dream, I hope?'

'I guess. Can't remember.'

Ella said, 'You miss him a lot, don't you?'

I could feel a well of emotion building, so I got up and packed my things away. I didn't want to talk about him and get asked questions I didn't want to answer. Turning to them, I made a mask of my face, and said, 'Come on, take me to that ocean.'

My zeal got us all moving and as we strode out, I swear I tasted salt in the air. The breeze flamed my face, and I tried to imagine what it would look like. Apart from its gentle meandering, the river struck a route directly west. Then, in the distance, I saw it: a vast blue ocean, ruffled on the top and at the edge, a band of yellow-fringed white where water met land. It was breathtaking. I stopped, mouth and eyes wide, staring. Joe came up beside me. 'Wait until you're up close.'

We walked, and it all got bigger and clearer and louder. Finally, we were on the beach. A breeze blew in off the water and I opened my arms and my mouth and let out a joyful yelp. I felt the need to shout, a mixture of release and joy. I ditched my boots and half skipped, half ran down the sand, which felt so nice, hot and rough at the top and cool and soft just below. Then I did something I have not done for ages; I turned a cartwheel. I stopped just where the water made a wet line in the pale sand. Then real slow I walked forward, dipping my toes in the gentle foaming water as it surged up the beach. I did not expect it to be so cold. Not so much as you would not want to get in, but colder than I thought it might be.

A moment later, Ella was beside me. She reached out her hand and I took it. She squeezed, looked out to the distant horizon, her shiny, pitch-black hair ruffled by the breeze. Her eyes shimmered. Her face set in a contented, peaceful smile. As the waves came and went, I noticed my feet dug themselves into the sand. It felt ducky, like I was becoming one with the land and the water.

Ella sighed and said, 'If ever I have to find a place to call home, I want it to be by the ocean.'

A swell of joy built inside me, and I flung out my arms. 'Holy smoke! It's so gigantic and fantastic!'

Ella joined in. 'Isn't it just?'

'Let's get in?'

'Race ya.'

We went back to our bags. I practically tore off my clothes. Free of them, I felt compelled to run as fast as I could. I ran splashing into the low waves, the cold water stinging at my hot naked skin. As it deepened, I found it hard to move my legs until, on the brink of falling, I leaped forward, diving into a breaking wave. The water boiled and frothed about me. It was like nothing I had ever experienced. As I surfaced, I was free of the wave, and I swam forward. The cold made me tingle all over. My skin felt like it was burning and made me feel alive. It was straightforward to swim through, lighter and more airy than regular water. After a while, I stopped my strokes and flipped over onto my back. It was simple to float, and I hardly needed to move my limbs. I whooped at the top of my lungs, then lay still, breathing hard. As the undulating water rolled past me, my body moved up and down. The salt stung my eyes, but not in a way that was unpleasant. I rolled my tongue around my lips, tasting brine. I felt like I could lie here forever just floating about, letting the water take me and all my problems far away.

I heard splashing, and Ella appeared. I righted myself to face her and began treading water, my legs finning away like a duck. She said, 'I'll never tire of this.'

I threw up my arms. 'Best thing ever. Here, look at this.' And I worked my arms and legs to spin me round as fast as I could. As I spun, I laughed until I felt dizzy and stopped, rolling on my back and spreading my arms and legs out like I was making a snow angel. Ella did the same, and spontaneously we maneuvered ourselves so our heads were almost touching. She said, 'Not too cold for you then?'

'Nope. I'm from the Idaho Panhandle. Cold winters, cold creeks, tough people. Anyway, if it ain't cold, it isn't any good for cooling you off, is it?'

We stayed like that for a bit before heading back to shore. As I neared the beach, a powerful, breaking wave picked me up, and I swam for all I was worth as the water boiled and roared around me. When it stopped and the water sucked back, it left me lying on the sand panting and laughing. I had not had so much fun in ages. For a while we sat at the water's edge, the sun warming our skin. The waves roared in, rushed up toward us, sizzling and frothing, and by the time they reached us, just a few inches of bubbling wet enveloped us, tickling my skin. I dug in the sand, pushing my hands and feet in deep.

Ella touched my back and slid her finger along several scars. She didn't speak. I didn't mind her touching me. In fact, it felt nice. I gazed at her. It was the first time I'd seen a grownup woman naked. My body had been changing, and it was good to know that I looked normal. She looked good, her breasts were appealing. I wanted to ask her things about the change but didn't know how.

She glanced at me and smiled. 'You okay, sweetheart?'

I nodded.

'You don't mind me touching you like that?'

'Uh-uh. It feels nice.'

'These marks got anything to do with why you left home?'

'Somewhat, yeah.'

I remembered once, a few days after pa had given me a whipping and the marks were still fresh, Jeremiah and I had been swimming and after, we lay next to one another on the bank, me on my front, and he had touched me just like Ella was doing now. He said, 'Why let him do it?'

'He's my pa.'

His moist, soft lips brushed my back. It tickled and sent a shiver down my spine and made me all goosebumpy.

'He goes too far. He shouldn't beat ya like that. It ain't right.'

I turned to him. 'Things are hard for him. He drinks, gets sore and lashes out. There's really not much I can do about it, is there?'

His eyes were heavy. 'One day, he'll go too far. I'm scared for ya, Fizz.'

I looked at him hard, our eyes locked together, and my love burned for him. Not wanting our moments together to be spoiled, I changed the subject. I sighed. 'Let's not talk about him, shall we? Just kiss me.'

Since that first kiss, we had kissed plenty more. We pressed our lips together, our eyes closed. It was nice to have him close. Then I lay back down, folding my arms under my head, and I closed my eyes. Ever so gently, he touched his lips to the welts and his hand caressed my back and ran over my ass and onto my thigh, which made my skin tingle and sent a warm surge through me. The feel and heat from his body aroused me and I felt this unaccustomed fire inside.

As Ella stroked my back, I felt that warm arousal again as memories of those last weeks between me and Jeremiah coursed through my mind. Losing him made me bitter sad. I shuffled closer to her and put my arm around her waist. I wanted to feel her warmth. She held me. For a time, we sat and let the water lap at us, the incessant waves mesmerizing. I lay my head on her shoulder and whispered, 'I'll tell you all about it sometime.'

(12)

— Joe —

I **watched the girls dump** their things and, like Undines, they ran with a careless surrender into the ocean. It put a big grin on my face. I figured they'd need a good fire to warm up when they were done, so I collected driftwood and found us a spot up on the dunes. By the time I got the fire going, they were sitting in the shallows next to one another. I lit a cigarette and watched. I saw Ella touch those scars on Heidi's back and I wondered if she was asking about them. I was certain they were the work of her pa. It made me desperate to think of her losing her mother and being left with a man who does that. If ever I got the chance to meet him, I'd make sure he'd never forget me. It was kinda dumb, but I couldn't think of any other justice than punching the beans outta him. One thing was for sure, I'd never let that happen to her again.

Heidi moved closer to Ella and put her arm around her. It was good to see they were getting along, and I hoped she could find in Ella what she needed. She'd never be her ma, but maybe the next best thing. I wondered where that left me. Our meeting had prized open my mind like a can, spilling out memories that were as fresh as the day I had packed them away. You go through life thinking you're the only one with crap piled so high it strains to bury you every day of your life. I can't say my life had been bad, or depressing, but I knew that it could have been better, and I did not want Heidi to end up like me: alone, growing old with nothing to show for any of it. She deserved more, but right now we were just marking time and dragging her along for the ride and I couldn't help thinking we might make it worse for her.

I figured Ella would make a great mom and reckoned she should have a chance. Since the attack on Heidi, she had been so caring and tender to her. I guess it was her maternal side. Over the years, Ella and I had used one another for sex and, I guess, a kinda comfort, at least, that is what I had thought. But now I was less sure, and I wondered whether all this time something had kept us from breaking the chains and making more of our love. Perhaps we were too afraid of being hurt and losing what we had. Then there was our age difference. I'd say I was good for my age, but she was still young. Perhaps all this time I had been selfishly stringing her along. Trouble is, I loved her and the times we spent together were always the best. The answers were few, the questions many, and I did not know how deep a hole we were digging.

They had grabbed their clothes and were heading toward me. I raised my hand and gave them my best face. Heidi forged ahead, but my eyes were on Ella. The wind blew her hair about and pushed her damp shirt against her body, and I saw her like I'd never seen her before, and it clean took my breath away.

Heidi ran up and dropped next to the fire with Ella close behind. They both glowed, their skin red from the cold. Heidi held out her hands and warmed them. 'Thanks for getting the fire going, Joe. Good thinking.'

'How was your first swim in the ocean?'

She closed her eyes and shook her head. 'Holy smoke, it was unforgettable! If I live to be a hundred, I'll never lose the memory. Creeks and rivers are nice, but the ocean is something else. Kinda scary too. The power of those waves and it's so big you feel like a speck of dust. Aren't you coming in?'

'Maybe later. You should try swimming in the dark, then it's scary, you know, in a good way. Like being spooked, but you know it's safe, really.'

'I'm up for that, but not on my own.'

Heidi leaned back, resting her weight on her elbows. Her head wound was almost gone. I don't know whether it was the location, with the blue ocean and the pale-yellow sand, but her eyes seemed more intense, like dark sapphires. They were hypnotic.

'You alright, Joe?' said Ella.

'Sorry, I was miles away.'

Heidi said, 'It's funny to think that across the ocean there may be people just like us sitting on a beach by a fire, talking another language, eating different food, yet I bet they like the ocean in the same way, and want the same things as us, too.'

I asked, 'What things do you want, Heidi?'

She shrugged. 'Oh—I dunno. To be loved, I guess, and to love back. To be safe, have a way to live content and free. Have some fun along the way. Not too much to ask, is it?'

I shook my head.

Ella said, 'Where do you think those things will be?'

Heidi cocked her head, looking at Ella, askance. 'I don't know. Maybe one day with Jeremiah.'

She smiled. 'He's your nirvana, isn't he?'

'Nirvana? What's that mean?'

'Heaven, I guess. Like your ideal place in the world. Yeah, I like that better. Heaven has too much religion attached to it, doesn't it?'

Heidi frowned, then nodded. 'I can't imagine meeting anyone else who'd make me feel the way I do about him.'

'I used to think that way about David, but—'

Heidi cut in. 'You have married no one else, though, have you?'

'No, that's true. But that doesn't mean I don't have the same love for someone else. You just got to keep an open mind, and don't fear following your heart.'

Heidi looked between me and Ella, working those eyes. 'How come you two don't spend more time together? I can see the way you are and I reckon you love one another.'

I looked at Ella. She raised her eyebrows. I chose my words carefully. 'Maybe we're still getting to know one another. I always was a late developer.' I grinned, and it cut the tension. Heidi laughed out loud and rolled on her side. 'Holy smoke, Joe, you're killing me.'

I loved the way she said "holy smoke", like a catch phrase. She had such character and despite everything she'd gone through, had bundles to give. I realized Ella was looking at me hard and I wondered if my answer to Heidi's question had riled her. 'You good, Ella?'

She nodded. 'Maybe we know one another better than you think.'

I smiled. 'I guess—maybe, you're right.'

Heidi looked between us. Her eyes told me what she thought, and I figured I'd reached a critical point in my life. Get it wrong now and there would be no other chances. I felt anxious. Guess that's what responsibility feels like.

Ella began fixing food. She didn't want help and Heidi said she fancied a walk alone and she'd collect more firewood. I watched her walk up the beach, and felt blessed that we had met and, in some ways, I reckoned it was a lifeline. Not your regular kind, because this lifeline had two souls attached, and I wondered who was pulling us in and whether the line would hold such a weight. And I surmised if one let go, so would the other. I felt way out of my depth but also I relished the dilemma and I guess it was best to let the ride keep going and hope we'd know when to get off.

At least we had a few weeks to kick back and spend time together, and it sure was nice to be by the ocean again. It brought to mind some verse, and I lay back, closed my eyes and plundered my memory in search of the words.

(13)

— Heidi —

I walked aways up the beach and reveled in the location. Everything seemed so vast; the beach stretched away to the distance; the ocean hugged the land like some colossal blue desert; the infinite sky sat atop of it all, and it made me feel minuscule. I suppose in the scheme of it I was. The further I traveled, the more remote seemed Jeremiah, home and everything it had meant to me. I loved the adventure and experiencing these incredible places, but I did not travel alone: my constant companions, dread and despair, stalked me. Momentarily, I might forget them but then, without warning, they'd be back weighing heavy and escape from them seemed impossible.

By the time I returned to camp with an armful of wood, the sun was setting. The food smelled delicious. The fresh air, swimming and walking had given me a healthy appetite. I sat down and tried to push my dark companions aside. While we ate, we watched the mighty red sun sink into the ocean, and I swear I could hear sizzling as it hit the surface. The shimmering rose pink and ever darkening blue took my breath away. The sounds seemed strident in the dark, and the ocean turned inky-black. Moonlight washed waves came endlessly rolling onto the beach, their repetitive crash-roar-whoosh-hiss comforting. The stars shone bright, and the fire cracked-n-popped. I stared into its glowering heart and told myself I was safe with Joe and Ella and they offered new horizons. All I had to do was let go of my past and embrace this brave new world. Joe's voice broke my trance.

'Such things are hard to put into words and only the greatest of writers dare it.'

Ella and I looked at him. She said, 'You've got some verse for us, haven't you?'
He nodded.

'Have I heard it before?'

'I can't recall.'

I asked, 'Is it about the ocean?'

'In part. It's a type of verse they call a sonnet, by an English poet named John Keats, about his reaction on first reading a translation of Homer by a man called Chapman. Among other things, he likens his experience to the moment in history when the first Europeans saw the Pacific Ocean.'

I said, 'Never heard of him. And what or who is Homer?'

Joe chuckled. 'Well, let's taste the words first and if you like what you hear, we can dig deeper.' He looked out to the cloaked, roaring ocean and while we sat captive with a sense of anticipation, he gave up the verse.

> *'Much have I travell'd in the realms of gold,*
> *And many goodly states and kingdoms seen;*
> *Round many western islands have I been*
> *Which bards in fealty to Apollo hold.*
> *Oft of one wide expanse had I been told*
> *That deep-brow'd Homer ruled as his demesne;*
> *Yet did I never breathe its pure serene*
> *Till I heard Chapman speak out loud and bold:*
> *Then felt I like some watcher of the skies*
> *When a new planet swims into his ken;*
> *Or like stout Cortez when with eagle eyes*
> *He star'd at the Pacific—and all his men*
> *Look'd at each other with a wild surmise—*
> *Silent, upon a peak in Darien.'*

He said it over, and I clung to each word, trying to figure it out. He watched me. He said, 'Beautiful, isn't it?'

I nodded. 'It is. I don't know some words, which makes it tricky to understand fully, but I love the sound of it.'

'I'll write it out. You can study it. You'll figure it out.'

'I like the reference to the men staring at the Pacific.'

He smiled and lit a cigarette. 'Do you think they felt like you did, even though they lived hundreds of years ago?'

'I guess. Don't suppose we've changed that much, have we?'

Joe leaned back on one elbow. 'Not in the way we see wonders of nature.'

I lay back on the sand and looked at the stars like the sky watcher from the poem and pieced together what it was the poet was trying to relate in those few vivid words. I wondered how you could say so much with so little. I said, 'I guess this Keats fella must have had lots of practice to write such words. Sounds like the wisdom of a man who has lived a long time—like you, maybe?'

Joe said, 'Ah. We've all got our own kinda wisdom, even a youngster like you. You think of all the things you have done in your brief life, even since the time we met a few weeks back. The trick is how to put them into words that condense the soul of the experience. That is what a man like Keats mastered, only he wrote that poem when he was just twenty. He died a few years later. Crazy, hey?'

'How'd he die so young?'

'Sickness, I guess. The reason I like those words is they're about the transportive effect that stories, poems, and books can have. Now, I'm willing to bet that you'll never forget today and your first sight of, and swim in the great Pacific Ocean. Am I right?'

'Sure.'

'Well, that was how Keats felt about reading Chapman's translation of Homer, and he went straight off, sat down and put it into those words.'

'You should have been a teacher, Joe.'

'Isn't that what we're doing here?'

'Yeah, I guess.'

'Teaching and learning is what you do all the time. You don't need to put it in a schoolhouse or some fancy college. I teach and learn, so do you. Since I met you, well, you've taught me stuff and I hope I'm wiser for it.'

I frowned. 'What exactly have I taught you, Joe?'

He looked at me for a while. He flicked his cigarette end into the fire. 'Things that are hard to put into words.'

'Go on, try. I'm real curious.'

He sighed. 'Oh, okay, I guess it is like you've made me look at myself different. I've never spent much time with a person your age and I see that the world ain't exactly what I thought it was. Since I left home, I've drifted along like an island, but you've taught me I'm not.' He smiled, lay back and placed his hands behind his head and pushed his hat over his face, deflecting. 'Like I said, it ain't easy to put into words.'

Joe's verse and our chat had dispelled my dark companions, but I knew they'd be back. I yawned, the sea air and the long day pressed down on me, pulling me to sleep. I said, 'I'm glad something as good as you came out of my leaving home.'

Joe said, 'Likewise.'

I rolled on my side and pulled up my blanket. Ella stroked my hair. Then she did something she'd never done before, like a mother does for her child. She lent down, kissed my cheek, whispering. 'Goodnight, sweetheart, sleep well.'

I thought about Keat's words: explorers far from home, away from the people they loved. I guess many never made it back.

— Ella —

As soon as we were awake, Heidi disappeared off for a swim. We watched her distant figure run and dive into the rolling waves. It gave me pleasure seeing her have fun. I hoped that the time we'd have here before we had to head back and work would give her the chance to shake some demons. I'd opened the door, and she said she'd tell me about things, but I know that's easier said than done. Trust is hard earned, but when I laid my hand on her scars, I felt we had moved on in our relationship. All Joe and I could do was be the open arms when she was ready to talk.

Joe had packed stuff away, rolled a smoke, and was watching her. 'She sure likes to get back to nature, doesn't she? Swims like a fish too.'

'I think maybe water is her refuge.'

He looked across at me and nodded. 'I get that. It has a calming effect. And brings out the inner child, too.'

'You saw the marks on her back?'

His eyes darkened. 'Hard to miss. What kinda person does that to their child?'

'Yeah, I think it must have been her pa. I think in time she'll tell us. She's still trying to figure out if she can trust us. Maybe she isn't even sure she can trust herself.'

'I know that feeling.' He reached out his hand and took mine. 'Glad you're here with us. Seems right.'

I moved closer, and we sat there holding hands like love-struck teenagers. It was one of those moments that you cherish filing it away in the book of good. I knew he'd been doing a lot of thinking. We sat enjoying the moment. Heidi had made her way out beyond the breakers and was swimming parallel to the shore. She swam with confident, fluid strokes. I don't think I'd ever seen someone so poised in the water. After a while, she stopped and trod water. She spotted us and waved. We waved back, and that was when this feeling hit me like a bolt of lightning.

I felt bereft and vulnerable, like a child. Thoughts came to me, but I could not make sense of them, and it gladdened my heart that I was not alone. I dropped Joe's hand and put my arm around him.

He looked at me. 'You cold?'

'Nah. I'm—just—you know, having a scooch.'

'Well, you scooch away.'

Heidi turned and began swimming back. She must have been giving it everything because she cut through the water, covering the distance at great speed; it impressed me.

'Did I ever tell you about my family?'

I looked into his green eyes; they had a distant stare. 'I asked, but you never did.'

He moved his head in a slow nod. 'I had—have—a twin sister. She's called Florence, though of course, we always called her Flo. I don't know if it has anything to do with this but since I met Heidi and we all set off like some kinda makeshift family, Flo has come back to my mind and I have a powerful urge to find her.'

'Were you tight?'

'I'd say, as siblings go, we were. We got along fine. I know when I left home it was her I missed most, and believe me, I had plenty to miss.'

'Didn't you want to go back and see her?'

'It wasn't an option.'

'Oh, I see—kinda.'

He let go my hand. 'I think when we're done picking oranges, I want to go look for her.'

'You want to do that alone or with company?'

'Oh, I think maybe you know the answer to that.'

'Alright. I can take care of Heidi. But, and this is important, we need to discuss it with her, okay?'

'Yeah, of course. Maybe we can all give the past a good airing. This seems like the place.'

Heidi was running back up the beach. Some people look clumsy and out of sync when they run, but she was graceful, everything working in harmony. She scrambled up the dune. 'That was the best swim ever.' She dropped to the ground, panting, her wet hair plastered to her face. She had grown and filled out a little. You could see the woman ready to blossom. Even though she wasn't mine, I felt a great love for her and knew that my mission was to see her become a woman and be at peace with her past. It was the first time since my David passed that I had felt duty-bound to another human being and it felt empowering, but I didn't want to do this alone.

Heidi ruffled her hair, then gathered it up into a ponytail. 'Is there a beach at Carmel?'

'The town is right on a beach. If you move down the coast from there, it becomes wilder. When I was there, I camped near a beach a short distance south of the town. It was quiet, no one to bother me. If you two are agreeable, I reckon we should go back and check it out.'

Joe stood and stretched out. 'Sounds like a plan. Long walk ahead, I guess we should blow.'

We lifted our world on our backs and headed south. Heidi pushed on ahead.

Joe and I fell into step, the way hoboes do when padding-the-hoof. He asked, 'What's Carmel like for work?'

'There's a fishery nearby run by oriental folks and a quarry. I can't say if they'll still be there. Good chance they'll be laboring jobs around about. Aren't you going to take some time to kick back?'

'Maybe a few days, but seeing as it may take a while to find Flo, I reckon some extra scratch will come in handy, and I can leave some to help with Heidi.'

I put my arm around him. 'That's real thoughtful.'

He smiled. 'Feels kinda nice, having responsibility for others gives you a sense of purpose. Don't know much about fishing, so I guess I'll check out the quarry.'

By lunchtime we were still on the beach but had sight of the coast as it turned west. It looked wilder. I remember having been this way all those years ago and was sure that we could cut across the headland and save time. Heidi wanted to follow the coast road and as we weren't in any hurry, we hugged the shoreline that ran between small gullies of boiling surf on dark rocks, grand views, an invigorating sea breeze, and the taste of meeting our destination driving us on. Heidi never seemed to tire and spent most of the walk yards ahead, giving us time, which we spent equally in talk and thought. Though he was some quarter century older than me, he had plenty of life left in him. He was fit, unfettered by physical ailments, failing health, dull eyes or dimmed hearing. The years of outdoor living had weathered his skin, but he was still handsome, with a sharp mind and a kind heart.

I guess, like Joe, I had done a heap load of thinking, and as he said, the responsibility of Heidi had changed things. Though Joe and I had a special place in one another's hearts, after a time always we'd go our own way. I guess you might say we are itinerant lovers. But things were changing, and now I knew I wanted to be with him. He had never mentioned his family or his past. He was always a man of the moment, so I guess he needed to make some kinda peace before heading into uncharted territory. My worry was how I put it to him. Did he love me enough to want to make it permanent? Would it scare him off and leave me with Heidi? I was worried if he went off alone to find Florence we might never see him again, and then what?

Truth was, I guess I was worried about my own feelings. Life on your own is easy, but it has a cost, and I didn't want that anymore, like for the first time since David died I had a purpose: this girl with secrets had come into our lives out of the blue as though it had meant to be. You think about the chances of them meeting at that exact moment in the vast country that is America, riding the thousands of miles of track, and in all the multitude of boxcars. It sets your mind to thinking that other forces are at work, doesn't it? Then there was the way she had won him over almost in a flash, turned this loner traveler into a guardian without another thought. He'd fed her, clothed her, protected her, gave her his friendship, and without him even knowing it, she had somehow prized open his thinking and made him look back with a need to connect to lost family. A cynic might say it was just a coincidence, but I don't believe that. I must confess, after years of life set uncomplicated by the needs of others, it felt like we were heading into a new phase of our lives, and I found that thought to be equally exciting and unsettling. But the one thing that had struck me most was I yearned to be a mom.

Joe interrupted my thoughts. 'This place sure takes your breath away. And I'm wondering why you left here and traveled to Tucson, of all places.'

I laughed, like he had been reading my mind. 'I guess something guided me there to meet you.'

He grinned. 'Now that's the kinda answer that can set a jungle in deep discourse, can't it?'

'I learned from the best.'

He pointed toward Heidi. 'Looks like she's been driven on by something, doesn't she?'

'Yesterday, when we were swimming, she told me she had never been on a vacation. Never been more than a few miles from home. Now look at her.'

'It ain't stuff you can plan, is it? One minute we were lolling about in the middle of a small town in Iowa about as far away from the ocean as you can get, and the next we're making time on the fringe of the Pacific. And to get here she had to go through God knows what, run away, almost starve, run away again, almost get killed, and then put her trust in two homeless boes who'd never had to look out for anyone other than themselves.'

I swept my arms through the air. 'Yeah, so tell me that out there somewhere there isn't some guiding hand.'

He shrugged. 'Put that way, it seems reasonable.'

'Quite a story. Wonder how it will end?'

He put his arm around my waist. He'd never done that before when we were walking. It was like we had crossed a road and taken a rural lane rich with secret intimacy, and I reciprocated. 'It'll end the way we want it to, just needs us to take the right path as it comes along. Reckon we've been doing alright so far, don't you?'

His answer gave me hope, like it settled in his mind that we were part of his future. Up ahead, we saw Heidi had stopped. She turned and waved, yelling, 'Come on, I think we're almost there!'

As we joined her on the spit of land that stuck out like a viewing deck, a grand vista treated us, and there, almost close enough to touch, was Carmel. Just off the sandy beach you could see the neat town much as I remembered it, and the sight of it brought back an unexpected cocktail of memories.

(15)

— Ella —

We found an ideal spot for our camp in a shallow valley with fragrant trees flanking the slope, a stream nearby and a secluded, sandy cove just a few short steps away. We settled in and for the first two days, took our ease, improved our new home, and made use of the glorious beach and ocean. All along, Heidi had frequent, disturbing nightmares. Joe told me about the night in the hotel. He said that for a time after he left home, night horrors—as he called them—plagued him.

After David died, I used to dream about him, but they weren't nightmares as such, but more poignant and emotionally draining. Like, I'd dream I could see him on the other side of a road but could never get across to him, or he'd be walking and I tried to catch up and couldn't, no matter how hard I ran. Their meaning was easy to understand, and when I woke I'd feel sadness but nothing more. In time, the dreams ceased. Joe said his had too.

Heidi woke from her terrors, drenched in sweat, shivering, crying and breathless. I know it sounds odd, but it gave me and Joe an excuse to hold and comfort her, and I hoped it would speed the healing process. I asked her to tell me about them but she said she couldn't remember, just knew they were terrifying. It made me feel powerless and sad to see her so traumatized.

I noticed she was quiet and preferred spending time alone, swimming and lying in the sun. I put it down to fatigue and her need to recover from the epic journey, new experiences, and those lurking demons. It was a lot for someone so young to handle. Both Joe and I kept out a weather eye, but I felt frustrated at not knowing what I could do to get closer and earn her trust. Joe thought that patience and love would provide the answers, and we were conscientious not to pressure her.

On the third day, Joe went off in search of work. After breakfast, Heidi cleared up, as she always did. She came back from the stream with the cleaned tinware and sat down. I sat down beside her and handed her a cloth. 'Here, you dry and I'll put away.'

She nodded, and silently we set to work; her look distant. I said, 'Do you fancy strolling over to explore Carmel? I need to get some things, too.'

She looked up. Her eyes were dull with big dark circles underneath. She smiled weakly. 'Sure, I'd like that. Is there a library?'

'Don't recall there being one.'

She looked down, her shoulders slumping. 'What about a picture house? I'd love to see another movie, something funny.'

I shrugged. 'Things will have moved on in the years since I was here. Only one way to find out. Let's go see, shall we?'

We fell into step and made the twenty-minute walk in silence. The town ran along the edge of a glorious beach. We headed almost to the far end before turning inland and heading up the main drag—Ocean Avenue. I said, 'Shall we find a café and maybe we can ask where things are?'

It didn't take long to find an establishment. A young, bubbly waitress came over. 'Morning, ladies. What can I get for you?'

I said, 'Coffee and maybe a slice of cake.' I looked over at Heidi. 'What do you say?'

She nodded.

In just a few moments, the waitress was back. 'Here we are. Anything else I can get you folks?'

'Is there a movie house in town?'

She smiled, her face lighting up. 'Oh, I just love the flicks. Me and my beau, Frank, like to sit near the back, and—' She remembered where she was and blushed. 'Sorry, yes, of course. They have regular shows at the Golden Bough. It's just up the street, between Lincoln and Monte Verde. You can't miss it.'

'And is there a library?'

'Oh, sure, it's close to the theater, between Lincoln and Sixth. I love detective stories, don't you?'

Heidi gave me a look, and for a moment, I thought she was going to burst out laughing. It was a glimmer of joy, but in a flash, it was gone. I said, 'Why, thank you, Delores.'

She beamed, touching her hand to her name tag and said, 'Well, thank you. Maybe I'll see you at the movies.' She looked at Heidi. 'Has anyone ever said you have beautiful eyes?' At that, she turned and went over to a table just occupied by an elderly couple. We heard her say their names and a genial conversation struck up.

Heidi took a sip of coffee. 'Well, she's nice. If she's an example of the locals, I think this place will do just fine. I'm excited to see the library.' Her excitement did not translate to her tone, but at least she had found her voice.

It was in a delightful, wood-shingled cottage. Inside it was calm, with rows of books lining the walls. Heidi's eyes were like saucers. 'Holy smoke, Ella. I've never seen so many books. I think I've died and gone to heaven.' Her exclamation had drawn attention. A middle-aged woman with styled, dark hair and elegant eyeglasses came over. 'Why welcome, folks. I couldn't help overhearing your comment, miss. I'm always glad to have a young bookworm join us. I'm Miss Jennings, the librarian.'

'I'm Heidi. I've never heard of bookworms. Are they a good thing?'

Miss Jennings beamed and touched a finger to her nose. 'In here, they most surely are. Bookworms are people who love to devour books—' She put her hand up to her mouth and chortled. 'Not literally, of course, but with their eyes and minds.'

'Well, Miss Jennings, in that case, I am categorically a bookworm. Only it hasn't been easy getting books, us being on the road.'

I had not realized quite how much Heidi loved reading. She came alive.

She asked, 'How many books do you have here, Miss Jennings?'

Miss Jennings placed her hand on Heidi's back and guided her down the first row of shelving. As they walked, she ran her fingers along the books' spines like she was caressing a much loved pet. 'At the last count we had almost five thousand five hundred.'

I followed.

Heidi puffed out her cheeks. 'I never knew there were so many. Why if I read one a week—' I could see her working the math. 'It would take me over a hundred years to get through them. Holy smoke!'

I said, 'Well, you better get started. What say I leave you here while I run some errands?'

She turned and looked at me. Her eyes had their sparkle back. 'Is that okay, Miss Jennings?'

I was gone about an hour and when I returned, Heidi was sitting near a window, her nose buried in a book. I watched her for a while. She didn't notice me, lost in whatever world lay between the pages. She was a smart kid and needed to be in school, somewhere like this, with other kids and living a normal life. None of that fit with me and Joe, but seeing her there made me realize that I'd do anything to give her a better life. It was an eye-opener, like my existence would mean something if I helped her.

I joined her. She looked up and beamed.

'What you reading?'

'"Treasure Island". It's by the same author that wrote the poem I like, you know the one?'

I nodded. She closed the book. 'Miss Jennings said the coast near here gave him the inspiration for the story, that he stayed here. Apparently, he was lovesick.' She frowned, thinking. 'I like that word, lovesick. I think I have that for Jeremiah.' She laughed. 'I'm a lovesick bookworm from Idaho.'

I sat down, laid my hand on her arm. 'Oh, Heidi, sweetheart. It's good to hear you laugh and see you happy.'

She nodded. 'Thanks, Ella. I'll get there. I think.'

Miss Jennings told us there was no charge for Heidi to join the library, and with a few books in hand, we headed off to find the movie theater. The impressive building was just a few minutes' walk away. That evening, they were showing Harold Lloyd's "Girl Shy". 'Perfect,' I said. 'A comedy. Harold Lloyd is something. We gotta go see it.'

'Oh, can we?'

I bought three tickets for a buck and a quarter. We headed back for camp. I saw why Joe had thought about getting work. A youngster came with responsibility and not all things came free, but cash spent feeding her mind and giving her some fun was special. I don't think anyone had ever done that for her, and I got quite emotional thinking about it.

When we got back to camp, Joe was there. He'd been busy collecting a stash of firewood. 'Hey, you two. They took me on at the quarry.'

Heidi said, 'Hey, Joe, we're going to the movies tonight.'

'We are? What we seeing?'

'"Girl Shy". It's a Harold Lloyd film.'

He grinned. 'Oh, Harold Lloyd. Now he'll make you laugh, for sure.'

'Plus, they got a library in town and I've got this.' She showed him her book.

He took it and turned it over in his hands. 'A brilliant story. Hey you should read, Kidnapped, too.'

She nodded. 'They've got over five thousand books there, Joe. It's going to take me over a hundred years to read 'em all.' She giggled. 'If that's not a reason to live a long life, I don't know what is?'

He looked away, his voice dropping. 'Life is too short, that's for sure.'

After lunch, she disappeared to the beach. She asked us if we wanted to come, but I wanted an opportunity to talk to Joe, so I told her to have fun, but what happened next changed everything.

16

— Joe —

After two days of lolling around, I became restless. Heidi's night terrors were hard to take, and it reminded me of the time soon after I left home, of the endless nights clouded by dark dreams and darker awakenings. I don't recall how or why they ended, but I guess I made enough distance to settle my mind and bury them deep enough to stop the fretting. Since meeting Heidi, I'd dreamed again of my past. Not nightmares, just flashes of disorganized events but vivid enough to shake my heart, unleashing yearning and regret, the kind I didn't want to face but knew I had to. I'd reached the end of the road and before me lay a dark, thick, foreboding forest. Somewhere ahead lay a hidden path. I just had to find it and hack myself through. But what lay beyond? More darkness or wide sweeping pastures full of light and hope?

With all this on my back, I did what I always did: got a job, put my head down and buried it in the sand. The quarry wasn't far, and they offered me work and fair scratch, so I didn't bother looking elsewhere. Physical work was and always has been my therapist. The work was simple, my workmates short on words, and the location pleasant, with views of the ocean. It was my kinda place. While I humped rock, I worked my mind and stilled my heart, and somewhere among the broken boulders and honest sweat, I'd find that path through the dark forest. Maybe in the middle I'd find Heidi wandering lost and alone, and together, hand-in-hand, we'd find a way through to Ella's voice calling from the other side. Was that cowardly of me to expect her to aid my journey, or was it honest to humble myself and admit I needed her?

I swung the sledgehammer, a mighty clang as it made sweet contact with the iron wedge and the rock gave up and fell in two.

Banjo Bill looked at me, grinning. 'Damn, Scribbler, you hit that harder than a drunk hits the hooch. Yes sir, that boulder gave up like a girlie on her wedding night. Amen.'

I understood men like Banjo.

I understood hard work and the freedom it brought. All these years, it had served me well and never let me down. Men like Banjo didn't ask questions or waste time idly bumping their gums about stuff that clawed at your soul. They'd rip a yarn, spin a verse, sing a sad song, or tell a crude joke. It didn't mean they didn't care, have a heart or knew the time to shut their yap and just sit and let the quiet do the talking. For almost fifty years, men like Banjo were all I needed. In between, Ella gave me the sugar and a delicate reprieve just enough to stop my soul from dying. But now, right on this spot, I knew my time with the Banjos of this world was poor compensation for what was due me, and what I had to offer. The big sleep was at an end. It was time to wake up and become Joe Reisen once more.

Banjo helped me smash the two halves and load them on the cart. He said, 'Take five, I'll hump this lot, then I need to have me a movement.' He hefted the barrow and headed off. Yeah, there was more to life than Banjo, work and selfish solitude. All that time ago, I had abandoned those that needed me and I was damned if I was going round a second time. But standing on the fringe of that dense forest terrified me. I could hear Ella calling, and I knew Heidi wandered lost within the darkness, and only we could save her. But truth was, I did not know how to.

As I walked back to camp, my mind and body calmed by the physical work, I recognized I looked forward to finding people there that I loved and who loved me. Did they love me? Was love the wrong word? Too strong, maybe? I remembered telling Heidi that it depended what you meant by love. I knew for sure that I loved Ella. Heidi, I wanted to protect and help, but isn't that love, too? I enjoyed her company, intelligence, playfulness, and her spirit. I wanted to stop her from having to live the life I had. I was sure she had run from a violent, abusive father and her torment came from knowing that to get back to Jeremiah meant going back to him as well. I resolved that before I could sort out my stuff, I must take her home and make sure she would never again fear her pa.

I figured time was not our ally. She was awful quiet and the dreams more frequent, so I reckoned I should front it up and suggest we get right back to Idaho and nip it in the bud. After, she could still come with us to pick oranges and what have you. Maybe she could bring Jeremiah with her, too. It was a loose plan, but from my experience, I considered it was the best for all. With a heady resolve, I held my head high and strode home.

When I got back to camp, Heidi and Ella had been into town, and Heidi seemed chirpier. And it caused me to falter. Yes, believe it or not, I was that weak, and it changed my resolution and I thought maybe the vacation would be the answer, so I kept my peace, and in the end fate had another hand to play. Doesn't it always?

17

— Heidi —

I left Joe and Ella and made my way to the beach. I stripped off and lay in the sun. Night after night of those awful dreams, each becoming more vivid, had consumed me. Then the living nightmares had begun. I'd be doing something or other and images would flood my mind and I was back there, in my house, the whole hideous event playing out like I was a helpless spectator. I could hear Jeremiah calling out, see the look in my father's cold, blue eyes. Smell things as I remembered them: the sweat, the blood, and the cheap moonshine. But most of all, I bore the fear: raw, malevolent fear.

I felt utterly powerless and despite being here with all its peace and beauty being looked after by Ella and Joe, I knew it would never go away and I'd spend the rest of my life looking over my shoulder, my past stalking me like some hateful predator. I missed Jeremiah so much it pressed me down with overwhelming sadness. I felt horrible guilt that I'd left him to face the music while I, like some criminal coward, had fled, and was here sitting pretty, having the time of my life; except I wasn't.

To shake off my melancholy, I swam and as I pushed out through the surf into calmer water, began heading further out. I had made no plan. I just kept going, and as I tired, I stopped, and treading water spun round to look back at the now distant shore. Then it came to me. Just keep going and make a hole in the water. It would look like an accident, and I would pay my dues. I lay on my back pointing my head out to sea and began gently sculling my arms, propelling myself into destiny's embrace. As time passed, I had not noticed the cold sapping my strength and before I knew it, violent shivering took hold, and I could hardly think. My arms and legs stopped working properly. I struggled to keep afloat. Of course, that was the moment I realized I did not want to die and from somewhere found a little strength to keep me going. I do not know how long this went on, as I drifted into lethargy. Each time my head went under water I saw Jeremiah's pleading face and his hand reaching out to me, and I'd wake and break the surface, coughing and spluttering. But each time I swallowed a mouthful or two and knew it was hopeless. I'd just got to where I could not feel my limbs and my mind had found a peace, that these powerful arms were pulling at me, and my world went blank.

Someone was tapping my face. I woke, spluttering and choking. I did not know where I was. I could hear this loud droning, rumbling noise, and there was a powerful smell of something like oil. A man was holding me, my body wrapped in blankets. He looked different to other men, had a strange accent that I could not place. I just wanted to sleep, but every time I closed my eyes, he would tap my face and shake me, not roughly, but just enough to bring me back. It irritated me and I got angry, which made him smile. Then another man came over. He too looked different, and I realized they were foreign, oriental looking. It confused me. Had I swum all the way to another country? Who were these people? Would I get back to Joe, Ella, and Jeremiah?

Maybe I was in heaven, but then I don't believe in all that and anyway sinners like me don't go to heaven. Hell then? If this was hell, it didn't seem too bad. The man did not look like the pictures of devils I had seen and read about in books. There were no flames, though the oily, fishy smell was unpleasant. The man that held me took the cup the other one gave him. He lifted my head and put the hot cup to my trembling lips. 'Drink, it will help.' His voice was soothing, which didn't fit with hell, either. I sipped the hot, sweet liquid. It was good. I closed my eyes again. The tapping on my face returned, a little harder this time. The strange oriental accent. 'No, no, come on child, try.' He lifted my head and sat me up, holding me tight. 'Drink.' Then shouted something in another language. The droning, rumbling sound increased. He made me drink more, and when the cup was empty, another came, then another. It helped, and I felt better. I was shivering, though less so than I had been in that icy water. I focused some and looked at his face. He had kind eyes, like Joe's. I thought about Joe and Ella and how sad they would be at my passing. How could I do that to them after everything they had done for me? And Jeremiah, how could I leave him without saying goodbye?

I thought about the movies and the library and was mad at myself for being so stupid. But the pain was there. Perhaps that was what happened to sinners after they died, left to an eternity of regret and misery.

The droning sound faded, and the man picked me up and stood. I realized we were on a boat and must be near to shore. But where was I? Some foreign land? Clawing fatigue drowned me and I closed my eyes.

The voice, loud this time, broke through. 'Wake up, stay awake or you'll die.' The words "or you'll die" nudged me. So I was alive, or was it another trick to keep me awake and suffering? Never again would they allow me to sleep. Dread flooded through my aching, exhausted body.

All you have to do, Heidi, is go to sleep and it will end: no shouting, fear, or gut-wrenching sadness. Just peace.

But try as I might whenever I closed my eyes, he brought me back, each time with more urgency.

He sat with me on his lap, now bumping along, more droning mechanical sounds. It was daytime, but everything seemed hazy. I kept trying to shut down, and he kept at me, over and over. Then the bumping and joggling stopped and once more he carried me. The light reflected from the bright white walls. It was quiet, the unpleasant smells were gone. There were other people, women dressed funny, but they weren't oriental, they sounded American.

The loud, brutal man disappeared, and the strangely dressed women took me. They removed the blankets and put my cold, naked body in water so hot I thought I was to be cooked. It hurt, like my skin was peeling off, but when I looked it seemed fine. After a bit, they pulled me out, dried me and then laid me in a big, soft bed. The coverings felt heavy and warm and, finally, blissfully. Sleep.

part
three

— Joe —

Through the night and well into the next day, Ella and I sat beside Heidi's bed and it killed me we were doing so for the second time in just a handful of weeks, though this time it seemed worse because I could not imagine life without her. It had been a miracle that the Japanese fisherman, Katsura Hikomori, had plucked her freezing and half-drowned from the ocean. His long experience and knowledge saved her life. Wrapping her in blankets, he held her to the warmth of his body and sitting near the boat's motor, forced hot, sweet tea down her and kept her awake. On coming to shore, he took her straight to the monastery, knowing the sisters had an infirmary and the right care.

Once safe, she had drifted into unconsciousness, and now we sat, waiting. I cannot say why, but I knew she would be alright because she's one of the good ones and a fighter and I was damned if I'd let her die.

Sister Catherine entered the room. She came over and checked Heidi's pulse and temperature.

'How's she doing?'

'She's doing well. Her heart is strong, her lungs clear, and her temperature is normal. She just needs rest. Why don't you both go home and get some sleep? You won't be any good to her if you get sick.' Ella and I glanced at one another. Sister Catherine glared at us as a parent might their errant child. 'Don't worry, we'll take good care of her. I promise. If she wakes I'll send for you. Now go.' And she stepped aside and pointed at the doorway.

Stepping out into the warm, calm of the afternoon, I felt strangely disconnected. We walked, heads down, pondering.

After a bit, Ella said, 'Do you think she tried to drown herself?'

I'd thought about little else since they had sent for us. 'Not that it's saying much, but she is the most confident swimmer I have ever met.'

'The ocean is a fickle place. Perhaps the current took her and she couldn't fight it?'

'Maybe. She has been gloomy and quiet these last days. And we both know she is carrying guilt, or trauma that rears up at her and she changes from a confident girl to one that is scared and troubled. And those nightmares. Almost every night now she wakes screaming. It's exhausting her, and if I'm truthful, me too.'

'Yeah. Well, let's be practical and assume the worst, that she purposefully put herself in harm's way. Maybe she did not intend to end it, but we can't let her carry on like this. We must get her to open up.'

'And if she won't?'

Ella took my hand. 'We show her the way, tell her that no matter what may have befallen her, we're here for her, no strings or conditions. It's essential we make her believe that.'

I nodded. 'I have seldom felt such a sense of love and responsibility to another than I do to her, even if it's in my own broken, clumsy way.' I stopped and turned to her. 'I've been thinking a lot about my past and about you, too. About us.'

She laid her hand on my cheek. 'Me too. Things have changed, Joe. I realize I want things I never thought about. Like being a mom, and—' She broke off and began walking slowly.

I fell into step. 'And?'

She glanced across. 'And I don't want to be doing that alone.'

I let the words sink in. 'Dammit, Ella, I'm a sixty-four-year-old homeless man with no past and no future—'

'You don't have to be those things anymore, though, do you?'

'I'm old and set in my ways.'

'Yes, you're getting on, Joe, but you're not old. Look at yourself. You have lots of life in you. Look at the way you play with her in the water. The way you talk to her. You're healthy, you don't need eyeglasses, or a cane, the years of work and clean living have made you strong. But most of all, you are a kind, intelligent, caring man. So, give yourself a break, wilya?'

I smiled. I guess she was right. 'I know things you don't. About me.'

'I don't give a rat's ass about your past. All I see is what I got right in front of me, which is a good, dependable man. Folk like you aren't easy to come by, believe me, I've looked. I guess that's why I kept coming back to you and taking what you could give. You're good-looking, and I enjoy having sex with you because— dammit, you're good at that, too.'

I held up my hand. 'You really think all those things?'

'Of course I do, Joe. Don't you love me?'

I pulled her to me, and we kissed. 'I always thought you were too good for me. I didn't deserve someone as beautiful, warm and bright as you. The sex is good because you light my fire, you're goddamn gorgeous, and having you is special.'

We walked. For a while we didn't speak. In all the years we had been together, we had never declared our feelings, not truly. But then life goes on and sets its own rhythm and before you know it, two decades have passed. I genuinely didn't understand she felt that way. How stupid could I be? All these years I had been drifting like a blind-deaf-mute. I thought I had buried my past, but I hadn't; it had buried me. It had stopped me from seeing what was right before me. And there it was, the hidden path through the dense forest, except Ella wasn't calling on the other side. She was standing right next to me to take my hand and hasten forward, find Heidi and get us clear.

By now we had met the beach and headed along the sand. Then I was alone.

She had stopped. She called after me, 'I love you. I always have, but I was afraid to say it.' I turned and stood, blinking. She looked vulnerable, and more beautiful than I'd ever seen her. 'Well Joe Reisen, say something, dammit!'

I walked to her, cupped her face, looked deep inside her deep brown eyes and planted my lips on hers. She opened her mouth, and we kissed passionately, in a way we'd never done before. The moment took us and we made love on the beach like it was the first time, full of wild passion and newness. After, we lay together as the sun slipped toward the ocean, bathing it crimson red. And I said, 'Sorry.'

'For what?'

'Sorry for wasting all them years.'

We kissed again. She looked deep into my eyes. 'Maybe it was meant to be, but let's not waste any more time, shall we?'

When the sun had slipped away, the moon bathed the landscape in a harsh chromium light. Hand-in-hand, we walked naked into the ocean. It felt like I was washing away all those years in the wilderness and when we came out and sat on the cooling sand, were reborn. It was late when we made the walk back to our camp. Sleep was a million miles away, so we made love again and then, exhausted, fell asleep entwined.

19

— Ella —

When I woke, I was alone. I felt renewed, like I was eighteen years old. I guessed Joe had gone to work, so I dressed and made up a breakfast lump and strolled over to the quarry, stopping on the way for a quick swim to wash the sweat away. It was a cooler day, but he stood there stripped to the waist, his lean, muscular frame hauling a large barrow of rock. Seeing me, he laid it down and came over. He kissed my cheek. 'I didn't want to wake ya.' I smelled the sweat and heat on him. I laid my hand on his glistening chest and handed him the food. 'Can you take a few minutes to eat?'

'Sure, let's sit up over there.'

He unwrapped the lump, and we tucked in. In the last day-or-so, we'd hardly eaten. We were famished and for a while ate in silence. After, Joe said, 'How do you feel this morning—you know—about us?'

I wanted to keep things light. 'Well, I'd say that was the best sex we've ever had, so if that's a sign, I reckon I feel good about it. You?'

'I feel like I can see some kinda future for us all. You know, like, maybe we're supposed to be together. I won't deny I'm worried about me becoming a burden on you.'

I laughed and gave him a nudge. 'That's okay. When the time comes, I'll just trade you in for a younger model.'

He chuckled. 'I'll hold you to that, you know.'

I ran my hand through my untidy, salt-stiffened hair. 'No point in worrying about stuff like that, and besides, our future is about what we do today, not tomorrow.'

He turned to me. 'Give me your hand.' I did as he asked. 'If we were together, and I don't mean just a declaration of love, but really together—'

'You mean married?'

'Hell, yes, why not?'

'What, get married and roam the land, the perfect homeless couple? I can see them writing songs about us.'

He shook his head, his expression serious. 'No, I mean get married and find a place to call home.'

I frowned, looked at him, and our glistening eyes met. 'Really? You'd want that?'

'Sure. It'll take some getting used to, but I can't see it working any other way, particularly with Heidi to consider. So, I've been thinking about that. How would you feel if we offered to adopt her, legal like?'

I hadn't expected him to suggest all this at once. 'What about her father?'

'We'll have to take some advice, but I reckon if it's her decision, why not?'

'So, are you asking me to marry you so we can adopt her?'

'Well, yes, and no. I want to marry you because I love you and I want to make what's left of my life with you. But I feel like having Heidi as a part of us would be good for her and us both.'

I dropped his hand and stood up. 'Ask me again, Joe Reisen.'

He stood and then went down on one knee. I put my hand to my face to stifle a laugh. But I felt like a girl again, and my heart thumped in my chest. He cleared his throat. 'Luella Frank, would you do me the honor of marrying me?'

He looked at me with puppy eyes and I knew he meant it and it was for the right reasons. 'Yes. Joseph Reisen, I will, dammit.'

We kissed. Strangely, all I could think about was I hoped it would last longer than my first marriage. We broke away. I laid my hand on his scrubby cheek. 'You better get back to work. You've got a load more responsibility now.' I giggled and tapped his cheek. Then I kissed him; he tasted salty. 'I'm going over to the monastery. I'll see you later.'

'Give her my love, wilya?'

'Course.' As I walked away, I felt his fiery eyes boring through me. I liked it.

As I made my way, I thought about where we were and how we could best help her. I knew I wanted her in my life. What person wouldn't? She was smart, kind, attractive, but also vulnerable, young and she so deserved to have a proper mother and father and a home. She needed to have friends her age and enjoy the last years of childhood. I felt like everything was happening so fast, but also like it was our destiny. If Heidi could see we could offer her a proper home and be parents, then maybe that would be enough to help her get better.

My route had taken me along a path I had not traveled before. About a half-mile inland, I came to a large, scrubby field in a low wooded valley. I couldn't see any sign of life. It was a peaceful spot, and stuck in the ground was a post, with a sign pinned to it:

"For sale, Ye Old Realty, enquire to M. Escott, South Pacific St. Phone 768".

I looked around. It was a glorious spot. I closed my eyes and imagined us here. *Now, wouldn't that be something?*

I sat down by the field and took a few minutes to think things through. Truth was that my mind was all over the place. On the one hand, I felt like I had started fresh with Joe and it felt bizarre and bewildering. I knew him, but not that well. I had told him I didn't care about his past, but of course I did, and I needed to know. I told myself that whatever it was, it wouldn't make one speck of difference, but then how can you say that until you have the facts? Then there was Heidi, almost fifteen and carrying baggage so heavy it had almost killed her. I was an open book, no secrets, no unpacked bags, or complication but it scared the crap outta me; I was between two people I loved so much but knew so little about. A few weeks earlier, I would have hefted my world on my back, headed off, hopped a ride and made like dust. But I didn't want to keep running, and I had to find from somewhere the strength to get them to confide in me.

I mused about what it was they had hidden. Had Joe killed someone, maybe? Had he done something so terrible it had made him go on the run, a fugitive? What about her? Maybe someone raped her, or after years of abuse from her pa—then the thought struck me. It made my blood run cold. Maybe he'd raped her and Jeremiah had tried to fight him off and that's how he'd gotten injured. Knowing how much she loved Jeremiah, it was not something trivial that had caused her to run. And what about Jeremiah? She was goofy for him, said she loved him like no one else. So, wouldn't she be better off going back and being with her boy? Maybe we could go with her and sort things out? But sort out what? I needed to know, and one thing was for sure, I was going to make her tell me and I didn't care what it was. She was mine, and I'd do anything for her. I felt like an outraged bear defending its cub from a pack of snarling, salivating wolves. It was like I had woken up from a twenty-year trance.

My mind set, I hastened to the monastery. When I got there, she was awake but didn't want to talk. I told her to take her time, and that Joe had sent his love and would be along later. I so wanted to tell her about us, and how we wanted her, but I didn't wish to put her under any pressure. I lay down next to her and stroked her hair and put my arm around her. She placed her hand on mine and relaxed.

— Heidi —

I woke up lying in a soft bed and I wondered if I was back at Doc Moon's and had dreamed it all. Then I looked and knew I was somewhere else. The room had stark white walls and light flooded in. I let my eyes wander around and they came to rest on a black wooden cross with the crucified Jesus set in silver on it. There were other beds, none of which were occupied. At the far end of the room was a small desk at which sat a lady dressed in black, wearing a type of white bonnet the like of which I had never seen. I did not know how I had got here. Maybe I was dead and in heaven. But, if this were heaven, wouldn't my ma be here by my side? I sat up. A voice said, 'Well bless the lord, you are awake.' It was the lady at the desk. She came over. 'Now don't rouse yourself, lay back and rest.' She had soft eyes and beautiful, pale skin that looked so smooth. She smelled of soap and something else, like the tree resin did back home. I lay back down, and she lay her cool hand on my forehead. I asked, 'Where am I? Am I dead?'

She smiled, stroked my cheek. 'Dead? No, you're fine now. I'm Sister Catherine. You are in the infirmary of the Carmelite Monastery. You're safe here.'

I furrowed my brow. Then I recalled the monastery near our camp, and I felt relieved that they had not taken me from Carmel. I looked at her. 'Ella and Joe?'

She smiled again. 'They were here all yesterday and all night. I sent them home because their vigil exhausted them, and you were out of danger. I'll send for them, don't worry.'

I felt relieved beyond imagination. 'Thanks.'

'They love you so much, you know. They told me how they found you, too. I'm so sorry you have been through things that are hard. Try to let them help, won't you?'

I was all jingle-brained, with waves of powerful emotion surging through me. Tears pooled in my eyes and swept down my cheeks. 'I'm sorry, I'm so sorry.' I screwed my eyes shut, trying to halt the waterworks.

I turned away from her, lay on my side and let the hot tears fall on the cotton pillow that smelled of something floral, like the cleanest thing I had ever smelled. My body shook and silently she stroked my back and I questioned why people were so good to me now I had done this terrible thing, where before few people had given me a kind thought. It was too much for me to make sense of.

Soon after, Ella arrived. 'Hey, sweetheart, you're awake. How you feeling?'

'Okay, I guess. Tired and confused.' It was good to have her here, but I didn't know what to say. The hours drifted by and she lay next to me, ever patient, not asking questions or pressing me. I told her how sorry I was and she told me not to worry, that she loved me, no matter what. I wondered if she would change her mind when she knew the truth. The doctor came and went, said I had been lucky not to drown and my lungs and heart were strong. I must have slept again. When I woke, she was still beside me. I turned to face her. 'You stayed.'

She smiled and laid her hand on my cheek. Her chocolate eyes radiated warmth. It made me feel like an impostor. She said, 'Of course. Getting you better is more important to me than anything.'

I fixed her gaze. Her eyes drew me in. I was inside them. I believed her. You can't fake stuff like that, and I knew she really cared about me. Later, Joe returned, and the sister left us. I looked at his kind green eyes painted with sadness, and I realized I had wounded him. 'I'm so sorry.'

He took my hand. 'It's okay Heidi, you got nothing to be sorry for. Nothing at all.'

I shook my head. 'No, I do. I need to take responsibility. I'm not a little kid anymore and you both have been so kind and you don't deserve the worry and trouble I have brought with me.'

Ella said, 'We've all got stuff, Heidi. All you need to know is we love you like family, and that type of love comes without strings or conditions, and it does not end. Never!'

I looked up at them. If I didn't trust them now, I'd trust no one again. So, I sat up in that soft bed, in that calm, holy place, and made my confession.

— Heidi —

Joe and Ella pulled up chairs and sat. They looked at one another and I wondered how they'd react when they knew. But I had to trust them. And I had to give them the complete story, chapter and verse. I closed my eyes for a beat, then I chose a spot on the far wall, and began.

'Well, it began like most days. I had woken early. Pa was still sleeping it off, so I got on quietly with my chores. I fixed the coffee. There wasn't much food about, so I made griddle cakes, and though I had been quiet as the grave, pa had come out of his room. His grim face gave me fair warning I'd riled him. He looked at me like I was dirt. "Christ, girl, you're crashing around like a graceless elephant. Hell, I don't know why the Lord cursed me with such an ungrateful *dummkopf* like you."

'I apologized, like I always did. I told him I had made coffee and fixed breakfast.

'He made a face and sat down in his filthy underwear, muttering something in German, his mean eyes roving over my body. I tried with all my might to keep from trembling. I looked away and poured the coffee. I placed a couple of cakes on a platter and put them down in front of him. He slurped his coffee and grimaced. "Ugh, your coffee tastes like your ma's did: river dirt." He picked up a cake, sniffed it, then threw it at me. "*Mein Gott in Himmel* girl, you expect a working man to eat this for breakfast? Fix me some bacon."

'I swallowed. And muttered, "Sorry pa, we've got none."

'That was it. He exploded from the bench and fell upon me, grabbing my throat, pushing me on the table, and thrusting his rank-smelling face in mine. "You selfish little cow! What use are you to me, anyway? You're an ugly, scrawny *hündin*, not even good enough to lick my boots."

'I screwed my eyes shut and waited for the blow to come. But he let me go.

That was part of it, the power he had. My throat hurt and my heart pounded. I stood and went over to the wall and watched him as his blood-shot, booze-riddled, cold blue eyes—the same eyes he gave to me—bored through me, and I prayed to God that was all he had given me. He glowered and growled, "Go get my clothes. I'm going out to get a proper breakfast."

'As he dressed, I cleared up. He came out of his room and watched me, like he was trying to find an excuse. I felt his passion sucking the air outta the room, and I wanted to run and never stop. Then he headed for the door and turned. "If this place ain't spotless when I get back, you know what you'll get, don't ya?" Then he was gone, and I breathed again.

'I sat and drank some coffee and ate a cake. It tasted fine. I cleaned up and climbed the ladder to the loft gallery where I slept. I picked up the photo of ma and me I kept hidden in a box under my bed. I was just a baby, but you could see the love in her eyes. I ran my finger over her face and wished she was here. That photo, a lock of her hair and a few bits of jewelry were all I had of her. There was a knock on the door, then I heard Jeremiah's voice. "Hey, Fizz, you here? I saw him on the road. Whoo-hee, oh boy, he looked like a rabid dog that an irritable bee had stung square on the butt."

'I poked my head over the edge of the loft and beamed. He had a way of saying things. I said: "Hey, handsome."

'He laughed. "Come on down. I want to take you somewhere."

'We headed off to the Big Creek, but when we got to our usual swimming spot, he took my hand and led me down the path aways. We walked for about fifteen minutes before we came to this wider part of the creek. I had not been here for a long time. He stopped. "Remember this?"

'"Yeah, why don't we come here anymore?"

'"We got lazy, I guess. It's why I thought about it, seeing as none of the other kids come here much." He nudged me and raised his eyebrows twice. "It's a beautiful, hot day. I thought we could be alone."

'I looked at him for a while. He had a beautiful face. To me, he was perfect. I stepped forward and kissed him. He opened his mouth a little, relaxed like, our lips squashed together and our tongues touched. He tasted and smelled nice, made me feel warm inside and I wanted to dive in. We pressed ourselves together, and I knew more than anything that I wanted to be with him always. We stripped off and lay on the grassy bank. Over time, tentatively, we explored one another. It had made us giggle childishly, and it had been scary, like I felt we were doing something wrong. When he touched me, the pleasure it had brought had surprised.

I'd never really touched myself before, hardly given a thought about my private parts and didn't have any idea or understanding of sexual pleasure. I kinda knew where babies came from, but I did not know, or to be honest, understand, why the act of touching and caressing needed to feel so good, though I was mighty relieved it did. Somehow, our exploits seemed sinful, but it was fun, with arousing urges overtaking my fear.

'We kinda figured out how sex worked, but I wasn't ready for that. And truthfully, I don't think he was either. We were happy as we were, fumbling around, wrapping ourselves up together, holding tight, and smooching.

'Over the years, few people hugged me. Most of my contact had been violent, so I took from Jeremiah what I needed. Sometimes I wanted to hold him so close I thought we might bond. I liked to feel his hot, soft skin against me and for us to share one another without feeling ashamed.

'That last day, we spent together, swimming, laying out in the sun, and talking about this and that. After a time, he said, "I got a plan how to get you away from your pa."

'I looked away, miffed at him for bringing up the subject, like it had poisoned the air. "You're wasting your time. He ain't going anywhere. Let's just be content with the time we got together. Let me deal with him."

'This time, I could not put him off. Honestly, his plan was smack-dab crazy. He wanted to rile up my pa so that he would hit him; you know, hard enough to mark him. He said that then he would go to Chief Banyard and make a complaint and my pa would go to court and get sent to jail for causing harm.

'As Jeremiah lay there telling me about his hare-brained scheme, I could not help but feel honored and loved that he would put himself in harm's way to help me. I turned to him, tracing my finger down his chest and resting my palm on his warm, flat belly. "It is a brave thing you are proposing, but you don't know my pa. He may be a drunk, but he is strong, and I am afraid that he would go too far and kill ya. I'd have no way of stopping him, would I?"

'"I thought about that. I am sure he would just give me a good hiding and throw me out."

'I shook my head. "It's too risky. Besides, why would I want you hurt?"

'We turned to face one another, our eyes locked together. "But Fizz, he's been getting more violent with you, beating up on you more often. Are you going to wait until one day he kills you? We've got to do something today."

'Desperate to put him off this crazy plan, I said, "Look, I could run away and go somewhere where I would be safe, but not too far, so as we can still see one another."

'He pursed his lips and frowned. "Got somewhere in mind?"

'I shook my head. "No, but we could find somewhere."

"'How would you survive?"

'I shrugged. "Find some work. If I went to a bigger town, say Bonners Ferry."

'I could see his mind working. "What if someone recognized you?"

"'I could cut my hair short and dress like a boy; who'd give me a second glance then?"

'He leaned forward and placed his hand on my cheek. We locked eyes. "Sounds crazy enough that it might just work." He rolled on his back, placing his hands behind his head. His lean boyish body glistened in the scorching sun, a small bead of sweat tracked down to his belly button. "Okay, how about we get you out today? We go back to your house to get clothes and whatever food you need. Then we go to mine, get a picnic for us and tell ma we're going to camp out for the night, you know like we did a while back. Then we'll go to Bonners Ferry and get you fixed up. What do you say?"

'I sighed. "Oh, I don't know, it all sounds kinda extreme, doesn't it? I mean, how long would I have to hide? Besides, I enjoy going to school, and Miss Hannah, and I'd not see your ma and pa anymore. I'm not sure."

"'Hey, maybe we could go to Chief Banyard, get my ma and pa to come with us. Tell him how your pa's been treating you bad, show him the marks on you, and that you need to come live with us."

'He stared at me, his chocolate eyes pleading. "My pa would talk himself out of it somehow and then I'll be worse off."

'He screwed his eyes shut and banged his hand on the ground. Then he looked at me, his eyes watering, and it softened my resolve. I knew he was right. Pa was getting worse and lately he'd been taking a more sinister interest in me, which I had not confided in anyone because it terrified me so. A couple times he'd got back late, drunk and hauled me from my bed, then made me strip and dance for him. It had been demeaning, and it petrified me where it might lead.

"'Oh hell! Let's try it. The running away idea mind, not the going to Ted Banyard, okay?"

'He propped himself up on his elbow, his eyes wide. "Really?"

'I nodded. "Yes. Really.'"

— Heidi —

I **glanced at Joe, but** could not read him. He gave me a slight nod, and the flicker of a smile danced around his mouth. I looked back at my spot on the wall and swallowed. It felt good to talk about that day and get things off my chest. I turned my gaze to Ella. Her eyes were soft, and she reached out and took my hand and gave it a squeeze.

'Go on, sweetheart, you're doing great. What happened next?'

I looked back at my spot on the wall. 'It wasn't much of a plan, was it? But you can imagine that my predicament was none too rosy, and I did not want Jeremiah to play the hero and get himself killed. As we walked back to get my things, I reasoned we were fifteen soon and so long as I could find work and keep my head down, it would not be too many years before we could make our own way in the world. I reckoned I could do that, and he was worth waiting for. I cannot deny that the prospect perturbed me, but now my pa was more terrifying than heading down this uncharted path. I think it is what they call being stuck between a rock and a hard place.

'When we got to my house, I told Jeremiah to wait while I checked the coast was clear. Tentatively, I opened the door and called out. The house was empty, so I waved him up. I looked around the small space. I kept it clean and cared for as best I could. It was the only home I had ever known. Good or bad, I felt a pang of guilt and sadness that I may never see it again.

'See, before ma died, I had happy memories here. Even pa had his moments before the darkness took him. I never spoke of it, but I believe he killed her. The day before she fell ill, they had this horrific fight. I can't remember what set it off. Ma shouted at me to go up to my bed and I had scooted up the ladder, lain flat on the floor, peeping over the edge, watching. I had seen him hit her plenty of times, but this was more ferocious. At one point, she screamed and launched herself at him, thrashing her fists on his chest and face. But he just laughed. Then he pushed her down and kicked her hard in the belly twice. I'll never forget the look in his eyes: demonic hatred. I remember her coughing, choking, and retching. He looked at her and I remember him shouting, *"Du willst mehr Schlampe?"* Then he spat on her and left.

'The tears were streaming down my cheeks. His violence shocked me. I had never seen him so wild and enraged. Sobbing, I came down and fell on my knees beside her stricken body. She saw my distress and, despite the pain she was in, pulled herself up and held me tight, kissing my head, saying, "Sorry, sorry, *mein kleiner Engel, vergib mir mein süßer Kleiner Schatz."* The next day, she could not get out of bed. She had a terrible fever. Then she was gone. It was why I never riled at him. I knew what he was capable of.

'Jeremiah came through the door and broke my cogitation. He saw me standing in the middle of the room. "Best not hang around, Fizz. I'll grab food while you go get your things."

I climbed the ladder and pulled the cloth bag from under my bed and began stuffing a few clothes inside. I looked at Lotti, my old rag doll lying on my pillow. For a moment I hesitated, then picked her up and put her in the bag too. I was about to pick up the box that contained a little money, ma's photo, and a few other personal items when the door crashed open, and pa reeled in. He did not see me, but Jeremiah was pulling stuff out of the cupboards and putting them in a sack. As the door banged, he looked over, saw my pa, and froze. I could see pa had been drinking, so there was little hope of talking reason. Before I could say anything, he fell upon Jeremiah. He punched him in the face, shouting, "You come here stealing my food! You sonuvabitch-low-life-rat!" I could hear the crack and Jeremiah went down, his hands clutching his face. A second later, blood began leaking through his fingers. Pa was on him again. He pulled him up and hit him and down he went. Then pa pulled him to his feet and flung him across the room like he was nothing. Pa had become a crazed animal. He overwhelmed Jeremiah who attempted to scrabble away, but once more pa was on him, like a cougar on a lamb, wrapping his powerful hands around Jeremiah's throat.

'I do not know how I got down the ladder or how the boning knife came to be in my hand, but the next moment I buried it to the handle in the back of pa's neck. It stopped him like some invisible force. One second, he was choking the life out of Jeremiah, the next he just slumped down on top of him. I stood there, looking down at them. I was panting hard, my head swimming, tears streaming down my face. After the storm of brutality and noise, the room fell silent. You could hear a pin drop. No one moved. Then Jeremiah, coughing and retching, struggled underneath pa's motionless body.

'I dropped next to them and helped pull him free. He rolled onto his knees trying to get up but yelled in pain and rolled back down. He was in a frightful state. His face was bloody from his nose, a gashed lip and a cut on his cheek right down to the bone, which was so swollen his left eye was closed shut. Gently, I pulled him up, resting him against the wall. I could smell the sharp metallic tang of blood. I got some clean rags, soaked them in water, and cleaned him up. My hands were shaking. I said, "I know it's a stupid question, but are you alright?"

'His one good eye looked at me, and he nodded once.

"Don't move. I'll go get help." As I stood, he grabbed my arm and pulled me back.

'Through gritted teeth, he said, "No—no, wait. Your pa."

'I had been so focused on Jeremiah that I had given my pa no thought. We both looked at his motionless form, his head turned toward us, his dimming blue eyes with big round black pupils, stared at us accusingly. I turned to Jeremiah. "I think I killed him."

'Jeremiah's one good eye was wide and flickering, but he remained calm. His breathing had slowed down. "He—he was going to kill me."

'I nodded. "I can't remember doing it. I must have just, you know—"

"Well, I'm glad you did."

'I stroked his swollen cheek, and he winced. "Sorry. Anything feel broken?"

"My shoulder feels weird."

'I pulled down his blood-soaked shirt and I could see the bone stuck out, not through the skin, just lumpy and odd looking.

"I think he busted your collarbone. Anything else?"

"Only everything."

'The bleeding had reduced to a trickle. His clothes were soaked red, and I wondered at how much blood there was. It terrified me. "I've got to go get help for you."

'He held my arm again. His powerful grip shocked me. "Then what? How do we explain all this?"

'I frowned. "We—we tell the truth."

'Jeremiah's eye was dark and focused. He whispered, "They execute killers in Idaho. You want to take that chance?"

'I felt hot tears rising. I sat back on my haunches. My mind a mishmash.

"But—but he was going to kill you. I didn't mean to kill him. I just wanted him to stop."

'A tear ran from his eye. He trembled. I'd never seen such a look of stark determination. "You've got to get away like we planned, but now you go far away from here. And I mean, far away! As far as you can get. I'll protect you. Protect both of us. I'll say we stumbled on a man what broke into the house, and I tried to stop him and it was him done all this. I can say that maybe it was that man that killed those girls last year just over the State line. Yes, that would work. Why not? And—and then your pa came back and there was a fight and the man killed him and left me for dead. I'll say that when I came round, you and the man were gone. You know—like he took you."

'Jeremiah's chilling words hung in the air like a death sentence. I'd forgotten about the dead girls and how, for a time, the thought of this child killer had scarred people, making them keep their kids close. If they thought he had taken me, then—the thought iced my veins. Then they'd think he'd kill me and they'd not come looking, would they? Case closed.

'I furrowed my brow. It sounded like madness. "But—but Jeremiah—it's a lie. You'd be living a lie. We'd be living a lie. And not some little white lie, neither. It's one fat, gobstopping, treacherous lie that could get us both in a shitheap of trouble."

'Jeremiah's stabbing gaze fixed on my dancing eyes, arresting them. He gripped my arm. He stared at me with one bloodshot eye. "Please, I beg you. I can't see you in jail or worse, because you saved me. Get away, it's your chance to start off new somewhere. We'll find a way of getting back in touch and—" Tears rolled down his sticky, bloodied cheek. "Please, Fizz, please! If you love me, just go. I'll be alright. I'll give you as long as I can before I raise the alarm."

'At such times, it is odd how the mind works. He begged me to go, and the truth was I too was confused and petrified that they'd send me to jail, or worse. Me rotting in jail would be my pa's revenge. So I kissed him and told him that one day soon we'd be together, no matter what. I scurried back up the ladder, grabbed my bag and fled the scene like a thief in the night, except I was worse. I'd murdered my pa, and left the boy I loved all alone to take the rap.'

Puffing out my cheeks, I let out a big breath of air. I felt relieved that I had unburdened myself. Hearing it all spoken out loud, I appreciated how horrific it had been. I looked up at Ella and then Joe. 'About a week later, you found me in that boxcar. I think I've got to go back to put things right, and to see Jeremiah. Truth is, I don't even know if he's alive.'

Ella had her hand over her mouth, her eyes wide. She reached out and laid a hand on my shoulder. 'Oh my goodness, sweetheart, how in heaven have you carried that all alone?'

Joe took my hand. 'Oh my sweet girl, I am so, so sorry you had to go through all that on your own. Not just that, but him mistreating you, and losing your ma, and feeling so alone you felt you couldn't carry on. Only, you aren't alone because we love you like family, and we're here now to help you. Anything you need. Anything.'

'Even after you heard what I did?'

Ella looked into my eyes. 'Listen to me, Heidi, if you hadn't lifted that knife and killed your pa, he would have killed that innocent boy and then done the same to you. You can't even remember doing it, can you?'

I closed my eyes and shook my head. 'It's just not there. I know it must have been me that stuck the knife in and I've tried over and over to figure it out, but I can't, truly.'

Ella hugged me tight, and I held her and cried like a small child, heaving sobs. She stroked my hair and whispered in my ear that everything would be alright. She let go and sat beside me and put her arm around me. I laid my head on her chest and let the tears flow.

Joe said, 'I'm relieved beyond words that you've told us. It took real courage, and I don't think any the less of you, far from it. I'm proud and thankful I met you on that boxcar, and I want you to know that you mean the world to me.'

For the first time since that day, I recognized I was not alone. 'Well, you mean the world to me. Both of you do.'

Joe's eyes shone with warmth and determination that fired my soul. 'First, we've got to get you back on your feet. Then we all have some serious talking to do. Me and Ella have got some things we need to tell you, good things. Promise me, Heidi, promise me, you won't do anything, like running off or the like, until we've had time to discuss things like grownups, okay?'

I nodded. 'I promise, Joe, cross my heart and swear on that crucifix above my head, no more dumb stuff.'

He bent over, kissed my forehead, and whispered, 'Thank you. It'll be alright, you'll see.'

I said, 'I don't know how I can fix things. It's like I'm drowning in guilt and shame.'

Ella said, 'You got to put that to one side and start again, only this time you aren't carrying it on your own. We'll fix things and I promise we won't rest until we do, okay?'

I nodded. Clawing fatigue racked my body. I closed my eyes. Ella made a fuss and made me comfortable. I said, 'Will you stay until I fall asleep?'

'Try to stop me.' She lay down next to me. I looked into her chocolate eyes that were so loving. I felt like a small lost child and I was glad she was here. I closed my eyes and tried to empty the clutter from my head. I concentrated hard on the sound that waves make when they break on the beach; I love that sound. I let the whoosh and hiss of the sea fill my mind and I drifted into a dreamless sleep. It had been a long time coming.

— Heidi —

I **don't know how long** I slept, but when I woke up, it was dark. I was alone. For a moment panic gripped me as I wondered whether I had dreamed telling them my story and now it was too late. A shaft of light from the partially open door bathed the room in gentle illumination. I lay with the covers tucked up to my chin. No. I had not dreamed it. They knew it all.

I thought about Jeremiah. I concentrated my thoughts on a spot on the ceiling and tried to empty everything from my mind but him: his face, his smell, the touch of his lips, his hot sweet breath and his body pressing against mine when we cuddled. I thought about the way he swept his fringe of brown hair from out of his eyes with a flick of his head; of how he ran naked, laughing and whooping along the bank before leaping, turning a somersault in the air and splashing feet first into the creek, and his big boyish grin when he surfaced, shouting, "Come on in Fizz, it's perfect!" I thought about his gentleness after I'd taken a beating, how he held me and said it would be alright. I thought so hard about all these things that I conjured up this feeling inside that he was here with me. I wanted so badly to say sorry I had tried to end my life, and that I had left him not knowing where I was. I wanted to tell him I was fine, and that now I'd told of my suffocating secret, I could make things right and get back on my feet and move forward.

I knew I had to get back home, see him again, and face up to what I'd done. But I felt confused and exhausted. I guess I had to be kind to myself and take some time to work stuff out. I thought maybe I could write a letter to him so he'd know I was alright and that I'd come home soon. But where could I send the letter so that only he would see it? Answerless questions drifted through my mind.

As I lay there, I wondered whether he was moving on with his life. I worried maybe that with time and absence, he'd let me go. Maybe he'd find someone new. The thought hurt me but I did not want him to live in a kinda limbo. I guess we all need some certainty and circumstances had meant that we had parted, unable to communicate, make a proper plan, or say goodbye. We had kissed and promised to see one another again, but I was not sure what that meant. All I knew was that all the cards lay in my hand. Do I go back or let him go?

Let him go!

Those haunting words tumbled around my head. I thought about what that meant. How long did it take to let the person go you most loved in all the world? Is it ever possible to do that, or will there always be this wound inside that when you pay it heed, bleeds a little?

I thought about what Ella had said about David, that she had left him in the past, accepted that he was gone rather than trying to live forever in a state of miserable loss. I knew what that was like and it was eating me alive. I felt if it was best to let him go, the thing that would hurt most of all would be that I had not said goodbye but had left on the promise of reunion, to keep the flame of love burning for him. And then it hit me, hit me so hard I felt sick that if I never said goodbye, I'd never be at peace.

You can't say goodbye in a letter, not really. That's the coward's way, or when you have no other choice. I had promised not to do anything until Joe, Ella and I had talked things through, "like grownups," he'd said. It had moved me. And it surprised me when they declared their love for me, that they saw me as family. It had been so long since I had felt that sense of belonging that it had, maybe, given me a way to move forward and let Jeremiah go. But that meant never knowing him again, never going back home, even if home was some Idaho backwater. It was where I was from, and just as beautiful as anywhere.

I had got to that part of idle thought when your mind sets off on perilous paths of speculation, desire, fear and romance. Thoughts riddled my mind of going home to Jeremiah, back with my people. But I saw their pointing fingers and heard their whispers behind my back about my brutally stabbing my pa to death and running off, leaving a near-dead boy who supposedly I loved. Maybe I'd go back and find that Jeremiah, too, was dead. What then?

I knew he would have waited for as long as he could to give me time to get away. Maybe he waited too long and did not have the strength to get home, and by the time they found him, it was too late. Tears filled my eyes and rolled down my temples, wetting my soft pillow. I did not know what it was I was weeping for. I lay there and my mind went numb at the endless possibilities, none of which had a wholly satisfactory ending. And anyway, right now, I did not have the spirit to face up to it.

Joe was right. We needed to talk, and I needed their help. I understood that was what family was about, which was new to me. I had to trust them to guide me. I knew nothing about Joe before the day we met. I knew I loved him and I reckoned that fate had brought him and Ella to me because I had too much burden for one so young. I had to grow up but also accept that I needed help to do that, take responsibility and set things right.

I must have drifted off again. I dreamed of my ma. She stroked my cheek and sang to me in German. I dreamed of swimming in the creek and laughing with my buds. I looked for him, but I could not find Jeremiah. I called his name, but he did not answer. When I woke, I felt empty. Daylight spilled round the edges of the drapes. Sister Catherine was back at her desk. She saw I was awake and came over. She had a wonderful, serene face. She laid her cool hand on my forehead. 'How you feeling?'

I didn't want to hide anymore. 'Sad.'

She smiled. 'I know. Would you like to get up? I can take you around the monastery. The gardens are beautiful and you can sit and look at the ocean.'

Truthfully, I did not want to get up or see people. But I had to begin somewhere, so I nodded my head, and said I would. She said, 'That's good. You've been through a lot. Just take it one step and one day at a time.'

When I stood, I felt a little shaky, my pins unsteady. She took me to the refectory, where the amiable sister in charge of the kitchen made a terrible fuss of me and gave me a delicious bowl of soup and a freshly baked roll that tasted better than any bread I'd ever had. I was famished and wolfed it down. I forgot my manners and wiped my mouth with the back of my hand. I looked up at her beaming, rosy face and said sorry. She shook her head, laughing. Her jolliness infused me. I felt better. Sister Catherine took me to the grounds, and we walked among the shrubs, grasses, and flowers. We sat on the bench that looked out to the ocean and I felt foolish but glad to be alive to make things right. I felt maybe that a minor part of me, the lost girl, the child, had drowned out there. There had to be a reason that Mr. Hikomori had been there right when I needed him. I glanced over at Sister Catherine and said, 'I think I know where to make a beginning in putting things right.'

Her eyes were closed. She radiated peace. 'That sounds good.'

'I want to thank Mr. Hikomori for saving me and I want to do something for you and the monastery.'

She opened her eyes and looked at me. 'Well, I am sure Mr. Hikomori will be very pleased to see you. He is a good man. I believe he has a daughter the same age as you. Maybe it will help to have someone your own age to spend time with. You don't need to do anything for us here. Our mission is to serve Christ, and he brought you to us in his love and compassion for a soul in need of comfort and charged us with giving you a place to come back. Life is love, you see?'

I shook my head. 'I never thought about it like that before.'

'You have a long and beautiful life ahead of you, Heidi. Keep your mind open and your heart full of joy and love. Do that, and you will follow the path intended for you, whatever that might be.'

I knotted my brow. Her words challenged me, yet made it sound easy. 'How do you know if you believe in God?'

She placed her hand on my shoulder, laughing lightly. The sound floated off on the ocean breeze. 'Now there's a question.' She lifted the crucifix that hung from a chain around her neck and said, 'God gave his son to save our world, to give us a path, and an earthly figure we can relate to. In order to believe, you must accept, and be open to God, to hear his word and understand it.'

My frown had deepened. 'I don't know what that means. I wasn't good at going to church.'

'You don't have to go to church to find God. You can find him everywhere. Just keep an open mind so that you will hear him when he speaks.'

I looked out at the rolling waves and the beautiful blue water and thought about being out there as I slipped under, my body numb and lifeless. 'So, did God save me out there?'

'Do you think he did?'

I thought about what it was she was asking me. 'Well, Mr. Hikomori saved me. He pulled me out of the water and warmed me back up and kept me awake. But I guess he is not God, is he? Maybe God guided him? You know, like he can't do it himself because he isn't—' I paused, getting lost in my thoughts. 'Because he isn't real like made of flesh and bone like us, but he can make things happen.'

Sister Catherine smiled. 'I think maybe you get the idea. You know what I think?'

I shook my head.

'I think we can't go through the complexity of life on our own. If we try, then we fail. We need to open our hearts and minds to spiritual guidance. For me, that is in God, Jesus Christ, and the Holy Spirit. The word of God. I believe, for others, it may be in some other way. You must not overthink things, Heidi. Listen to your head, but follow your heart.'

It was strange for me to think this way and I was glad that Sister Catherine had given me something on which to ponder. From the moment I was born to now, I have been through many things, both good and bad. I guess bad things come for a reason. I tried to figure out if the good and bad had balanced each other. I had lost my ma when I needed her so much. Her passing had left me with a father filled with bitterness, his soul devoid of love. Then, right when I lost my ma, I had found Jeremiah. He did not replace what I had lost, but his goodness helped me endure the misery of my pa and losing her. I thought back to the people in my town and remembered that many, in their own way, looked out for me. Abigail's pa would let me have food when I had no money. Ted Banyard had sometimes locked up my pa when he was at his most dangerous. The Chief would come to the house to see if I was alright and tell me that my pa was sleeping it off. Miss Hannah was kind to me, encouraging me to learn and gave me responsibility to help the younger kids so that I knew I had worth. It was like there was this host looking out for me. All that good to balance the bad of losing a mom and enduring my pa.

But then the bad won out, and I struck it down and ran out into the wasteland. But rather than being left alone, I found Joe and Ella and, without knowing me, they supported me, no questions asked.

As I sat and thought about it, I thought about how precious and finely balanced are our lives and the lives of those around us. It was like an epiphany giving me something to cling to, and I vowed never again to take my gift of life for granted.

— Ella —

Heidi's story filled me with intense sadness, dredging up past emotions I had buried along with David. It made me and Joe feel helpless that she had been through such an horrific ordeal and then carried it alone, far from home. Telling it exhausted her and it was good to see her sleep. We stayed a while, just sitting quietly alone with our thoughts. The color from Joe's face had drained away, and he shed a few tears.

We left her in the care of Sister Catherine, telling her I'd come back first thing in the morning. We walked along the shore. It was a while before either of us spoke. Joe broke the silence. 'If she hadn't killed him, I'd go there myself and do it for her. What kinda man does that to his own daughter, his wife, and then almost beats a boy to death?'

I could feel his passion. By way of calming him, I took his hand. 'Well, looking on the bright side, if there is one, we don't have to worry about her father anymore, do we? And we should adopt her. No one has ever needed a family like she does. I've never been so certain of anything.'

'What if she doesn't want that?'

I sighed. I felt exhausted. I sat down and lay out on the sand. Joe dropped next to me. 'We'll have to cross that bridge when we get there, won't we, Joe?' I rolled over and draped my arm across his chest and lay my weary head on his shoulder. 'You still want to get hitched?'

'More than ever. I feel like we have mountains to climb, but with you at my side, anything seems possible.'

'We'll make a good team, won't we, Joe?'

We lay there a while, cuddling and listening to the waves, then headed back to camp. We ate, then fell into bed. Despite the day's epic revelations, I slept like the dead. I woke first. I nudged Joe. He, too, said he'd slept.

I kissed him. 'I'm going to the monastery to see if she's okay and can come home. I won't talk to her about us or the adoption. We can do that together, okay?'

'Sure. I'll go earn some scratch. Look forward to seeing you both later. Fresh start, eh?'

I nodded, shrugged, and smiled. 'Uncharted territory.'

I walked back along the beach and took a swim to freshen up. When I got to the infirmary, she wasn't there. I walked along the white corridor and made my way outside. I found her sitting alone, looking out at the ocean. She looked peaceful. The sun shone from her golden hair, which danced in the light breeze. Before joining her, I watched for a while. I can't explain why, but I felt a hint of anxiety. I took a breath. 'Hey you.'

She turned. Her face broke into this broad smile, and she stood. She hugged me. I reciprocated and kissed her hair. It felt like we were where we were supposed to be, and it dispelled my anguish. At last, she looked up at me. 'Can we begin again?'

I nodded. 'You took the words out of my mouth.'

We sat down. For a while, we held our counsel, letting the ocean breeze carry its salty tang over us. With her gaze set far out over the ocean, she said, 'When I was out there and I felt like I was at the end, just before Mr. Hikomori pulled me out, it was like this great weight lifted from me and I was sinking but floating at the same time. It felt warm and I couldn't hear any sound save the slow beat of my heart and my shallow breath. It was peaceful and beautiful, and it seemed to last forever.' She brushed her hand through her hair and turned to me, her sapphire eyes so clear. 'Do you think that's what death is like? Because if it is, then there's nothing to fear. And if you don't fear death, then you shouldn't fear living either, should you?'

I held her enthralling gaze. 'You can't go through life being afraid. I guess death and life are strange bedfellows and neither should hold any terror for us.'

She put her arm around me. 'I had a good chat with Sister Catherine. I think I understand things better. I don't really know how to move on, but I guess I must try. Will you and Joe be able to help me?'

I gave her a squeeze. 'We'd like nothing more. You mean the world to us.'

We sat like that for a while. It felt like we belonged. I had a new, deeper love for her. Perhaps losing David and all my years in the wilderness led to this moment. I did not know how long it would last, but it felt righteous and beautiful.

The emotion surprised me, almost overwhelmed me, and a lone tear rolled down my cheek. She said, 'I hope we can stay together. I'd really like that.'

'Me too. I think we all need it.'

We sat with our thoughts. It was good just being. At last, she said, 'I think I'm ready to leave. I know our camp isn't much, but it's home.'

While we had been sitting in the garden, Sister Catherine had sent for the doc. He checked Heidi over and gave her the all clear. She hugged Sister Catherine, holding her for a long time. She told her she'd come and visit and Sister Catherine said she'd look forward to it. Heidi had a gift: a gift of acceptance and friendship. I'd never seen her give out anything but love and kindness.

We took our leave and as we walked along the beach, I asked her, 'How do you feel about going back into the ocean again?'

She grinned. 'Try to stop me.' She laughed and ran off down the beach. Her youthful flourish suffused me, and I chased after. She was fleet-footed and ran as well as she swam. Her blond hair flowed behind her and soon she was running with a purpose and I could not catch her. Breathless, I slowed and watched her disappear down the golden sand. I did not know what was going to happen and where we'd all end up. I knew that somewhere along the line we'd go with her to Idaho and stand with her and I knew that whatever that led to, I'd stay with her as long as she needed me, and I knew Joe would too.

I found her at the end of the beach sitting on a rock, her face red, her chest heaving. 'That was fun!' She called out. 'Last time I ran like that was when I chased Jeremiah down the creek bank. He dived, flying like a dart and punctured the clear water and I stopped on the bank and watched his body, a trail of bubbles behind it, cutting a path like he belonged there. He surfaced, squirting out a fountain of water. His arms and legs were gently pumping to keep him afloat, and shouted, "What you waiting for, Fizz?" And I stood there a while and watched him. He said, "I'll come get you if you don't come in." I was teasing him. I said, "You'll never catch me." He began swimming toward me. He shouted, "Will so." I waited until he was at the bank and about to haul out when I leaped over his head and swam as hard as I could. The water was always freezing, taking your breath away, and I loved the way it made me feel. Seconds after I stopped, he was on me, pushing me under the water. He was ticklish, so I dug my hands into his sides and he let go and pushed away. And we splashed around on the surface laughing.' She paused her story. She shrugged. 'I wonder if we'll ever get to do that again?'

'If you don't, it's a wonderful memory.'

She nodded, swept her hair out of her face, and looked away. 'He'd love it here.'

We made it back to camp and ate. After, she lay on her bedroll and removed an old rag doll from her bag. I asked, 'Is that Lotti?'

She nodded. 'Mom made her. I think.' She held the doll out at arm's length, studying it. 'I've never been much into dolls or girlie things. Once me and Jeremiah became friends, I played with the boys more. They seemed less complicated than the girls.' Suddenly, she held the doll to her chest and let out a little laugh. 'Even though we went swimming buck naked, they all wanted to see inside my panties, if you know what I mean?' She turned, her eyes twinkling. 'But only Jeremiah got that privilege. It's only ever been him.' She giggled. 'There was one boy, Gerome. Now he admired me, but he wasn't interested in me like that. He just enjoyed larking about. I think he liked boys. He looked at some of them like I looked at Jeremiah. The others never noticed, but I did. I admired him, too. He was the best tree climber, and he could run us all into the ground.' The twinkle vanished, and she frowned. 'I miss them.'

I came over, lay down beside her and turned on my side, holding her gaze. 'When I was about thirteen, I fell for this boy called Jeff Howard. I wasn't ready for anything romantic, just those first tentative steps. But he wanted too much, you know? He was only interested in my body. I recall he pressured me, making me think I was cold and that most girls were happy to do more. I'm glad I resisted, but it was a salutary lesson for me.'

Heidi rolled on her back. 'I worry Jeremiah will find someone else. I know a few of the other girls like him. It's a small town and well—you know?'

'From what you're saying, I think he'll wait. You can't cancel out all those years easy, trust me.'

'Truth is, I don't even know if he is alive. My pa beat him real bad and maybe Jeremiah waited too long to get help. The thought of it kills me.'

'Close your eyes and ask your heart. What does it tell you?'

She sat cross-legged, closed her eyes and clutched Lotti to her chest. She looked like she was praying. After a few moments, she opened her eyes. 'I think he's still with us.' She laid down Lotti, rolled onto her back again and placed her hands behind her head. 'I need to get a message to him that won't get him in trouble. Got any ideas?'

I thought about it. 'Apart from a letter, I don't see how there's a way short of you going back. I guess you can't write to him direct, can you?'

She shook her head.

'Did he have other family living elsewhere, you know, like an aunt?'

'I don't know. He mentioned no one. It's an idea, though.'

The approach of a man and girl interrupted our conversation. 'Hello!' He called, waving. 'May we enter your camp?'

Heidi and I stood up. I said, 'Please.'

The man was well-dressed and carried a leather bag, like a satchel, and the girl wore an elegant blue dress. She had light-brown, slightly wavy hair, gray eyes, and an enchanting smile. She looked all around, then closely at Heidi. 'Wow, this is fantastic, what a camp. I'm Betty. Betty Reed and this is my papa, William.'

It surprised me how forward she was, but there was something about her I liked. For a moment, we all stood looking at each other. 'Sorry,' I said, 'Please sit down.' We all sat. 'I'm Corbeau and this is Straw Blue. What can we do for you?'

Betty said, 'What unusual names, so exotic.'

William cleared his throat as though he were about to make a speech, and all the while Betty couldn't take her eyes from Heidi. 'We just wanted to come and say hello, really. I run the local newspaper, "The Cypress Chronicle". We heard about Mr. Hikomori rescuing you from the sea— er—' He nodded toward Heidi.

Heidi said, 'Straw Blue.'

'Yes—yes, Straw Blue. As I said, we don't want to intrude, but when we heard it was a young girl saved, Betty wanted to come and see if you were alright, really.'

Heidi wore a blank expression. 'Yes, as you can see I am. Thank you.'

An awkward silence followed. I said, 'You're not going to write about it in the paper, are you?'

'Well, only if you wanted me to.' He held up his hand. 'Of course, we at the Cypress are always interested in such stories, particularly with a happy ending, but—'

Betty cut in. 'Mr. Hikomori's daughter Mayumi goes to my school. She mentioned the rescue, and that you were camping here, and I wanted to come and meet you.' She gave this light laugh and brushed her hand through her wavy hair and beamed. 'I'm joyful I did. You're lovely.'

Heidi's eyes widened. 'Oh—thank you. So are you, but I don't think I want to be in the paper.'

Betty smiled. 'That's okay, isn't it papa?' He nodded. She looked back at Heidi. 'You're so beautiful. I love your hair. Where are you from?'

Heidi looked at me like she didn't know what to say and whether we should trust them. I said, 'We travel for work, but right now we came here for a vacation. In a few weeks, we're going to Fresno for the orange harvest.'

Betty looked impressed. 'So, you travel and look for work? But where's home?'

'That's right, we do, and wherever we are, is home. Right now, it's here.'

Betty frowned. 'Don't you have a home, you know, like a base?' I shook my head. Betty bit her lower lip. 'Oh—I see—You're—homeless, then?'

I smiled. 'Well, I guess we don't see it that way.'

Betty shook her head. 'This is so exciting.' She looked at Heidi again. 'Don't you go to school?'

'I do. When I can. I read lots and—'

'Oh, I love books. We have a magnificent library in the town—'

'Yes, I've been. Miss Jennings loaned me a copy of Treasure Island. There are so many books there.' Talk of books animated Heidi.

Betty said, 'I loved Treasure Island. Did you know the author stayed near here and took inspiration from the location?'

Normally I'd be wary of strangers, but I trusted William and his precocious, charming daughter and I thought it would be good for Heidi to have a girlfriend.

Betty plonked herself down next to Heidi and they began chatting and laughing. Betty kept nudging Heidi and giggling, her animated face intoxicating, and her bubbling enthusiasm washed off on Heidi. It made my heart soar to see her amused. I turned to William, who was looking at them with this benign, satisfied expression. To no one in particular, he said, 'Such clever girls, aren't they?'

I nodded. 'They are, William. Would you like some coffee?'

He looked at me, smiled, and bobbed his head. 'Why, that would be delightful, Mam.'

I asked William many questions about Carmel, including what he knew about the agent selling the land I had seen. He was a wealth of information. I told how I came here twenty years ago to recover from my loss.

'Ah, yes, Carmel is a place to slow down and take stock. There are many people here taking refuge, many artists and writers.'

I appreciated him and I was sure their visit had been out of curiosity with the chance of a story, and I felt he would honor his word not to write about us. Time slipped away. At last, he said they must be off and that we must come to their home to meet his wife, Bethan.

'Come on Betty, we must be going.'

We all stood. Betty gazed at Heidi and then gave her an enormous hug like she wanted to gather her up and spirit her away. Heidi looked astonished and for a moment hesitated before putting her arms around the younger girl. Betty held on for a bit and then they were gone. Before they disappeared, Betty looked over her shoulder, grinned and with tremendous flamboyance waved, shouting, 'Cheerio!'

I turned to Heidi. She had wet cheeks. 'Oh, what's wrong?'

She shook her head. 'Sorry, it's silly. It's just—I guess I've missed kids.'

We chatted about it for a while. Heidi told me Betty was twelve, and like her, was an only child. I asked her, 'What do you want to do this afternoon?'

She thought about it. 'I'd like to go and say thanks to Mr. Hikomori and meet Mayumi. Betty told me how pleasant and clever she is. Besides, I've met no one from Japan before.'

(25)

— Heidi —

We made our way over to Bluff Cove, where the Hikomoris lived and worked. It was a gorgeous stretch of coast and the bay perfect for drying fish. Ella and I walked past rows of wooden frames holding the pungent, drying flesh. Two workers looked up as we walked by, but they paid us little attention. At the far end of the cove were some buildings, and set back a little was the house where Mr. Hikomori and his family lived. There was a cute little girl playing out front and when she spotted us, she ran on inside and a few moments later, a man came out. I recognized him from the boat. He came down the steps and walked over to meet us. He stopped a few feet from us and gave this formal bow. At school I remembered reading that Japanese people bowed to one another like a kinda handshake, and their society had lots of formal rules and customs that I did not understand. I did not know what I was supposed to do, and he was intimidating, so I emulated him and bowed back. His eyes softened, a warm smile filled his stately face. He offered his hand. We shook. His hands had done plenty of work and his grip was firm and I recalled those powerful arms pulling me from the freezing ocean.

He said, 'I am Katsura Hikomori. I am gratified to see you back on your feet and looking well again, Heidi-san.'

I bowed again. 'Words cannot express my gratitude that you were there to help me, Mr. Hikomori. Thank you so much.'

He nodded. 'I lost my brother to the sea, so I am overjoyed we did not lose you.'

'Oh. I'm sorry for your loss.'

He nodded, a flick of sadness around his gentle tawny eyes. 'Would you like to meet my family?'

The house was elegant but not flamboyant and laid out in a combination of American and, what I guessed, was Japanese style. I'd seen the pictures of the type of clothes Japanese people wore but the Hikomoris dressed like Americans. His wife, Fuku, greeted us with warmth, and introduced her children. She named them but apart from Mayumi, their Japanese names did not stick. I felt awkward and tried to catch Mayumi's eye. She did not look at all as Betty described her, seeming to me reserved and serious. But what struck me was her beauty. I'd not seen anyone so beguiling, and I longed to get to know her. I don't know why but I didn't want to use my hobo name. 'I'm Heidi. I'm from Idaho.'

Mayumi frowned. 'Idaho? That's way up north. You're a long way from home.'

'Yes, I suppose I am. My ma and pa died. Joe and Ella take care of me now.'

She looked away and lowered her head a little. 'I'm sorry about your parents. That must be hard.'

I told her, thank you, like you do, but you never really know what to say about something so big. We sat and had something to eat and drink while Ella and I asked questions about Japan and how they came to live here. I thought I had come a long way, but it was nothing to Mr. Hikomori's adventure, a true pioneer. After he settled here, more of his countrymen had followed to take advantage of the ocean's rich bounty. His story inspired me, and I grasped that there was a realm of possibilities and the thought of forging out into the world seemed enticing. I asked if they ever planned to go back to Japan, but they said that America was their home. 'Besides,' said Mr. Hikomori, 'why would we wish to leave such a beautiful place as this? When first I came here, it reminded me of my home.'

I said, 'I like it here too. Before I came, I'd never seen the ocean. I love to swim.'

Fuku said, 'But you must be careful not to swim too far like you did the other day.'

I felt stupid. 'Of course, yes. I think I've learned my lesson. I am lucky your husband was there when I needed him.'

She looked at me with her bright cinnamon eyes. Her almond skin was so delicate. She said, 'It is odd, though. These days Katsura does not go out on the boats often, but that day he said he wanted to check a new area.'

A shivery feeling ran down my spine. 'Oh—I see—how odd.'

She looked right at me and pointed her finger at my heart. 'Someone was looking out for you.'

Mr. Hikomori said, 'That is the way of things.' He turned to Mayumi and said something in what I guessed was Japanese. It was the same language I heard him use on the boat.

She looked at me and smiled. My heart skipped a beat. She replied in English, 'Of course, papa.' She pecked him on the cheek. The closeness and harmony of this beautiful family touched me. She brushed my arm. 'Come, Heidi, I'll show you outside first.'

While shy before, now alone with me, she was chatty and confident as befitted Betty's description. Her oval face and delicate pale skin that reminded me of moonlight enchanted me. Her silken, black hair was perfectly straight, symmetrically bordering her head, falling just short of her shoulders. It shone in the afternoon sun, and I craved to run my hands through it. Her light accent was a mix of Japanese and American, and I loved the way it had this lyrical tone to it. The shape of her eyes was different to mine, and it fascinated me how we could look so distinct yet we were teenage girls and as we walked and talked, I realized, though outwardly different, inside we were alike. After we had looked around the compound, she took me for a walk along the cliffs.

I admired her straight off, and it was fun to spend time with a girl my age. It did not take long for me to tell her about Jeremiah and some of my life back home. Not having a boyfriend herself, she had lots of questions about him. Mostly, she played with her siblings. Like me, she loved school, worked hard, and we shared a passion for reading.

As we strolled, I said, 'I met Betty. She said you're at school together.'

She looked surprised. 'How'd you meet her?'

'She came to our camp with her father. They heard about your pa rescuing me and wanted to know if I was alright. Betty said you had mentioned it.'

'Oh, Betty, always about other people's business. Are they going to put you in the paper?'

I shook my head. 'They said not. I believe them. I liked Betty. She was fun and easy to talk to. Like you, I guess.' I paused and reached out and touched Mayumi's arm. 'I like you too.'

As we walked back to her home, I figured she may have the answer to my dilemma of contacting Jeremiah. I wasn't sure how it might work, and I did not yet know her well enough to open my heart and tell her how I had come to be here, but I felt I could trust her. We had a few weeks before heading to Fresno, so I had time to think it through. Reaching the headland, we paused, looking down over Bluff Cove. I asked, 'Do you swim in the ocean? I mean, do you like to?'

She brushed her beautiful hair from her face. 'Yes, of course.'

'Would you like to go tomorrow?'

For a moment, she studied me. 'I have school in the morning—' Then she paused, thinking and a wisp of a mischievous look brushed across her face. 'Hey, why don't you come with me? I am sure Miss McLaughten would be happy for you to join us while you're here. It would be such fun and we'd get to know one another better.'

I had not thought about school or that I'd ever go back. It seemed like a rare opportunity and a place to restart, and the thought of spending time with Mayumi was too good an opportunity to dismiss. I said, 'I'll ask Joe and Ella. But I think that sounds like the bees.'

This decision seemed to create a bond, and she pulled me down and we sat opposite one another. 'How did you find your—' she hesitated. I guess not sure what they were to me. It made me think about that too. We had become loosely attached, but I thought of them as much more than that. She continued, 'How did you all meet and get here?'

I puffed out a sclunch of air and laughed. 'It's a long story. I'll tell you another day when we have time, okay?'

She smiled, nodding. For a while, we sat and gazed at the ocean. It still took my breath away at its immensity and beauty. After, we walked back down, and I left her at her house and she told me to come back in the morning. It felt wonderful to have friends once more. I walked back alone and thought about her, Betty, and going to school and being a kid again. I had forgotten those things. I wondered whether the little kids, those I helped Miss Hannah with, were missing me. Thinking about them made me smile and feel sad, and I know I missed them. I walked down to a quiet cove, stripped off and slipped into the cold water. I wasn't sure after my experience how I would feel. For a while I stayed in the shallows playing in the waves. I'd wait for a good roller to arrive and just as it broke, I'd leap on top trying to ride it in. I loved when the water took me and tumbled me around like I was nothing and then dump me on the beach. For a while, I'd lie there on my front waiting for the whoosh of water from the next wave to crash into me, lifting me up a little and rolling me over and closer to shore. After a bit, I needed to stretch out, so I swam out beyond the breaking waves to calmer water. I swam parallel to the shore for a while, then flipped over onto my back and spread my limbs out starfish like, floating on the gently rolling water.

I had been like that for a while, just floating and thinking, when this sound startled me. It was like someone breathing out real loud and blowing water at the same time. It happened several times in quick succession. I righted myself and spun around to look in the sound's direction. About fifty yards away, these shiny, black shapes broke the surface and when they did, they made the sound I heard, a small fountain of spray coming from the top of their heads. On their backs, they had a pointy fin that was lighter, and they slipped through the water like they were part of it. They moved closer. They appeared quite large. I felt afraid, vulnerable, but kept treading water and watching them. They swam past me just a few feet away, close enough almost for me to reach out and touch them. I could see their quizzical, intelligent eyes looking at me and realized I had nothing to fear. They had two more fins near the front on their sides, a big white patch on the underside, and a broad flat tail that was also lighter. They were striking and moved through the water like an arrow does through air. They looked solid and powerful, yet sleek and beautiful, made perfect for the ocean. Dawdling, they circled. I rotated to keep eye contact. They stayed a bit, then with a few strokes of their tails they were off at terrific speed, breaking the surface as they went, like jumping fences. Stunned by their grace and beauty, I watched them go and thought about what it must be like to roam free across the ocean, swimming at such ferocious speed. I read stories about mermaids and wondered whether they were based on such creatures as these. They looked at me with curiosity and intelligence, like they wanted to know what I was, and when satisfied, took off.

I swam back to shore, pulled my clothes over my damp body, and with an unfamiliar feeling of joy, hurried back to camp.

— Heidi —

When I got there, Ella had got a good fire going, cooking supper. Joe had gone down to the river to wash after his hard day's toil. I threw myself down and said, 'Hey, anything I can do to help?'

She looked at me and grinned. 'Been swimming, I see?'

I told her about Mayumi and the fish I had seen.

'Those aren't fish. They must have been dolphins or porpoises.'

I frowned. 'They looked like fish. If they aren't fish, what are they, then?'

She stirred the Mulligan. It smelled good. I was ready to eat. 'They breathe air like you and me; they're mammals.'

'Oh, okay, that explains the blowing sound they made from the top of their heads. I guess that's where they breathe from?'

'Can you describe what they looked like?'

I did so.

Shaking her head, she said, 'Don't know what they are. Maybe you can ask Mr. Hikomori?'

Joe came back and when he saw me, he came over and hugged me, pushed my head to his chest and I held him close. He felt robust, like a tree. He said nothing. He kissed my head, then looked at me for a while. We sat down and ate well. After, he lit a cigarette, and I cleared up. I took the plates and things down to the water and cleaned them. It was a pleasant evening. The wind had dropped. We sat around the fire and I stared right into it, focusing on the shimmering red coals. Ella told Joe about our visit to the Hikomoris and I told him about Betty, Mayumi, my animal encounter, and about school.

He said, 'Well, you all both had a more interesting day than I did, that's for sure.' He looked at me and smiled. 'It's wonderful to have you back and you go spend as much time with those girlies as you want. It'll do you good.'

'It'll be interesting to see another school and Mayumi seems to like me. I like her. She's so pretty and smart.'

Ella turned to Joe. 'Mr. Hikomori offered us work if we want it. Be less back breaking than the quarry and he offers a better wage, too.'

Joe thought about it. 'Sure. I'll go see him tomorrow.'

Ella laid her hand on my back. 'You up to us having that talk, Heidi?'

I looked at them both and nodded, but a thread of apprehension seeped through my gut.

Ella turned to Joe. 'Alrighty, then. Who wants to go first?'

He took the cue, thinking a moment. 'Well, okay. I guess proper introductions are a good start. I was born on the third day in January, 1861 in a town in Indiana called Lagonda. I have a twin sister, Florence.'

I pointed at myself. 'I was born an only child, October Thirtieth, 1910, in Sitwell, Idaho.'

Ella said, 'Hey, that makes your birthday a couple of weeks away. We'll have to make sure we have a celebration. You're only fifteen once.'

'Last few years my pa didn't remember my birthday, well, either that or he chose not to pay it any mind. Jeremiah and his parents always did, and if your birthday fell on a school day, Miss Hannah would make a fuss. I guess her not having children made us more of a focus for times like that.'

Joe said, 'Well, we won't forget your birthday, ever. Let's make sure you remember your fifteenth birthday here by the ocean as something special.'

I beamed.

Ella said, 'Well, okey dokey then, I'm Luella, but prefer to go by, Ella. I was born in Black Hill, Wyoming on June Eleventh, 1887.'

I said, 'Ella suits you. But how'd you get your moniker?'

She and Joe exchanged knowing looks and chuckled. 'Do you want to tell it or shall I?'

He shook his head. 'No, you.'

She, too, sat cross-legged and shuffled a bit to get comfortable. 'Alrighty. So in the beginning they gave me the nickname Carmel because—well, I'm sure you get it. So, we met in Tucson and then spent that winter picking fruit in California and after we went our own ways for a bit. I had some walking-around money, and I wanted to travel and see how it would be on my own. Joe was going to wend his way to work lumber, or some such. He told me about the annual festival in Britt and we agreed to meet up there. It felt so good to roam free but know that there was someone out there who cared about me. Anyway, we met at the festival, of course you know what that's like. Well, there was this old bo there, a French Canadian. Everyone called him Salut, because that's what he said to anyone he met.'

Laughing Joe said, 'Yeah it was always, hey *Salut Monsieur*: that's Frenchie for Hi Mister. If he really liked you, he'd kiss you on both cheeks.'

'Oh, and with the ladies, and there weren't many of us, he liked to kiss and grab a feel of your ass at the same time. Let's say he was a character. Anyway, when first he met me and after he'd given me the full meet-and-greet, he looked at me hard then ran his hand through my hair, which shocked me; I can tell you. He said, "*Mon Dieu*, I have never seen such hair! So shiny and black, *c'est comme Le Corbeau*." The French bit means it is like the raven. For the rest of the festival every time he saw me, which was often, he'd say, "Ah, *salut Le Corbeau*," and it stuck, from then on in, I was Corbeau.'

I said, 'So you and me both got our hobo names from our hair. I wonder what French for Straw Blue is?' Absent-mindedly, I ran my hand through my hair and for the first time saw how it helped define me. It was more intense and brighter than most other blond hair I had seen, but until now, I'd not really considered it. As for my eyes, I had always assumed they were cold, like my pa's. 'Do you think my eyes are cold?'

Ella frowned, shaking her head. 'Cold? Why no, sweetheart. Some blue eyes are, but you have a deeper color that gives off warmth. Why do you say that, anyway?'

'My pa had cold, blue eyes, and I always thought he'd given them to me.'

Joe said, 'Well, what color eyes did you ma have?'

'They were blue too.'

He made an open-handed gesture and bobbed his head. 'There you go then.' Then he sighed and looked at me. 'You know, it was your eyes and hair that kinda got me thinking about my past. You reminded me of someone—two someones—'

He stopped talking, and the silence hung in the air like a dust cloud, and I so wanted him to say more. He glazed over. 'I'm still working it out. Be patient. Anyway, tell us more about you.'

'Well, let's see now. Like I said, ma and pa came from Germany. I remember ma spoke German to me, and pa cussed good in German, but after she died he didn't teach me about the old country or my grandparents and it all faded away. Pa had this strange German accent with just a hint of American. I know that my family name in German means bat, like something you hit a ball with.' I laughed. 'In American I'm Heidi Bat but I think Schlager sounds better, don't you?'

By now it was dark and the firelight made shadows of us that would catch your eye and make you think there were dark figures lurking among the trees. Ella said, 'Well, Heidi, we know you've been through a hard time, and you still got a load of things to get through so, me and Joe want you to know some stuff, okay?'

I nodded. I did not know where this was going, and it made me fretful. Ella looked at me and a lightness around her mouth made me feel like this was good news. 'Well—me and Joe—how can I put this? We've been lovers, I guess, for a long time but we've both been drifting through life and we don't really know why but since the three of us have been together and all that has happened has made us realize we love one another and we want to be together, you know, permanent like.'

This big grin splashed across my face and I felt my heart soar. 'You're going to get married?'

They looked at one another, just a glance, but their eyes betrayed them. 'Well, we haven't quite got that far, but—hell yes, married in the sense we are partners, lovers, best friends.'

My grin was stuck fast. 'Well, that's the bees; you two should be together.'

Joe said, 'You're not wrong, we should, but then it wouldn't feel right if you weren't part of the deal, so we were wondering how you would feel about us adopting you as our daughter.'

Well, kiss me sideways. You could have knocked me down with a feather. I sat staring at them. I had not expected this. It was overwhelming to think that just a few weeks back I had killed my pa and run away, and now here I was sitting far from home being offered a new life. Of course, those old tears came flowing again. And I sat there and let them flow, but I could not find the words. Ella gathered me to her and hugged me. I surrendered to her like a child does to their mother. It had been so long since I felt that way I had forgotten how it was. My tears wet her shirt. She whispered, 'I'm proud of you and we love you and having you as our daughter would complete us.'

I took some control and looked up at her. 'Really? You'd want me even though I did something so terrible?'

She wiped a tear from my cheek. 'Of course we do. You're growing up, but you still need a family. You've been too long on your own, we all have. Meeting you got Joe and me to think about what we need, too. I know it's quick, but we don't want to waste any more time. So, what do ya say to becoming Heidi Reisen?'

'I'd love you and Joe to be my ma and pa. And—I—I won't let you down.'

She kissed me. Her eyes burning bright. 'Nor we you. Whatever happens, we'll be here for you.'

I went over and hugged Joe and saw his eyes were watery. I said, 'I knew when we met you were special. I've always felt real comfortable with you: safe, and loved. I'll go anywhere with you, Joe Reisen. Being with you both is home now.'

Ella came over and joined us and the three of us sat together like families do. We didn't speak because there aren't words for such things. We had nothing other than what we carried on our backs, but in that moment, I felt like the most blessed, well-to-do person in the world.

Before I went to sleep, I took ma's lock of hair in my hand and as I lay in bed, thought back to the day I got on that boxcar and gave up that childish prayer. I don't know who or what heard me, but they'd answered my prayer in ways I could not fathom. I reckoned there were still payments due, but now I was no longer alone. I reckoned I could face an uncertain future.

The next morning, I woke early before it was light. It was cool. A soft breeze carried the sound of the waves to me. I walked to the beach and headed down the sand and up to the little promontory that overlooked the bay. I watched the sun come up, and finding a suitable spot, got a stick and dug a little hole in the ground. When I reckoned it was deep enough, I dropped in ma's lock of hair, gently covering it up and patting it down. I didn't remember ma's burial, and it had been a while since I had visited her grave in the little cemetery at the foot of the hills that rolled up from our valley home.

'Hey ma, reckon this is a good place to leave that last bit of you that isn't memories. You can look out over the ocean and see the creatures and feel the breeze and taste the salt. But most of all, I know I'll come back and when I do, I'll come talk to you and tell you about my life that you have missed.'

My tears fell on the newly dug ground, melding with it. I found some small stones and placed them over the dirt, then I stood up, turned and walked back to camp.

part
four

(27)

— Joe —

Doubt and guilt had made me worry she wouldn't want us to adopt her and it was with immeasurable relief that she had reacted so positive. I hoped it wasn't because she felt we were the best thing on offer. I knew that among the families here, we'd find a suitable home for her. Maybe even Mr. Hikomori would take her, or that newspaper man. Someone would because she was a great kid. But despite all my failings and how I felt, I wanted her in my life more than anything. I guess, though, I was worried that I wanted her in my life for the wrong reasons. I figured if it was all clear cut, it would mean we weren't being honest, which kinda justified my fretting.

For someone who'd spent almost fifty years going about his business, the last few weeks had been an emotional tsunami, and part of me was ill prepared for the uncertainty of what lay ahead. Getting hitched with Ella was one thing, but adding Heidi to that was quite another. Practically all her life, she'd lived under the shadow of abuse, and I don't think she had ever mourned the loss of her mother, and I reckoned that because I had lost too and had done what she had: bury it. You think it won't come back at ya, but it always does.

Until I met Heidi, who reminded me of beautiful people I had left, I'd trivialized the events that set me on my life of roaming unable to commit to anyone or anything, because being alone was simpler and I thought I knew exactly how the rest of my life would pan out. I guess I saw it as just punishment, maybe like Heidi did for the guilt she carried. But I know I was wrong and so was she. I'd done nothing wrong but make a stupid mistake, but it had set in motion events so traumatic and catastrophic I simply could not handle them. She hadn't even made a mistake. It took courage I did not comprehend for her to stand up to her pa and strike him down to save Jeremiah and herself. But taking a life, even in those circumstances, is irreversible, and she'd have to find a way to live with it. I guess we all would because now her baggage was our baggage.

Right now, I did not know how Ella and I could help her move on. Yes, we'd love her, and show that love. We'd give her a home and help her use that beautiful mind of hers. But how in the heck do you make sure that leads to her making peace with her past? I hadn't done it, thought I had, but then the day I hopped that ride and she was there like a ghost from my past, the past emerged like a malignant spirit and sat itself right down next to me. It mocked me and everything I had ever done. They say if you don't have a past; you don't have a future. And until that day I had never understood that, and it took a courageous girl to show me the way. I felt ashamed and foolish. But, if Heidi could tell us her story warts and all, I must as well. I owed them the truth. Easier said than done, though. It didn't make pretty, and I was afraid they would see my true character: weak, cowardly, and selfish. I had so long worn my mask that I wasn't even sure I could rip it off and show them my truth. But of one thing I was certain, if I didn't, then I could never be a part of them. I had a simple choice: tell or run.

Ella and Heidi had gone to bed, but I was a million miles away from sleep. I grabbed my coat and wandered off down the coast and hit the beach. There is something about the sound of breaking waves and the immensity of the ocean that quietens the soul. I sat down and rolled a cigarette. I inhaled deep and then looked at it. I wasn't right sure why I smoked. I never had before I left home. One day while sitting around a jungle fire, an old hobo had rolled me a smoke. Practically everyone there had a pipe, cheroot or rolled cigarette, so I joined them. I don't know why anyone ever has a second cigarette because the first made me feel sick and I coughed my lungs out. Hell, how they'd laughed, and they warmed to me. So, for whatever reason, you smoke another and so on until they are part of you, a comforting ritual and uncomplaining friend. I chuckled at the craziness of it. I guess sucking all that smoke in my lungs for all those years probably hadn't been a good thing, and it got me thinking. There wasn't much I could control, but I could stop smoking and make sure I took care of myself to be there for as long as possible, leastways until I was no longer needed. I chucked my smoke away, opened the pouch, took out the makins and made a little bonfire of them. The fragrant smoke rose and floated off on the breeze and with it went a lesser part of Bo Scribbler, and the first step to unmasking the man with the hidden past.

I lay back, listened to the waves and thought about Florence, Melissa and little Sophia. I let the tears come: it was time to grieve and face it and I had to get that straight in my head before I could tell Ella and Heidi, and I reckoned that if they loved me, then it would be alright. Ella would be mad as hell, and I'd deserve that. Maybe my story might even help Heidi know she wasn't alone in carrying a heavy load. I figured she was the kinda human being that gave more than they took, and she'd want to help me as I wished to help her because that's what family does.

I tried to push away the blues and think about all the good things we could do for one another, and for the first time for ever I thought about a future worth fighting for.

I must have dropped off. When I woke the sun was pushing at the dark, forcing its way up behind the beach, a smudge of silver gray. I watched as it turned a pale yellow, growing darker to rose pink. Then the edge of the big, round orange sun broke the surface, casting a veil of hot pink across the sky and washing gold hues over the ocean until the sun rose, bright yellow flooding the world with glorious life-giving light. I stood and scattered the ashes from my tobacco bonfire and, full of resolve, strode back to camp.

㉘

— Heidi —

After **I had buried ma's** lock of hair, I ambled back to camp. A few minutes after I arrived, Joe appeared. He had a jauntiness to his step. He greeted me with this huge boyish grin. 'Hey, morning, Heidi. You sleep good?' Before I could answer, he scooped me up in his arms and held me tight. He didn't speak. He didn't need to. At last he put me down and took a deep breath and, closing his eyes, said, 'Think it's going to be a beautiful day. What say we eat? I get a better job, and you get back to school and make some friends.'

I nodded and, raising myself on tiptoes, kissed his stubbly cheek. The three of us had breakfast. Ella kept looking at me and Joe and it made me laugh and I knew that from that day forward she was the one in charge and me and Joe were the kids. I didn't think that in a bad way; it was just the dynamic. Ella kissed me goodbye, and it made me feel good to have her say, 'Have a great day at school,' like someone cared about how my day went.

Joe walked over with me to the Hikomoris to see about the work. Mayumi was ready. She took my hand and looked me up and down. I had fixed up my hair and put on the best clothes I had, but I guess I was what you might call ramshackle, and I won't deny I was feeling kinda apprehensive. Save the glow in her pecan eyes her face was hard to read. 'You look perfect. Come on, it isn't far.'

It took us about thirty minutes to make it over to the local schoolroom. It was bigger and grander than the one back home, but in all other ways, similar. Just like at home, the kids gathered outside, the younger ones running around ragging one another, and us older kids made a group. A short while after we arrived, I saw Betty approaching. As soon as she saw me, her face lit up, and she ran over and gave me a hug. 'Straw Blue, you came to school. Wow, that's made my day!'

Mayumi said, 'Straw Blue? What?'

I laughed. 'It's my hobo name. From my hair and eyes.'

Betty frowned. 'I thought you had a weird name. What's your real name?'

'Heidi. Heidi Schlager. I'm from Idaho.'

Betty said. 'I like that better. It suits you. Where exactly is Idaho?'

One of the other kids snickered, and I heard someone say something about potatoes. They were all curious about me, and young Betty got pushed to the fringes of the group. They looked somewhat more prosperous than my Idaho school mates. Mayumi did a grand job of protecting me, not that anyone was unpleasant or such, but as though she understood maybe what it was like to be an outsider. The questions fired at me from every side and I'd only got as far as my name and where I was from when this elegant lady appeared at the school door and rang a handbell, which worked like a magnet quieting the mob and pulling it inside. Mayumi and I hung back and were the last to approach.

The woman smiled. 'Well, good morning, Mayumi.' She looked at me. 'And who is this?'

'Morning Miss McLaughten, this here is Heidi, and she's staying for a few weeks with her family and I was wondering whether she could come join in while she's here?'

Miss McLaughten gave me a quick look over, nodded, and stood to one side. 'Welcome to Bay School, Heidi.'

We entered the tidy, cool interior. There was space for us at the back. We sat. The younger kids at the front, who earlier had paid me no attention, now turned and stared. My face flushed hot. Miss McLaughten went to the front. 'Children, this is Heidi and she's a friend of Mayumi and will join us for a while.' She looked at me and said, 'Perhaps you can stand and introduce yourself.'

I had long forgotten my first day at school and it was kinda scary being here amongst all these strangers and, for a minute, I felt like running. I stood. The faces stared back. I thought about what I should say. I plucked up courage and began. 'Hi, I'm Heidi Schlager and I'm from a small town in Northern Idaho called Sitwell. When my ma and pa died, I had to leave and now I'm with my new family and right now we're traveling and working and looking for somewhere to call home. Before I came here, I had never seen the ocean and you're all real lucky to be living by it. Back home, my best friend was a boy called Jeremiah and I miss him a lot and I miss my old teacher, Miss Hannah. I like school and I enjoy learning stuff. I love to read and you have a real nice library here in town. Mayumi is the first person I ever met from Japan and it's kind of Miss McLaughten to let me come and join you all.' I sat down. The faces stared. Then this little girl, I guess she was about ten, asked, 'Is Jeremiah your boyfriend? And how did your parents die?' The questions surprised me.

Betty came to my rescue. 'What kind of question is that, Mary? Mind your own, why don't you?'

Mary bridled. 'That's rich coming from you, Betty. You're the biggest nosy parker in the whole town—' The class laughed. Betty colored red, and I felt bad for her. Miss McLaughten intervened.

She split us into groups and set us to different tasks, just like Miss Hannah did. Betty kept looking over at me and when she caught my eye, she'd smile and I'd smile back. At one point I mouthed the words, thank you, to her. Mayumi said, 'Betty seems really struck on you.'

I blushed. Truth was both Betty and Mayumi had sparked my interest. It felt kinda nice that Betty took a shine to me, and I didn't mind one bit.

It did not take me long to finish the set tasks. Miss McLaughten looked at my work. 'You have neat writing, Heidi. Good work, well done.'

At recess, we sat under a cypress tree. It wasn't long before Betty came over. Mayumi said, 'What do you want, Betty?'

'Can I sit with you, please?'

'Can't you go play with one of the other kids?'

Betty looked forlorn.

I guess were our places switched, I'd have said the same thing. But I said, 'It's okay, Mayumi, I don't mind.'

Betty beamed and sat down next to me and moved close so we were touching. 'Thanks, Heidi. You're so pretty.'

'Why thank you, Betty. You look lovely, too.'

'I do? Wow.' She took my hand. I was happy to let her, enjoying the attention and it made me feel good about myself.

She asked, 'What does Jeremiah look like?'

I described him. It made me feel nostalgic.

'Have you kissed him?'

Mayumi said, 'Betty, you shouldn't ask questions like that; it's private.'

I nudged her. 'Have you kissed a boy yet, Betty?'

She made a face. 'No fear, not with the boys around here, yuck!'

Mayumi and I laughed out loud. I gave Betty a nudge. 'You're funny, Betty. I like you.'

She seemed pleased when I told her that. She put her arm around me. It felt nice, and I remembered some of the younger kids doing the same. We chatted away until we went back in. After school, Mayumi whisked me off quick so we got away and ran laughing back to her house. It was such fun to be with kids again.

When we got home, she said, 'Still want to go swimming?'

'You betcha.'

We went inside and her mother gave us something to eat and drink. After, we walked down to the same cove I had swum in many times. She had a bag with her and took out a towel and swimsuit. I realized I had nothing to wear, hadn't even occurred to me. She said, 'Where're your things?'

I shrugged. 'Mostly, I swim naked. But I don't mind, I can wear my undergarments.'

She scrutinized me, and you could see she was kinda interested. I had never been self-conscious about my body. I figured all those years at home, swimming naked in the creek meant I never gave it a second thought. 'Have you ever swum naked?'

She shook her head.

'Well, there's nothing to be ashamed of. Try it; it's real nice, makes you feel alive.' I held her gaze for a moment and grinned. 'I don't mind if you want to try.'

To encourage her, I stripped off and stood there. Her eyes ran down my body and I felt a shiver of arousal. I smirked and shrugged. 'I guess you got the same as me.' And turning, I ran laughing into the water, disappearing into a wave and, not wanting to embarrass her, swam out for a minute. When I stopped and looked back, she was entering the water, her swimsuit still on the beach. My heart leapt and a giddy feeling came over me. She swam confidently, and it was not long before she caught up and we faced one another, treading water. I giggled and splashed her. 'So, how's it feel?'

She made a face. 'Weird. Naughty. And I feel a little vulnerable.'

I spun around, throwing my arms in the air, and shouted, 'They ain't no one around but us!' And I moved closer. Her breasts were a little bigger than mine. Her wet skin and silky black hair plastered on her head and face were so beautiful, and I realized, confusingly, how attractive I found her. Odd feelings went through me. I shook my head. 'Let's swim.'

We swam parallel to the shore, moving a little away from the beach. She said, 'It's cold but I'm getting used to it. You're right, though, it feels liberating. My legs and body feel lighter, less constricted.'

'Well, that swimsuit's awful big, even got a kinda skirt to it. Must make it difficult to swim proper.'

For a time, we swam and mucked about in the waves. She was past her fear of being naked. For a while we sat side-by-side on the beach, letting the waves wash over us. I dug in the sand with my hands, burying them, and stole glances at her. I said, 'I like the feeling of my hands being in the sand.'

She nodded and smiled. 'This is fun.'

In the end, the cold water defeated us. She let me share her towel, and we dried one another's hair. I loved the closeness this allowed me. As I messaged her head, an overwhelming urge to kiss her and stroke her body came over me, and fearing she'd show me the icy mitt, I buried the urge. Instead, I dallied, savoring the moment. She turned to face me. 'Thanks, Heidi.'

'What for?'

'The swim and you know, making me try something new.'

I beamed and kissed her cheek, lingering just a moment. 'Thanks for being my friend and taking me to school. You didn't have to do that. I've been through a lot and having someone like you has made me understand how much I miss being with friends. I mean, I love Joe and Ella and they've been real good to me, but it can be lonely.'

We got dressed, and I asked her to come back to camp. Joe and Ella weren't there, so I got a fire going and we sat down.

She sat, propped herself up on her elbows, and looked around. 'This is home?'

'Yeah. I know it's not much, but we've got everything we need. Most of all, we have each other.'

'Papa always says that family and being together are more important than anything else. I think maybe I take things for granted.' She looked at me with her rich pecan eyes. 'How did your parents die?'

I thought about it for a second. 'Can I tell you in a day or two? Assuming, that is, you want to spend more time with this wicked girl?'

She giggled. 'Oh, you are a wicked girl, but then, I'm not so good either.'

'Oh yeah, really? That sounds intriguing.'

I told her about how I got attacked and met Sam and Booker. It reminded me and I went and got the game they had gifted me. She didn't know it. I said we should play it another day. I said, 'Sam told me that some white people hated black people and did awful things to them. It shocked me to hear that. I mean, I know folk can be mean to one another, but that shook me.'

'Most people round here accept us, and we are part of the community, but some people think of us as inferior. We get called names.'

I frowned. 'What kinda names?'

She shrugged. 'I've been called yellow and slanty-eyed. Some people think we're Chinese, like we all look the same. There was this boy at school used to call me Chin-Chong. In Japan they call foreigners, Gaijin.'

'Well, that doesn't sound too bad. Am I Gaijin?'

She nodded. 'But I'd never call you that. I'm an American first. I was born here.'

I poked the fire. 'Well, I don't get it. My ma and pa were from another country. Folks back home came from all kinda places.' I looked at her. She met my gaze. 'Anyway, you're the most beautiful person I have ever met, and your skin isn't yellow. Only a dumb Dora would say a thing like that. We might look different, but then doesn't everyone? I mean, I'm blond and blue eyed and Jeremiah is brown-haired, has lovely chocolate brown eyes and his skin is darker than mine, and yours, for that matter. Sam and Booker are real handsome boys, and I just loved their smooth, black skin and how it shone in the light, and their tight, black curly hair. Hey, if it weren't for them, I might have died.'

She looked at me hard with quizzical eyes. 'You think I'm beautiful?'

'Course you are, don't you think so?'

'My parents think so. I don't like my nose and my lips are too big.'

I laughed. 'Well, for what it's worth, you look perfect to me. If I was a boy, I'd want to be with you and kiss those gorgeous red lips.'

She blushed. 'You're funny, Heidi. I've met no one like you before.'

'See, we're all unique. I've met no one like you either.' We giggled. A voice made us look round.

'Glad someone's happy.' We saw Ella approaching. She was carrying a bag, and I guessed holding provisions. 'It's real nice to see you again, Mayumi. How was school?'

I think I had been waiting a thousand years to be sitting at home with a friend and for someone I called ma to ask me how school was. I turned to Mayumi and could not help laughing.

Mayumi gave me a look. 'Heidi's got a little admirer.'

Ella sat the bag down. 'Oh, has she now? Do tell!'

I let Mayumi tell her about it and our day at school. She even told about how I'd got her to swim naked. I lay back, savoring the moment, and watched a few whimsical, wispy clouds float in the blue sky.

— Heidi —

We slipped into a routine that had been missing from my life. Joe and I would walk over to Bluff Cove, where I'd meet Mayumi and go to school. Joe enjoyed working for Mr. Hikomori. I hoped that like many hoboes do, he'd make a good contact here and it would give us a reason to return. Ella was doing yard work up at the monastery, so maybe there had been a positive from my foolish attempt to end my life. School was fine, but mostly I wanted to spend time with Mayumi and Betty. I found it difficult to find my place among the other kids, most of whom were growing up with all the things that I had missed out on. I guess it made me feel different and the things I had been through had made me grow up quick, or at least that is how it felt. I did not know whether this was a good thing and I guess if you had pushed me to choose, I would have wanted to be like them.

Sometimes, I longed to go home to my sad little house and climb up my ladder to the space where I slept and had my things. In some ways, I even missed my pa, though I found that difficult to get my head around. I wondered whether it was from guilt. I guess that despite knowing that Joe and Ella wanted and loved me, I still had a lot of confusing stuff in my head and wondered how I'd ever make sense of it all. I kept reminding myself what Sister Catherine had said about taking it slow and being kind to myself. The night terrors and bad dreams were still there, though they came less often, and when they did, Ella would be there to hold me and tell me I was safe and then comfort me as I fell back to sleep. Every morning when I woke, I felt this little hollow in my stomach and I'd lie there and try to drive it off by thinking of all the positive things in my life. Sometimes it exhausted me, but I promised myself to keep trying.

That morning, as Joe and I strolled along in silence, enjoying the morning sun,

I reflected on how little I knew about him. I hoped he would find his way to tell me more. I think he had been so long on his own he needed time to get his head around being a father and a husband, just as I was processing the idea of calling them ma and pa. They were just words, but it isn't until you think about them you understand their power. Can a person who hasn't made you ever be your parent? I guess by now, with everything we'd been through and them knowing what I had done, they knew me as well as they needed to. Perhaps love is enough? Maybe if you love someone wholly, you can love them like you made them, like Joe said, no strings attached, no agenda, no conditions, just love. Joe had been more of a father to me than my pa had ever been. It had nothing to do with my pa being mean or beating me, for that was like an aberration, which didn't make it right. No one should treat another person like that, and I'd carry those scars, physical and mental, for the rest of my life. No, Joe had given me something my pa never had: love and respect. I trusted him. The day we met, he could have given me food and even a little money and then walked away. But he chose not to, and I believe he did that because he needed me. It's just, he didn't know it then. Fate had thrown us together at that moment, and I guess love and some hidden need had done the rest.

Then Ella came along. I think I knew they should be together when I first saw them that day she arrived at Britt and Joe had stood up and hugged her tight; it was the look they had, and the body language. They'd been discreet, but I knew they were sleeping together, and I was happy for them. I had taken to going off after our evening meal for a walk to give them time together. I guess it was a problem with us all living cheek-by-jowl.

I needed the alone time, too. Sometimes I'd just walk and think about stuff, other times I'd find a spot either up on the cliffs or away in the trees where I'd sit and read. The more time I spent with Mayumi the more confused I was about my attraction to her. I'd always been with and liked boys. I liked their openness and the physical nature of our play together. I knew I loved Jeremiah. I enjoyed kissing him and being with him.

It was one of those times when I was up in among the fragrant cypress trees, just leaning against a trunk. I was reading a Japanese novel—"Kokoro"—loaned to me by Mr. Hikomori. Though tricky in places, it absorbed and intrigued me and gave me an insight into Japanese culture and literature. But that day I could not concentrate and kept having to go back and reread sentences. At last, I gave up and closed my eyes, and as I daydreamed, this weird, disturbing thought came to me. It was so peculiar it startled me, and I sat upright, my eyes now wide open, staring. What if I was a boy in a girl's body? Was such a thing possible? Was that why Betty was so attracted to me and I to Mayumi? Was it why I preferred ragging around with the boys and was best friend with one? But then, Jeremiah attracted me as well. So, what did that make me? Was it why my pa hated me so? He could see something that disturbed him. The more I thought about it, the more muddled I became. It was a crazy idea, wasn't it? I mean, I didn't mind being a girl and was sure I didn't want to be a boy. But boys got the better deal, and I wanted what they had.

I told myself I was being silly. There were girls that liked boy's stuff. What did they call them? Tomboys. Yes, that was it, tomboys. Maybe I was one of them and I just enjoyed doing boyish stuff more than girlie things. It didn't make me a boy, did it? But then, if I am all girl, then why was I attracted to Mayumi?

These thoughts drove me crazy. Why was it so complicated? I wondered whether there were books that might help. But then, who do I ask? I could not imagine asking Miss Jennings, or anyone. As it transpired, my old friend serendipity paid me another visit, when a few days later nature played a card that gave rise to such an opportunity.

A few days before my fifteenth birthday, I had my first period. It was a Sunday. I was on my own and swimming. Throughout the day, my belly had felt crampy, but the cold water and swim seemed to soothe it. But when I got out of the water, I noticed blood coming from inside me and running down my leg. It shocked and scared me and I thought maybe it was a punishment. With feverish panic, I grabbed my clothes and, not wanting to get my dungarees all bloody, I rolled up my underwear and pushed them between my legs and then dressed. I hastened back to camp, but it was awkward walking fast while trying to keep the makeshift pad from slipping. I was relieved that Joe wasn't there, but Ella was. She glanced up and my anxious horror plastered expression made her drop what she was doing. 'What's wrong?'

I pointed. 'I'm bleeding from down there.'

To my surprise, she nodded and smiled and took my hand. 'It's fine, sweetheart. It happens to all girls. I get that too. Come on, we'll get you sorted and we better have a chat.'

I sat riveted as Ella laid out the facts of life and about becoming a woman. She left nothing out, saying she didn't want me to get any surprises. Her openness and kindness gave me the courage to ask about the stuff that was so confusing me. She sat and listened, and the more she listened, the more I talked. The questions blurted out nineteen to the dozen. At last, I stopped and looked at her. 'Am I weird?'

She frowned and shook her head. 'No, sweetheart, of course you're not.' She came and sat next to me. 'Look, all this stuff might seem real confusing, but you'll work it out in time. You don't have to be anyone you don't want to. If you like girls, then that's fine. Thing is, right now, your body and mind are going through this vast change and all your yearnings are kicking in. Give it time and things will work themselves out. Don't worry about it. Take your time and I'm sure that as you grow and adapt, it will become clearer. Enjoy being young and embrace the adventure.'

I nodded. 'I don't want to be different. People hate—you know—people that have sex with—don't they?'

'Yes, there are people that think that. But they don't matter, do they? Me and Joe will love you for the person you are. I promise you. Those Bluenoses that think themselves so superior don't matter. Your friends will love you for who you are and if they don't, they aren't friends, are they?'

'I guess.'

'Just take your time and I'm here if you have questions. You can ask me anything.'

I looked at her. 'Is it wrong to touch yourself, you know, down there?'

'No. Of course not. Just, you know, what with them Bluenoses about, keep that to yourself. But it isn't sinful even if that is what some folk will tell you. And you know what?'

I shook my head. 'Huh-huh?'

'I bet you all the water in that ocean that they may tell you it's a sin to touch yourself, but they're at it, too. Men in particular; they can't help themselves.'

I snorted. 'Kinda hypocritical, isn't it?'

'Oh, sure. But then they tell themselves one thing and do another. That counts for all kinda things, not just sex.'

'Wow. I never knew it was all so—secretive.'

'People feel embarrassed, I guess. But there's nothing to feel embarrassed about. So, be yourself and don't go fretting about it. It's complicated, but it'll work itself out, you'll see.'

By the time Joe returned from work, Ella and I had been through one of those important moments that reached the very heart of the word trust. I guess had I been back home I'd have gone to Jeremiah's ma, though I cannot imagine she would have been as easy to talk with nor as forthcoming, so I was thankful my first period it had happened here and now. It was the first time I had hugged her and called her ma at the same time. She had looked at me. 'I know I didn't make you, but I feel about you as though I did. I'm always here for you.'

On his return from work, Joe had looked at us fixing the meal. He said, 'I am one lucky son of a gun.' He dropped his bag, adding, 'So what you all been doing today?' Ella and I had glanced at one another and giggled. She said, 'Oh, just the usual.'

He'd frowned and then shrugged and a part of me felt guilty we excluded him. That evening, as always, I took myself off. I walked up to the spot I'd buried ma's hair and sat and looked out to the ocean. I chatted to her about my day and my change. It felt like she should know. I knew in church they talked about heaven and hell and such. I did not believe in all that, though I could not deny that I felt her presence now more than ever before.

The wind blew my hair, flapping it about my face and it felt good against my skin and when I ran my tongue over my lips, I tasted the salt. My belly ached a bit; Ella told me I might expect that. In a few days, I would be fifteen and I felt like little Heidi, that Idaho motherless girl with a mean father, the girl that ran free and despite the hand they had dealt her, loved life and found love in a boy just enough to keep the flame burning, was history now. A part of me felt sad that the child in me was fading, but I felt enthusiastic about becoming a woman and exploring life to its full. I wondered what it would be like to make a life and grow it inside me, feel it moving. It was kinda nice to have something else to think about.

The following morning, as Joe and I walked to Bluff Cove, he had asked me how I was and I knew Ella had told him about my period and I was fine about that. I was quiet at school, partly because I was a little sore but also because I felt sad and low. I was happy to spend recess sitting listening to Betty tell me all about the town's gossip. She brought me a copy of her pa's paper. It was the previous Saturday's issue. Thanking her, I took it and began leafing through. A short item on page five caught my eye. Entitled "Carmel Reading Circle", it read:

> The Carmel Reading Circle has chosen "China" as the subject of the winter.
> The present reading is "Sun Yat Sen and the Awakening of China"—which will be finished early November. The subject promises to be interesting as well as profitable, and those interested will be welcome Tuesday evenings at eight, at "Gray Gables" corner of Lincoln and Seventh.

I glanced at Betty. 'Hey that sounds interesting.' She looked at me with lost, dull eyes and shrugged. I put down the paper. 'What's up, Betts.'

'Can I tell you something? Only you mustn't tell anyone else.'

I frowned and placed my hand on her arm. 'Of course. And I won't tell a soul. I promise.'

She told me how lonely she was. All her life, her mom had been unwell, given to fits of severe despair that sent her to bed for days at a time. Betty loved her pa, but he treated her like a peer and was all wrapped up in the newspaper, expecting Betty to take over one day. Some kids teased her because she was so forward and she said that when she met me, she couldn't help her attraction to me, how kind I was, and I didn't judge. I knew what she meant, and I felt for her. 'Well, Betts, I promise I won't tell and I'll always be your friend.'

'You will, really?'

'Yeah, of course. Even if I'm not here.'

'You don't mind me spending time with you?'

'Don't be silly, I'm fond of you and you're funny and interesting.'

'I help at the office sometimes. Would you like to come over after school one day and see?'

'Actually Betty, that would be real interesting; I'd love to.'

She smiled. 'Oh, great, you'll love it.' And she hugged me, which she did often, only now I got why. I liked her, and I loved how she held a torch for me, wanted me as a friend, and looked up to me.

That day, after school, I walked back with Mayumi and told her about getting my first period. I asked her whether she had, too. She looked at me, a knowing twinkle in her eyes. 'I guess that explains why you're quiet today.' She stopped and turned me to face her. 'Yes, I have. A few months back. I am still getting used to it. Though truthfully, I'm not sure I ever will.' Then she laughed and said, 'We Japanese call it the arrival of Matthew Perry.'

I frowned and giggled. 'What? Where does it come from? What does it even mean?'

'I don't know. It's just what we call it.'

'Oh, okay. I guess it is like a kinda code seeing as it is so private. Do you get belly pains?'

She nodded. 'Last time I stayed off school for a day. It soon passes though.' She gave me a sisterly hug and as we walked on, she put her arm around me. 'You'll be well for your birthday on Friday.'

'I hope so.' We walked on a bit. 'Look, I need to tell you something, but you've got to promise me you won't tell anyone else.'

She stopped and looked at me. 'Okay, sure.'

'No, you got to promise because this isn't something little. It's real big and you may not like me after, so I need to know.'

She frowned but regarded me with warm, trusting eyes. 'Sure, I promise with all that is sacred, your secret will be safe with me, and I won't hate you ever.'

We went on further and found a quiet spot and sat down cross-legged opposite one another. I told her everything that had happened. About Jeremiah and me, about our plan, and how it turned to disaster and led me here. I told her how I planned to drown and it wasn't an accident and how alone I'd felt. I told her how much she meant to me, how good it was to have a girlfriend, and that I loved and trusted her. And she sat and listened with unblinking eyes, her brow furrowed. Then her eyes softened. My words moved her as fat tears trailed down her cheeks that gave away her shock and compassion, and I knew she would stand by me. When I'd finished, I felt drained but relieved. I took a deep breath and said, ' I do not want our friendship to be a lie.'

She took my hands; her touch felt electric. 'My goodness, Heidi, I'm so sorry. It's okay now. I'm honored you told me, trusted me.'

'I'm glad I told you.' She rubbed my hands. Her hands were soft and warm. I reached across and kissed her lightly on her cheek and whispered a thank you.

She wiped her wet cheeks with the back of her hand and lowered her eyes. 'You'll be gone soon, and then what will I do? I wish you could stay.'

'I'd like nothing more, but there are things I must do. I promise with all my heart that even if you can't write to me, I will write to you and as soon as I can I'll come back, though—' then it hit me like a brick in my face that when I went back, they might put me on trial and send me to jail. I looked at her and sighed. 'It's just that might be some time.'

She took a deep breath, and a flicker of a smile washed her face. 'We'll have to make the most of the time we have, won't we?'

'Sure. We will.'

I walked her back home. I was tired and wanted to get back to camp and lay down. When I got back, I told Ella about the Matthew Perry thing and she laughed and told me a few more code words for it, most of which didn't seem pleasant. We agreed from then on, that between us we'd refer to it as the arrival of Matthew Perry.

— Ella —

It meant loads that Heidi trusted me by discussing such personal things. For me, it was like a test. I remembered my first period and going to my mom, which had been of little help. Back then it was all brushed under the carpet and made to seem shameful. I had not been told about the facts of life and how and why my body was changing, and it wasn't until I met David that I had the full picture of things. He was a kind man and a wonderful lover and wanted me to enjoy sex as well. I remember the first time he went down on me. Of course, it shocked me, but then he went to work, and my goodness, I had never imagined such a thing. So, after I got Heidi sorted, we sat down and I told her everything I knew, and I mean everything.

She asked about Joe and me and knew we were having sex, said it was why she went off in the evenings to give us space.

I leaned back my eyes wide. 'Wow, I did not know you knew that, and you had the maturity to give us space.'

She shrugged. 'It's okay. I don't want to cramp your style. It must be tough having me—you know—'

'No. No, never say that. You're never in the way, and never will be.'

She nodded. 'I know.' She looked down, picked up a stick and began drawing in the dirt. 'Can I ask you something, you know, about feelings?'

'Sure, anything.'

She stopped doodling and looked at me. 'Is it normal to be attracted to boys and girls?'

'I think at your age, when your body is going through such a massive change, it is not unusual to feel that way. Truth is, I find some women attractive and I'm sure I'd enjoy having sex with them. Is this about Betty and Mayumi?'

'More about Mayumi. When we went swimming, you know, her body attracted me. I wanted to—well—' My mind hunted for the right words. 'I guess—mess about—you know, like I have with Jeremiah. Is that wicked?'

'Wicked? No. Are you talking about find things out, you mean?'

She nodded. 'I guess.'

'Well, I'd say if she's interested too, and don't assume she won't be, then you should talk to her about it. Ask her questions and I'm sure she'll have some for you. I've seen the way you two are together and if you think it'll help, then don't be afraid. It doesn't mean you're odd and I know some women like being with both genders, and I guess some men do as well.'

'What if I really like girls more and don't want to be with a boy?'

I smiled and laid my hand on her soft cheek. 'Sweetheart, take it as it comes. You'll know what's right for you, and whatever that may be, we'll support you.'

She gave me a hug. 'Thanks, ma. You're the best.'

It did not surprise me she was struggling with her sexuality. She seemed far from a typical girl and I had seen the way she looked at Mayumi and how much she enjoyed being with Betty. I wasn't sure whether Betty's infatuation with Heidi was just a girlie crush or that Betty was that way inclined. I suppose time would tell and either way, made little difference to the good that came from their friendship.

I felt like our conversation was a giant stride in my feeling like a mother to her. I found it gut-wrenching, and it made me think about the children David and I may have had. I tried to hold back the tears, but they came in floods and for a brief time she became the mother and held me. It was like nothing I'd experienced before. She said, 'I love you so much, ma.' It was a defining moment in our relationship, and I cannot tell you how proud I felt.

Every day, as I walked to the monastery for work, I passed the field that was for sale. I had made discreet inquiries to the agent and mentioned it to Joe and we went to look. We stood by the field that, with each visit, felt to me like our place.

I nudged him. 'Well, what do you think?'

'I think it's terrifying, but I know it's what we have to do.'

'Don't you want to stop roaming and make this gorgeous place your home?'

He smiled and put his arm around me. 'If I'm with you and Heidi, anywhere is home. But here feels special, and we seem to have made friends outside the hobo community and I've never done that before, not really.'

'Yeah, me neither.'

'Trouble is, we can't make that decision right now, can we? Heidi needs to go home and make peace with her past. Maybe she'll want to stay there and be with

Jeremiah. I guess putting down roots there would work for me as well. Like I said, so long as we're together, it'll be right. And, don't forget, we've got a job picking them oranges for Luther, and when all that's done, I need to find Florence and clean up my mess. Of course, I can do that after we've put down somewhere.'

'What if they send her to jail?'

'Ah, shoot, I don't know. She killed him in self defense. Jeremiah will speak to that.'

'What if he died and they make out she killed her pa in revenge?'

Joe held up his hand. 'We get her an outstanding lawyer and she tells the truth. I figure a jury will see it for what it was.'

'She might still do time.'

'She might. And if she does, we'll be there for her.'

'What if we persuade her not to go back? We can get Jeremiah to come here.' I realized I was clutching at straws. He looked at me like I'd gone soft. I turned away. 'Dammit all to hell. I know—I know. We must do right by her.'

He turned me to face him and held me. 'No one said it would be easy, but I have a feeling it will work out fine. She isn't alone and neither are we. We plan for the worst and hope for the best, eh?'

I nodded. 'The whole damn thing gives me the jitters. We'll have to get her to say one of those prayers of hers.'

We walked.

Joe said, 'You know what I think?'

I shook my head. 'Go on, what do you think?'

'That girl's been to hell and back, hasn't she? Yet, she's still got so much fortitude and an energy about her. See how she wins people over? So, I think when she stands up and tells her story and when people know how he beat her, and her ma, too, they will know the truth. I don't know squat about the law, but I know if you kill another in self defense, then you stand a good chance of going free. She killed him in a moment of terror. There was no planning or desire to see him killed. She just plucked up the knife that was probably lying on the table and struck once. Admittedly, it was a lucky strike to kill him like that, but it stopped him and she didn't carry on. It proves all she wanted to do was stop the assault on Jeremiah. Now I know we're biased, but if you look at the cold hard facts, she's no murderer.'

'Yeah, I guess you're right. Still, when we get back to Idaho and before she goes to see the police, we get to a lawyer first, right?'

'Definitely.'

We stopped. I turned to him. 'Perhaps, when we can see daylight, we can come back here and find a place. What do you think?'

'It's good to have a goal. We'll keep this to ourselves for now, shall we?'

I took his hand; we walked on. It was like we had just met and fallen in love, planning a future together. I suppose we were. 'Those nightmares are still coming regular.'

'Not as bad as just before she took that swim. I think she understands it's going to take time. And now, she has a mom to comfort her, doesn't she? That makes a big difference, you can tell.'

I felt emotion building. I wasn't used to it. 'We've really bonded since we discussed the adoption.' I laughed. 'It was kinda lucky she had her first period when she did, and we did the mother and daughter stuff. It felt like a test.'

'Well, I'd say you passed that with flying colors, don't you?'

'Yeah, I think I did. Even a little proud of myself. Maybe I can be a mom.'

He pushed back his hat and took a deep breath. 'Dammit, I could use a smoke right now—'

We stopped. It was quiet, like we were the last people alive. I placed my hand on his cheek. 'Well, I'm proud of you for quitting.'

He nodded. 'You know, you are a special mother and partner. We could try for a kid, couldn't we?'

Well, you could have run me down with a herd of beef cattle. 'Are you serious, Joe Reisen? Have a baby?'

'Hell, yes, why not? Least we can have fun trying, can't we?'

'Oh, I dunno, Joe, maybe when we've settled and Heidi is too, eh? Also, I'm kinda old for having a kid.'

'Yeah, you're right, bad idea.'

'Nice thought, though.' I smiled and wobbled my eyebrows. 'Like you say, in the meantime, we can put in plenty of practice.'

We kissed. I wanted him, could feel his passion.

He said, 'There's no one around, how about—'

We were like a couple of newlyweds on honeymoon. After, we lay on the grass, our glistening bodies cooling off, our clothes strewn around. He let out an enormous sigh. 'Now I really need a smoke. Never knew it would be such hell quitting.'

'Well, you stick to it, Joe.' I laughed, propped myself up on one elbow, and laid my hand on his chest. 'Hey, you know when Heidi goes off in the evening and sometimes we take advantage?'

'Yeah, what of it?'

'She knows and goes off to give us space.'

'Oh boy, well I'll be. She is an observant girl; I'll give her that.'

'I mean, I thought we'd been real discreet. She said it was the time in Britt, that first day we were back together, that she'd gone for a wander and came back and almost barged in on us.'

Joe roared with laughter. 'Well hell, it makes sense now, you know, that she says, "Well, I'm off for a walk now, back in about an hour or so." Doesn't it?'

'She said she enjoyed knowing we were having fun. She's real interested in sex, though she said she was confused, being attracted to Jeremiah and Mayumi, both.'

Joe raised himself on an elbow. We faced one another, and he cupped my right breast, giving it a gentle squeeze, then caressed the nipple with his thumb. A shiver ran through me, and he ran his hand and eyes down and stroked my belly, resting it there. He glanced back up. 'She'll work it out. Maybe spending time with Mayumi will help get her back on her feet. She's a pretty girl that Mayumi. Smart, too.'

I kissed him and lay my hand on his and pushed it down between my legs.

By the time we got back to camp, Heidi was back too. She looked at us and waved. 'Hey, where've you been? I got supper going.'

Joe said, 'Oh, we just took a walk, been an hour or so.' Heidi made a face and rolled her eyes. Joe looked at me and we burst out laughing. She shook her head, rucking her brows, and went on back to stirring the pot, saying, 'Reckon you've both had way too much sun.'

— Heidi —

My birthday fell on a Friday. I woke early. I didn't feel different; you never do, do ya? Except, rather than that hollow sensation in my stomach, there was a flutter of excitement. I could hear Joe outside by the fire and smell the bacon. I joined him.

He looked up, and his beautiful, warm, craggy smile spread across his handsome face. 'Hey, happy birthday.' He stood and gave me a hug. I could smell Ella on him. Since their commitment to one another, they'd been closer physically and emotionally. It had made me think about what love was and what it meant. They both seemed younger and more playful than when we'd first met. I worried I was still in the way, and they had offered to adopt me because they felt obliged. I knew they cared for me, but I could not shake the nagging doubt. He let go. 'So, how's it feel to be fifteen because I'm darned if I can remember?'

I chuckled. 'It feels good—old man!'

He grinned and gave me a gentle nudge. 'Old man, is it? That's harsh! You hungry?'

Ella joined us and she made a fuss, and we sat in the early morning sunshine, ate bacon with griddle cakes and drank coffee. After breakfast, she went inside and returned with a large parcel wrapped in paper, tied with a blue ribbon, and held it out. 'Here, happy birthday. This is from us.'

I took the package and sat back down and held it on my lap. It was heavy. 'What is it?'

Joe waved his hand at me. 'Open it up and find out, girl.'

I pulled the bow; It was real pretty. Ella said it matched my eyes and I could use it for my hair. I set it aside and laid open the parcel. Inside were a leather-bound notebook, four pencils painted yellow, a small penknife, a leather pouch, and a book inside of which was a tooled piece of leather to keep your place. I studied them. 'Holy smoke! I love them. Thank you, thank you so much.'

I put the things down and got up and hugged them both, kissed their cheeks. 'Best present ever. I mean it. Thanks.'

Joe grinned. 'The knife is to keep them pencils sharp, and the pouch will keep 'em safe, and you can write stuff in that notebook. I hope the book is to your liking.'

I looked it over again: "Jane Eyre" by a lady called Charlotte Brontë. Inside, Joe and Ella had made an inscription:

To Heidi on her fifteenth birthday, many happy returns, love ma and pa.

Underneath those words, Joe had written a quote from R L Stevenson:

I kept always two books in my pocket, one to read, one to write in.

I ran my finger over the words and lingered a moment over the ma and pa, and I lost the emotional battle, and tears of joy sprang forth. I said, 'I love the words you wrote. I have not read this. How did you know what to get?'

'Miss Jennings helped us out with that, didn't she, Joe? Said it would suit you well.'

'Have you read it?'

They both shook their heads. 'Well, that's good. We can all enjoy it.' I held the book to my chest. It smelled good. 'It's the first book I can call mine.'

'Well, I'm glad you like the gifts. I've got to go to work. You going to school?'

I wiped my eyes, laughing. 'Do squirrels like nuts?'

Joe chuckled and shook his head. 'Well, that's one way to put it.'

Ella said she'd clear up, and I went off and got myself ready. As we walked over to Bluff Cove, I felt a lightness in my step. I had put my notebook, book and pencil case in my bag. They told me to be back early as they had a surprise, which drove me wacky the rest of the day trying to think what it might be. Mayumi was waiting for me.

She gave me a hug and kissed my cheek. She smelled so good. Now it felt like my birthday. 'Happy Birthday. I have something for you, but I'll let you have it later.'

At school, while I sat red-faced wishing a void would open in the floor and swallow me whole, Miss McLaughten had everyone sing me happy birthday. Then I had to make a speech, so I told them about the book I got. She said it was a fine novel, but a grownup book, which made me feel special and more intrigued to read it.

Betty gave me a sweet-smelling handkerchief with a pretty, gold flower embroidered on it. She told me it was a California Poppy, and that she had put a little of her ma's perfume on it. I felt spoiled, and it was nice to have something feminine and the perfume smelled so good. I told her I did not know if Idaho had a special flower, but I was sure it could not be as lovely as her poppy. I thanked her by kissing her cheek. I don't think I had ever kissed anything so dainty. She beamed and held her hand up to the spot. 'Your lips feel so nice. They tickled.' We laughed. She kissed me back and hugged me and held me for a while. I put my arms around her. Her hair smelled so clean and soft. I could tell she needed the contact, and truthfully, so did I.

It was a fun day and not unlike birthdays at school back home, only back home I had known all the kids for a long time and we belonged together. As Mayumi and I strolled back to Bluff Cove, I told her I had to be home early, and she almost gave up the surprise by saying she'd see me later but covered her tracks and I was none the wiser. The weather was warm, which made me want to have a swim, but I did not want to spoil the plans so I made tracks and when I got back Ella was there laying on the grass, eyes closed, taking in the sun. She had a stalk of grass in her mouth and one hand behind her head while the other stroked her belly. I watched for a bit. She looked contented. She must have sensed someone was near, as she lifted her head and looked across. I beamed. 'Hey, you looked so peaceful; I didn't want to disturb you.'

'How was school?' I still appreciated hearing her say that. I showed her the handkerchief Betty had given me and what the flower was. She put it to her nose and inhaled. 'Smells as good as it looks.'

I sat. 'Well, what's the plan, ma?'

She sat herself up. 'We're going to get dressed up as well as we can, go to a restaurant in Carmel and have a party.'

My eyes were wide. 'A party, really? Just us?'

'Yes, just us.'

'Sounds great. Have I got time for a swim?'

'Sure. We need to leave here about six, so you've time.' I needed no more prompting. A birthday without a swim would have been no birthday at all.

— § —

Ella had another surprise: she'd bought me a dress and some white canvas shoes. The dress had a white scalloped collar, the main body was lilac with small red flowers and green leaves set over a pattern of white foliage. It was elegant without being too girlie. It buttoned up from the waist with a row of delicate white buttons. The skirt part was pleated and ended just above my knee. The fit was perfect. It made me feel feminine and made my breasts seem bigger. But I was so unused to wearing a dress, it took a while to get accustomed to it and I had to remind myself to keep my legs together when I sat. She worked on my hair, brushed it out and put it in a ponytail, tying it with the blue ribbon. When she was done, she twirled me around. It will not surprise you to hear that I had never had such fine or feminine attire.

Ella held her hand up to her mouth as her eyes glowed. 'My goodness, you look beautiful! I mean, you always do, but now it shows you off properly.' She was a natural at being a ma. The canvas shoes were comfortable, and it was nice not to wear boots. She said, 'Do you like them?'

I nodded, beaming. 'I love 'em. It's good to have something stylish to wear for special.'

We hugged. She pushed away and held me at arm's length, her eyes glistening. 'Glad rags!'

I laughed. 'Yes, I like that—glad rags.'

When Joe returned, he took a double take. I stood there and splayed out my arms and gave him a twirl. I felt blissful and my face had the biggest, most stupid grin on it. I could see him look at me differently. He pushed his hat back on his head. 'I don't have my own words so I'll pinch these from the French writer, Anatole France: "If the path be beautiful, let us not ask where it leads".'

It was typical of him to put what he saw into a word riddle for me. I was glad he did not say I was pretty or beautiful because I know I look nice, and I don't mean that in a showy way. It is one thing I have never questioned or bothered much about. Even when my pa was hitting me and calling me hateful names about how I looked and behaved, I saw myself in the reflection of those that liked me and how I liked them. Of course, we all have things we don't like about ourselves and I reckon no matter what you change, you'll never find peace in the business of physical perfection. A smile can make you look perfect and a frown ugly, which kinda gets you to thinking that your mind makes you what you are. But standing there and seeing how I affected Joe made me feel extraordinary.

He looked at himself and made a face. 'Well, I best go see whether I can polish some respectability into this old bo.'

He managed just fine. But it didn't matter what he wore; he was handsome and dignified.

— Heidi —

Joe and Ella had made table reservations at the Carmel Restaurant, whose advertisement in the newspaper Betty had given me had caught my eye. It read:

Positively not a tearoom, just a place to eat, BUT A GOOD ONE!

I loved the honesty and had shown it to them and they must have taken that as a hint, which of course it was not. We walked into town, arms linked, me in the middle, joining other folk taking the evening air on this most fine of days. I saw some of them give us a look and we exchanged a nod and smile. It was that kinda town.

When we arrived, I got another surprise: it was not a party for just us. I had made a few friends since I had been here, people who had, well, I guess the words would be, helped save me and reset my compass. Save is a strong word, but in its literal sense, it was true. Mayumi was there with her mother and father. She was wearing this blue dress that made her looked so grown up and for a time I could not take my eyes off her. Sister Catherine had come, so had Miss Jennings. She gave me a book called "Heidi" by Johanna Spyri, saying, 'Here, it's the only thing you can give a bookworm for their birthday. I couldn't resist this story. Maybe a little young for you, but it's a fine tale.' I thanked her and looked it over. It was uncanny because it had my name as the title and its author had the same first name as my ma and in the story Heidi's father was called Tobias, just like my pa. Of course, Betty was there, and us three girls sat together: Mayumi opposite and Betty, as ever, next to me.

Betty, Oh little Betty! So confident and chatty, like she had a grownup inside her. She regaled us with popular gossip. She knew many of the guests at the other tables and would say things like, 'that's Mable Shaw whose husband is having an affair with Mrs. O'Keefe; and that there is Mr. and Mrs. Butterworth, their son, Cedric, who was a brilliant musician, died in the Great War; and that's Miss Santiago from the east coast, who was heir to a fortune but ran away with the yard boy and came here, only he found his way into the bed of Mrs. Bradley, the richest woman in Monterey County.' She made me and Mayumi giggle and gasp and I loved her for it. I knew she had great affection for me, and since confiding in me about how lonely she was, we'd grown closer.

Joe and Miss Jennings talked books and poetry, and it animated him. He told her about some of his stories. Ella was more of a spectator, though she found good discourse with Sister Catherine for a time, and in between I'd catch her with those gentle, smiling, chocolate eyes watching me having a ball with my girlfriends.

The best bit was when they carried from the kitchen a cake topped with icing and fifteen candles. I don't recall ever having had candles. The whole restaurant assembly sang happy birthday as I stood there, my face red and grinning, then they clapped as I blew out those mesmerizing, dancing flames.

'Make a wish!' shouted Mayumi.

The room went quiet. I sensed all eyes locked on me and I heard Mrs. Butterworth—whose son lay far away and forever young—whisper to her husband, 'Such beautiful eyes.'

Betty gave me a nudge. 'Go on.'

I cleared my throat. 'Well, I don't rightly know what to say. This is the best birthday I've ever had bar none, and I mean that. But I want to say that wherever you might be on one of these special days, there are always folk that can't be with you. So, I want to say that even though they aren't here in person, I know they are in spirit because we think about them at these times.' I paused and took a deep breath because a wave of emotion filled me. I saw Mrs. Butterworth take a handkerchief from her bag and dab her eyes and her husband place his hand on hers. I caught Sister Catherine's gleaming eyes, and she nodded. The silence felt thick, and I wondered whether I'd said the wrong thing. Then Joe, my gallant knight, came to my rescue.

He stood. 'I could not have put it better myself. Here's to Heidi, happy birthday sweet girl, and here's to all those we love who can't be with us.' Everyone stood and raised their glasses and drank what I found out later, was called a toast.

Mr. Hikomori's gift had been the booking of a group of local musicians and we invited everyone in the restaurant to join in. Tables moved aside, the music struck up, and it wasn't long before the room blossomed as we danced. I knew little about dancing, but Mayumi and Betty made excellent instructors and the three of us moved to the music with gay abandon, like stylish young flappers. I took turns with them both and it surprised me how romantic it felt to hold them and lose myself in the music.

I think I danced with almost everyone that night. When I took my turn with Joe, he said that my speech was moving and showed how grownup I was. He said he knew how much it hurt to miss folk and he'd tell me more soon. I put my arms around him and laid my head on his chest and slowly we moved distant from the music's tempo. I could hear his heartbeat. He felt strong and I could not think of a better rock on which to have secured my battered craft.

Just before the end, Mayumi grabbed me and took me to one side. Her eyes sparkled mischievously. 'I haven't given you my gift yet.' She handed me a small packet wrapped in tissue paper. She kissed my cheek and said, 'Happy birthday, Heidi.' Inside was a delicate silver chain and pendant on which was an old man carrying a boy on his shoulders. In his hand he carried a stick and it looked like they were wading across water.

'It's beautiful. I love it, thank you.'

She took it from me, unlinked the clasp, and asked me to turn around. She placed it around my neck and fastened it, then turned me back. 'There. The pendant is of St. Christopher. He is the patron saint of travelers. Lots of sailors carry something like this to protect them from a watery death.'

I held the pendant up and studied it. 'Gosh, you think it was him that's looked out for me all this time?'

She smiled. 'We all need things to believe in. I'm dreading when you go and I'll miss you like crazy, so I wanted to give you something for you to remember me and keep you safe.' She had a tear in her eye, she wiped it away. 'Look what you've done: made me cry.'

I hugged her and pressed my lips to her soft cheek. She smelled like sweet almond and fresh mown hay. I whispered in her ear. 'I'll wear it always. Every night when I go to bed, I'll think of you and send my love.'

When I broke off, like a butterfly landing, she placed her fingertips on my arm. 'Hey, let's spend the day together tomorrow. We can have a picnic. I'll take you to a special place.'

I felt this surge of heat run through me and I swear I felt so happy I could have died. I pushed my arm through hers, pulling her close. 'That would be the bees.'

    Joe, Ella, and I walked back in the moonlight. I took off my dress, folded it and tucked my good shoes back in their box. I hoped that one day soon I'd be able to wear them for Jeremiah and hold him while we moved to music. I hunkered myself under my blankets and thought of him. I did not think he would forget what day this was, so as I fell asleep, I projected my thoughts at him. But strangely, as my thoughts turned to the coming day with Mayumi, he kept drifting away.

33

— Heidi —

Picnic in hand, Mayumi led me a few miles south to a remote cove with a sandy beach. We left our clothes on the beach and swam in the water and gamboled in the rolling waves until the cold drove us out and we threw ourselves, panting and laughing, on the rug she'd brought with her. We lay on our sides, facing one another. The sun warmed our goose-pimpled bodies and dried our hair. Hers shone in the sunlight. Gently, I ran my hand through it. 'Your hair is so fine and soft.' I looked into her eyes and she into mine. We did not speak, just enjoyed being, our eyes doing the talking.

After a time, I bit my lower lip and looked hard into her eyes. 'Do you want to know what it's like to be kissed?'

She half giggled, then gave the slightest of nods. She had her arms held across her chest. She closed her eyes and the tip of her tongue ran over her lips. I moved close and brushed my lips over hers. They felt soft and moist. I could feel the heat from her face and breath. I tasted the salt and her skin still smelled a little of almonds. She opened her eyes. Again, the tip of her tongue ran across her lip, but this time more slowly, like she was tasting me.

I swallowed. I had this peculiar feeling in my belly. I felt emboldened like something possessed me and I knew what I must do. I looked into her glowing pecan eyes; the pupils dilated. 'Just do what I do.' I kissed her again and opened my mouth a little and let my tongue stroke her lips and she opened her mouth and our tongues touched. She tasted sweet and her mouth was hot. As we kissed, her arms lowered, and we moved together, our bodies touching and we held one another and I stroked my hand down her back and over her behind. She did not resist. We kissed again, lingering. I whispered, 'This feels nice.' And I felt her relax.

I placed her hand on my right breast, and she allowed herself to explore my upper body. After a few moments, I pulled away and looked at her. She smiled, squeezed her lips together, and looked down. 'It feels wrong, but I like it. I thought it would be revolting touching tongues, but it isn't. You smell good and feel so soft.'

'I've kinda done this with Jeremiah, but it's different from you.' Then I laughed out loud and threw back my head. 'For one thing, you don't have a dick sticking out and getting in the way.'

She gasped, wide eyed and then giggled. 'What's it like being with a boy?'

'It's fun I guess.' We sat up and faced one another crossed-legged, her eyes sparkling with inquisitiveness. 'They're really easy to arouse and they like it when you touch their dicks, you know, rub them up and down.' Her hand went up to her open mouth, and she snickered. 'They feel tougher and rougher than us and they have a kinda animal quality about them that is kinda thrilling. At least that's what Jeremiah is like.'

She said, 'I caught my brother playing with himself once. He was mad as hell. I couldn't believe how big they get when they get hard. I mean, how do you put that inside you? Doesn't it hurt?'

I laughed out loud. 'How should I know?'

Her eyes flared. She giggled, and we fell into one another's arms and fell about.

'I asked Ella about, you know, that stuff. She said it can hurt, particularly the first time, or if you're not ready, but then it's okay.'

'You talk to your mom about sex?'

I shrugged. 'Sure, why not? She's got the answers and anyway, it felt right, made us feel close, like we trust one another. Just like we do now, don't we?'

'Sure, of course I trust you. I love being with you. But I can't ever imagine asking my mum about stuff like that.'

I placed my hand on her cheek. 'Being with you takes my breath away.'

She looked at me and frowned a little. 'Oh—'

I lowered my voice. 'Do you touch yourself?'

Locked together, our eyes moved, searching. There was a slight flicker of intrigue around her mouth and in her eyes. 'Sometimes. It feels wrong, but nice, too. Do you?'

I nodded. 'Yeah. I don't think its wrong to know yourself.' I placed my hand on her left breast. Her breathing had quickened. She closed her eyes again. I pulled her down next to me.

It was an exhilarating experience, an education, and I can think of no better way to find out such intimate things. Since I'd last been with Jeremiah, I had changed both physically and emotionally. I had so missed lying naked with another person feeling such intimacy. I had not expected our day to be like this. It did not feel wrong, naughty, or dirty, but just loving, fun, and to me it felt as natural to be with a girl as it did with a boy.

We swam again, ate our picnic, then lay in the sun, she on her front and I caressed her back. I said, 'I think I've thought of a way you can help me contact Jeremiah.'

She looked across, squinting in the sun. 'How?'

'When we go to school on Monday, we can ask Miss McLaughten if we can write letters to my old classmates, you know, like a writing exercise and information exchange.'

She sat up. 'Okay, that may be tricky as you wouldn't want your old school to know that you are here, would you? So how would we have come across the names of the kids there?'

'Yeah, I thought about that. You remember when Miss McLaughten let me join the class she had to fill in a form for the county education department, a record of my attendance? Well, Miss Hannah does the same, so there must be a record with each county of the kids in their schools. That's how.'

'But if we involve Miss McLaughten, then she'd have to write to the school board and she might mention you and then—'

'Huh, good point. How about we get a few of the others to write to my old friends like an out-of-school project? I'm sure Betty would do it, and you, and well, who else do you suggest?' I gabbled, seeing my plan crumbling away. 'It doesn't have to be many, maybe four or five. I'd tell you all who to write to, and we'd send the letters to the school care of Miss Hannah.'

Mayumi pursed her lips. I could see her figuring things. She shook her head 'Too many people involved and they'll ask questions. I mean, we love her and all, but you know what Betty's like. Plus, what happens if your Miss Hannah writes back to Miss McLaughten?'

I slapped my hand down on the blanket and lay back. I sighed. 'You're right. It's one big fat dumb Dora of an idea.'

For a while we lay, thinking. Then she rolled over on her side and nudged me. 'Look, why don't I just write to Jeremiah using some code in my letter that he'll understand, something only you and he would know. I send it to the school using my home address and say it is a local idea to educate Japanese settlers, and they gave me his name from a list of Idaho school pupils. It's simple and believable.

Who'd suspect that? I mean, they won't even know I'm a girl, right?'

I grinned and sat up. 'Oh, Mayumi, that's genius. I must learn to keep things simple.'

She shrugged. 'Lies work best when they are almost true.' She touched my face, brushing my hair aside. 'So, what am I going to write?'

'Let me think about it tonight and I'll write it out for you.' I felt a weight lift. I cannot describe the pleasure that came from having an ally like Mayumi. We glanced at one another and both smiled. I put my arm around her and we sat and looked at the waves.

She said, 'If he writes back, we may write more freely, so let me know what things I can tell him and what not to.'

I pulled her tighter to me. I said, 'This is so kind of you. It will be an enormous relief for him to know I'm safe.'

The sun was burning my skin, so I draped the towel about us and we snuggled up. I thought about things and then I felt bad. 'Look, I hope you don't think I befriended you just for this. I mean, I love you like a sister, well you know a girlfriend—' I felt flustered, like I was digging a hole. 'I mean, I don't want you to feel used.'

She laughed. 'Heidi, it's okay. I don't. You trusted me with your secrets. You barely know anything about me and you did that. That means so much to me. You're my best friend. And I've learned things today about—well—you know.'

I grinned. 'Thanks, me too. I'm going to be broken up to leave you.'

She nodded. 'I don't know what I'll do without you. You've changed my life.'

And once more, we kissed.

A proper kiss.

— Ella —

When Heidi came back from her day with Mayumi, she had a serene calm about her. I don't think I'd ever seen her so relaxed. She sat down and sighed.

'Well, someone's had a good day. I'm guessing you and Mayumi had fun?'

She laughed, almost to herself. 'Yeah, I guess you could say that. She's special. I've never really had a girlfriend before, not like that. You know, I can tell her stuff I can't tell anyone else. Even Jeremiah.'

I knew exactly what she meant. I looked up from the chopping board. 'I had a close girlfriend when I was your age. We did everything together like we were sisters, but more too.' Heidi looked at me, her eyes like darts. I tapped my nose. 'She was my first proper kiss.'

'Really? What happened to her?'

I gave Heidi a knife and she began chopping some carrots.

'She got married a few weeks before me and almost straight away got pregnant. He was from the next town; she went there, and I saw less of her. Then I married David. The rest, you know.'

She stopped chopping and frowned. 'What was her name?'

'Celest.'

She took a slice of carrot and popped it in her mouth. 'That's a beautiful name. What was she like?'

'She was kinda ordinary looking, really. You know, brown hair, dark eyes. That look you see everywhere. She was kind and fun and I guess we just connected in a way people do, like you can't explain it, can you?'

She shook her head. 'You said she was your first kiss, but you did more?'

'I guess. She was my first sexual experience with another person.' I looked up from stirring the pot. 'How'd it go with Mayumi? Did you talk to her?'

She nodded and paused for a moment, her glowing eyes hinting at her depth of feeling for Mayumi. I worried Heidi might fall in love too easily. She changed the subject. 'When you lost David, why didn't you stay with Celest?'

'I was broken-hearted, and she had everything I'd lost, and it would have hurt too much. I didn't want to spoil things for her. Before I left, I said goodbye and promised to write.'

'And did you?'

I shook my head and a flush of sadness flowed through me; it had been a while since last I had thought of her. 'No, I never did.'

She looked at me, eyes wide. 'Why?'

I stopped stirring and wiped the perspiration from my forehead. 'I had to leave her in the past with my old life.' I smiled, added the carrots to the pot, stirred, and closed the lid. 'I still miss her, though. Sometimes.' We sat down and I stretched out my legs. I enjoyed these conversations with Heidi. Since leaving home, she was the first female I had intimate discussions with. It's odd how you can put things in compartments and shut them away. But as the memory of Celest flooded back, I recognized it was a mistake not keeping in touch with her.

'Didn't you ever want to go back?'

'Sure, from time-to-time. Once Joe and I were traveling through Wyoming and he asked me if I cared to look. I think he was more curious than I. I thought it would just dredge up memories and make me sad. It was stuff I thought I had dealt with.'

'But you hadn't?'

'In some ways not, I guess.'

'So, do you think I should go back and, you know—'

'I do. You can't change what's happened, but you make sure it doesn't dog you for the rest of your life.'

'You can still go back and find Celest. I'd come with you.'

And that was it, Heidi in a nutshell. With everything she'd been through, she always had enough for others. I put my arm around her and pulled her to me, and she placed her head on my shoulder. 'Thanks,' I said. 'You know what I think?'

'Uh-uh.'

'Right now I'm good with my past and I want more than anything for us to help you and for us to find a place to call home. Maybe, when the time is right, I'll take you to where I grew up and we'll find Celest.'

'What about Joe?'

'Give him a little time. He's getting there. You first, us later. And don't go worrying about us, wilya?'

For a while, we sat watching the flames. She told me about her idea to get Mayumi to write to Jeremiah and asked what I thought.

'I guess it can't harm. If it eases your mind, you should do it.'

'I worry about him not knowing where I am and whether I'm alive and I don't want him to lose hope. It would be so much easier if I could just write to him and tell him what I think and intend to do.'

'So why don't you?'

'If I do, his ma and pa will know. His ma will recognize my writing. They'll want to know what it says, putting him in a tight spot. Also, I don't know what he told them about that day. It might put him in danger with the police, and his ma and pa. If I get Mayumi to write, he'll know I am okay. If it were me, that's all I'd need to know.'

'You haven't pressured her to do this, have you?'

She shook her head. 'It was her idea, really.'

I lay back, and the fragrant steam from the pot drifted in the air, making my mouth water. 'If it were me, I'd want to give him peace of mind, too.'

'Mayumi really wants to help, and I made sure she didn't feel like I was using her. I'd do it for her in a heartbeat.'

'Sounds like a plan, sweetheart.'

Over our meal, we discussed it with Joe, who looked tired, the kinda tiredness that isn't physical. He said, 'I guess if you can get a dialogue going with him through Mayumi, then you may find out the lay of the land before you return. I'll give you Luther's address so you two can keep in touch.'

Her face lit up. 'Holy smoke, that would be the bees. I can write to her and it will keep us buzzing while I'm gone.'

Joe closed his eyes and nodded.

Heidi looked at him. 'Are you alright? You look bushed, pa.'

'I didn't sleep too well last night.' He chuckled. 'I think I was dancing still.'

Heidi sighed and laughed. 'It was something, wasn't it? Can't wait until we can do that again; best day of my life.'

He lay back, and I lay beside him and placed my head on his shoulder. Heidi looked at us and grinned. 'I'll go take a walk and sort out in my head what the letter should say. Back soon.'

She grabbed her coat and a water bottle and headed off. We watched her as she disappeared down the track. Joe grinned. 'Not tonight, Josephine, I'm all-in.'

And we both laughed. I don't think we'd ever laughed like we did now, like we had a new language between us, and the same thing was happening between us and Heidi.

I wondered whether this is the true language of peace that is lost to you until unlocked by that mystical, spiritual presence of pure love? It may strike unexpectedly, cutting deep and laying open your heart, leaving you breathless and gasping. It made no sense: undefinable, unteachable, or indescribable, but you know it when it comes and there is nothing more beautiful or precious. Now, I felt its presence embolden me, and I knew that whatever lay ahead, together, we would vanquish.

(35)

— Heidi —

I took my coat and some water and made off. I walked up among the cypress and pine trees with their tangy-sweet, pungent smell, found a spot, sat down, leaned my back on a trunk and closed my eyes. The sound of the ocean, insects, and the light rustle of the breeze infused my mind. I thought about Mayumi and Jeremiah. I felt so relaxed I drifted into a trance. I speculated whether Jeremiah had made a new friend to confide in and I worked my mind through all the other kids, testing each. I was sure that none of the boys would provide a confidant. Of the girls, only two came to mind: Abigail and Mary Ann. I knew Abigail had eyes for Jeremiah and she was a beauty, all tall and elegant. I liked her but always felt overawed by her. Of all the girls I knew from home, she was the only one I'd call a genuine friend. Her pa was kind to me and on the occasions I worked in the store, Abigail always joined in and never looked down on me. I wished now I had made more effort with her.

Mary Ann was also pretty and from the same background as Jeremiah. Their mothers were tight, and Mary Ann's ma would have been concerned when he got injured. Jeremiah had never shown much interest in her, but she was quiet and could keep a secret, and I knew she fancied him. I had watched her after we'd been swimming in the creek. Her bright bronze quizzical eyes roving over his wet, naked body. The thought sent a pang of acidic jealousy through me.

Thinking about him with either of them made me feel helpless. I talked myself down, told myself not to be silly, that what we had was special, and you don't break that so easy. He loved me. Really loved me. Didn't he? Didn't I feel that way about him? I thought about how I'd feel if he told me he'd kissed another girl or been intimate with her. It was confusing. After all, had I not just spent the day being intimate with Mayumi? We had done things that even he and I hadn't.

I still loved him like no one else, but I needed to be held and touched and I was so attracted to her. Hell, what was that all about?

Maybe today, with Mayumi, had been about me wanting to know if I was the same as other girls. I loved her and she had a gorgeous body and sweet face and I relished what we did. I wondered if other kids did this to find out stuff. I guess everyone went at their own pace, but if you liked a person that way, and given the opportunity, there wasn't much going to stop you, was there?

I sighed. Hell, life was real complicated. I shook my head, saying out loud. 'Don't go mulling too much, Heidi.'

I turned my thoughts to the letter and began drafting ideas in my head. I reckoned it was best to keep it simple. Satisfied, I made my way back to camp before it got too dark. Joe had gone to bed, but Ella was sitting by the fire reading the book Miss Jennings had given me. I was deep into "Jane Eyre", so had not read it yet. I asked, 'Is it good?'

She nodded. 'I love the descriptions of the Swiss mountains, and there are things here that you and this Heidi have in common.'

'I can't wait to read it, though I'm going slow with "Jane Eyre", savoring every word. England seems kinda grim.'

'I'm sure it's not at all like that. I hear it is a beautiful country, but there's nothing better than a book that drags you into its world and carries you away. How was your walk?'

'Peaceful. I have a lot to think about, but I'm trying not to let it bog me down.'

'That sounds like a fine idea.' The fire was fading but still gave off light, and I was not quite ready for my bed. 'Can you read me a bit from "Heidi"?'

She flicked through the pages. 'Here, you'll like this, and it won't spoil any surprises.'

She began reading, and I lay down and let the words breeze over me. Joe had read aloud some of his stories, many of which were about lonely mountain men, trappers, and the animals that roamed the northern wilderness. He wrote well, descriptively, but he kept his sentences and words to the point, kinda like him: no frills, but with hidden depths. My favorite of all his stories was about a young man rescued by a Native American outcast, ostracized by his tribe. The two men forged a friendship and traveled the land looking for work until an angry mob mistaking him for another man lynch the Native American. His distraught young friend exacts a terrible revenge but ends up alone. It was a powerful story, and I wondered how much of it was based on fact. Joe always said he had a vivid imagination and that his life was just as simple as could be, but I figured you don't roam this great country for as many years as he has without witnessing and experiencing a good deal of colorful events. I hoped one day he'd tell me his story and hated the idea that it might die with him.

After my unusual but beautiful day and all that listening, reading, and thinking, I was exhausted. I slept like a hibernating bear from one of Joe's stories. I was up at first light and got the fire going. Joe followed quickly. Other than a customary greeting, we went about our morning routine in silent calm. I scribbled a draft of my ideas for the letter and told Joe I was heading off early as I wanted to have time with Mayumi before school.

She had walked part of the way and met me along the coast path. When she saw me, she waved, but her expression and eyes seemed distant and I wondered if she had some regrets about what we had done. We fell into step and made our way close to the school before we sat down and I showed her what I had written. She looked it over. 'Yes, nice and simple. You think he'll know it's from you?'

I shrugged. 'I think so. See, he always calls me Fizz—'

She giggled. 'Fizz! Where did that come from?'

'Oh, well, when we were little, I used to run around jumping and rolling on the ground like a crazy ball of energy. One day we were playing at his house and his pa said, "you full of Fizz girl." Jeremiah liked the word and from then on, I was to them, Fizz or sometimes Fizzy. Silly ain't it?'

She smiled. 'No. I like it. Fizz!' She gave me a playful nudge. It sounded strange coming from her. 'He sounds fun. If I'm honest, I'm jealous. Wish I had someone like him.'

'You will. The right person will come when you least expect it. I mean, did you ever imagine you'd meet a runaway-orphaned-murderer from Idaho who wanted to kiss and touch you like that?' I raised my eyebrows and gestured with open hands. She shook her head, blushed, and laughed. 'Anyway, I haven't got him anymore and in a few days I won't have you either. I don't know where I'll be at the end of all this, but I hope more than anything I'll still be in both your lives. Whatever happens, I'll never forget you and what you've done for me.'

After school, she wrote out her letter:

Dear Jeremiah Bell.
My name is Mayumi.
I am fourteen years old and I live with my family in Monterey county in California. My mother and father came from Japan and settled here. I am writing to

you as part of a scheme in our community to find out
more about life in other parts of the United States.
I have black hair and brown eyes. I have a
brother and two sisters. Sometimes they can be a
pain. Do you have any? My father runs a fishing
company and we live and work near the ocean.
I go to school, which I like very much.
I like to read and do math.
The nearest town to me is Carmel-By-The-Sea. It is
friendly and has a fantastic library. It is where I met
a new girl in the area. We have become good friends.
She is full of fizz and fun. She is beautiful, aged fifteen
and loves swimming. She told me that her best friend
from back home loves to swim underwater and pull
her under by her ankles, but she always gets away by
tickling them. I think, maybe, she is in love. She goes
to my school and is very good at composition and
reading. Please write to me and tell me about your
home and I promise to write back. Let me know what
you want to know about where I live, and my life.
Your friend,
Mayumi Hikomori.

I read it over twice. I said, 'If he doesn't get that, then he never will. It'll work. Thank you.' I kissed her on the cheek and felt fervent passion flood my body. 'Thank you so much.'

We looked at one another. She touched her hand to her face; her eyes flashed a deep nut brown, and a glimmer of a smile flared at the corners of her mouth.

36

— Heidi —

It was my last day at Carmel. I had told Mayumi that I would meet her at school because on my way in I'd wanted to do something to which I had given much consideration. I walked over to Betty's house and knocked on the door. Moments later, the door was flung open and there she stood. She almost took a step back and looked at me with hooded eyes. 'Heidi! What are you doing here?'

'I wanted to walk with you to school. I've got something to tell you.'

Her eyes lit up. 'Ooh, really?' She grabbed my arm and pulled me inside. 'Come in. Give me a minute.'

While she rushed off, I stood in the elegant hallway. Decorative tiles covered the floor, and a long, dark wood, sumptuously carpeted staircase swept away to the upper landing. Clearly, there was money in newspapers. A moment later, she appeared with her bag. 'Let's go.' She dragged me through the door, slamming it behind her. 'Wow, this is such a treat, and it's your last day, isn't it? I'm miserable about that.'

'It's why I wanted to speak to you, Betts.'

We walked and chatted. Well, she did, and I listened, which made me appreciate how much I would miss Betty's enlightening stories. At last, we came to a quiet spot near to school. I stopped her. 'This is perfect. Let's sit.'

We sat opposite one another and for a moment I looked at her, our eyes locked together. 'We're friends, aren't we, Betts?'

'You bet. I love you Heidi, you're my best friend. I know you're older, and all that, but the kids my age aren't interesting like you and Mayumi. Thanks to you, I've made friends with her, too. Mama said I seem happier. Do you think I am? I feel happier. But I'm so wretched you're leaving tomorrow. I'm going to miss you more than you know.' Her words tumbled out. I loved the way she wore her heart on her sleeve.

'How is your ma?'

She shrugged. 'The same. I go sit with her when I get back from school, if she's awake, that is. I wish I could take away what makes her so despondent.'

'I think some people just can't find their way out of the dark. In a way, my pa was like that.'

'Oh, really? Maybe that's why we connect; we understand things others don't. What was it you wanted to tell me? I'm intrigued.'

I took her hot, soft hands. 'I don't know what you were like before we met that day you came to our camp. You're a positive spirit, Betts. You always think the best of people and I love how you are interested in what's going on, but I need to tell you about me, so you understand why I must leave and why I may not come back for a while—'

'You are coming back then? For sure!'

I nodded and crossed my heart. 'I promise. I trust you, Betts, but you've got to promise that what I tell you, you must keep to yourself. The only person you can discuss it with is Mayumi.'

Betty knotted her brows and made a locking motion by her mouth 'I promise, Heidi. Despite what people think, I can keep a secret. I won't tell a soul.'

I told her about how I came to run away from home and everything in between. As I related my tale, a gamut of emotion swept across her sweet face. At times, her hand raised to her mouth, eyes wide, and by the end of my tale, she sat looking wrung out, her wet eyes cast down. She sniffed. 'Oh, heavens, what a story. You've been through all that. How does anyone get through all that and still be so—so—' She rocked forward and grabbed me, hugging me tight. 'I'm so sorry.' After a bit, she let go and sat back. 'I feel so proud you trusted me and I promise I'll never let you down.'

'I know you like me. I hope you still do—'

'Oh, of course I do. Of course. It wasn't your fault, it was your papa. He's the grownup and he should have taken care of you, not done those horrific things. It was his own hand that struck him down, not yours.'

Her eloquence and maturity surprised me. I had never thought of it that way. Perhaps something had forced my hand, and that was why no matter how hard I tried, I could not remember picking up the knife and killing him. Did *I* do it? But then, if not me, who? Or what?

With each retelling, the event became clearer. 'I understand it better now, which is why I must go back and sort it out. I love you and Mayumi and this place, but I love Jeremiah as well. It's bewildering and I think if I go, it'll help me work things out. We can write to one another.' I reached into my bag and pulled out a slip of paper. 'Here, this is the address of the orange grove near Fresno. When we move, I'll let you know how to contact me.'

She took the paper and stared at it, like it was something awe-inspiring. 'Oh wow! I'll write often and give you all the news. I'll ask papa to send some copies of the paper, too, shall I?'

'Thank you, that would be kind. Knowing you hold a torch for me will help me get through things.'

For a while we sat in silence, our wet, red eyes locked together, and I rubbed her hands. We had sat down as friends but stood up as sisters. She took my hand, and we strolled to school. I said, 'You and Mayumi look out for one another, won't you?'

'We will.'

Just as we had on my first day at Bay School, on the bench under the Cypress tree, me in the middle, the three of us sat.

Mayumi said, 'How long do you plan to stay picking oranges?'

'About twelve weeks, maybe a bit more. I'm looking forward to earning some money and helping Joe and Ella.'

It was small talk. It's the kinda talk you make when you face a difficult parting and no one knows what to say because words are useless and never fill the void.

I gave them both a nudge. 'Look on the bright side. We've had fun, haven't we? And we're friends now. Even if we don't see each other for a while, we'll always have that, won't we? And next time we meet, we'll have lots to talk about. It is good to have things to look forward to.'

I was relieved when the school day ended. We walked Betty home and said goodbye. It was emotional, gut-wrenching and horrible, but it sealed the bond and you can't fake that depth of feeling. Mayumi came with me to say goodbye to Sister Catherine and then we walked to the library and did the same with Miss Jennings, who gave me another book: "The Call of the Wild" by Jack London, saying, 'I think you'll enjoy this thrilling tale.' I told her how much I would miss my time in the library and our little chats and how much she had opened my eyes. She said, 'Books ask for nothing, our constant friends and the greatest of teachers.'

As we headed down the main drag to the beach, I took Mayumi's hand and we walked together. I savored the contact. Once on the shore, we turned left and made our way toward Bluff Cove. Our generous friend, Mr. Hikomori, had asked us all to stay in one of the guest lodges for our last night and, despite Joe's protestations, had insisted on driving us back to Salinas.

We passed the place where we had camped; there was little evidence we'd been there. I liked that. In no time, nature would take back what we had borrowed. I said, 'Do you mind if we go up to Johanna's point?'

It wasn't far to the place where I had buried ma's lock of hair, and Mayumi had suggested we call it Johanna's Point. Only we knew about it. We sat and put our arms around one another and looked out to the ocean and felt the breeze that carried the tang of salt and clean air. I breathed it in and prayed it would not be long before I was back here. Perhaps next time I would be with Jeremiah. Mayumi said, 'You promise you'll come back.'

'With all my heart.'

'If they send you to jail, I'll find a way to come and see you.'

We looked at one another with wet eyes. I said, 'Thank you. Thank you for being here and being my friend and—' The words stuck in my throat. I leaned across, delicately our lips touched. I pushed her down, and we lay together holding one another. I stroked her hair and breathed her in so that I would remember. I don't know how long we stayed like that. Of course, I wanted the moment to go on. At last, I kissed her one more time, lingering on the act and tasting her, allowing all my senses to indulge their need. When I broke off, she said, 'Wow, Heidi, that was some kiss.'

I smiled and touched a finger to her lips. 'So you won't forget me.'

'Oh, I'll never forget you; of that you can be sure.'

I sat up. 'Best be getting along.'

The last evening went by in a blur. The Hikomoris gave us a wonderful meal, and we talked into the night. They told us there was always a welcome for us.

In the morning I went to say a final thanks to Mr. Hikomori. I could not help but break formality and I gave him a hug. He held me like a father might his daughter. I said, 'Thank you. If you hadn't been there that day, I would have missed my life.' Gently, he pushed me away and held my face in his warm, rough hands. He said, 'We have a saying in Japan, Heidi-san. When it rains, earth hardens. Thank you for being a good friend to Mayumi. She has come out of herself and you make her happy.'

After the last tearful hugs and goodbyes, we loaded ourselves and our bags, all of which had gained weight, on Mr. Hikomori's truck. Joe rode up front and me and Ella sat in among our things on the flatbed. It was the best seat. As the truck joggled and swayed on the rough road, Ella put her arm around me and it felt good to be with her. We did not speak. My hair fluttered about my face and I watched the world go by. I had been so certain about the things I needed and wanted, but now my mind was a mess of unresolved ideas and thoughts. We'd talked at length about the prospect of jail, and I had got used to the idea of being shut away and serving my time to pay my debt. It was good to be on the move again and I forced out the black bile of the parting, replacing it with a stoic fortitude, resigning myself to what fate had in store.

part five

37

— JOE —

As Katsura Hikomori had eased our return to Fresno, we had time in hand before we were due back at Luther and Eliza van de Berg's orange grove. We camped out near the spot we had some weeks back, though now that seemed like a lifetime ago. I left the girls at camp and went on up to see when we might begin our work. Luther had done us proud and made available our own accommodation and said we could come up the following day. I walked back with a light step and as I neared our camp, a tune I'd not thought about in years entered my mind and I whistled it. I came over the rise and took a moment to savor the scene of Heidi and Ella sitting by the fire and shooting the breeze. They looked over and waved. I joined them and sat down.

Heidi looked at me. 'What was that tune you were whistling?'

'Dixie. If you whistle Dixie, it's a kinda slang expression for folk unrealistically fantasizing about their expectations. Got popular during the civil war. My pa used to whistle it sometimes.'

A veil came over her face, and her sapphire eyes locked on me. 'Tell me more about your pa, Joe.'

There it was. I'd walked right into it. She missed nothing. I did not know whether it was because we were once more on the move, out in the wild and in my natural habitat, but I guessed that now was that time to unload the baggage. I looked at her and nodded. 'Let's eat, then I'll give you chapter and verse.'

After eating and clearing up, we made ourselves comfortable around the fire, the way we did when we talked turkey. They sat watching me like buzzards waiting for a man to die. Our pool of orange, oscillating firelight danced on their eyes, and beyond our sanctuary, the dark enveloped us, and save the fire's delicate melody, deep silence shrouded our world. I sat for a while, thinking, not sure where to start. As I tried to form it into words, the past lay on me like a vast rock.

Heidi broke the impasse. 'Well, whatever it is, it won't be as bad as what I did.'

Ella nudged her.

The silence pressed in on us.

Nothing but the three of us existed.

'Where to start? Okay, right, so you know when and where I was born and that I have a twin sister. My pa was a good man and always tried his best. Then came that loathsome war. When he went off to fight for the Union, me and Florence were just small. Honestly, I remember little about him before he went, other than he was kind to us. He didn't really know how to play with little kids, but like I said, he did his best. We worshiped him and I remember he read to us before we went to sleep. He loved a good story. I guess that's where I get it from.'

'When he came back, the war took something from him that left a dark void. He wasn't cruel like your pa, Heidi, but it was like he had this black cloud enveloping him. He couldn't work much and he took to drinking real hard. Sometimes he'd just sit and stare into the distance for hours at a time. Ma had to be mother and father to us and she had to work more and little by little that and his mood swings wore her out. By this time, me and Flo had turned twelve, and because ma and pa had little left in them, we got sent off to work so we'd not starve. I liked school and was sad to leave, but it was thrilling to get working.'

'I got taken on by the county's primary employer, a mighty firm that made cartwheels and barrels and all kinds of stuff outta wood and metal. I liked the work and put my head down, beavered away and learned a trade, which has helped me all these years. After I'd been there a few years, the firm that had grown prosperous from the war landed a big government contract and, by way of celebration, the boss arranged for a community party. The firm employed a good deal of the town's working men and supported many other trades and businesses. The boss, Ambrose Davenport, was a hard man, equally respected and feared across the state. He had the governor's ear and powerful contacts at the heart of the government. The picnic was a big deal, kinda like a fair with stalls and pony rides for the little kids, and some amusements. There was a country band and pretty soon, with the liquor flowing and music playing, folks were dancing and having a good time.'

'I was a good-looking boy, I guess. I had a good job. Now, although most of my wages went into the family pot, I had a little walking-around money, enough to treat the girls. I was with my sister and a few other friends when this cutie-pie comes over to say hi. I had seen her looking at me, and Flo reckoned she was sweet on me. Well, this cutie was real grownup-looking and drop-dead gorgeous, and I remember reeling, my head spinning. I was smitten. Fatefully, I tickled her desires as well, and it wasn't long before the two of us had snuck off to get to know one another better.' I glanced at Heidi. She had a knowing look in her eye.

'She wasn't the first girl I kissed, but it was the first kiss that meant anything. There was just one tiny, wee problem: she was the boss's daughter. Now, she was all set for us to keep on seeing one another and I appreciated little about how her father might view his beloved only daughter hanging out with a lowly apprentice boy from his firm. It never entered my simple mind. Melissa—that was her name—made me promise to keep our liaisons secret, and we went on seeing one another. We were hopelessly in love and it wasn't long before nature and wild passion got us in a heap of trouble and she fell pregnant.'

Heidi raised her hand to her mouth. 'Oh, holy smoke, no!'

I smiled and looked down. Now I had begun, I wanted to get it all out. 'See, no one really gave me the facts and, well, we didn't think it through. We were the same age as you are now, Heidi. Just kids, but old enough to know we were in a heap loada trouble. It was a dark time as we tried to figure what was best to do. I was all for going to her folks and telling them the truth and say that we'd marry and I'd always love her and so on. Melissa said that would just get me killed. Actually, she said that when her pa found out like as not, he'd kill me anyway and her too.'

'Of course, I thought she was being melodramatic, but I guess she knew him better than I did. So there came a time some weeks later when she could no longer hide her condition and her folks got to know. At first, she refused to tell them who the father was, but I guess they wore her down. I don't blame her. I knew I loved her and thought that was what counted. The first I knew about it is I got fired from my job and, on my way home, got dragged into an alleyway by three heavies who worked me over like they were tenderizing an old beefsteak. I was told to leave town, and that I was never to see Melissa again.'

'I made it home. My bloodied face and broken heart were impossible to hide, and I spilled the beans. I give credit to my folks that even though they were angry and ashamed, they stood by me. Ma cried and pa got drunk. Florence was the only one who I could talk to. She pleaded with me not to go. She said that they were bluffing and that if I just kept my head down and stayed away from Melissa, the dust would settle.'

I looked at the girls. Heidi's eyes were wide, and it seemed like she was holding her breath, but I could feel her empathy, and it gave me strength. I said, 'Guess you both know that when you are in love it ain't that easy to just let it go, is it?' They shook their heads. 'For some months, I did just that. I found some work out of town laboring on a railroad project. It was my first taste of the open road. It kept me away for a while, but I came home from time to time. Like Flo had said, it seemed like the dust had settled. I heard Melissa had given birth to a little girl, Sophia. It broke my heart that I couldn't see them. First time I ever cried so long and hard. One Saturday morning I had to go down to the store to pick up some things for ma and this little kid came up to me and said, "You Joe Reisen?" I told him I was, and he gave me this letter from Melissa saying she's arranged for me to see the baby and her. I would have gone to the ends of the earth to see them, so I jumped at the chance.'

'A week later came the day. Her pa was out of town and she had arranged to go over to a friend's house for tea, and it was there we met. I had to sneak in through the back. I remember being so excited to see them, it felt like I was floating on air. I was there right on time and they ushered me in through the back and into the parlor where Melissa and Sophia were. Melissa was more lovely than I'd remembered, like she had bloomed by becoming a mother. We kissed like folk in love do when they haven't seen one another for an age. Then she said, "Come, meet your daughter." Sophia was just perfect, and my heart melted the moment I saw her. It was such deep love. I can't really explain it. I held her, and, like new parents do, I wondered at her button nose, tiny toes and fingers. We sat, and I held her to me and smelled her head and drank her in. I savored the time. It was all too short, and I had to sneak away like a thief in the night, but I didn't care, as we had agreed to run away as soon as we could.'

I stopped speaking for a bit, surprised by the emotion welling up in me. Maybe time doesn't heal all wounds. I reached in my pocket for my makins, then remembered and sighed. The girls were silent, their eyes urging me on. I gathered myself and continued. 'So it went okay for a while and we met twice more. Each time Sophia was bigger and my love grew deeper. I don't know how, but her pa found out. She sent me a note to warn me he was hell bent on having me killed. I was still working the railroad job, so I went off for a while, you know, to see if time would calm things down like it did before. I was a foolish boy still, and it turned out Melissa's pa had someone watching the house. The night I came back, they set it ablaze. Me and Florence got out unscathed save some minor injuries, but our parents died. There wasn't much left to bury.'

I glanced across at Ella. She sat still; her face impassive, her eyes dark.

'Holy smoke, pa, he tried to kill you all just because you made a mistake. What kinda man does that?'

'A jealous father who is used to getting things the way he wants. A man who can get others to do his bidding and who rules with fear. That's who.'

'I'm so sorry. What happened then?'

'Ambrose soon found out he had failed to kill me and was determined to finish the job. Florence had breathed in smoke, so they'd kept her in the hospital. I was on my way to see her when these two big fellas waylaid me. They put a hood over my head and I got pushed in a cart and driven off. We rode for about two, maybe three, hours. Then we stopped, and they pulled me out and threw me on the ground. They ripped the hood off. The light hurt my eyes. When I could open them and focus, I saw Ambrose there and just behind him were two fresh dug graves. I thought that this was how it ended. I've never been so scared. I cried and begged him. He made me kneel beside one grave. He stood behind me and I heard him cock his pistol. Then the barrel pushed hard into the back of my head. It's funny but at that moment I felt calm. I stopped trembling, reconciled to die. A bullet in the brain would be quick. But that day I found out there are fates worse than death.'

I glanced at Ella. The color had drained from her face.

'Ambrose told me I was never to come back to the county. He said he'd put the word around and if I ever tried to come back or contact either Flo or Melissa, he'd kill Flo and my bastard daughter and put them in those graves. I felt a gush of anger and made to move. I wanted to get up and lay into him, but he gave me a pistol-whipping. Then he bent down and pulled me up, right in his face. I could feel and smell his hot, sour breath. He told me he had people in the postal service who'd open every letter to Flo, his daughter, and all the other folk that were my friends. His last words were that before he had Florence killed, he'd pass her around.'

The fire flickered. The smothering quiet was a perfect backdrop to such a grim tale. Heidi sat, her cheeks wet, radiating emotion. I said, 'You alright, sweetheart?'

She nodded. 'I'm fine. Go on.'

'Before they left me miles from anywhere, they roughed me up good and dumped me in a grave. When I came to, I could see these enormous birds circling. I don't know why, but it made me laugh. Perhaps it was because I wasn't dead. They had taken my boots. I had no food, water or possessions, and they took the few coins I had in my pockets. But as you know, I'm no quitter. After I got my head together, I headed west. I don't know how long I'd been stumbling along, but I kept thinking someone was watching me. Just before nightfall, I made it to a creek and collapsed, buried my face in the water and drank deep. As I pulled my face from that life-giving water, I heard this noise, spun around and there was this Native American on a pony. A young guy, maybe a few years older than me. We just looked at one another. Then he gets down and comes over. He holds out his hand and I grab on and he pulls me up. I would like to think I could have made it on my own, but he saved me. He patched me up, gave me food and friendship. That type of kindness gives you a reason to keep going, doesn't it?'

Heidi asked, 'What was his name?'

'You remember that story of mine you like so much—'

'The Indian that rescued the young guy?'

'That's the one. You remember the name?'

'Of course. Tetinchoua. He was from the Miami people, right?'

I nodded. 'Well, that was where the idea came for the story and that was his real name. By then, they had moved all the Indiana tribes from their lands. Shameful.' I shook my head. 'That day I realized we are all just people, the same. We all want the same things: peace, love, a little place to call home and to live with dignity. Alas, some folks want to take it all for themselves. Tetinchoua led me to the railroad. I jumped a loco and found my way to a jungle and got taken in. No one cared what I'd done or where I'd come from. In no time, I had some boots, extra clothing, and the stuff I needed to survive. This old bo named Missouri Bygone took me under his wing, learned me the ropes, and for almost fifty years I thought that was that. Then I hopped that Big-G and found you, Heidi. See, Melissa and Sophia have golden hair and blue eyes and I guess seeing you there all vulnerable ignited things inside me I had buried deep.'

'Holy smoke, pa. You've got a daughter and a sister and lover out there. Don't you need to go back and find them?'

I felt forlorn. Then, she was round my side of the fire like a mountain lion on a deer and hugged me tight. Ella didn't move. After a bit, we composed ourselves. I watched her, the firelight dancing on her pale face.

After a bit, she took a deep breath and shook her head, a softness at the edge of her mouth. She looked at me. 'Dammit, Joe, why in the hell didn't you tell me this long ago?'

I shrugged. 'I should have. I'm sorry. Truth is, I'd buried it so deep I thought it was gone forever. Can you forgive me?'

She looked down, shaking her head again. Then her eyes were on me, a spark in them. 'Don't be soft. There's nothing to forgive. I'm just—well—I'm just in shock. Didn't you think that maybe after some years you'd be able to sneak on back and see what-was-what?'

'I did. But by then I convinced myself that they were better off without me. I didn't want to risk it. It was cowardly.'

Ella stood and joined us and knelt in front of me, taking my face in her hands. 'I love you, Joe Reisen, and nothing will change that. You must go back and put this to rest. It's been almost fifty years, so it's high time, you hear me?'

I nodded. We hugged and kissed. I was relieved. We three sat side-by-side deep in thought. After a bit, Heidi said, 'What are winters like in Indiana?'

'Not like they are in Idaho.'

She looked at me and fixed my gaze with a look so penetrating it would have stopped a wolf in its tracks. 'After we're done here, let's find your people. My stuff can wait. I owe you that.'

— Ella —

At first, Joe protested Heidi's suggestion, saying. 'My stuff has been waiting all this time, so a few more months won't make any difference, will it?'

Heidi shook her head, pursing her lips. 'I'd like nothing more than to go home and sort things out, see Jeremiah, and hug him. But by the time we finish working here, the weather back home will be bad. If they send me to jail, what will you do with no work and no place to stay?'

Joe frowned. 'Then we go now. Luther will understand.'

Heidi shook her head. 'Winter's just round the corner—'

I touched her arm. 'What if you stay here, Joe, and work while I take Heidi home?'

Heidi turned to me, her eyes flaring. 'No, no! We can't be apart. I don't want that. Besides, I'm not sure I'm ready yet. Being here with you, working, will give me time, will give us all time to be together and take stock. And we need to earn some scratch, don't we?'

Joe held up his hand, nodding. 'You're right. This is serious stuff and we've got to do it right.'

The firelight danced about us. We sat silent for a time. After a bit I said, 'Joe, you said we hope for the best but we plan for the worst. So, I agree with Heidi that we can't go back to Idaho until the spring. If she gets jail time, then we can stay and find work. So, how about we stop here until the harvest is over? Then go to Indiana and find your people, or at least make a start. And come the Spring, no matter where we are, we go to Idaho. That's my vote.'

Joe thought about it. 'Okay, agreed. Me too.'

Heidi looked relieved. 'Yeah, me three.'

On that we turned in, though sleep evaded me. At least now I knew the secrets were out. How he managed all these years to deny his past floored me. I tried to get my head around the mountain we had to climb, and I could not help but worry that, once back with Melissa, Joe might not want me. I knew it was silly, but I guess I was less sure of myself than I thought. They had a daughter together and chances were she would have married and had children. It was one unholy mess.

The following day, we began work. Time flew by and the routine and calm had a positive effect on us all. Heidi loved the work. She was the only youngster among the laborers, and both Luther and Eliza took a shine to her like people did. Eliza opened her library and asked Heidi to babysit her grandkids, which she loved doing. She worked, swam in the river, read books, and brought a light to our lives, and having made our plan, none of us discussed what lay ahead.

A few weeks in, I began getting sick. I hid it for a while, but then it got worse and I collapsed. They sent for a doctor. With comforting words, Eliza took Heidi. I told her I'd be okay, but her face betrayed her fear and it made me understand how important it was that I fight. When the doc arrived, a fretful Joe sat by my bed. The doc said, 'Best if you give us some space, so I can do my work.' With gentle persuasion, I got Joe to leave, though he stood in the doorway for a time looking lost, and I realized how much he loved me. Then he turned, closed the door, and I felt alone.

The doc went to work, taking temperature, pulse, blood pressure, and he asked a lot of questions. Then, to my surprise, he asked to carry out an intimate examination. I was too weak and tired to object. He was gentle and professional. When he finished, he put on his jacket and asked one last question. 'When did you last have your menstrual cycle?'

I thought about it for a while. 'I'm late.' I frowned. 'Very late, actually—' Then I realized and I felt like a giant idiot. 'Oh, my goodness, do you?'

'Think you're pregnant? I do. Your blood pressure is sky-high and you need to rest. I will keep an eye out, but all being well, you're going to be fine.'

My head swam at this added complication. I thought maybe I was too old to get pregnant, but the thought of being a mom excited me. But then, what about Heidi and Joe? How would they take it? There was no hiding and as soon as the doc left, Joe returned, and I put him out of his misery. For a while, he stared at me, dumbstruck. Then that boyish grin of his flooded his face. 'We're having a baby? Well, how the hell did that happen?'

I smiled weakly. A fat tear ran down my cheek. He hugged me all gentle like. I needed to sleep. I said, 'Get Heidi, we need to tell her.'

She came in with Joe; her face tight with anxious eyes darting in her pretty head. 'Hey, sweetheart.' She hung back, fear plastered on her face like jam. I told her to sit on the bed. 'I'm okay. I just need some rest for a bit.'

She looked at me like she could tell I was holding back. 'What's wrong with you?'

There was no beating about the bush. 'I'm pregnant. You're going to have a brother or sister.'

Her chin hit the floor. 'Holy smoke! Oh, my gosh!' She shrieked. 'Really? A baby. You're not dying, you're having a baby. You and Joe made a baby.' She jumped up and hugged me. 'When?'

'We figure around June.'

'June. That's a long way off.'

Joe still had that dumb grin on his face. I was so relieved they were happy about it. 'Pa, this is amazing. I always wanted a brother or sister. And I can help loads.'

I looked at them and knew I should never have doubted. Despite all they had been through, they were wonderful people, unselfish, loving, and I was lucky to have them.

A few days later, the doc came back, and I got back to work, though Eliza and Luther gave me a soft job. They were kind people, and I could see why Joe had stuck with them. They treated us like family and it was a happy place to work. Luther said, 'You get the best out of people if you treat them right.' He wasn't wrong. Joe and Heidi worked with a new fervor, and the baby excited them. I had to stop them from fussing over me, but it was good to feel special and it seemed to bind us yet closer.

— Heidi —

By the time we learned of the thrilling news of the baby, Mayumi, Betty, and I had exchanged several letters. At first Jeremiah had not been sure and had written back to confirm that Mayumi was talking about me, and with a little to-and-fro a line of communication opened and I received my first letter from him. With my heart in my mouth and dancing butterfiles in my belly, I went off somewhere quiet to read it. My hands shook as I looked down at his handwriting.

> Howdy Fizz, or should I say, Straw Blue ha-ha-ha!! Holy smoke, you're a hobo!!! Id of never gessed at it. I always new you would be alive! Its the bees. I'm goofy-happy turning cartwheels. Ive missed you more than you know. I hung on until late to raise the alarm and I told Chief Banyard that a man who had beaten on me and killed your pa took you. For a long ol time I do not think he beleeved me. He told me what he thought hapened, and he darn near got it spot on. But I had to keep to my story and to this day that is what I have done! I know you would have done that for me also. A few weeks after you left they found a girl dead as stone near Loon Lake just over the state line. Timmy Barton told me she had worms in her eyes. Yuck! I was terified it was you, and I gave thanks when I found out it wernt. Was that horrible of me? Then they found another body, even closer, and Chief Banyard changed his view and beleeved

my story. Everyone in town thinks you got took and are lying dead some place. It has sadened many, patickly my ma and pa, and Miss Hannah. I keep saying I am sure you are ok but they all think I gone soft in the head. I hate lying to them but dont see another way. Besides I am deep in the swamp aint I? Then another girl went missing and last week, they found her body just thirty miles from here. Naked as the day she were born she was and all her cloths gone missing. Timmy who seems to know stuff said the man that killed her molested her also. He herd his ma and pa say it. Horrible horrible!! Everyone is bumping gums about it and mighty scared. When I tell folks I know you are safe they look at me funny and won't talk about you. leastways it means your in the clear being dead an' all! Save a few scars I am over my injurys. Hell darn your pa hit me so hard and I still gets bad dreems about that day. They planted him in the far corner of the cemetry. Only Chief Banyard and the preacher were there. Ithort youd want to now. He gone left this bump on my cheek. I have been drawing more to help me get over you being gone. Even been getting paid by folk to paint their families. Hey you'll love this. Bernie Hoggle even had me draw a picture of his sow Gertie. You remember feeding her bacon that time? Gosh darn I felt blue about that, making her a canibal an' all. He cried when I showed it him. Big softy!! But it pleased ma mighty good cause he paid me in pork belly. Of course life aint the same with you gone but I now time will sort things out. Im ok and knock around with my buds so you must not worry none. Just nowing you are out there and being looked after by Joe and Ella makes me buzz. Can't wait to meet em. I now one day we will be together. Above all you get on home when you can and dont fret about me none.
loads and loads and loads of love - I miss your sweet cherry lips. I am your one and only rolldog. J xx

I read his words several times. I held the paper to my nose and cried at the thought of what he was doing for me. The murdered girls were startling. I was glad it gave credence to our story, but I cannot say it felt comfortable hiding within such a ghoulish business. Back before I'd killed my pa, when someone murdered the first two girls, I had thought little about it. I did not know them and they had no connection with my life. But now I wondered who they were and who had done that to them. Hiding under the cover of their misfortune made me more determined to go back.

Without delay, I wrote him back and told him of our plan to return in the spring and promised we'd sort everything out. It delighted me he was using his amazing talent in art to get over the trauma. I reminded him of the drawing he had made of me lying naked by the Big Creek. I was lying on my side, my lower arm stretched out with my head laid on it, while the other arm covered my chest, though you could still see one breast, which he had exaggerated somewhat. My top leg was bent forward covering my modesty while the other was laid out straight. He'd captured something in me I'd never seen. I looked kinda vulnerable, distant, ethereal almost, and it made me look grown up. I ended my letter by telling him he must get on with his life as I was and not be afraid to enjoy himself.

Both Betty and Mayumi wrote to me at least once a week. Their news made me laugh and cry and kept me always thinking of them and I yearned to be with them as much as I longed to be with Jeremiah. I answered each letter with what news I had and found it a good way to express my feelings and, despite our separation, our friendship blossomed. Several copies of the Cypress Courier arrived, and I devoured every word. I wrote to Miss Jennings telling her what I was reading, and she wrote back the most interesting letters about literature and it became like a correspondence course for me.

In the days I spent deftly plucking the fragrant oranges under the sweet, California sunshine, I had plenty of time to think. I thought about how Joe had left behind the girl he loved, as I had with Jeremiah. But Joe had left a sister and baby daughter, too. He had made a new life, sacrificing his happiness to protect them from a vile man full of hate. He had found Ella and for years fallen almost trance-like in a life he understood. It put my stuff in perspective and made me appreciate what I had believed I wanted was not necessarily what I needed.

For the first time since the day I had killed my pa and run, I was settling and regaining some control. I took R. L. Stevenson's advice and always carried with me two books: one to read and one to write in. During breaks from the picking, I began writing out everything that had happened to me since my ma died. It was cathartic and harrowing to relive events no child should experience.

But then, a few weeks after the news of the baby, something happened that wrenched open memories and woke me up.

— Heidi —

It is hot and hard work picking fruit. So, oftentimes, when done for the day, I'd take myself off to the river to unwind and have some Heidi time. We had washing facilities at the bunkhouse, but as you know, I love to swim. I had found this spot not too far aways that had high banks, giving some privacy. I had been in the water some while and was thinking of coming out and lying in the sun with my book, when these four young fellas appeared on the bank. I turned to look at them and covered myself as best as I could and deftly put some more distance between us.

They were right by my clothes. One of them knelt, picking his way through them. I shouted, 'Hey, what you doing, mister? Those are mine!'

The group leered at one another. Then one stepped forward. 'Well, what have we here? She's a pretty kitty, ain't she?'

Dark memories of Sioux Falls returned, making my blood run cold, fear enveloping me. I sculled toward the far bank. I watched them. The one that had been going through my stuff stood with my panties in his hand. He buried his face in them, which made me feel sick. He passed the garment to his friends. 'Here, get you a taste of these.' Their leering, cruel faces transfixed me. I had nowhere to run and no one to help me. But despite my terror, this rage boiled up inside.

The one that rifled through my clothes seemed to be the leader. He pushed back his hat and grinned. 'Come on girlie, don't be shy. We won't hurt ya, we just want a look-see. Maybe a feel of them nice little titties.'

They guffawed.

Another grabbed at his crotch. 'Bet you never been with a real man before.'

I hunted around for some way of protecting myself. My anger boiled, and there was no way I was coming out. If they wanted me, they'd have to come get me and I was going to fight with everything I had. For a while, there was a standoff.

The leader took off his hat and dropped it on the ground. 'We don't mind coming in and joining you, if that's what you want?' Then he turned to his mates. 'Hey, I think she's playing hard-to-get and wants us to come in and take a cooling dip with her. I mean, woo-hee, the smell of them panties has made me real hot and hard.'

His words acted like a spark. They pulled off their boots and began stripping off down to their filthy underwear. With panic rising and adrenaline pumping, I felt around on the river bottom for a rock or something to use as a weapon. They advanced and just as they entered the water, my foot found a rock. I ducked down and grabbed it, holding it beneath the surface. I no longer tried to cover my modesty, but stood firm, trying to control my shaking. They were up to their knees and were moving apart, making it difficult to keep track. I saw the look in their eyes: predatory, ravenous, and ugly. I was so focused on them and they on me we did not notice the horse and rider.

'That's far enough, boys!' called out a calm voice.

It came from behind me. I spun round, but the sun was behind him and all I could see was his silhouette. I looked back at my would-be attackers. They had stopped. I could see them weighing up their options.

The leader, who was just a few yards from me and close enough that I could smell him, said, 'This ain't your business, mister. If you want your turn, you'll have to wait.'

The horseman spoke again. 'Beggin' your pardon, miss, but it seems like these here boys have more than bathing on their minds. Did you invite these here boys to take a swim with you?'

His words surprised me. I shaded my eyes, squinting at him. 'No, sir, I did not!'

I saw he had a rifle, and he cocked it. All eyes rested on the weapon.

'Well, you heard her boys. Me and my friend Winchester here going to give you the count of twenty Mississippis by which time you all need to haul out of the water and make like dust over that rise.' His horse dragged a front hoof along the ground and snorted. The rider held the rifle rock steady. 'Or you can stay and make good eating for the buzzards. Your choice.' He leaned across and spat in the dirt. I looked back at my would-be attackers. Their eyes were wide and darting. They looked between me and the rifle held steady and aimed for their leader, but they did not move. The horseman began counting. 'One Mississippi, two

Mississippi—' Which put a rattle among the group, and while the three of them turned and splashed their way out, and grabbed their things and ran scared, the leader stood his ground. His cruel, proud eyes raped my body and before turning he licked his lips and said, 'We'll do this another time, girlie.' And to my relief, he made off. I guess it is hard to argue with a rifle.

With the threat gone, I dropped my rock and shook, my teeth chattering. My legs felt like wet cotton. I wished I had a gun or something to protect myself. What was I supposed to do in a world full of men like that who wanted to use me like meat?

The horseman's voice broke through my panic. 'You okay, miss?'

I couldn't speak. I nodded.

He said, 'There's a crossing further down. Go get your things and I'll meet you on the other side.'

He tipped his hat, turned his horse and trotted off up the bank. As soon as he was clear, I got out and dressed. I didn't put my panties on, stuffing them in my pocket. I was worried those men were watching and waiting, so I picked up another rock, my darting, saucer eyes scanning the rise over which they had departed. A few minutes later, my savior appeared, and he brought the horse to a stop. I could see him well now. He had dark skin, a mess of stubble, and a cowboy hat. The rifle was back in a long holster attached to the horse. He had a gun on his hip and a long, broad blade in a sheath slung across his back. All he had to do was reach his hand behind his head and the handle was right there. I had seen no one so well armed. He said, 'I'm going to get off my horse. I won't hurt you. Okay?'

I nodded. He got down. He was tall, but there was gentleness around his crow-footed, nut-brown eyes. The horse walked itself down to the river and began drinking. It was a handsome beast. The horseman came closer. 'Where are you from?'

'Luther and Eliza's grove. I'm picking fruit for them. You know 'em?'

He shook his head. 'I'm not from these parts. Just passing through.' He popped a cheroot in his mouth and lit it. I noticed a gold tooth. He blew smoke up into the clear blue sky. 'Lucky I did.'

'You've got a lot of weapons, mister. Wish I had something to protect myself.'

He regarded me for a moment then walked over to his horse; it looked up a beat then went back to drinking. He reached into a saddlebag and brought out something. He came back and held open his hand. In it lay what looked like a much bigger version of the penknife I'd had for my birthday. He said, 'This here is a flylock twin-bladed knife. Press this button here and the long blade deploys and this here for the smaller one.' He showed me. 'Easy to carry, easy to deploy. You can have it.'

He held it out, and I took it. I pressed the button. The blade snapped out, making me jump a little. The long, thin, cruel steel glinted in the sunlight and this curious feeling coursed through me like I was in a living dream. I was back in Idaho, in my home. In front of me was my pa bent over Jeremiah, choking him. I could see Jeremiah's bloodshot, pleading eyes and hear my pa grunting. I had the boning knife gripped tight. I could see the white of my knuckles. I raised it up high and, with both hands wrapped around the handle, rammed it down into my pa's neck.

The horseman's voice penetrated my consciousness. 'Miss—miss—you okay?' I came to, shaking my head. He said, 'You kinda checked out there a moment, must be the shock.'

I looked at the blade in my quivering hand. I handed it back. 'Thanks, but I wouldn't know how to use it, probably just injure myself.'

Taking it, he said, 'That's the thing with a weapon. Once you take it out, you must be prepared to use it and accept the cost. Let's get you home, shall we?'

I had ridden in a horse-drawn cart a few times but never on the back of the animal. It felt high up. I could feel the heat and smell of the beast. It was strong, noble, yet gentle. I said, 'I like your horse.'

'He's called Flare.'

'I'm Heidi.'

'Good to meet ya, Heidi. Where are you from originally?'

'Sitwell, Idaho.'

He let out a low whistle. 'You're a long ways from home, Heidi.' For a while, we moved on and save the gentle fall of the horse's hoofs, all was silent. Then he added, 'I guess we all are.'

The rhythm of the horse, the heat and shock tired me out, and I ran out of talk. I held him and rested my head on his back and closed my eyes. When we got to the ranch gates, he got down and helped me off. I was about to turn and walk down the lane when he said, 'Hey, Heidi, you're right, you know?'

'Right about what?'

'No one can protect you, apart from you. Next time, when they get close enough, eyes and testicles.'

I frowned. 'Eyes and what?'

He remounted. 'That is where you hit them, hard and fast, no hesitation. Jab the eye with a finger and then knee or kick them hard in the groin. Then you run.'

He tipped his hat and, with a kick of his heels, took off. I watched him go, the dying light making a silhouette of him. I never asked his name or thanked him. I think that's how he wanted it.

Luther called the police. I gave them a description of the men and what they'd done. The officers seemed little bothered. One said, 'Seems to me like they were just larking around. Anyway, missy, you shouldn't be out swimming on your own unclothed like that, should you?'

They seemed more interested in my heavily armed rescuer. It shocked me with what they had said and how they'd made me feel. I thought the police were there to protect. It was a lesson I would not forget.

When they had gone, Joe said, 'Don't listen to them. It wasn't your fault. Next time I'll come with you.'

I never swam there again. On our day off, we'd go to sleep under the stars in our camping spot and I'd get my swim, but I was always nervous and that wasn't right. You shouldn't have to live in fear. It took a long time to get my confidence back. Also, it was when I began experiencing a series of vivid flashbacks to the day I killed my pa and other times he'd beaten me. I even had a couple reliving the day he attacked ma. I was certain he had killed her and it made more sense of what I'd done. He was a miserable, dangerous man and given time, he would have used me like meat, and one day put me in the grave. The experience hardened me and I lost a little more of the child. But above all I understood now, I lived in a world of lowlife-predators lurking cloaked among the good men.

By the time we were ready to leave, we'd filled our pockets. I had never had or seen so much money. It was more than enough for us to set off east into the past. Although fond of them, I did not feel the same sadness at leaving Luther and Eliza. They told us to come back next year and there would always be a welcome for us. Eliza gave me a hug and told me that if I ever needed a refuge for any reason, I could come to them. It was sweet of her.

Ella was fine and fit to travel and as we headed off, I felt a million miles away from that little runaway girl. A part of me wished I was still that person: unworldly, contained, knew what she wanted and where she was from.

In Fresno, we hopped a ride heading east. We sat in a row, leaning our backs against the warm wall of the boxcar, our bodies swaying to the loco's rhythm. I gave Joe a nudge. 'Hey, Joe, can you teach me to whistle Dixie?'

— Heidi —

To keep clear of tough weather, we took a southerly route. Though it was a detour, we dipped as far south as Tucson in Arizona. They wanted to show me where they had met. I could see it meant something to them and I reckon Joe needed to make a kinda pilgrimage. It was a long ways over vast arid states, but as we forged eastward, the land turned greener. We scythed our way through Missouri, crossing the mighty Mississippi at Cape Girardeau aboard the brand spanking new A. C. Jaynes ferryboat; another first for me, and as we sailed over the huge river my captivated mind filled with tales of travel and adventure. Heading north east, we hopped rides on the myriad railroads, making good speed crossing the state of Illinois, and by the time we traversed the state line into Indiana, we were foot-sore, and traveled out. It had been quite a journey, but we had used the time and distance to beneficial effect and as we hopped off the loco at the nearest water stop to Lagonda, we had in our minds a plan.

Although I was worried about what we might find and how it would affect Joe, the sense of adventure enthused me. I felt a little like Mrs. Paschal, an English lady detective from a book Eliza had loaned me. She was not a typical lady of the time. She smoked cigarettes and carried a colt revolver. She trailed suspects and made entry into houses and searched them for clues, and it made me appreciate you don't have to be what others think you should be.

We found a good place a mile outside of town to make camp. After we'd settled in and eaten, we sat round our fire. Ella poured the coffee and handed a mug to pa. 'How you feeling, Joe?'

He took the cup and cradled it. 'Most of me yearns to get back on that loco and keep going, but there's just enough that needs to know.'

'I need to know, pa. After all, if your sister is here, that would make her my aunt, at least in principle. Do you think she would have stayed here?'

'People didn't move round so much then and she was going steady with this boy. With me gone, she'd have been alone, and we had little cash. I'd like to think she would have stayed in case I came back. But your guess is as good as mine.'

That night I slept poorly. Restless dreams featuring a muddled cast of folk I knew, and all taken out of context, beset the little sleep I had. When I woke, Joe was sitting by the fire. I propped myself up on my elbows and blinked away the sleep. 'You too, I guess?'

He nodded. 'Not a wink.'

After breakfast, Ella and I dressed nice and, with the aid of Joe's handmade map, set off into town to get the lay of the land. The town had grown some and had better roads. Automobiles scooted around and it wasn't long before I almost got mowed down, just stepping back in time as the machine whirled past, sounding its horn and frightening the life outta me. We made for the county hall. Once there, the receptionist directed us to the records office where a homely, middle-aged woman, dressed in sober colors, manned the desk. She looked up. 'How may I help?'

Ella cleared her throat. 'I'm looking for my husband's sister. I got important news about him for her. It's been a long time, so we don't know exactly where she is living right now. Do you think you can help us?'

She scrutinized us and thought about it. I gave her my best sweet girlie smile. It seemed to help. She smiled back and directed us to sit. 'What name is it?'

'Florence Matilda Reisen. She was born here on January third, 1861. Her father was William Henry Reisen and her mother, Emeline Mary Reisen, both born here as well.' Ella gave her the last known address. We gave our names as Luella and Heidi Reisen. It sounded strange, and I wondered whether my thoughts betrayed me. But she seemed satisfied and told us to come back in an hour while she had someone investigate it.

As we stepped out onto the street, I turned to ma. 'Well, that was easier than I thought.'

She shrugged. 'We'll see. Let's go explore.'

We found the Davenport factory in the same place as on Joe's map. It was imposing and looked prosperous. We stood outside the ornate gates the name Davenport Engineering set above in two foot tall gold painted, iron letters. I thought about Joe as a boy coming here to learn a trade and then make a silly mistake that sent him off on a fresh path in life. Ella looked at me. She had this twinkle in her chocolate eyes. 'What do you think? Shall we go see if there are any jobs going?'

I grinned. 'Oh—yeah. Good idea.'

We followed the signs and made our way through a yard, where sat a row of imposing looking automobiles, and just beyond we found the office. There was a main desk with a stuffy looking, fat man sitting behind it. The room was hot and airless. He looked up, his forehead glistening with sweat like morning dew. 'Well, good morning, ladies. What can I do for you?' I had not expected him to be so welcoming.

Ella bobbed her head and almost did this weird kinda stoop. 'Me and my daughter are looking for work.'

He leaned back in his chair, which groaned like it was screaming from holding the weight, and looked us over. For a moment, his eyes rested on my face and we regarded one another. Then his greedy eyes traveled down my body, sending a shiver down my spine. His gaze linger awhile too long, then he shook his head. 'Sorry, ladies, don't think we've got anything to suit. Try the clothing firm on the south side.'

Ella nodded. 'Why, thank you, sir. We will.'

He nodded back. 'Well, you're welcome. You all have a nice day now.' His ravenous eyes came to rest on my chest and he leered. He let his cloak fall. I know you, mister. I can read your filthy thoughts and I see you.

He moistened his flaccid lips. 'Pretty girl.'

I twist of bile rose within me. I took Ella's hand. 'Let's go, ma.'

As we turned to go, Ella stopped and said, 'Sorry to bother you but my ma was from here and she went to school with a Melissa Davenport, they were friends. You know her?'

He scowled, sitting upright. 'Miss Davenport? Why I do. She's on the board of directors.'

'Does she still live in town?'

He narrowed his eyes a little, his voice striking a cautious tone. 'A little ways outta town.'

Hearing this, my mind went into a twizzle. Ella pursued her interrogation. 'Does she work here every day?' He nodded. Then he looked at the papers on his desk and began reading. The audience was over. 'Thank you, sir. Good day.'

We made our way back out to the street where I turned a full circle and threw my arms into the air. 'Holy smoke, ma. She's here! What are we going to do?'

'Let's go buy a coffee and then see what we get about Florence.'

We found a café just round the corner from the county building. We said little, but my mind jumped fences. Would Sophia be here too? Did Melissa get married and have other children? Did Florence get married? I figured there might be an entire family waiting for Joe. I did the math. He might even be a grandpa. I giggled at the thought. Ella broke me outta my daydreaming. 'What's tickled your fancy?'

'Joe might be a grandpa.'

She rolled her eyes. 'He could at that. Let's hope we aren't opening a whole can of worms here.'

She looked a little stressed, and I appreciated this might be hard for her. I lay my hand on hers. 'It'll be fine, ma, you'll see.'

Right on time, we were back at the county building. They kept us waiting, which gave me time to look around the cavernous room, with high ceilings and fine detailing picked out in rich timber. It said: this place has power and money. It wore an air of sophisticated calm about it, like a church. This woman appeared and bid us follow her into an office. We sat opposite her, a neat desk between us with a few heavy books set upon it. She laid one hand on them. 'I've been through the records and I found entries for the Reisen family you were asking about.'

My heart beat fast and I felt lightheaded. The office was warm and kinda airless. I guess I was so used to being outdoors I was susceptible to the closed feeling of it. She said, 'You were asking about Florence?' She looked down at the form the first lady had filled in, adding, 'your husband's sister, that right?' Ella nodded. The woman glanced at me and then back at Ella. 'I'm sorry to tell you that Florence died five years ago.'

I covered my mouth with my hand and screwed my eyes shut. The bleak news stabbed me like a blade through my heart. I had not expected that. It was so final. The woman turned to me. 'You okay, miss?'

I nodded. But emotion welled up, and my eyes filled with unsolicited tears. She said, 'Oh my goodness! I am so sorry for your loss.' She seemed somewhat panicked by my reaction. 'I—I know it's not much, but there is family.' She looked down at another sheet of paper. 'Florence was married to Edward Hamel and they have three children. I haven't looked further into each of them, but I'm sure there are grandkids. They laid Florence to rest in the local cemetery on the eastside of town.'

Ella took my hand and squeezed it gently. 'Do you have an address for Edward?'

The lady thought about it. It looked like she was deciding maybe to give out information that customarily she would not do. She glanced at my distressed face and her expression softened. She tapped the enormous book twice with her fingertips. 'I know Edward. Not well, but I know him. He worked here managing the finance department. He retired last year. I can see you are good people. I know he is a family man and I think he'd want to know about you. Come back tomorrow at noon. I'll have an address for you; you have my word on it. How's that sound?'

'You're too kind. It means a lot to us.'

We stood up, and she shook our hands. 'Forgive me for asking, but we want to call on Miss Melissa Davenport and I believe she lives just outside of town. Can you point us in the right direction?'

I glimpsed her eyes widen a little at the hearing of Melissa's name.

She retrieved the large tomes from the desk and pushed her chair neatly under the desk. 'Take the main road out west about half a mile. You can't miss it.'

We opened the door. Ella paused, turning back to the lady. 'Oh, one more favor. It's a shock to hear about Florence and I know my husband, Joe, will need to think about things, so please don't inform Mr. Hamel that we're here, if that's agreeable to you?'

She nodded. 'Oh, yes, of course, I quite understand.'

'Thank you. You've been so very kind. Good day.'

We stepped back outside. I took a deep breath. I felt despondent yet exhilarated, my mind in turmoil. 'Joe's going to be real sad. Shall we go find Melissa's house?'

'No, sweetheart. We best get back and break the news.'

— Joe —

When Ella and Heidi returned, I read it in their eyes. I went off on my own and wept hot, bitter tears not just for my loss but for all that I had missed. The grief had been so long coming it felt more painful than any other emotion I had ever experienced and felt like righteous retribution for my cowardice. When I returned, I hugged my girls. They shared my grief.

Though upset, Heidi rallied. 'She got married, pa, and had kids. I bet she missed you like crazy, but it didn't stop her living and finding happiness.'

'Flo was my last link to my childhood. Feels like it's died with her. I had so many questions.'

Ella sat beside me and put her arm around me. 'Maybe Edward can answer some.'

It felt like my heart had shriveled. 'That's what happens when you go digging in the past.'

Heidi told us to take a walk while she prepared food. We walked in silence as I corralled my thoughts. Ella held my hand. She and Heidi had lost, so they knew my loss, and it made me appreciate that life goes on. After a time strolling we found the road heading west of out of town. I stopped. A deep curiosity emboldened me. I turned to Ella. 'Let's go see if we can find Melissa's house.'

She looked at me and smiled. 'That's a fine idea, Joe.'

When we returned to camp, a pleasant aroma greeted us. Heidi put down her book. 'Hey, how was your walk?'

We sat. 'We went to find Melissa's house.'

'Really? And did you?'

'You can't miss it.'

'Oh, I see. Grand, is it?'

I grinned. 'What I'd call a mansion. There were lights on, drapes closed. Looked like a family home.'

'Weren't you tempted to go knock?'

'Every fiber of my being wanted to. The thing is, I still love her.' Heidi glanced at Ella. 'But Melissa's not going anywhere, and I need to get my head around Flo and I guess we need to meet Edward and find out stuff, don't we?'

There was a flicker of a mischievous smile at the corner of Heidi's mouth. 'The water never stops flowing, pa. It's best to go with it.'

'You're getting philosophical in your old age, Heidi.' She shrugged. It was good to have them here; it would have been impossible on my own and the words of John Donne came into my mind: "no man is an island entire of itself". I shrugged off the gloom. 'Now, that Mulligan smells terrific. Let's eat.'

After another restless night, we woke early. It was still dark. I suggested we get breakfast in town. At daybreak, we arrived at the well-kept cemetery. The three of us stood looking at the last resting place of Florence Matilda Hamel. She'd died in the Fall of 1920, a beloved wife, mother and grandmother. It said nothing about sister. Had she forgotten me? I cast my gaze heavenward and wondered. It is times like this you think about life, death and the hereafter.

We stayed looking at Flo's grave for a while. It felt like a part of me died, too. The three of us reflected, shed a tear, and then left. We had time before our noon appointment and I wanted to look around, so we took a trip down memory lane. Much had changed, but you can always find the core of a place. I took them to the place where I had been born and grown up. The plot had several houses on it now. No one recognized me or paid us any mind. I took them to a restaurant called Early's, where I'd been many times. It pleased me it had changed little. A bright smiley waitress served us. 'John Early still own this joint?' I asked her.

She looked at me like I had a screw loose. 'You mean Peter Early.' She poured us coffee and we ordered breakfast, and I said to no one in particular, 'Who in the hell is Peter Early?'

Heidi laughed out loud. 'Aw, come on, pa, it has been fifty years.'

I loved her calling me that, and with the ice broken, I laughed with her. 'Dumb is my middle name.'

I looked around the bustling room and wondered if anyone was a relative of mine. No one looked at me. The world had moved on.

The fare was just as I remembered and the coffee exceptional.

Ella drained her cup and sat back. 'It's going to be one hell of a shock for him when we turn up on his doorstep.'

I called for the tab. 'Let's hope a pleasant shock.'

At noon, we were at the county building. Ella went in while Heidi and I waited outside. Ten minutes later, Ella was back, her smiling eyes telling of her success. It was a twenty-minute walk to the road where Edward Hamel lived. It was a pleasant street with houses set back from the road, sporting neat front yards and picket fences. Edward's house was an elegant two story building mostly of timber construction, the detail painted blue and white, a well-tended yard, and parked up front, a smart, black automobile. We stood in the road, considering the grandeur.

Heidi let out a soft whistle. 'Holy smoke! Sure is an elegant street. Florence did well for herself.'

We stood there unable to cross onto the property, like once we did, there would be no turning back. In the end, Edward decided for us. The front door opened, and this man dressed in a nice suit appeared. He looked older than me and was carrying a load more weight. I guess that came from easy living. He had steel gray hair and gold, wire-rimmed eyeglasses. He came down the steps from his porch and said, 'Can I help you folks? Only I see you standing there a while. You lost?'

We crossed onto the property and made up the path, stopping just a few feet from him. He scrutinized me. He was frowning a little and his eyes seemed to look right through me. He said, 'Do I know you?'

I took a deep breath. 'Are you Edward Hamel?'

'Yes, I am. I don't believe we've had the pleasure.' He spoke real fancy. It matched the look of the property. He had a kind face. The sun caught his eyeglasses, giving off a flash of light.

'I'm Joe, this is Ella and this here is Heidi.'

Edward's eyes narrowed, a web of crow's feet springing out. 'Joe?' You could almost hear his mind crunching the data.

I took a step closer and held out my hand. 'I'm Florence's brother.'

— § —

We sat in a room full of expensive-looking furniture. The walls had pictures on them and there were trinkets on the mantel next to a clock that tick-tocked away. The room smelled clean, like polish. Heidi looked about, her eyes wide. She perched on the edge of her seat, like she was afraid. Edward had a housekeeper. He asked her to make tea.

Like it was a necessary formality, it took a few minutes to work our way through the small talk. By the time we had a cup of tea in our hands, I figured we'd get down to brass tacks. I asked, 'How did she die?'

Edward's eyes glazed over and he looked down. 'It was the darnedest thing, really. She was fit and healthy, always loved being in the garden tending her roses. She got this silly minor cut on her finger and the next day she had a fever, burning her up. The doctor said she had blood poisoning. They tried various treatments, but she died a few days later. Even after all this time, I'm still trying to make sense of it. I miss her so.' He got up and left the room for a moment, coming back with some photographs and handed them to me. I looked at them and traced my finger over the figure of Florence. I choked back the tears at the cruelty of her demise. I passed the photos to Ella and Heidi.

'Wow, you look alike, pa. She's the feminine version of you.'

Tears rolled down her cheeks. I felt bad bringing more pain to her life. The somber atmosphere crushed in on me. No one knew what to say. No one apart from Ella, who was holding it together. She had a commanding side, like a jacket of steel. 'They told us at the records office that you and Florence have children.'

It perked him up. Edward nodded. 'Two boys and a girl, all grown up now. Sam, our eldest, is in the military, always had a sense of adventure. He hasn't settled down yet. Then there's Joe, who's thirty-nine.' Edward smiled at me, adding, 'Florence named him after you. She always talked about you. She said you'd come home one day.'

Edward poured more tea. When he took Heidi's cup, he put his hand on her shoulder, saying, 'She would have loved you.' He was right, she would have.

Fresh tea dispensed, he sat. 'So our Joe is married to Clara and they have four children, two of each, aged eight to sixteen. The older two are twins like you and Florence, Joe. They live nearby. Joe is a fine lawyer. Then our youngest is Catherine, thirty-six, also married, with three girls.'

More photos appeared, and the mood lightened as a now animated Edward poured out stories about my beautiful sister until I felt her presence. She never blamed me, people like her never do, the blame we lay at our own feet and Edward made plain that I should not be hard on myself. He said, 'You came back, Joe. Meeting you is like having a part of her back, too. We're brothers, you and me. You've brought your wonderful family to us. The past is done, unchangeable, but our family history now has a new chapter, and for that we give thanks.'

(43)

— Heidi —

I was relieved Edward did not go into more detail about names and ages, as I was having difficulty processing Joe's ever expanding family. More photos appeared and as we poured over them, I looked at the well-dressed, attractive people who had no connection to me. I was just a tag-along and felt overwhelmed by it. Reflecting, I observed Joe as he began making sense of what had happened in the years he had been away. They were strangers to me, but I could see the photos moved Joe who studied each image as though willing them to life. I recall little of the conversation and endless questions. The three grownups formed a unit, and I sat on the fringe content to sit and watch.

At some juncture Edward had his housekeeper serve sandwiches. I nibbled the elegant bready delicacies but could not tell you how they tasted or what the fillings were. I needed to pee, but was afraid to interrupt. I hoped Ella would need to go so I could go with her. In the end, nature won and forced my hand. I had expected to be sent to an outhouse, but the housekeeper took me upstairs to a room complete with a water closet, a bathtub and a fixed basin, both of which had faucets you turned to get water. It reminded me of the time Joe and I had spent at the hotel in Jusinca. Edward's bathroom looked so clean I was almost too scared to pee. I couldn't wait to leave and be back at our cozy camp, and though I would not have turned down an opportunity to take a long soak in his fancy bathtub, I prayed Edward would not ask us to stay.

It shocked Edward to learn that Joe had been homeless all this time. He got the edited version of our story with murder, suicide attempt, assault, and pending imprisonment left out. He told us he had plenty of room and he begged us to stay. Joe and Ella seemed reluctant, but he wore them down. No one asked what I thought. He wanted to drive us back to our camp, and I was glad that Joe said we'd welcome the walk and would return later, and as we wandered back, I consoled myself with the thought that I'd soon be able to kick back and have a long hot bath. Sitwell, Jusinca, Britt, Carmel, and the orange grove all appeared remote. Here it was like a foreign country where I had little idea of how things were done. I felt small and hemmed in. I don't know why I had these thoughts, and I tried to shake them. I didn't want to worry Ella and Joe, so I kept my fear to myself and tried to reason it out. Like I said to Joe, go with the flow.

Thing is, when you live with folk as close as we three did, it is impossible for a change in your demeanor to go unnoticed. When we got back to our camp and began packing up, Ella said, 'You're quiet, Heidi, everything alright?'

'Yeah, sure. Just tired. Two nights of poor sleep, I guess.'

'You can tell us anything, you know, don't bottle stuff up.'

For the first time since we'd been together, I felt furious, and I snapped back at her. 'Give me a break, wilya? I ain't bottling stuff up. I'm just tired is all.'

Joe looked at me, eyes wide and held up his hand. 'It's fine. I know it's all kinda new and stressful. If I was here on my own, I'd probably run a mile. But we've got each other, right? And we do what's right for us and whatever comes from this, we'll be together. I promise.'

I glanced at Ella. She nodded and smiled, her soft eyes glowing.

I made a face and shrugged. 'Sorry.'

She came over. 'I'm sorry, sweetheart. Sometimes having a good yell at someone clears the air, doesn't it?'

We packed up and made our way back. I guess we looked like what we were, and I knew in my heart, bathtub or no, that I would never feel at home here.

Mrs. Ellwood—the housekeeper—showed me to my room. It was airy and feminine. The iron-framed bed was big and high off the ground, with an immense fluffy towel draped over the ironwork. She told me it had been Catherine's room. I don't know why, but I told her I knew a nun named Catherine, to which she had smiled and said, "Well, our Catherine isn't that devout." And I pondered why she'd called her *our* Catherine. The room had a view into the backyard that was even more impressive than the front. It had a swing hanging from a mighty tree, I guess for the grandkids.

Mrs. Elwood tilted her head to one side, an easy smile forming around her mouth, and her eyes shone. 'You need anything, honey, you just ask.'

I nodded. She made for the door. 'Oh—there is one thing, Mrs. Elwood. Is it alright for me to have a bath?'

'Why, of course, honey, I'll run it for you.'

Ella and Joe were in a room across the landing. I guess it would be nice for them to be alone at night. I went across. The door was open. Ella saw me. 'How's your room?'

I nodded. 'Yeah, best I've ever been in. It was Catherine's room. There's a delightful view out back.' Their room looked out over the front. You could see across the street into the house opposite. I said, 'I'm having a bath. Mrs. Ellwood is running it for me.'

Joe laughed. 'Well la-di-da, look at you being waited on hand and foot. Guess we all need a good soaking.'

I gave him a shove and giggled.

Mrs. Ellwood knew her business. The water was just the right temperature. I lowered my tired, aching body into the hot water, surrendering myself to its comforting embrace. I felt better. There was a bar of perfumed soap of which I made good use.

After my delicious bath, I wondered what to wear. I had the benefit of a good-sized mirror in my room. I stood naked before it. It was the first time I had seen all of myself in reflection. It surprised me how feminine I looked. I cupped my small breasts, turning this way and that, taking me in. Side on, I liked the way my ass looked. I giggled. Then I turned round and viewed the scars on my back. There was one in particular that had left a clear impression of pa's belt buckle. I remembered the first time I went swimming with Mayumi. It horrified her when she saw them. I told her I was glad I couldn't see them, that it was like my pa had branded me as a farmer does his livestock. She had done what both Jeremiah and Ella had, tracing her finger over the welts. She said they had a noble quality about them and they weren't brands but marks of oppression and I should never be ashamed of them. As I looked at them, I could almost feel the delicate touch of her moist lips that far outweighed the memory of the searing pain as my pa's belt had flayed my back.

I wore the dress Ella had bought me for my birthday. It was a little creased but the best I could do. I fixed my hair in a ponytail and had one last look at myself. The dress did suit me, but it did not feel like me. I smelled good, and I was as polished up as well as ever. Even my nails were clean. I came downstairs, pausing by each of the paintings of Edward and Florence's children. There were two of each: one painted when they were children and one as grownups. I could see brief flashes of Joe in Sam and Catherine; both had his and Florence's coloring, while Joe looked more like Edward, and it delighted him we had named him Joe Junior.

I made my way to the parlor where Edward was sitting reading. He glanced up and beamed. 'Oh my, you look delightful, Heidi.' He did not look at me the way the man in the Davenport factory had. He fixed me up with a glass of lemonade and took me out back to look at the yard. He did most of the talking, saying that as it was winter, the garden was not at its best. We came to the tree with the swing.

'I hung this for my kids; now it's the grandkids that use it.' For a moment he looked rueful, adding, 'Florence liked to sit here and sway. I can picture her now, yes sirree.' He gestured. 'Here, Heidi, try it. Why don't you?'

He took my drink, and I hopped on. My feet just touched the ground like they made it for me. I got a little rhythm going and soon had a good swinging action. It had been an age since I had been on a swing and I had forgotten how good it felt. He shouted, 'Yes sir, there you go! You would have given the boys a run for their money.' He stood back and watched me, his face a picture, an admiring smile with a sense of genial contentment. As I swung, I enjoyed the feeling of lightness and freedom as though I were flying. The lady at the records office had been right, Edward was a family man and I guess now his family had grownup and fled the nest he missed them.

He watched for a few minutes, then placed my drink on the ground and set off down the path to the far end of the yard. He had a slight droop to his shoulders, and I guessed our appearance made him feel blue, maybe with mixed emotions. It brought me up and, feeling a little dizzy, I slowed to a gentle sway. I stayed there, swaying and letting my thoughts drift with the calm motion. Joe's voice startled me, and I turned. 'Hey, that looks fun.'

I hopped off the seat. 'Wow, pa, you've buffed up good. You look real handsome.'

He laughed. 'We're fit for royalty, eh?' He looked at me, a sudden flash of gloom in his eyes, and shook his head. 'Sorry, I'm dragging you all over the country.'

I frowned. 'Don't be silly. I love seeing stuff and traveling around with you both. Even with the bad things that have happened, I wouldn't change it.'

He gestured back to the house. 'Don't you want to be in a place like this with all the opportunities it can bring?'

I wondered where this was going. 'The only place I want to be right now is where you and Ella are. You're my ma and pa, aren't you? It isn't just a name I call you, it means something. And all this,' I added, pointing at the house, 'is just stuff. It isn't important, not really.'

He smiled the warmest smile and opened his arms. 'Come, give your pa a hug.' I wrapped my arms around his powerful body and held tight.

He said, 'You smell good.'

'So do you. Was there any soap left?'

We looked at each other and burst out laughing. 'Not much,' he said.

We walked back to the house hand-in-hand, and I felt proud to have him as my pa. He was worth a million times any amount of money and the stuff it could bring. We found Ella in the parlor. She looked elegant with a glow that took my breath away. A few minutes later, Edward joined us. His red-rimmed eyes betrayed him and I liked him all the more for it. He looked at the three of us and shone. 'It's fabulous to have such company and I wish Florence had been here to see you, Joe, with your family.'

Joe nodded. 'I'm sorry I left it too late. Always have been rubbish at timing things right. Main thing is she had you, your children and the grandkids. She was happy, wasn't she?'

Edward gestured for us to sit. 'Oh, always. She had a goodness about her and the patience of a saint.'

Joe nodded. 'I remember that well.'

Mrs. Ellwood called us to eat.

The food was the best kinda home cooked fare and Edward, a gracious host. He seemed delighted to have us in his house, and he said it was good to have a young person about. After supper, we returned to the parlor and made ourselves comfortable. Edward rubbed his hands. 'Well now, as this is such an auspicious occasion, I've got a little something stashed away.' He disappeared and came back with a bottle of clear copper-colored liquid. He set it down and fetched four bowl-shaped glasses. He rubbed his hands together and said, 'There's never been a better time to have a little fine French cognac.' He tapped his nose. 'Mom's the word.' I did not know what he meant by that. He pulled out the stopper, saying, 'Joe, Ella?'

Joe said, 'Well, it's been a long time, but I'll take a little oil of joy.'

Edward grinned. 'Oil of joy. I like that.'

Ella said, 'Yes please, don't mind if I do.'

Edward poured a measure into three of the glasses, then he turned to me and said, 'And how about you, Heidi?'

I shook my head. 'No, thank you.' I could smell the aroma. It was better smelling than the filth my pa drank.

I watched them as they sipped the dark liquid. It left an oily film on the side of the glass. After a bit Edward said, 'Now that is fine cognac indeed. Glad we had an occasion for it.' He looked at me, his expression pleading. 'Sure you won't try a sip? It won't bite.'

It smelled good, and they seemed to enjoy it, and I did not want to seem ungracious. 'I guess maybe a little would be okay.' He poured some in the glass, maybe a quarter inch. He told me how to hold the glass and how I should swirl the liquid around the bowl and then stick my nose in and take a sniff. Once I had it in my hand, it smelled stronger. All three of them were watching. I swirled like he said, stuck my nose in and took a big sniff. It was like a punch inside my nose, all hot and spicy, and then it burned the back of my throat, making me cough and my eyes water.

Joe laughed. 'You're not supposed to suck it up your nose, girl.'

I could see they were all amused, and I laughed with them. The liquid made me feel a little heady. I said, 'If it smells like that, God only knows what it tastes like.'

'Give it a go. Heidi,' said Joe. 'Take a tiny sip and let it rest on your tongue and breathe in through your mouth just a little.'

I did as he said. At first it tasted a little sweet, like caramel. Then it got hotter on my tongue. I tried to breathe in a little, but it felt like my mouth was burning, so I swallowed it down. I could feel its heat flowing down my throat like a dense ball of energy. It left a clean, pleasant taste in my mouth and little-by-little the heat faded, leaving my tongue feeling a little numb and tingly.

Edward said, 'Well, what do you think?'

I grimaced. 'You drink this for fun?'

'Well now, that's an interesting take on it. I think I would say not so much for the fun as for the pleasure of it. What do you say?'

I tried it again. This time I breathed in harder and it near choked me. I coughed and swallowed, nearly spraying it out of my mouth. A little went up my nose. It burned the back of my throat, worse this time. I recovered. 'Honestly, I can't say as it is fun or pleasurable. But thank you for letting me try it.'

Joe chuckled. 'I guess it takes a bit of getting used to, but you won't find a smoother or finer cognac than this.' He held up his glass, adding, 'To family and absent friends.' I drank with them, but this time I didn't let it rest or breathe in, I just swallowed.

I watched the three as they chatted away and I saw the cognac seemed to relax Joe and he looked happy. Booze had always made my pa sad and angry, but I was glad that it was illegal and difficult to come by. Sitting there with my belly full and the softening effects of the drink made me drowsy, so I excused myself and made my way up to my room.

Wanting to feel the outdoors, I threw open the window as wide as it would go and left the drapes apart. I undressed. Ordinarily I would sleep in my undergarments, but when I pulled back the sheets and felt how crisp and clean they were, I felt obliged to get back to nature. I climbed in, scooched down and pulled the covers up, the cool softness feeling sensual against my naked skin. My head sank into the pillow. It was almost too soft. I reached across and put out the light and the soft moonlight cast a chromium band across the room, making a shadow on the wall of the large tree from which hung the swing, the upper branches swaying in the light wind, and it was just enough of the outside for me. I could hear the muffled sounds of laughter and talk from the three grownups. As I did every night, I held the pendant Mayumi had gifted me and thought of her, Betty, and Jeremiah. I made a mental picture of the country. We were thousands of miles apart and tonight more than any other I felt faraway and disconnected from them, like I had crossed into another world or era, and an overwhelming feeling of homesickness flooded me, and hot, sweet tears rolled from my eyes.

— Heidi —

I woke to the sound of birdsong. Daylight spilled into the room and the breeze made the drapes sway. It took me a moment to remember where I was. For a while I lay in bed, almost too afraid to get up and face the world. I gave myself a good talking to.

It'll be fine, Heidi. Just get up, put on your best face, and feel the fear. Joe needs you to be strong and I need me to be strong.

When I came downstairs, Joe and Ella were in the dining room eating breakfast.

Ella looked up. 'Hey, sweetheart. You okay? You went off kinda sudden last night.'

'I'm fine. Was beat is all, you know. Better this morning.' I looked at the tempting spread, which gave me a lift. 'Well holy smoke, this looks good.'

Joe chuckled. 'Don't be shy, get a plate and dive on in.'

I made good use of Mrs. Ellwood's excellent fare. She had set the table with a large rack of toast, pots of conserves, elegant crockery, fine smelling coffee, and on the sideboard a range of plates with cooked fare, enough to sustain an army. It was how I imagined nobility lived. Was this us now? I sat and tucked in. 'Where's Edward?' I asked between mouthfuls.

Joe perked up. 'Ah, he's gone over to see Melissa, you know, break it to her all gentle like.'

I stopped eating and put down my cutlery. 'Oh. So, I guess he knows the story, eh?'

'Yes, all of it. He met Florence a couple of years after I had gone. He had heard the story about me and Davenport, everyone knew him, and when he met Florence at a dance that a girlfriend had dragged her to, he made a point of talking to her. He said she was sitting off to one side all alone, and he loved her at first sight. To begin with, she was blind to him, but he chipped away and dug her outta her sadness. They married a year later.'

'Wow, love at first sight. That's beautiful.'

Joe nodded. 'Florence kinda blamed Melissa for what had happened to me, so she didn't speak to her until one day they bumped into one another. Melissa was with Sophia, who by then was about four. All it took to break the standoff was one look at the cute little girl, innocent of the sins of her parents and grandparents. She had Melissa's blond hair and blue eyes, but Flo could see me in there too. She knew she had already missed too much and that little Sophia was her only connection to me. They went and took coffee and Flo understood Melissa had no choice or hand in the matter of my expulsion. Melissa said she hardly ever spoke to her father and never forgave him. He tried to win her back with money. He made her a director of the firm, a role she took serious and still does, but he understood little about people and what really matters, and he died unreconciled. Melissa said it was the only way she could punish him. After he died, she paid a private detective to go look for me.'

I puffed out my cheeks. 'Really? She must love you loads. I guess you were so far off the trail he'd never have found you. Imagine if he had?'

'Apparently her father paraded a load of moneyed suitors past her, but she rebuffed them all and never married. Sophia found a good husband in one of the town's doctors. They have a grownup boy and a girl, also both married and have five kids between them. Florence and Melissa became close, so Sophia grew up knowing who I was.'

I sat back with this stupid grin plastered on my face. 'Holy smoke, pa, you're a great-grandpa.' I laughed out loud. 'Heck, what does that make me?'

Joe and Ella joined in with the laughter. He said, 'Well, by my reckoning it makes you about the youngest great-aunt of all time. But I don't think I've got my head round it yet.'

I fell about and it relieved me to laugh so hard. 'I should say so. I mean, did you ever imagine this whole family sitting here and growing as you went about your hobo life?'

'That's the darnedest thing of all because once I had detached myself from the idea of ever being able to come back, I hardly ever gave it a thought.' He paused and pointed his knife at me, his eyes radiating. 'Until that is, I went and met you.'

I sobered up, remembering that moment we met. It seemed now like a lifetime ago. I fixed his gaze and there was a spark there I had not seen before. I swallowed.

'And was that a good thing, or would you rather have gone on as you were?'

He stood up and came over and kissed me on the top of my head. He said, 'Meeting you was the kick up the ass I needed. I want you to know you are so special to me, and I wonder whether some force put us together so that we could work stuff out. It would have been a tragedy if I had not come back and put an end to my running. I don't know how I can make it up to any of them, but at least I have time to start again.' He sat back down. 'Just wish I'd done that sooner.'

For a while we sat round that bounteous table, a table that most hoboes would give an arm for, and contemplated the true nature of our meeting.

I got back to my food. 'So, what's the plan?'

Joe sat back and sipped his coffee. 'If Melissa wants to meet Joe, Edward is going to telephone. All being well, she'll come here and—'

'Oh, don't you worry, pa, she'll want to see you.'

'Yeah. I know, but I'm terrified.'

I shoveled in the last piece of bacon and laid my knife and fork on the plate all tidy next to one another, and forgetting the stiff, linen napkin that lay untouched beside my plate, I wiped my mouth with the back of my hand, like I always did. I looked at Joe. 'I'd be terrified, too. But then, I'd be worried if you weren't.'

Ella took a coffee refill. 'I'm thinking it might be best if Heidi and I go out, give you some space. We need some things from town, so maybe we can go have a look around the stores and catch you later.'

I was relieved to hear that. I had not thought that coming back here would have such a dramatic effect on us. It delighted me Joe had found this vast, successful family sitting right here waiting for him. We'd gone from this self-contained threesome to something I had no comprehension of, and it worried me I might get lost in the crowd. After all, Joe had a proper daughter, two grandkids, five great grandkids, and an entire flock of nephews and nieces and so on. In a few months, he'd have another child with Ella bound to them by blood. I could not help reflecting on where I fitted in. I knew they loved me and I them, but I was an outsider, a mongrel stray with a tainted past. I tried to get a grip on my fear, but I was still a long way from mending. I was worried too that the whole family would get to hear my story and who I was, really. All I brought to the picnic was grief. Maybe it would be best if I went back to Idaho on my own. I had enough money to ride the cushions home and buy food. Once there, they could send me to jail and that would free Joe and Ella to get on with their lives here in Indiana. One day I'd get out and I could go somewhere no one knew me and start again.

One thing I knew for certain was I didn't want to live here. I knew I shouldn't be thinking like this. I tried to quieten the storm in my head and at least going out with Ella would give me some space and I told myself I must confide in her and not carry it on my own. Besides, she too was an outsider, and I worried Melissa might beguile Joe and draw him back. I hated the uncertainty.

45

— Heidi —

Leaving Joe to destiny, we set off into the morning sunshine. It pleased me to be with Ella away from the house, and for a while we walked in silence, during which I did a little math. In the years Joe had been gone, his family had grown from three to twenty-two, which gave me pause and made me think. I guess you could see it in miniature with us. A few months back, I had been on my own and so had Joe and Ella. Now we were a family, at least in theory. All being well by June, three would become four. I had never thought about the growth and evolution of a family. I knew nothing about my German ancestors. I didn't even know if my ma and pa had brothers and sisters. Maybe there was a town in Germany, just like this one, full of my relations. I don't know how I would ever find out or if I'd want to, but I guess the thought of it made me feel less lonesome.

Ella nudged me. 'You're miles away, a penny for your thoughts.'

'Just been doing the math about Joe's family.'

'Yeah, it's quite a crowd. You added them up, yet?'

'There's twenty-two of them. Mind you, it excludes any siblings of Edward and the folk his children and Sophia married. Could be double that or more.'

Ella gave this snorting kinda laugh. 'That's a scary thought. Small talk isn't my strong suit. Besides, when you tell straights you're a hobo, it can be a conversation stopper.'

It occurred to me I had thought little of or asked Ella about her wider family. 'Have you got family back home?'

'My ma and pa died when I was fifteen. They got sick and passed a week apart.'

'Holy smoke, that's awful! I'm so sorry. You lost them and then David. That's—that's so sad. Did you have siblings?'

'Like you, I was an only child. There had been a baby before me, but he died when he was just a few months old. I think it disappointed my father I was a girl. I have or had an aunt back east, but I know nothing about her.'

I took her hand. She looked at me and smiled. I said, 'Well, that's kinda odd, isn't it?'

'What is?'

'Well, you me and Joe all lost our parents when we were young.'

'Huh—yes. I guess we did, didn't we?'

'And it set us to leaving home.' I glanced over at her. 'I know nothing about my German family or if my ma and pa had brothers and sisters, not even what part of the country they were from. Never thought about it until now.'

'Does it make you want to go find out?'

I shrugged. 'I don't know, but it makes more sense of why Joe didn't come back.'

She frowned. 'What do you mean?'

'Well, he thought by staying away he was protecting the people he loved and it probably never occurred to him they were getting on with their lives and making a new family, you know, like what you don't know about, you can't miss. You think?'

'I guess. I think, as always, he's being hard on himself. He's the least cowardly person I know. It took courage to cut those ties and start again. Hell, when they left him unconscious in that grave, he didn't even have boots.'

'I guess we've all done that in our own ways, haven't we? Perhaps people like us have to keep moving forward like we're looking for something.'

She let go my hand, put her arm around me and gave me a look. 'Maybe we've already found what we're looking for. I'm so glad you're here with me.'

'Me too, ma.' She gave me a squeeze. I felt better.

We found the main drag and began window shopping. It wasn't long before we came to a bookstore. There was a sign in the window: "Help Wanted, inquire within". 'Hey, I'm going to browse the books. You coming?'

'No, I'll go get the things we need; I'll catch you later at the coffee shop.'

Heidi, this is your lucky day. My first book store.

I entered. A bell jingled, announcing my arrival. The store had that wonderful smell of books, which were laid out in two sections. One had new and used books, all arranged in shelves, like the library in Carmel, stretching on to the back. The other side had art supplies and stationery. About halfway down the store, there was a counter with a cash register. A youngish red-haired man sat on a stool, entering something in a ledger. He looked up. For an instant he seemed irked, but when he studied me his demeanor changed and he lay down his pen. 'Well, good day, miss. How may I assist you this fine morning?'

I gave him my best face. 'Good day, sir. I was wondering what kinda help you needed?'

He frowned. 'Help?'

I pointed over my shoulder. 'The sign in the window.'

He stood and nodded. 'Oh, yes, of course, that. Well—now—let me see. We need someone to help around the store, stacking shelves, serving customers, keeping things clean, you know, general duties.'

'I love books and reading. I am what they call a bookworm. I think working in a bookstore would be like a dream come true for me.'

He studied me. He rubbed his chin with a delicate hand. I'd never seen such clean nails or smooth skin on a man. He leaned his hands on the counter. 'What's your name?'

'Heidi Schlager, sir. '

'You ever worked in a store before?'

'Sometimes back home, I worked at the general store. I used to help my teacher, Miss Hannah, schooling the younger kids, and I got experience working an orange grove. I work hard, I learn fast, and I like people.' I beamed.

He sat back down, scratched his head, giving it some thought. 'How old are you, Heidi?'

'Fifteen.'

He nodded. 'Well, alright then. When can you start?'

My heart skipped a beat. 'Tomorrow.'

'Oh, tomorrow! Well, that's excellent. We've got a big order coming in. Okay, how about this? You come tomorrow morning at eight o'clock and we'll try you. You work hard and show me what you got and we'll talk terms. How does that sound?'

'Will I get paid for tomorrow?'

He grinned and pointed a finger at me. 'Oh, I like that. Shows you've got a good business head. But don't you worry, missy, whatever happens, you'll get paid. I take pride in the way I look after my employees, like we're all family.'

He held out his pale, elegant hand. 'Okay, Miss Heidi Schlager, do we have a deal?' We shook. The smoothness and warmth of his hand surprised me, as did the powerful grip.

'Thank you, sir. I won't let you down.'

Before releasing me, he held on to my hand for a beat. 'I'm Mr. Spaar. Timothy Spaar.'

'Pleased to meet you, sir. See you tomorrow, Mr. Spaar, and thank you.'

I went back out to the street feeling proud of myself. My feet felt like they were dancing down the sidewalk. I knew that we'd probably be here a while, so having a job would keep me busy and fill my pockets more. I reckoned a new outfit would make a good impression, so I wandered on down the street looking for a clothing store and soon found a suitable establishment. There was so much choice, I didn't know where to begin. Then this young female assistant came over. She looked a little older than me, but a good deal more sophisticated, being neatly attired and wearing red lipstick. She asked me if I needed assistance. I said, 'I've got a new job in the bookstore starting tomorrow and I need something to wear. What do you suggest?'

Her eyes narrowed. 'You mean the bookstore down the street aways?'

'That's the one, Spaar's Books and Art Supplies Emporium.'

She frowned. 'Oh there. Spaar's place.' For a moment, she seemed to check out with a faraway look. Then she shook her head. 'You're new here, aren't you?'

I nodded. She studied me, like she was gauging my size. Her eyes came to rest on my boots and her eyes widened. 'I guess you'll be needing shoes, too.' I smiled and shrugged. She took my hand. 'Alrighty then. Follow me.'

She parked me in a private booth at the back of the store and brought me outfits. I'd put them on and she'd tell me to come out and she looked me over and in the end I had three she said looked suitable for work but could double for walking about town too. It was an education. I chose two, bought some attractive panties—a first for me—and the pair of shoes that felt most comfortable. As I made my way to the door with a handful of bags, she said, 'What's your name?'

'Heidi Schlager.'

'Good luck in your new job. You be careful now, Heidi Schlager.'

I paused and turned. 'I will. Thank you again for your help. It was fun.'

She shrugged. 'It's what they pay me for.'

I went back outside. I had so little for so long I felt kinda guilty at having spent on new, but I'd earned the money and I wanted that job. I headed up the street and it wasn't long before I bumped into Ella as she came out of a chemist. Her eyes rested on my bags. 'Been spending?'

I nodded. 'New outfit for a new job.'

Her eyes widened, and she bobbed her head. 'New job? Tell me over coffee.'

We went back to Early's and slipped into a booth, our bags around us like well-to-do ladies about town. I felt kinda grownup having my own means. We ordered coffee and cake.

Ella caught my eye and raised an eyebrow. 'So, spill the beans.'

'I got a trial tomorrow at that bookstore.'

'Hmm, I can see you in a bookstore, made for you. What's he paying?'

'Well, we haven't agreed on terms. He said if I impressed, he'd take me on and discuss it. What do you reckon the rate should be?'

She thought about it. 'For a forty-hour week doing that kinda work, I reckon at your age you should get seventy-five cents an hour.'

'Gosh, that's thirty bucks a week. That sounds okay, doesn't it? Plus, I get to work with books and learn how a store operates. Like being paid to learn, isn't it?'

She smiled. 'I'm so proud of you, Heidi. You'll be independent before you know it. It'll delight Joe, too.'

'You think so?'

'I know so.'

'It'll keep me busy.' The coffee and cake arrived. We tucked in. 'I'm kinda nervous about meeting all that family. It's overwhelming. Me having a job means you and Joe have time to go see folk and not have to worry about me. Do you think Edward will let us stay with him?'

Ella sipped her coffee and tilted her head, looking at her cup. 'Damn, this is exceptional coffee.' She took another sip laid down her cup and tapped my hand. 'He said that we could stay as long as we wanted. Is that okay with you?'

'If you had asked me yesterday I'd have said no, but it's nice to have a few home comforts, isn't it? And, besides, I like Edward and you can see he's missed having folk in the house.'

'Yeah. We'll make sure we pay our way and help.'

I took a bite of the delicious cake. 'Wonder how Joe's getting on?'

Ella sipped her coffee. 'Hmm.'

'You're not worried, are you, about Joe and Melissa? I mean—you know—if they still love one another.'

She looked at me, set down her fork, and sat back. She sighed. 'I won't deny it is awkward but we've talked about it and yes he loves her, or the idea of her, but he said that you can't wind back time and he's known me a whole load longer and we're together. He can't do anything for Sophia as she's all grown up—' She made a face, twisting her mouth to one side, snorting. 'Hell's teeth, she's older than I am! Besides, we're having a baby and we got you. He won't throw all that away, of that, I am sure.'

'I guess we'll have to see what happens, won't we?'

Ella placed her hand on mine. 'Listen, don't go overthinking things. We love you so much. As much as we're going to love the baby when it comes.' I nodded.

'I can see all this has overwhelmed you, and Joe knows it. Truth is, we feel a little swamped, too.'

'You do? I mean, won't Joe want to stay here, seeing as he's got so much family?'

'Is that what you want? Be honest with me.'

I shook my head.

'Well, it may surprise you to hear that goes for the two of us as well. If we stop somewhere, it must be a place we all want to settle.'

'Do you think he'll ever want to settle?'

'I don't know, but he's got the best reason in the world now, hasn't he?'

'What about you?'

'I think this baby and you both need a home. I'd love to see you finish school and have time to heal properly, and that won't happen if we keep dragging you from pillar-to-post, will it?'

'But where?'

She drained her coffee and caught the waitress' eye for a refill. 'Well, that depends a little on what happens when you go back home, doesn't it?'

'Would it be better if I didn't go home?'

'Not if it means you spend the rest of your life living in regret. I think you're right to go back and me and Joe will be with you. Anyway, I think it would be nice to have the baby in Idaho, don't you?'

I felt so relieved to hear those words. The thought of the baby excited me and with the news we did not plan to stop, I felt annoyed with myself for thinking that Joe and Ella would abandon me. 'How long before the baby is born do you need to stop traveling?'

'Is there a good doctor in Sitwell?'

I nodded. 'Doc Jenner. He's helped more babies be born than I've had hot food. He helped me into this world. He's a kind man. If folk can't pay his bill, the charge vanishes. He'll look after you and the baby.'

She smiled. 'Well, that sounds great. It'll be something you and your brother or sister will have in common, won't it? And in answer to your question, I've never had a baby before, but I guess it would best to be there by late April or early May.'

I thought of home but for the first time I did not straight away think of Jeremiah. I said, 'The weather will be okay then.'

'What about Jeremiah? You haven't mentioned him so much recently.'

'I think about him and I miss him and I'm looking forward to seeing him again—'

'But?'

I shrugged. 'But a lot has happened since I left. Lots to think about.'

'Just remember to do what is right for you, okay?'

As we made our way back to Edward's house, I felt a load lifting. I was fine with spending time here so long as I knew we could leave. I was looking forward to my new job and meeting Melissa and Sophia. But most of all, I was looking forward to having lots of hot baths and sleeping naked in that comfortable bed in a room of my own.

(46)

— Joe —

fter almost five decades, the moment had come. I sat in the parlor, my heart thumping as I tried to think about what to say. What do you say after all those years? Were we even the same people? It was true she had never married. So, was she expecting me to come back and be with her? I felt sick, full of misgiving and it was all I could do not to run off, hit the railroad and keep going. But no, those days were gone. I heard the car arrive. Then the door. Then she was there. I stood like a boy on his first date. She looked fabulous. For a moment, we stood regarding one another like you might a beguiling sculpture in a museum. She seemed transfixed. I gave her my best smile. 'Hey, you.'

She stared. 'Oh, my God. It really is you.'

And that was it. She came over and took me in her arms and cried as she held me. I hugged her tight, and we stayed like that for what seemed an eternity, our tears flooding away the unspeakable emotion. At last, still embracing, she whispered, 'I'm so sorry, Joe. How am I ever going to make this up to you?'

Her words stunned me, and I pulled away and looked into her wet, sapphire eyes. 'What do you mean? It's me that's got the making up to do.'

We sat next to one another and poured out our stories. I wanted to know about Sophia. Melissa had brought photos, and we pored over them and I saw her growing, each pivotal moment captured in elegant studio portraits. I traced my finger over Sophia's beautiful, innocent face; It was the hardest and most poignant experience of my life, and it made us both weep and laugh as we shared the life of our child I had missed. I think the pain of it was our penance, and like some eternal confession, afterward we felt better.

'She's dying to meet you.'

'Likewise. I just hope she's forgiven me.'

Melissa placed her hand on my cheek. 'She never wanted for anything and she grew up knowing you had no choice. We've all suffered, and that was not our fault. I sent two investigators to find you. I couldn't understand how you had disappeared and in the end, we assumed you had died. Maybe that made it easier on us. We grieved your loss and made the best of things. Florence became a rock, and she gave so much love to Sophia. Florence's children became Sophia's siblings, and it was enough to fill the void you left. She grew up loved and happy.'

'And you? What about you? Why did you never marry?'

'No one was like you, Joe. But it's hard to explain.' She sighed and smiled. 'But look at us. Florence always said you would come back; I should have had her faith.'

'Are you okay I did? I feel maybe it's kinda selfish, and—'

'No! No, Joe, it draws a line in the sand. Just knowing you are alive changes everything for me. It means my father lost. It's over now.'

'I guess we can't change the past.'

'No, we can't, but the past can't hurt us now, do you see?'

I nodded. 'Sure. I guess.'

We hugged again. She said, 'Now, we have to forgive ourselves and one another. Can you do that, Joe?'

'I'm working on it, leastways the forgiving me part.'

She beamed and looked into my eyes. 'Me too.' She took a delicate hanky from her bag and wiped her eyes. 'Now, Sophia is here.'

'She's here, now?'

'Yes. The last time you saw her, she was just a few months old. She's with Edward, I'll go get her.'

Despite the photographs, I was ill prepared for the emotional impact of meeting her again. She was so beautiful. I saw flashes of my mother and sister, but she had all the elegance and beauty of her mother. After the briefest hesitation, she came over and threw her arms around me, and I held her tight. 'Is it really you, papa? You've come back to me.'

I did not think I had any tears left, but the water flowed and we held one another for the longest time. At last I felt able to speak. 'Sorry, so sorry I wasn't there to see you grow up. Can you ever forgive me?'

It was a while before she could answer. She stroked my face, and for a long time, looked at me. 'You're so handsome and strong.' She locked eyes with me. 'There's nothing to forgive, nothing at all. Thank you for coming back from the dead. It means the world to me, and mama.'

We could say little else. There were no words to describe the emotion.

Melissa and Edward joined us, and we took coffee and chatted, the room filled with a myriad of memories that sent us on a sentimental rollercoaster. I told how meeting Heidi had unleashed my past. We did not discuss the future. Rather, there was an unspoken acknowledgement we could never go back and be together, not like that, anyway. It was as Melissa said; we had drawn a line in the sand and all the suffering, madness, and pain must end in mutual forgiveness. I knew it would take time to forgive myself, but Ella, Heidi, and the new baby granted me a second chance, while being allowed to connect with my old life, like having two slices of pie with whipped cream and a goddamn cherry on top! I could not have asked for anything more, and it humbled me.

After they had gone, Edward took me to meet Joe Junior and Catherine. It was a less emotionally supercharged meeting, and mostly free of guilt. They were delightful, and it took my breath away how much Catherine looked like Florence; it was as though she were reborn to me, and I gave thanks that I had come back. We arranged for a big family reunion to take place the following Sunday and it excited me to meet Florence's grandkids.

As we drove back to Edward's house, the day's reunions filled me with joy and sadness, but more than anything it made me understand how important to me were Ella and Heidi, and I longed to hug them, because they were mine and I was theirs and I'd let nothing put us apart.

47

— Heidi —

Joe and Edward came back mid-afternoon. The weather had turned colder and light rain fell from leaden skies. I was up in my room, laid out on my bed, reading. I had the window open a little and could smell that wet earthiness that you get when it hasn't rained for a time. I love that smell. I heard the front door close and low voices. I rested the book on my chest and tried to gauge the tone. It sounded upbeat, so I popped my leather bookmark between the pages, set the volume down, and went on downstairs, eager to find out how Joe's day had gone.

They were in the parlor. When I appeared in the doorway, Joe got up, came over, and gave me a big hug. 'Hey, sweetheart, I've missed you. Hear you got a job.'

He took my hand and sat me down on the sofa next to him. I skipped through the details of my day, for I was eager to interrogate him. 'So, don't keep me in suspense. How's it gone for you?'

He gave me chapter and verse. The day had changed him somehow, like he had shed layers of armor. He seemed more vulnerable and kept telling me how important Ella and I were to him, and he'd never let us down. It moved me to see him so, and I knew it was our destiny to meet and everything that had happened had led to this moment. I had feared meeting Melissa would set him apart from us, but the opposite had occurred. It gave me pause and made me see my fate in a new light.

That evening, we climbed into Edward's automobile. I had never been inside one before. It smelled of leather. The doors clunked shut and when the engine fired up the inside seemed to come to life. We set off, and it felt like we were traveling at such speed, even more so than on the back of Mr. Hikomori's truck.

It was comfortable and I could see why folk that could afford it would want to travel this way.

I was ill prepared for the sight of Melissa's house. If Edward's had seemed opulent, this was on another scale. A solemn man dressed in a dark suit answered the door. He took our coats and ushered us into a vast room furnished and decorated in such finery that it made me gasp, but the object that most caught my eye was the piano. Even in this substantial room, it was dominant, but looked so elegant. It was shiny, jet black, with the name on the side, Steinway and Sons, picked out in gold. It so distracted me, I had not at first noticed the people in the room. When I did, I hung back. There were two ladies and a man, all dressed up. Both the ladies were blond-haired and blue eyed. I guessed they were Melissa and Sophia. They could have been sisters rather than mother and daughter. The man was tall, slim and had dark hair that was graying in places. He was well-groomed and dressed in a fine suit of clothes with shoes polished to a high gloss. I realized they all looked at me. I took a deep breath and Melissa smiled. 'And you must be Heidi. I'm Melissa.' She kissed my cheeks. She smelled floral and of something slightly spicy. Her elegance beguiled me. Sophia had everything her mother did, but with a little Joe thrown in. She was taller, darker skinned and had such nobility about her it made me feel plain. She took my hands, looked into my eyes, and whispered, 'And we have you to thank for bringing my papa back to us.'

This shocked me. I blushed. 'Oh—well—I, I don't know about all that.'

She led me to an opulent sofa. 'Now, don't be modest and come and sit by me. After all, we're sisters, aren't we?' She had Joe's heart, too. It was odd. We looked alike, and I could see why it jolted Joe to think of them when first we met.

The meal matched the house. The suited man, who had opened the door, served delicious food prepared by an unseen cook. I wondered what it was like to be a servant in such a grand house. I tried to imagine Joe playing host in such a setting, but I could not make him fit. I let the conversation flow about me, absorbing details of family and how they were all eager to meet us. Joe told them the full story of his expulsion and his rescue by Tetinchoua. Even in its retelling, it made stark listening. He gave me more credit than I was due for making him realize he had to come back and make his peace. We glossed over my story. It made me uncomfortable to veil myself in dishonesty, but in the most part, it was the truth, and it was hardly the time to declare my murderous act. They told me how brave I was and how glad they were to have me as part of their family. The conversation drifted to when Ella and Joe might marry, of my formal adoption—something of which I had not considered—and what they were going to call the baby. When they asked me whether I wanted a brother, or a sister, I said I was happy with either that I had always wanted a sibling and I had given no thought to names.

After, we returned to the room with the piano. Like at Edward's, illicit cognac appeared. I declined the booze but accepted the coffee, which was served with the most delicious chocolates imported from Belgium, a place in Europe that I'd heard about in connection with the Great War. There was a brief debate about whether the best chocolate came from there or Switzerland. I told them I knew about Switzerland from my Heidi book. That led to a lengthy discussion about books and it delighted me to discuss "Jane Eyre", which both Sophia and Melissa had read and loved.

During a lull, I plucked up the courage to ask about the piano. Both Melissa and Sophia played, though Melissa insisted Sophia was the better pianist, and it took little encouragement to persuade her to play. She lifted the top, revealing the fascinating interior that looked like a giant, golden, metal harp lying flat, and in raised letters on the front rail were the words Steinway and *Capo D'astro*. As she played, I could see the mesmerizing mechanics of it. The sound was rich and filled every particle of the room and I could feel the ringing vibrations throughout my body and I fell in love with it. Her fingers glided across the white and black keys while inside felted hammers raised up to strike each string. It was magical, and I so wanted to play like that.

When she finished, I asked if I might have a go. She tapped the seat. I smiled and sat beside her, my eyes feasting on the keys. There were so many. It surprised me how they felt when I pushed them. Depending on how hard you pressed related to the volume of the note. They felt exciting to the touch, weighty, yet sensually warm, and smooth, like they were alive. The others went and sat back down. Sophia showed me how to play the "Star-Spangled Banner" with my right hand and when I had got it, we played together; me picking out the tune while she added the chords. It sounded grand, and it made me grin and giggle. She said, 'You're a natural. You should learn how to play.'

'But we don't have a piano and—'

'Come here and I'll get you started. Edward has a piano at home, don't you Edward?'

'Yes, we do. It's in a room you haven't seen yet. It would be heaven to have it played again.'

'Who played it?'

'Well, Florence played and all the children, though only Catherine kept it up.'

So, we agreed I was to come over and play after I finished work at the bookstore every day. It filled me with determination, excited to have this rare opportunity.

That night I did not sleep well. I had music in my head and thoughts of my first day at the store. It did not stop me from jumping out of bed and a little before 8 a.m. I was at the bookstore.

48

— Heidi —

I was about to knock when a calling voice halted my poised hand. 'Wait, Heidi, wait! I must speak with you.'

I looked round. It was the girl from the clothes shop. 'Hello, what are you doing here?'

She pulled me to one side, a harried expression on her tired face, anxious eyes, pleading. 'Please, don't go in, leastways not until you hear me out. Oh heavens, I should have said something yesterday. I haven't slept a wink, you see?'

'I'll be late. What's so urgent?'

She caught her breath, and facing me, placed her hands on my shoulders, her eyes locked on mine. 'Please, just come with me for a coffee and I'll explain. I promise you'll thank me.' She lowered her voice. 'You're in grave danger, you see?'

A minute later, we sat in a booth at a nearby restaurant. We ordered. I said, 'Has this something to do with what you said about being careful?'

She nodded, bit her lower lip and took a deep breath. She picked up a napkin and began twiddling the cloth in her hands. 'I worked at the bookstore. At first it was okay. Then he got more familiar with me. One day, I was in the little restroom at the back when he came in. He told me he'd seen how I looked at him, and if I did what he wanted, he'd give me a little extra on my wage every week. At first I didn't get what he meant, so he spelled out for me and his suggestion disgusted and horrified me and I told him I wasn't interested, at which his expression changed, he got furious and the next thing I knew he pinned me to the wall—'

She stopped a moment, screwing her eyes shut. Fat tears rolled down her flushed cheeks. She scrunched tight the napkin in her hands, turning her knuckles white.

I reached out, took her hands and pushed the creased napkin to one side. 'Go on.'

She nodded, looked straight at me and whispered, 'He raped me.'

I shut my eyes and shuddered. For a moment, we didn't speak. I squeezed her hands. My heart was in my mouth. 'Oh, my goodness, I'm so sorry.' I realized I didn't know her name. 'What's your name?'

'Oh, sure. I'm Adelaid.'

'Adelaid, what happened then?'

'It seemed to go on for ages. Then, when he was done with his hateful business, he got up, pulled his trousers on, and took the envelope with my wages and threw it at me. He told me to clean myself up and go home and be back the next day for work as usual. He said it would be our little secret, and he knew I'd enjoyed it, really. I felt sick. As soon as he was gone, I sorted myself out and left. Needless to say, I never went back.'

I rubbed my thumbs on the back of her hands. 'Didn't you report him?' She shook her head. 'You told no one?'

'Only you know. Two days after, he came to my house and said that if I told, it would be my word against his. His exact phrase was: "No one will believe a little shop-girl slut like you against a respected business owner and treasurer of the church. Say one word and everyone will know you are a lying whore, and I'll say you stole from me, too." It made me doubt myself that maybe I had led him on somehow. But that was that. I put it behind me and moved on, only I haven't, really. When I met you and you told me you were going there, it all came back. I'm sorry I didn't tell you straight off.'

'No, I get it. It doesn't matter. You've told me now and that took such courage. I understand how it feels.' Her story brought back my two close calls and how lucky I'd been to have someone there to rescue me. I struggled to imagine how horrific it must have been for her. I told her about my encounters and said I knew how terrifying it was and that she did nothing to encourage him.

She took the napkin and dabbed her eyes.

'The nameless rider that saved me at the river told me to poke a finger in my attacker's eye and then kick or knee him in between his legs. And then run.'

'I wish I'd known that, though he was so fast and strong, I'm not sure I'd have been able to.' She dried her eyes. 'What will you do now?'

'Well, I'm going to the bookstore to tell him I won't be working there.'

Her eyes widened. 'What will you say when he asks why?'

I tapped my nose. 'Just I got a better offer, that's all. You saved me. I'd never put you in danger.'

Our coffees had gone cold, so we ordered fresh and chatted a while. I told her my story. It felt purgative to tell it to a stranger and I think all I had been through helped her feel less alone with her trauma. 'Listen,' I said, 'I'm here for a bit and I have got no friends, so maybe we can spend a little time together. What do you say?'

She smiled. 'I'd like that. This last year has been so lonesome.'

I nodded. 'I understand that. Hey, do you like the movies?'

'I love the movies. There's a comedy drama playing tonight at the pit.'

'The pit?'

She laughed. 'It's what us kids call the local movie theater. Do you fancy it?'

'Do bees love honey? How about I meet you there? What time and where is it?'

It was well gone 9 a.m. by the time I arrived at the bookstore. Timothy Spaar was sitting feathers when I told him I had changed my mind, and showed his true colors, saying: "Little bitches like you don't know their own silly little minds." And I gave thanks that Adelaid had told me and the thought of what he might have done filled me with dread. More than anything, I wanted justice for her, and wondered whether Joe Junior might help.

The following Sunday, we met the entire tribe. It was enjoyable but somewhat overwhelming. The kids found me fascinating, which I did not understand. They crowded round, asking loads of questions. One told me how much I looked like Sophia and was I sure we were not related. After a bit, the novelty wore off, and they dragged me away to play and it seemed like they accepted me.

It was after tea, and needing a little head space, that I found Joe Junior sitting chatting with his sister, Catherine, in the parlor. Everyone else was outside playing. It thrilled Joe and Ella being with the youngsters, all of whom wanted to play with their long-lost great uncle and his captivating wife, while grandpa Edward seemed to shed away the years chasing around the yard after the younger ones.

I stopped in the doorway, and Joe Junior glanced over. 'Heidi, come on in and join us.'

I Liked him as soon as we'd met. Catherine, too, was a product of her upbringing. They were people you could trust. I asked about their mother and found out how much she had missed her brother, but had compensated for that loss by showering Edward and her children with love and security. Catherine said, 'We haven't really got over losing her yet. I don't suppose we ever shall.'

Joe Junior nodded, adding, 'But then, Uncle Joe, you and Ella have come into our lives. Life goes on, doesn't it?' He exuded confidence and warmth.

Catherine said, 'We'd love to know more about you, Heidi.'

I thought about it and sighed. 'It's a long story, and it isn't pretty. I did a terrible thing. It's why I must go back to Idaho.' I paused. Joe Junior and Catherine glanced at one another. I looked at them and knew I didn't want to lie anymore. I wanted them to know me, warts and all. I took a deep breath and jumped in. 'I have to go back home and hand myself over to the police—'

Joe frowned and held up his hand. 'Just hang fire one minute, Heidi. Are you saying you may have committed a crime?'

I nodded. 'I—'

'Don't say another word. Have you got a dollar?'

I frowned. 'A dollar? Why?'

'Just trust me. Have you got a dollar?'

'Yes, in my room.'

'Get it, will you, please? We'll wait here.'

Intrigued, I went and fetched the money as requested, and handed it to him. 'Here. One shiny new dollar.'

He took it and slipped it into his pocket. 'Well Heidi, now you have a lawyer. By giving me that money you have retained my services, so anything you tell me now is confidential and protected under attorney-client privilege.' He grinned. 'Catherine has to leave now, don't you, sis?'

I had no idea what he meant.

Catherine patted my knee. 'Don't worry, Heidi. He'll look after you. He's the best, trust him.' She left, closing the door behind her.

Now alone, Joe sat opposite me. He leaned forward as though to share a secret. 'Now, Heidi, no stone unturned or detail left out. Tell me everything.'

I did. When I finished, I felt wrung out but relieved. With each telling, it got easier, and I began to understand that what I did had been out of my control. He made a steeple with his hands and placed them in front of his lips, thinking. Then he smiled to himself. 'First, I am deeply sorry for what happened. It's a profound and painful story and not one you should have endured. I'm overjoyed you met Uncle Joe and ended up here. Second, I promise you'll never see the inside of a jail cell, leastways not long term.'

My heart skipped a beat. 'Really?'

His face hardened and his eyes grew darker. 'Yes, really. You acted in self defense, and your father had a long history of abusing you. I doubt the police or the state attorney will prosecute. If they do, I will defend you with every breath in my body, and we will win, no question. It's what I do. Going back and putting this business to rest is vital. If, and I doubt it shall happen, they charge you, then you call to me and I will execute my duty of care to you. Do you trust me?'

I nodded. 'Of course. Thanks, Joe.'

He smiled at me, his sharp eyes focused. 'I like you, Heidi Schlager, and I see why my uncle took you under his wing.'

'I don't know the correct etiquette, but is it permitted to hug your lawyer?'

His face softened, his eyes lost their brooding hue, and he laughed out loud. 'In your case, Miss Schlager, it would be my privilege and honor.'

We hugged. 'You do talk funny.'

He waved his hand in the air as though swatting an imaginary fly. 'It's a lawyer thing.'

For a while, we sat in silence as I absorbed what had just happened. I remembered Adelaid. 'Can I ask you a question, Joe?'

'Sure, shoot.'

I told him Adelaid's story. It troubled him. He knew Timothy Spaar, and it shocked him to hear what he'd done.

'Is there anything you can do for her, Joe?'

'Does she know you're asking me?'

I shook my head. 'I want to get justice for her, and I think maybe he had the same in mind for me, and if so, I wondered has he done this before? Are there others living in fear of him?'

Joe Junior sat back, frowning, the dark pall once again filling his eyes. 'You're right. I can't ignore this. Let's meet with her and see what can be done, shall we?'

— Ella —

The three months we spent in Lagonda were memorable and cemented the family. Heidi and Adelaid became friends, and Joe Junior went to work on her case. In the end, he found four other girls who'd suffered the same fate. For a time Heidi struggled, knowing what Spaar had planned for her. Like the events in Sioux Falls and at the ranch, it set her back and some nights I slept with her when she was low. She called them her black dog days. When Joe Junior presented his evidence to the police, they arrested and charged Spaar. Confronted with a line of witnesses and the reputation of Joe Hamel, Spaar saw the hopelessness of his situation. Facing disgrace and ruin, he hanged himself in his cell. At least that is what the official report said. A rumor flew round town one victim's father had paid a guard to kill Spaar. Either way, it released the girls from having to relive their horrible ordeal in court.

A few days after Spaar died, several boys from the church came forward to say they, too, had been victims of his abuse, leading Heidi to comment, 'When these things happen, we must learn to speak up. For years, I pretended that what my pa did was okay. If I'd had the courage to stand up to him, he'd never put me in the position to kill him. Despite everything, I don't think I'll ever truly forgive myself for that..

At least once a week, Adelaid stayed over and it always gave me joy to see Heidi come alive when she was with her. I could hear them talking and giggling late into the night. Melissa gave Adelaid a job working in her office as a trainee assistant and Heidi went to work in Joe's law firm. He commented on how smart she was and she'd make a brilliant lawyer, though I thought she'd be a wonderful teacher. She took to the piano like a duck to water, and it bonded her and Sophia. Regularly, Heidi stayed at her house looking after the kids, a role she relished.

One day, I was taking a rest in my room when there was a tap on the door and Heidi appeared. 'Come on in, sweetheart.' She climbed on the bed and we cuddled. She liked to feel my bump and the baby kicking. She said, 'I can't wait for him to be born.'

'Him? What makes you think it will be a boy?'

She giggled. 'I don't know, really. I just think it. Plus, you said how much he kicks and keeps you awake. Only a boy would do that.' I laughed with her. We lay there for a while. We'd all come a long way in such a short time. Glancing over, I noticed she was crying. 'Sweetheart, what's up?'

She shook her head. 'Nothing, really. I was thinking about Mayumi and Carmel and how much I love it there, but now we have so much family here, and then there's Sitwell where I'm from and where Jeremiah is. I'm confused. I don't know where I belong or where I should be.'

'What does your heart tell you? You know, if you had to choose between those three places.'

She sighed. 'I love being here with the family, but I don't like the town. I feel like too much bad has happened here. I love Adelaid, but not like I do Mayumi, Betty or Jeremiah. Truth is, I'm confused about who I want to be with and for what reasons. But as far as places to live, I'd love to go back to Carmel. We can always come here to visit and even if Jeremiah can't or won't come with me, we can still be friends, can't we?'

'You know what I think?'

'Uh-uh.'

'I think when the time comes, you'll know. Until then you must look after yourself and you have me and Joe and—' she tapped her belly, 'this little fella, too. You're still young and you don't have to decide anything in a hurry.'

'What about you and Joe? Where do you want to be?'

'We like Carmel, too. But right now, we should take it one day and one bridge at a time.'

'That's what sister Catherine said.'

'Well, it's good advice and I swear by it. Look at how patient Joe and I have been, but we got there in the end, didn't we?' I stroked her cheek. 'Thanks to you.'

She laughed. 'Holy smoke, I hope I don't have to wait that long to know what I want.'

'I doubt that. You have the advantage of knowing there are choices and you have us and we love each other.'

We fell asleep together. I treasured those moments when she confided in me and let herself be a child and I mothered her. It was still emotional for me and I too couldn't wait for the baby to come because I knew it would bond us tighter and force Joe's hand to settle. We didn't tell Heidi about the land in Carmel because I did not want to influence her decision.

Heidi continued to send and receive letters from Betty and Mayumi. Most she read out to us. In particular, Betty's letters were priceless, full of amusing stories, and she wrote so well. I think Heidi loved how Betty made her feel as in every letter she said how much she missed Heidi and counted the days until they would see one another. It made her feel warm to have the younger girl hold a torch for her and I think she thought of her as a sister. Whereas with Mayumi I sensed a deeper attraction as strong if not stronger than that she had with Jeremiah, and I wondered who'd win the battle for her affection. Heidi did not talk about Jeremiah as much as she had, though I knew she still loved him. He'd sent her a self-portrait—the boy had talent—and she had it next to her bed and she wrote to him, too. He wasn't so good at writing back, but then one day in mid-March she got a letter from him that shocked her. She brought it down to breakfast and read it out.

'Howdy Fizz,
Im dead sorry I have written little. Well you know writing aint my thing. I count the days until your home and I can see you. I miss you so much. I dunno how to say this so Ill just blurt it right on out. They have declared you dead. All ofishul like. They held a memorial service an all for you which was kinda creepy. Most of the town folk went. It was darn difficult being there nowing you are alive and well. It killed me to see my ma and pa, Miss Hannah and Mr Garity and others crying for you. Truth is I cried like a baby also and I thought Id breakdown and confess but knowing you are back soon has kept me grounded and trufuly I am scared what they will do to me when they find out Ive been lying all this time. Corse I dont blame you none of this is our fult. I just want you to come home so we can sort it out. Im all good, so dont fret. They have done nothing with your house. They boarded it up but I gone snuck in and just in case sneeked out your keepsake box. It is safe for

when you come home. This darn kills me but I
promise I have not read your secret diery.
I have to confess sumthing to you and it has been the
darndest hardest thing keeping our secret alone and I had
to tell someone. I told Abigail. She promises on her life not
to tell and I trust her. It helped me share my burdon and
she says to send her love to you. I hope you understand
and forgive me. When you come back, there will be one
hell of a crap storm for shure. You must not worry as I
will make shure I am there for you and will be ready like
you to take whatever comes to us. I dont think neither of us
deserves to be punished cause being apart from you has
been plenty punishment. I feel like I have lost you and I hope
we can put all of this behind us and pick up our lives again.
Come back soon and I look forward to meeting Joe and Ella.
Loads and loads and loads of loving
from your only rolldog. J xxx
Oh I almost forgot. It is the bees the baby will be born
here. You'll be one humdinger of a big sis!!!"

She folded the letter and set it on the table. It stunned us to hear that they had declared her dead. She looked crushed. Then she said, 'I can't believe they all came to my memorial service. And why do they think I'm dead? They can't have found my body! It makes little sense, does it?'

Joe said, 'Maybe they feel, after all this time, they need to move on. You know, what with those other murdered girls, I can see why they figure you're another victim. After all, it was kinda what Jeremiah told them. But there isn't much we can do right now. When we go back, it'll get straightened out, don't you worry. At the very least, we'll put that lovely boy of yours out of his misery, won't we? He is quite something, and I can see why you think so much of him.'

'It feels weird being dead. I mean, if I don't go back, it doesn't matter now, does it?'

I said, 'It will to Jeremiah and all those people that love you. Plus, I don't think you'll find peace if you leave it like that, will you?'

She nodded. 'I know that. It just seems like they gave up on me, is all.'

For a few days, the news subdued her. She spent the night over at Sophia's house and then had Adelaid over, as though she didn't want to be alone. She made jokes about being a ghost and going back to haunt Sitwell for giving up on her. After a few days, she seemed better, and a night at the movies and a meal out found her back on an even keel. It made me appreciate I'd have to watch her closely, for I feared it would not take much for her to plunge into despair, and it was for this reason I so wanted to return to Idaho and draw a line under this miserable business.

Bit-by-bit Joe came to terms with the loss of his sister and relaxed into his role among his wonderful family. Being Joe, he was never idle, and it did not take him long to find work at a local wood shop run by a man with whom he had gone to school. He remembered the events that led to Joe's exile and it delighted him to see Joe back and the two resumed their friendship.

And me? With forbearance, I watched things and took it easy as the baby grew and I considered my past. Sophia's husband, Thomas, looked after my medical needs and it was nice to have time to take stock. I tended Edward's garden and helped Mrs. Ellwood, though mostly she resisted all my attempts to ease her work.

I guess had things been different, we might have stopped here and made roots, but the day came to leave. The farewells were long and difficult. In particular, Adelaid was distraught at losing Heidi, which shocked her, but Melissa promised to keep an eye out and Heidi added another girlfriend to her unstinting letter-writing circle.

We paid passage back to Bonners Ferry. As we came to the sharp bend where all those months back Joe had hopped on that boxcar and found a frightened, starving girl, he gave her nudge and put his arm around her and the two stared out of the window as we tracked along the southern bank of the Kootenay River. We hopped a ride to Sitwell, and I wondered after all the years whether this might be our last hobo adventure. The journey was somber. Although Heidi knew Joe Junior had her back, the idea of confessing and facing the unknown filled her with dark apprehension.

part
six

— Heidi —

We hopped off the freight to be greeted by a dazzling, full moon bathing everything in an ethereal, chromium glow that lit our way. Though it felt outlandish to walk this well-trod road once more, it was as if I had been away for years, not months. The house looked much as I had left it, though the land looked neglected and the vegetable patch I tended was in ruins. It did not take long for Joe to get the front door open and the three of us entered the melancholy interior. Just like Jeremiah said in his letter, they had boarded up the windows, and the gaps between the planks caused sharp slashes of silver moonlight to fill the gloomy, musty interior. I went over to the old dresser, found some candles and we had light.

We stood in the forlorn space.

I sighed. 'Well, this is it.'

Ella and Joe looked around. She said, 'This will do just fine, soon have it spick-n-span, won't we?'

Joe smiled. 'Luxury.'

I pointed. 'The room out back is the bedroom and I sleep up there.'

Joe turned to me, his eyes somber. 'Are you sure you're okay being here, you know—'

'Where else shall we go? It's fine, don't worry.'

There was a dark stain on the floor where pa had been bent over Jeremiah. I closed my eyes, steeling myself. It was time to put back some happy memories into this old house. I climbed the ladder to my space. It looked small. I unrolled the bedding, sat down, and took a moment.

It was time to look destiny right in the eye.

I went on back down. Joe and Ella were sorting out stuff in the bedroom. I popped my head around the door. 'I'd better get going.'

Joe looked at me, regarding me with uneasy eyes. 'You sure you don't want me to come with?'

'Sure. I got to do this on my own. If Chief Banyard locks me up, I'll ask him to come tell you.'

'Okay. You got this. Justice will serve.'

We hugged, and they wished me luck and I went out into the moonlight and made my way to Ted Banyard's house and thirty minutes later I was at his door. The lights were on.

The truth will set you free. Just knock and tell it like it was.

My heart was in my mouth. I took a deep breath and knocked.

I heard movement then the door opened, spilling a sharp rectangle of warm, yellow light onto the stoop. Ted was about to speak, but froze. His jaw dropped. His eyes like saucers. He stared. Transfixed.

I lifted my hand. 'Hey, Chief.'

The color had drained from his face. He blew out his cheeks. 'Heidi? Well heaven be praised, Heidi Schlager is alive and well—or, are you a ghost come back to haunt me for failing?'

'No, I'm real alright. Sorry it's late. May I come in? I've got stuff I need to tell you.'

He nodded and stood to one side, ushering me in. Before closing the door, he peered into the dark. With the door shut, we stood in the cozy interior. 'Now, let me take a proper look at ya, Heidi.' He stepped back and puffed out his cheeks once more. 'You look so well and I know it's a cliché and all, but you've got bigger, almost a woman. I can not tell you how happy I am to see you. Come, come sit down.'

He fixed us some coffee and sat opposite me. With my heart thumping, I tapped my fingers on the table. He looked at me with his kind, smiling eyes. 'So—I guess I'll just get right to it. It hasn't been easy coming back, and a lot has happened—but, where to start?'

'I've nowhere else to be, Heidi, so you take your time and start at the beginning.'

I fixed a spot on the table and began. I told him everything that had happened from the time by the creek Jeremiah and I had plotted to get me away, to my coming back and knocking on his door. By the time I finished, our untouched coffee had gone stone cold.

He made some fresh and sat back down. 'Oh brother, Heidi, that is some story. I mean, you are something, my girl.'

'I'm ready to face up to what I did. Only if you lock me up, please tell Joe and Ella. They're back up at my house. I hope it's okay for them to be there, you know, seeing as she's having a baby soon. Oh, and Joe, my lawyer, said you would allow me a phone call and to call him and—'

Ted held up his hands, shook his head, and sat back. 'And why would I be wanting to lock up you, of all people, Heidi?'

I frowned. 'Well, because I stuck a knife in my pa and killed him. Then I skipped town and ran.'

He folded his arms. His eyes had a faraway look. 'Oh—that—yes, of course.' He leaned forward and fixed my gaze. 'Thing is, Heidi, that case is closed.'

'Closed, why?'

He gave me a knowing smile and took a sip of his coffee. 'The fella that killed five girls just over the state line got caught abducting another near to here. He told us he killed your pa and took you. He said you're buried somewhere up in the wilderness, and we'd never find ya. He gave an excellent description of you. When they searched his house in Lamb Creek, they found a missing person poster that Jeremiah and Abigail had put up. We assumed it was like a trophy, but I guess it accounts for how he knew what you looked like.'

'Jeremiah and Abigail put up posters for me?'

Ted leaned back and chuckled. 'That boy loves you. He drew your likeness, looked exactly like you. He's been making a name for himself, doing portraits of folk. I believe he used some of the money he earned to pay for the posters. Abigail's father drove them all over the county, putting them up.'

I shook my head. 'Holy smoke, I guess he never gave up on me. So, everyone thinks I'm dead, right?'

'They do.'

'I don't get why that man would say he killed me and how did he know my pa was dead?'

'At first, he just confessed to you, but when we asked him about your pa, he said he'd done that, too. I asked him how he did it and he said, and I quote, "I stuck him good, like a pig." A lucky guess, don't you think? Or was it? Anyway, he went on to tell me in sickening detail what he did to you before killing you.'

I swallowed and nodded once, trying to take it all in.

Ted smiled. 'Guess you must have got away from him and he was lying. I'd say you had a lucky escape, don't you?'

'But no. No, that's not what happened. I did it and Jeremiah—' I remembered it wasn't just me that might be in trouble.

Ted held up his hands again. 'You know, just after it happened, I reckoned it went down the way you said it did. Only Jeremiah was adamant that this man had killed your pa and taken you. So what with the two girls that he took and murdered previous and then more of them turning up after. I thought I was wrong and should have trusted Jeremiah. Now you come here and tell me I was right and Jeremiah was lying, which means our killer is lying as well.'

I didn't speak. I felt like I was digging a hole for myself and Jeremiah. But I needed the truth to come out.

Ted smiled again. 'However, like I said, the case is closed and I think that's how it should stay, don't you? Hell of a fuss and paperwork to backtrack now. And besides, our man abducted, molested, and killed five innocent little girls, and he'll die for it. Makes no difference if he takes the rap for your pa, and seeing what he told me he would have done to you, it seems like justice has served.'

The silence hung thick. I thought about it. I looked at him with wide eyes. 'But what about the truth?'

He poured another coffee. 'I like the story I've got. I don't like your truth. No one else will neither.'

'Oh, really? I don't understand. Are you saying you'll never arrest and prosecute me?'

'Well, not for killing your pa. Can't say ever as I don't know what you're going to do in the future, though I'm willing to bet you're a model citizen, aren't you, Heidi Schlager?'

I felt dizzy. This was not going as I had thought it would. 'No court or jail time?'

He leaned forward and put his warm hand on mine. He smiled. 'I think you've done enough time, don't you?'

I swallowed again and nodded. 'That's it then, all over?'

His eyes glimmered, and he patted my hand. 'Of course folk will want to know how you got away and why you didn't come back straight off. My advice is to keep it simple and near to the truth as is possible. And never, ever, tell anyone else what really happened, you hear? Forget about it.'

'Are you sure about this, Chief?'

'It's all in the past. Apart from me, not one person came to your pa's funeral. No one is asking questions and everyone thought he got what he deserved. We all knew he was mistreating you and I have a niggling feeling he had something to do with your ma's death. Truth is, there was an unbroken line of folk would have stuck that knife in, me included. So, I'm sure, and Amen!'

'You're right about my ma. He gave her a good kicking the day before she fell ill. I'm sure that's what killed her.'

He frowned, his eyes darkening, and he looked down. 'See, I told you I failed you. And her. Dammit. Truth is, I was a little in love with your ma. She was the sweetest, kindest woman and she loved you and I'll regret to the end of my days that I didn't work harder to give her justice. Where I'm standing, I reckon it was you that delivered her that justice. I'm just sorry it took so long. Can you forgive me?'

He almost had tears in his eyes and, for the first time, I saw what I had done from a different perspective. 'You were in love with her?'

He nodded. 'After she died, I kicked myself for not trying—you know, to let her know how I felt. But I guess what with me being older, I felt foolish. Then she was gone. I should have done more for you. If I had, you'd never have killed him. So, I'm as much to blame as you are, aren't I?'

I stared at him. My mind reeling. 'I guess things would be easy if we could see what's coming, but that isn't how it is. So it's okay Chief, she would have been the first to forgive you and, for what it's worth, I forgive you with all my heart. You're a good man, Ted Banyard, and the town is lucky to have you.'

I got up, went round the table, and hugged him. 'Thank you. You've given me my life back. Ma would thank you too.'

He held me for a bit. He said, 'You didn't deserve all that pain.' We broke away, and he looked at me with that kinda proud look a parent has for a child. 'Now I know you're okay, life is better, and I'm beyond relieved you're home. Now, Heidi Schlager, you're all free to go and no looking back, eh? And the house is yours. I'll stop by to meet your new family.'

'Thanks Chief. You're always welcome.'

I turned and walked to the door. 'Before I go, I got to ask you. If that man hadn't said he killed my pa and the case was still open and you knew I'd done it, what would have happened tonight?'

He stood up. 'Does it matter?'

I shrugged. 'I guess not. Oh, please don't tell anyone I'm back, will ya?'

He shook his head and did a key-locking motion over his mouth. I opened the door. 'See ya around, Chief.' And I slipped out into the silvery night.

I ran back home. It felt like everything was so much lighter, and now I could get on with my life. I burst through the door. Joe had got the range going, they had tidied up and got the boards off the windows. Ella had some food warming, and the place felt different. You could feel the love that had been missing so long.

Joe stood. 'Hey, there you are. We were worried. You've been gone so long. But I get by your expression it went well?'

I was so excited I could hardly speak. They got me sat down and I told them what happened.

Ella's eyes were wide. 'So, you're free, and it's over. No court or—'

I held up my hands. 'That's it, all done.'

Joe puffed out his cheeks and sat down. 'Well hallelujah. Now it makes sense why they thought you were dead. Jeremiah didn't have the full story, did he? Wish I had a little of that cognac right now.'

'And the house is mine, I—I mean, ours.'

Joe let out a low whistle. 'Jeez, I've spent nearly fifty years homeless and scratching a living to put a few dollars away and since I met you—' words failed him.

I looked at him. It still gave me a jolt thinking of all the people I might have encountered on that boxcar it was him. 'The day I met you, Joe, I never felt so rich because I knew you were going to take care of me and that means more than any house or money. You're the richest man I know, Joe. All this stuff,' I gestured around the room with my hand, 'it only means something if you can share it with those you love. My pa had lost his love; he had nothing.'

You could feel the mood lift and, my appetite restored, we tucked into a hearty meal. Ella said, 'So when are you going to see that boy of yours? We're dying to meet him.'

I paused between mouthfuls. 'All of me wants to run over to his house, hammer on his door, wrap my arms around him and plant a big kiss on his stupid, gorgeous mouth. But see, I've got one cunning plan all worked out and I'm going to wait until morning. On the route he takes to school, there's a tree I can hide in and I'm gonna drop out of the sky scaring the beJesus out of him. Then I'm gonna go to school and come back from the grave. By the end of the day, all the tongues will have done their wagging and everyone will know I'm back and I won't have to tell the story over-and-over, will I?'

(51)

— Heidi —

I was good and early. I scooted up the tree and made myself comfortable. There was already a little warmth in the sun and a gentle breeze made the new leaves rustle. As I sat waiting, trying to make myself believe all the madness had never happened, that I'd seen him only yesterday, and we'd start over where we left off. Voices broke my daydreaming. I looked down the path, and he was there, unmistakable. My heart skipped a beat. He was taller and his voice deeper. He wasn't alone. They walked hand-in-hand, their arms swinging, a lightness in their step. They were laughing and smiling, a prattle of teenage talk bubbling about them. They looked good together, happy. As they neared the tree, I could hear the words: 'No, she didn't say that. She said she wanted to kiss him.' Jeremiah laughed: 'That's not what he said. He reckoned they did more than kiss.' Abigail giggled. They stopped almost under me and she pushed him against the tree and kissed him and he kissed her back like he meant it. It was so blatant I thought they'd seen me and were making a point. Shock flooded me. I thought I was going to pass out, but steadied myself. I watched them go and everything about their body language told me what I needed to know. I stayed where I was, incredulous, green-eyed, wounded, and bewildered. It was horrible to see him with someone else and so blissful, like I'd never existed.

After a time, I came down and speculated on what to do. Had I really come back to face up to killing pa or had I returned to claim back Jeremiah and take up where we'd left off, like nothing had happened? Was I that stupid? I needed thinking time, so I took off to the spot on the Deep Creek, where we had spent that last day before everything changed, and I gave myself a fine old talking to. I don't know how long I sat, my feet dangling in the cold water, as I unscrambled the muddy tangle in my head until I could see clear through to the other side.

And I sat there for a while, my head full of all those wholesome memories of us kids playing here. All those times me and Jeremiah had built a bond. If I closed my eyes, I could see us young cubs, naked as on the day we were born, charging along the banks, throwing ourselves in the water, fighting, pushing, ducking, the sound of laughter: exuberant, carefree moments. A lifetime of stuff. And I knew my time here was done. All those things that happened had been the road to this day and me sitting here alone. And it shocked me, knowing I felt at peace that this is how it was supposed to be.

— § —

The school room looked just the same. The door was open, and I could hear Miss Hannah's voice. It warmed my heart to hear her sweet tone and encouraging words. I walked up and stood in the doorway. She glanced my way and stopped dead and stared. Her hand went up to her mouth, her expression a mix of confusion, horror, and surprise. 'Oh my lord, it's Heidi!' She'd gone so pale I thought she was going to faint. At that moment, every kid turned around and stared at me, wide-eyed. No one spoke. I lifted my hand and waved. 'Hey. I'm back.'

One of the younger kids, Beth, burst into tears and, terrified, ran behind Miss Hannah.

When everyone recovered, I stood at the front and, with selective editing, told what had happened. Miss Hannah sat with Beth on her lap and cried. Jeremiah and Abigail looked sheepish and awkward, and neither could make eye contact with me. The rest of the kids seemed happy to see me and were all curious about my new ma and pa and Japanese friends.

After school ended, I stayed to talk to Miss Hannah. She hugged me so tight and said, 'This is the happiest day of my life. The thought of you buried in some lonely grave was too much to endure.' She burst into tears and it set me off. We both had a good cry. Then she held me at arm's length. 'And look at you. So grownup and beautiful, you look so healthy and—' words failed her, and she held me again. It grieved me to have put her through such pain. She sat me down and interrogated me, wanting every detail, and I figured I owed her that, and despite what Ted Banyard had said, gave her the truth. She marveled at how far I had traveled and all the people I had met. When I finished, she said, 'Heavens, Heidi, what an adventure.'

I nodded. 'It was, and this morning when I saw Jeremiah with Abigail, I knew I had to go through all that to find out who I was. Isn't that screwy?'

She stroked my cheek. 'Don't be too hard on him, will you? He went through hell and all that time he never betrayed you. In the end, he just moved on. I don't know what went on, but Abigail stood by him when he was so low and missed you so much. I can't believe she used it as an opportunity, they just—'

'I don't think they wanted to hurt me and I know now Jeremiah and I aren't supposed to be together. I'm glad he had someone to help him, because I did too. And, honestly, I'm not even sure I'm that attracted to boys, you know, that way.'

Her eyes narrowed, and she studied me for a while, as though contemplating something important, but not sure she could or should trust me. At last she said, 'I understand that. I don't like men that way, either. That's why I never got married. I have a special friend in Bonners Ferry.'

My eyes popped. 'Holy smoke, I never knew that. Although, to be honest, when you're a kid you don't really think about the private affairs of grownups, do you?'

'Nor should you have to burden yourself with such things. If you *are* like me, Heidi, then it will be hard. Society and all those Bluenoses do not approve. If the school board knew about me, I'd like as not lose my job. So, be careful who you tell and if you want to talk about it, I'm here for you.'

'Thanks, Miss Hannah.'

She reached out and touched my arm and looked at me like she was seeing me for the first time. 'Out of school, call me Lucy.'

I mouthed her name. It sounded unfamiliar, but I realized to me she was more than a teacher. In all the time my home life had been barren, she had always been there. School became my refuge with its routine and camaraderie. I could always rely on it and she never let me down.

I hugged her again. 'Sorry, I put you through all that. Is it okay if, while I'm here, I come back to school?'

She smiled. 'You have already. No one is as good with the little ones as you are, and you are my best student, too.'

'I've been learning to play the piano.'

'Your mother was musical, you know? Come here anytime and practice. I'll give you a key.'

We chatted for a time. She told me about her partner in Bonners Ferry and her life outside of school and it gave me courage knowing I was not alone.

By the time I left, we were no longer child and teacher. I had so much to thank her for as she had, over the years, watched over me. Guardian angels have nothing to do with religion or God. By the time I left Lucy Hannah, it felt like someone had sucked my insides out. I felt exhausted, but most of all, relieved. But before I could go home, I knew I must find Jeremiah and put him out of his misery.

Despite how much time had passed, he was waiting by the tree. I stopped. He looked beat up and contrite. I looked at him with glowing eyes and gave him my best I missed you face. I went over and kissed his cheek and held him tight. He trembled. I broke away, and we locked eyes and I saw he did not have the words. He had a scar where my pa had whacked him. I ran my finger down it. I whispered, 'It's okay. I know.'

We held one another, and I realized he was crying. I pushed away and looked into his wet, chocolate eyes. 'I'm so glad you recovered and got on with your life.'

'How did you know?'

I told how I had been up the tree waiting to surprise him but it had been me who got the surprise.

'I never meant it to happen and—I, I still love you.'

We sat by the tree. It felt blissful to be with him. 'I've been gone a long time and I know what you did with the posters and the letters you wrote helped me, and of course I love you too. I always will.'

'I'm sorry.'

I smiled. 'No need. I'm glad I found out the way I did. It gave me time to think about it. Abigail is gorgeous and fun. Are you happy together?'

'Yes. I wouldn't have survived without her help. I guess along the way we fell for one another.'

'Well, I'm pleased for you both, truly. Maybe all this was a twisted way to set us on our true path. But nothing can take away our friendship and everything we mean to one another, you hear me?'

'She's really worried that you'll want me back. She knows I still love you, but I love her, too. It's so bloody confusing and—' He took my hand. 'What do you want, Fizz?'

'Honestly, J, I don't know what I want, but you should tell her you love her and don't make her suffer. Too much has happened and we can't go back, can we? Everything changed that day. Maybe all for the best.'

We strolled back to town. I told him the things in my story I had left out in the schoolroom. I told him about the attempted rapes, and how I had been with Mayumi and that I loved her too. Knowing it made him feel better and I could see a flash of jealousy in his eyes, which I enjoyed. I said, 'See, life meant for us to experience other people and other things. I think you and Abigail look right for one another. I saw the way she kissed you this morning. She's a real catch, you know? Don't let her get away.'

'I won't.'

'Do your ma and pa like her?'

'Yes, they really do.' He stopped and thought for a moment. 'It devastated them when they thought you were dead. It was the hardest thing lying to them. In the end, I think I got so used to the lie I thought it the truth. Then Mayumi's letter came, and I was—' he had tears in his eyes again, he added, 'words can't say how I felt.'

'I didn't know you were alive, either. I was terrified you would have waited too long.' We looked at one another but did not have the words. We hugged, holding tight and wept tears of relief and unburdened pain. In that moment, I loved him more than ever, but it was pure love that has nothing to do with sex or passion, the love a mother has for her child, love that can never break. And it marked the end of my journey and it gave me heart knowing we'd never be able to hurt one another again.

We stayed like that for what seemed an eternity. It was a goodbye, the best kind of goodbye, and I knew above everything, it was why I had returned. At last, we went to find Abigail.

He said, 'After you left, Chief Banyard had men scouring the woods looking for you. They spent weeks searching. Nearly the whole town came to your memorial service.'

'Really? Holy smoke! That makes me feel a bit of an ass.' We laughed, falling against one another like we used to.

He looked at me, his scar made him looked hard. 'If you knew what you know now, would you have stayed?'

'Gosh, J, I don't know. We were terrified and confused and we did what we thought was right. I've grown up loads since then. I don't know whether what we did was right or wrong and it doesn't matter now. While I was away, after I almost drowned myself, a nun looked after me. She told me to take it one day at a time, and that's what I do now.'

He took my hand. 'How's today been?'

I smiled. 'So far, more good than bad, so that makes it a fine day.'

'Mayumi seems real nice. She likes you lots.'

'I know. She's special. Then there's Betty, and Adelaid, too.'

He stopped, looking aghast. 'Who in the name of sweet Jesus are Betty and Adelaid?' He shook his head. 'That's so you, befriending everyone.' We laughed out loud, and I pushed him away. I realized that despite all the time apart, we were now right back where we should be.

'I'll tell you about them another day.'

By the time we made our way to the general store we had passed the awkwardness and had fallen back to those parts of our old self that I had so missed, friends with the deepest, most meaningful roots, the kind that are impossible to sever. No matter what, where or when, we knew we'd always be there for one another.

We entered the store, and Abigail's father, with tears flowing down his cheeks, gathered me up like some long-lost daughter. He set me off again. I could see Abigail hanging back, anxiousness spread across her face like butter. I went over and hugged her. I whispered, 'Thanks for taking care of him. I haven't come back to take him.' I broke away, and she was frowning.

It was hard to leave the store as folk coming in to shop got a surprise and word flew around town. In the end, I agreed that I'd go to church on Sunday and tell my story, although the idea of standing there among the faithful lying my ass off didn't sit easy. I guess I was getting used to it. At last I could leave and it made me happy to see the release on Abigail's face when she understood Jeremiah was hers.

She ran after me. 'Wait—wait, Heidi, wait.' I turned, and she stopped, breathing hard, her face red. 'I'm—I'm sorry. I never meant it—'

'There's nothing to be sorry for, Abigail.'

She frowned. 'Are we friends still?'

'Jeremiah told me how you helped him recover from his injuries and losing me. How you held back when first he fell for you. How could I not be friends with someone like that? It would have broken my heart to think of him going through that on his own.' I hugged her again and kissed her soft cheek, lingering a while. She smelled so good. I whispered, 'He's a lucky boy.'

As I walked off, a strange feeling came over me, one I had not had since I left California. I found Abigail more attractive than Jeremiah. As we hugged, I'd wanted to kiss her passionately. I shook my head, saying to myself, 'Holy smoke, Heidi, you do like girls. Life sure is complicated.' It had been quite a day, full of surprises, and ahead lay an empty road full of openings I'd never dreamed of.

When I got home, Ella and Joe had been busy cleaning the place from top to bottom, even the dark stain now just a pale patch. Joe looked up. 'Hey, you look bushed, but also happy.' I told them about my eventful day.

Joe let out a low whistle. 'Wow. That's some day.'

I looked at them both with fresh eyes. 'Come. I want to show you something.'

— Joe —

Heidi led us to the cemetery on the valley side overlooking the town: a well kept space full of tidy crosses and headstones dating back to the time of the town's origin, a timeless roll call of souls with names echoing faraway places and you could not help but wonder what had brought them here. We strolled among these until she stopped. She pointed to a simple headstone. 'This is ma's grave.'

The inscription read:

JOHANNA HELGA SCHLAGER
BORN AUG 28 1890
DIED SEPT 4 1917
AGE 27
BELOVED WIFE AND MOTHER
MIT DEN ENGELN

We stood together in silent contemplation. It brought to mind the day me and Flo had buried the charred remains of my parents and I thought about how two fathers had caused so much pain.

Heidi took our hands, like she was showing her ma she was with us now. 'I haven't been here for years, but in the last few months I've thought about her so much and remembered things I didn't even know I had in my head. I know she would be happy to see me with you.'

Ella voiced my thoughts. 'She'd be so proud of you, you know?'

'Yeah, I think she would. I hope I keep recalling these wonderful, hidden memories. One was this song she used to sing to me. I've pieced some of it together. It's called *Hänschen Klein*.'

She sang.

> *'Hänschen klein*
> *Ging allein*
> *In die weite Welt hinein*
> *Stock und Hut*
> *Stehn ihm gut,*
> *Ist gar wohlgemut.*
> *Aber Mutter weinet sehr*
> *Hat ja nun kein Hänschen mehr*
> *Da besinnt sich das Kind,*
> *Läuft nach Haus geschwind.*
> *Liebe Mutter, ich bin da*
> *Dein Hänschen tra la la*
> *Bin bei dir,*
> *Bleib' bei dir*
> *Freue dich mit mir.'*

She chortled. 'Wacky, what you remember, isn't it?'

'You have a lovely singing voice, you know? What do the words mean?'

'I don't know exactly, pa. Just, it's about a boy who leaves home but then realizes that his mother will miss him and be sad, so he goes back and they live happily ever after, or some such story. The last line means rejoice with me. Ma used to speak German to me and I remember a few words. Maybe I should learn again, keep that link with her.'

I squeezed her hand. 'You should. It's good to know where you come from.'

Ella looked away. 'It's a lovely resting place, peaceful.'

'I don't think I'll ever come back. All the bits of her I need are in my head.' She knelt and touched her hand to the ground and said a quiet goodbye. Strangely, I felt a powerful responsibility to Johanna Schlager to take care of her daughter.

Heidi got up. 'Now—' she began walking. We followed. She looked over her shoulder. 'One more.' We went to the far corner of the cemetery where they had buried her pa. The simple wooden cross had his name and dates and the words "now at peace".

We stood a while. She stared at the cross. 'I've been trying to remember the good parts of him. All the pain and hurt died with him.' She placed her hand on the rough-hewn cross. 'I'm sorry, pa. I hope you forgive me, and I hope you are at peace now.'

Her words surprised me. After everything he put her through, she asked for his forgiveness. Ella put her arm around Heidi. It was like an official handover from her old guardians to her new, and I prayed we'd not let her down. I gave thanks she had come into my life and wondered at the power a random meeting can have on your destiny.

We returned to the house and settled into a domestic routine quite alien to me. I knew it would take time to adjust, but as always, I got on with life. I landed a job in the timber yard where Heidi's pa had worked. When home, I mended the house and worked the land. It was good to have some land to make something of and I realized in all the years I had been a hobo I had left nothing bar a handful of tags on water towers, bridges and railway crossings. For most of my life, I had felt I did not deserve to have what most people take for granted. It filled me with a sense of purpose and joy to earn a second chance. The imminent birth of the baby filled me with excitement and awe, and I was relieved that Heidi, too, was full of joyful enthusiasm.

Doc Jenner was a gentleman and a fine doctor. He visited often to check on Ella, who got bigger, and Heidi and I drove her mad, fussing over her and stopping her from doing too much. Heidi mothered her. 'Come on, ma, you know what Doc Jenner said. Rest and let me do that.' It cheered me she was there, and I saw it did her good to give something back. It delighted her and further helped bond us, and it felt like she had always been mine.

The day came when Ella went into labor. Doc Jenner, together with Jeremiah's ma, came over and Heidi and I were told to make ourselves scarce. We sat at the table, neither knowing what to do. The sounds coming from the bedroom pasted terror on Heidi's face. 'Holy smoke, pa, that can't be right. Sounds like she's dying.' I took her hand and told it would be okay, and that childbearing was painful, but after a bit, she got up and left. It was no use sitting around, so I followed her to keep an eye. I guess, if I was honest, the state of her mind worried me still. She had gotten a hoe and was jabbing at the vegetable patch. I leaned on the fence and wished to God I hadn't quit smoking.

After what seemed an age, things in the house went quiet. Heidi stopped her jabbing and stood still, poised like a hunting dog. I could almost taste her fear. Then, that wondrous tone of a baby's first breath projecting out a sound so delightful it is hard to describe. A new life, one I helped create. Heidi dropped the hoe and ran back in. For a time, I could not move. I thought about Sophia and how I had missed it all. After a bit, I took a deep breath and made my way back to the house. Doc Jenner was in the kitchen cleaning up. He beamed. 'Never get bored with this, the best part of my job. Now, go on in, Joe, and meet your son.'

I stood in the doorway. Ella looked so beautiful, radiating love, and held the baby in her arms. Heidi was crying and smiling. She said, 'Look what you two have made. He's perfect.' For a time, we sat and marveled. We took turns to hold our new family member, and it did not escape me the importance of his role in cementing us, as I truly believed that had it not been for Heidi he would not exist nor would we be a family. When she held him, her eyes shone, glowing with an ethereal warmth. She said, 'It's weird. He's pig ugly, but also the most beautiful thing I have ever seen.' She made us laugh, and I dared glimpse a future full of joy. She said, 'So, what are we calling him?'

Ella and I exchanged a glance. She nodded. I said, 'What do you say to Benjamin Johann?'

She looked at the baby and mouthed the names. 'Yeah, I like that. He looks like a Benjamin. She stroked his tiny, chubby cheek. 'Hi, Benjy, I'm Heidi, your big sister.'

The words 'big sister' made my heart skip a beat. 'We thought of Johann for your ma.'

She looked at us. 'Wow, that's lovely, thanks. Benjamin Johann Reisen. Sounds nice. Weird though, after everything that's happened, he was born in the same house I was. Blood may not relate us but spiritually you don't get closer, do you?'

After a while, Benjy needed feeding again, and she handed him back and told us she would prepare a meal. We heard her singing and saying: 'I've got a baby brother, I've got a baby brother.' It made us smile and Ella told me it had worried her Heidi would feel on the outside.

I felt a great calm come over me, like a thousand generations of pain washing away. 'I think she knows she helped make that child happen. Like she said, spiritually they are as close as you can get, and in my eyes that's every bit as powerful as being bonded by blood.'

Benjy latched on and took a good long feed. Ella looked tired but ecstatic, and as I sat and looked at them, I let tears of joy and sadness mingle.

Ella stroked Benjy's tiny hand. 'Are you happy, Joe?'

'Happy? I'm over the goddamn moon and back again, and I thank the day you came into my life and I'm sorry it took so long.'

She shook her head. 'No more regrets, Joe, or raking the dying embers of what's gone. We can't change that. I love you so much and couldn't ask for a better husband and father for our son.'

I leaned down and kissed her glistening forehead. I smelled the baby and the milk and it was like something holy. Is there a finer thing than creating a new life? I think not.

A few days later, after supper, we had gone outside to sit around our fire pit. Well, you know, old habits and all. The sky was clear and bursting with a myriad of sparkling jewels.

I poked at the fire. 'So we need to think about what we want to do, where we wish to live and make our lives. Have you given it any thought, Heidi?'

'I can't see myself wanting to stay here. It seems so small and there's too much I'd rather leave behind. And, if I stay the thing with me and Jeremiah will always be there.' She laughed almost to herself. 'Plus, if I'm honest, I'm kinda falling for Abigail myself. That would be real awkward, now wouldn't it?'

'Won't you miss them, and school?'

She nodded. 'Sure, of course I will. But I've seen something of the world and I want more. Is that allowed, do you think?'

I put my arm around her and pulled her to me. 'You betcha, sweetheart.'

Ella glanced at me and played the ace we'd held up our sleeves. 'How would you feel about going back to Carmel?'

Heidi's face lit up. 'Really? That would be the bees.'

'Ella found this plot of land for sale near to where we were camping. We have enough savings between us to buy it, build a house and put down roots. You can go back to school, and I can't think of a better place for little Benjy to grow up.'

'I've written to the agent, and the land is available,' said Ella. 'If we want it, I can write back and set things in motion. We left some money with Mr. Hikomori, you know, just in case.'

Heidi frowned. 'Why didn't you mention this before?'

'We didn't want to get your hopes up and we needed to see how things went back here, and we wanted the baby born, too. We've crossed all those bridges and now safely on the other side, we can make plans, special plans. Carmel has everything we need, doesn't it?'

Heidi beamed. 'And more. Plus, I can put this place up for sale and we can add that scratch to the family pot.'

I was going to refuse, but saw how important it was to her. I lifted my coffee cup and said, 'Well, here's to the Reisen family. Carmel, here we come.' And we knocked our mugs together to seal the deal.

53

— Ella —

Now, for the first time, living together in Heidi's home, we had pause to feel like a surefire family. A few months back, I had never thought I would be a mom, nor even thought I'd want to. But now I had an adopted teenage daughter and a baby boy, both of whom had changed me, unearthing long suppressed emotions and desires. Simply, I'd learned to love again. It had been a long time since I'd thought about David the way I was now, like I had never grieved for him and got over that he was gone and we never got the chance to grow together, have a family, and for him to be a father. And for my suppressed anger at his senseless death that left me alone and broken. Now I yearned for Carmel, our home and to begin again, and I knew we'd never take for granted our life together.

We decided to give Benjy a few months before making the journey back west. It allowed Heidi time to make peace with leaving behind such a big part of her life, and to find a buyer for her property. It was good to see her back at school with the kids she had grown up with, being a teenager, except now she had a loving home to come back to. A few times she stayed over at Abigail's and the two of them became closer. She told me they never talked about Jeremiah, but discussed, in fine detail, everything else under the sun.

Heidi was goofy in love with little Benjy. She'd sit holding him, just gazing in his eyes, chatting away, or nuzzling him. When he was clamorous, and it wasn't food he wanted, she could always calm him by singing songs she remembered or made up. It gladdened my heart to see my two beautiful kids bonding, and I knew the cement of love that hardened between them would serve them well. At times, I had to pinch myself lest I'd wake up back in a jungle somewhere drifting between jobs like a ball of lonesome tumbleweed. So much had happened it took time to believe that what we had was real.

When Benjy was a couple of weeks old, Heidi and I took him into town to show him off. She said, 'We need some supplies from the store and I can put up a notice about selling the property.'

When we got there, Mr. Garity, Abigail and others cooed over Benjy and it touched me how friendly were the folks of Sitwell. Heidi looked at Frank Garity with glowing eyes. 'Hey, Mr. Garity—'

He beamed and wagged a finger at her. 'Now, you call me Frank, Heidi.'

She smiled. 'Oh—really? I don't know, that seems peculiar. You've always been Mr. Garity or Abigail's pa.' She shrugged. 'But—I guess, well—why not? So, I was wondering—Frank, if I could put up a notice about selling my property?'

He frowned, thinking for a moment. Then he stepped aside and lifted the counter flap. 'Come on through.'

Heidi and I looked at one another and we followed him into a cozy office. He closed the door and invited us to sit. And said straight out, 'How much you asking for your property?'

Heidi cut straight to the chase. 'I'm thinking fifteen hundred.'

He nodded and thought about it. 'Hmm—fifteen hundred, eh?'

Then the conversation shifted, and it was like I wasn't there.

He looked her square in the eye. 'You know, when you came back, it petrified Abigail she'd lose Jeremiah. He's such a respectable boy and we like him, but most of all, she's struck on him. She came out of herself and it made her happy.' He glanced down and paused, thinking a moment, his elegant fingers tapping the desk. 'She's been through some stuff, you know, in the past, so it was agreeable she didn't have another setback.'

Heidi leaned forward. He looked up, she fixed his gaze, and in a soft voice said, 'She told me about Jimmy.'

His eyes widened, he crossed his arms, and the color drained from his cheeks. 'She—she told you about that?'

'It's okay. I won't tell anyone else, but I told her if she's serious about Jeremiah that she should let him know. You can trust him with that.'

I didn't have a clue what they were talking about, but I could tell from Frank's expression it was painful.

He sat back and sighed. 'It broke my heart. I know you're all just kids still, but it doesn't mean you don't have genuine feelings, does it?'

'No, it doesn't.'

For a moment, he was silent, a wounded expression on his face. 'Anyhow, I'm truly grateful you accepted them and didn't make trouble.'

'I love them both and I could see that things had changed and if I'm honest, I did it for selfish reasons as well.'

His haunted expression vanished, and the color returned to his cheeks. 'We all do that, of course. Anyway, I still thank you for it. Also, I wanted to say sorry that we all let you down with the way your pa was. We all knew. We should have done more, you know—'

'You did and besides, it's easy saying that after the fact. It doesn't matter now.'

He shook his head and smiled. 'You've grown up so much, not that you weren't like that before, but you're growing into a fine woman. Your ma would have been so proud of you.'

'You know, despite everything, there isn't much I would want to change. If I hadn't gone away, I would never have found myself. I have these visions of me and Jeremiah getting married and growing old together and never leaving here. There isn't anything wrong with that, but I see now it isn't my destiny. Does that make sense?'

'Sure it does. You know, every person who lives in Sitwell came here on the back of an adventure or a dream, like your ma and pa did. Follow your own path, that's what I say.'

She laughed. 'Joe told me that if you don't know where you are going, then any path will take you there. I took his advice.'

'I like that.' In the pause, Frank glanced at me, like I was back in the room. He grinned and rubbed his hands together. 'Anyway, I want to buy your property and I'll give two thousand for it.'

Heidi considered. 'You don't have to do that. Fifteen hundred is the price.'

'I know. Call the extra five hundred a thank you and a sorry. I can afford it and the property is worth that.' He looked at Benjy. 'Besides, you all have an extra mouth to feed. It isn't charity. It's a fine piece of land and just good business. What do ya say?'

We could see there was no use in protesting, so we stood up and shook on it.

I said, 'We expect to be off early October if it's alright for us to stay until then, Frank?'

He nodded. 'Sure, of course. Stay as long as you need. I'll get the papers drawn up.'

We walked out to the store. Frank said, 'Will you come back one day and see us?' I wasn't sure who he was asking, but Heidi was quick to jump in, her answer unexpected. 'I don't think so, Frank.'

He gave her a hug. 'We won't forget you, Heidi Schlager.'

She held him for a time. 'Thanks Frank, I won't forget you, and look after that beautiful girl of yours.'

On our way home, she was quiet, which did not surprise me. It was like a long goodbye as thread-by-thread she severed the past. But my curiosity burned. 'So, are you going to tell me about Abigail and Jimmy? You know what you mentioned to Frank?'

She took my hand. 'I promised her I wouldn't tell anyone, but you're not anyone, are you? I don't want us to have secrets.'

'I'm glad to hear that.'

She glanced at me. 'No, I mean it, ma. You got to promise me that whatever happens, you always tell me the truth, no matter what.'

I squeezed her hand. 'I promise with all my heart.'

She took a deep breath. 'When Abigail was eleven, her brother, Jimmy—he's the youngest of her three brothers—came to her room one night, got in bed, threatened her and then made her do— stuff, you know—'

I stopped dead in my tracks. 'Oh, crap! Really? Jeez, her own brother! How old was he?'

'Nineteen. We all liked him, you know. He was real friendly, handsome, cocky and he always like to chat, particularly to us girls. I thought nothing of it, but now I see—' she trailed off. She didn't need to say it. 'Anyway, the next day at breakfast, he behaved as though nothing had happened. It petrified her he'd do it again, so she told her ma, who at first didn't believe her. I mean, what mother would want to believe their beloved son had done that to his little sister? Anyway, she came around and told Frank. It incensed and bewildered him. He loved Jimmy, but Abigail, as you can tell, is the apple of his eye and when Jimmy came home that day, they ordered him to leave and never come back, and they told everyone he had gone north in search of adventure.'

I sighed. 'Poor Abigail. So much suffering. Can't have been easy unburdening herself. She trusts you.'

'I told her about my experience with predatory men, and what my pa made me do. But her thing is way scarier. It's hard to trust men. I mean, how do you know which ones are good?'

'I see that. But look at Joe, he'd never do that to a woman, now would he?'

She shrugged. 'I know that, but maybe he's the exception. Look at what Timothy Spaar had in mind for me, and what would have happened those two times had someone not been there to help me? And I'm sure my pa was—'

'You've had bad luck is all, sweetheart. In all the years I crossed the country traveling, hanging out in jungles, working jobs I never had that happen to me, even when I was much younger. Sure, I've had my ass pinched and my boobs groped, and that's bad enough, but I've been round men all my life and—'

'But isn't being groped and having your ass pinched just as bad? I don't want boys to think they can do that to me. Anyway, the point is, I'm going to be real careful from now on, and I want to learn how to defend myself. Like the nameless-rider that saved me at the river that time said, no one can protect you, but you.'

I stopped, and she turned to face me, her eyes dark and mouth set firm. 'You mean it, don't you?' She nodded. 'Okay, I get it, and you're right.'

We strolled on and she said, 'Good. Because the next time anyone tries it on, they're going to wish they hadn't.'

Her defiance and fire made me realize I had been lucky. I had never thought about how vulnerable I'd been back when first I took to the hobo life. Maybe those times I had my ass and breast groped were bad enough, but I'd always brushed it off as men being men, but now I was not so certain. I vowed to make sure I'd support her, and to bring up Benjy to respect women as equals.

I put my arm around her, and she turned and half-smiled at me. 'Don't let it darken your life, though, sweetheart. Keep that beautiful flame of love you have burning. It's what got us all here, you know?'

'You and Joe would have ended up together without me.'

I shook my head. 'Wish I could believe that. But it doesn't matter now because, well, just look at us. Are you happy?'

'Sure—of course I am, ma.' She smiled. 'Just can't wait to get back to Carmel, though.'

(54)

— Joe —

One Sunday, about two weeks prior to our departure back west. Heidi had gone off to the Big Creek with her buds and Ella was busy in the yard, leaving me at a loose end. I was sitting at the table drinking coffee, deciding what to do, when I glanced at the old dresser. I'd never really paid it much heed, but for some reason, I looked to see if I could tidy it up a bit for the new owner. I pulled it away from the wall and set to mending the broken door and sticky drawers. I was about to shove it back in place when I noticed the floor in the middle cupboard was loose and, on closer inspection, saw a faint pencil inscription that read "for Heidi". Well, I could not ignore that, so I grabbed a screwdriver and lifted the board. Inside, I found a stout locked box. It was real heavy. I set it on the table, and to no avail, went looking for a key. It sat there mocking with my curiosity burning, but I decided to wait for Heidi's return before opening it.

Some hours later, Ella was prepping supper, dead keen to find out what was inside, when at last Heidi came back tired and happy. She scooped up Benjy and sat down and put him on her lap. The box sat on the table. Her eyes rested on it. 'What's that?'

'I found it under the floor of that old dresser.' I told her about the inscription. She frowned. 'Really? What's in it?'

'We waited for you to open it. After all, I guess it's yours.'

She looked closer. 'Is there a key?'

'Can't find one but I can get it open.'

She nodded. A little fettling saw the lock pop, and the box revealed its treasure. There was a letter addressed to Heidi from her ma. Heidi put her hand up to her mouth. 'Holy smoke. Ma left this for me. Why?'

'Well, read the letter and find out.'

She shook her head. 'No—you read it.'

I smoothed the page and began.

> Oct 31 1911
> Meine liebste Heidi,
> Oh my tiny girl, today you are one. What a joyful year
> it has been since you came into my life. We made you in
> Germany, but I bore you in America! Things, though, are
> difficult and I fear your pa gets worse and I don't know what
> I can do, so I have made this package to make sure you have
> something to help you and to know about where we came
> from. It wasn't easy finding a place to hide the box, but your
> pa never goes in the dresser and I figured that somehow you'd
> find it because you are supposed to. Does that make sense?
> You are such a joy to me and the greatest gift, and watching
> you grow up will fill my every waking hour with pleasure.
> I'd do anything for you and I hope one day you will
> have children and understand the love they bring. The
> documents in the box will give you a connection to our
> German family and my past. I don't know when you will
> read this, but please write to my sister Gretchen to tell her
> I am gone and introduce yourself. We were close. She said
> she would try to visit one day, but after that awful war in
> Europe began, that became impossible. You'll find out
> more in the enclosed documents, and I have written a brief
> history and made a simple family tree for you. I hope you
> will find answers to your questions, but make sure you do
> not let your pa find this box. When you open the leather
> pouch, you will know why. It is for you and your future.
> I hope you find happiness and thank you for the
> gift you gave me the day you came into my life. I
> love you with all my heart, and always shall.
> Gottes Segen sei mit dir. Ich liebe dich für immer
> Deine liebevolle, Mutti xxx

I passed it to her. She looked at it with wet eyes. 'It was like she knew something bad might happen and—' she cried. Benjy looked worried.

After a while, she wiped her eyes. 'Sorry Benjy, I'm a crier. You'll get used to it.' She set the letter down but laid her hand on it a while. 'Well, let's look, shall we?'

I pushed the box across. She handed Benjy over and began pulling out the contents. Mostly it was documents, letters and some old photos, which Johanna had annotated on the backs. Heidi looked at them. 'Holy smoke, these are my German family. Look, here, this is Gretchen. She looks so much like ma, doesn't she?'

She passed the photos around and we all looked, just as we had in Edward's house. I said, 'Maybe one day you can go find them.'

She nodded and bit her lower lip. 'Maybe.'

The last item in the box was a large leather pouch. She picked it up. 'Gosh, this is heavy.' She opened it and poured out the contents, and dozens of gold coins spilled glitteringly across the table. We all sat, eyes wide. Dumbstruck.

I picked one up. 'These are German gold coins. Look here, it says Deutsches Reich, a date of 1894 and a value of twenty marks.'

Heidi picked one up and studied it. 'They're beautiful. I wonder what they're worth?'

We counted five hundred identical coins. We got the kitchen scales, split them into five equal lots and weighed them. Each lot was just over twenty-eight ounces.

I sat back and whistled. 'You've got almost nine pounds of gold here, Heidi.'

She shrugged. 'So, how much is gold worth?'

'Could be a couple thousand dollars here.'

Her jaw dropped. 'Holy smoke! That's one heap of cash. Where did she get them from? And how come she left them for me? And how did she know?'

Ella sat down next to her. 'Maybe some of those answers will be in the documents, but all you need to know is she loved you so much.'

Heidi looked at me. 'What made you go looking in the dresser, anyway?'

I grinned. 'The devil makes work for idle hands, except this time I don't think the devil had anything to do with it, do you?'

To all of us, the cash was a grand thing, but truthfully, those documents, photos, and letters were worth more than gold.

That night, as we sat around our campfire, and save the pop-n-crackle as the flames worked the wood, all was quiet. We were quiet. Then Ella said, 'Funny, but after all those years I feel now like truly the past is being laid to rest.'

I lost my thoughts in the glowing embers. 'You can almost sense them, can't you?'

Heidi looked at me. 'Sense who?'

I smiled. 'You know who.'

She thought about it and nodded. 'You think she always watched over me?'

'In a way. It's kinda hard to get your head around it, isn't it?'

'I've been thinking about the day I killed my pa and how I couldn't remember coming down from my loft, taking up the knife, and where I got the power and nerve to stab him. I'd always been so fearful of him, like when he was beating on me, I'd just cower and take it. You think that day she helped me?'

Ella looked at Heidi, the fire dancing in her eyes. 'Do you think she did?'

Heidi sighed. 'I don't know. I don't believe in ghosts, or spirits, but I think that maybe, when she died, something of her came to me. And after I had killed him, I felt her presence more strongly and began remembering stuff about her. Is that possible or is it just stuff locked up in our heads?'

'When we went back to Lagonda, even though Florence had been dead five years, I could feel her everywhere. So, yeah, I think maybe there is something that carries on. I guess you just gotta believe in it and open your mind.'

Ella leaned forward and poked the fire. 'Well, one thing is for sure, I swear all the stuff that's happened this last year isn't just coincidence.'

We chatted on late into the night, trying to make sense of stuff that you can't rightly figure out. And that night, for the first time in decades, I dreamed of my mother back before the war that changed my pa, and when the world lay at our feet. The next morning when I woke, I felt like much of the darkness from my past had gone to rest and I could remember happy times again. It felt redemptive.

— Heidi —

The day came to leave Sitwell. You can imagine how hard were some goodbyes but made softer by the feign promise of reunion. We left early. Frank drove us to the station, and as we passed the end of the road where Jeremiah lived, he was standing, waiting. When he saw us, he ran after the car, shouting and waving. I turned, kneeling on the seat, and waved back, watching until he disappeared, and a bit of my heart broke off to remain in Sitwell where it belonged.

The journey west was epic, and I appreciated the changing scenery as though it were my first encounter. We stopped off en route and three days later we arrived in Salinas. We camped by the river, and it was Benjy's first taste of living wild. It was warm and good to be out under the stars again. I could almost taste the ocean. We walked the same route we had the year previous, and as soon as I saw that vast expanse of liquid bliss foaming and crashing against the golden sand, I had to get in. I didn't care who was looking. I stripped off, ran into the cold, frothy, bubbling water, swam as hard as I could through the breakers and out to where it was calmer. I yelled with joy and splashed around. Ella stood holding Benjy. I could see her talking to him and pointing his hand to where I was. She took him to the shallows and tried to dip his toes in the water, but every time she did, he would pull them out and gurgle. The waves and the sound mesmerized him. I came to shore and took him from her and sat in the shallow water. He wasn't sure about it. I think maybe it was too cold. But he sat on my lap, laughing at the waves as they broke against us, his hazel eyes wide and sparkling.

Taking turns to carry him, we walked hard all day and that evening we arrived at Bluff Cove tired but happy. We were home. The Hikomoris were there to greet us and insisted we stay. I threw myself into Mayumi's arms. We did not speak but held one another for the longest time. At last, we broke off, and she cupped my face in her hands. 'I'm so happy to see you.'

'I promised I'd come back and this time we're staying.'

She took my hand, and we went off to catch up. 'Betty can't wait to see you. She practically burst when I told her you were coming back.'

'I've missed her. Where else will I get my gossip from?' She laughed and told me how, despite the age difference, they had become close. The return celebration went long into the night and the joy of it balanced the melancholy of leaving Sitwell.

The following morning, we went to look at the land and began planning. As Joe strode around pointing here and there reeling off ideas, it animated him in ways I'd never seen before, and he seemed brighter and happier, like it had stripped years from him. We began by making temporary accommodation, comprising a simple wooden structure and canvas. Mr. Hikomori had two of his men make a Japanese-style bathing tub for us and, in just a few days, we moved in and began our new life.

Now settled, Joe and Ella got married. The ceremony took place on the beach. Betty's pa, William, gave Ella away and Mr. Hikomori acted as Joe's best man. I was the maid of honor, with Mayumi and Betty as bridesmaids. It was an unforgettable day and Joe said a fitting wedding for hoboes. Just after my sixteenth birthday, they adopted me formally, and I became Heidi Reisen. It was the first time I could remember truly belonging and, though I'd left Sitwell only a few weeks back, it was already sinking into the past; the ache diminishing.

We worked on the house and it rose just as we planned. On weekends, some of the Japanese community would come and help. They were the finest of woodworkers and, as a result, the structure had a Japanese flavor. I had my room with a view and a bed big enough for friends to stay over. The first thing I put out was the picture of my ma holding me as a baby. Joe made me a bookcase for my growing library. Of course, I made haste to go see Miss Jennings and reacquaint myself with Carmel's wonderful books, and acquired some German texts to teach myself the language of my ancestors.

When the house was complete, I used some of my money to buy a piano and our home was often full of music. Joe and Ella liked a singalong. She had a pleasant voice, but while Joe had many gifts, the gift of song was not one of them, but I never minded because everyone should be able to sing any way they can.

Betty became a regular fixture in the house and like a sister to me. Joe and Ella never minded folks calling in and happily shared their food, sat quietly and listened to stories, moans, and reminiscences. I guess their years of living in jungles made them so hospitable. I appreciated it because it was a home full of life.

Benjy was growing fast and was the sweetest, most content of babies. He never minded me dragging him off for walks or sitting in the cold ocean splashing around in the waves. He loved to sit on my lap while I was playing the piano. I translated the *Hänschen Klein* song, but it never sounded right when sung in English. Benji loved being sung to and I could see him studying my lips as I sang and often he would burble along. I loved every second we spent together. I guess it was for me a chance to experience vicariously some of the childhood I had missed.

We fell into a contented, domestic routine that was, to all of us, alien. I think it took Joe the longest to adapt. Sometimes I'd care for Benjy while the two of them took off for a bit. On those occasions Mayumi and Betty would come and stay over and we'd stay up late talking, laughing and being kids. I always knew Joe and Ella would come back and little-by-little his feet itched less as he relaxed into his role as father and husband.

He set up his own carpentry business and soon began attracting commissions. We all pitched in to work our land and soon had produce growing, chickens in a run, and had planted a dozen fruit trees. One day, Joe came back with a puppy. It was a cute Dachshund. Joe said he could protect the chickens and I don't know why, but the idea of it made me laugh hysterically. We called our little pup, Waldi. I guess it was the last addition to our family.

I joined Mayumi at the Monterey High School and my education resumed. I had a little catching up to do, but I put my head down and soon found my way. One teacher was German and offered to give me lessons. I was lucky that I loved to learn. It was never a chore, and I soon had a working grasp. When I took Benjy out for a walk or swim, I'd speak only German to him. Both Betty and Mayumi adored him, too, and he'd often come with us on our picnics, and, of course, Waldi followed us around and never missed out and was, much to my joy and amusement, an accomplished swimmer.

In the evenings, I still liked to go off on my own and take a walk. I'd venture off on fresh paths and it was on one of these excursions that I found the answer to my need for self protection. I came to a small bay with a modest patch of golden sand on which stood two Japanese men engaged in some kinda unusual exercise. Not wishing to disturb them, I took cover behind some rocks and watched. It mesmerized me as they moved with elegant fluidity. It seemed part dance, part combat. They'd stand opposite one another and move their arms and legs like you would in some exotic dance. Each move seemed calculated and powerful. Then one would make a noise and launch himself at the other. Who'd deflect the attack, put down his opponent in some head or body lock until he tapped the ground to surrender. Each graceful lunge and attack occurred at such speed and ferocity that it took my breath away.

After a time, they stopped, stood opposite one another and bowed. I don't know why, but they had so entertained me I stood up and clapped. They turned to me and bowed, and I knew that despite them never having looked in my direction, they had noticed me watching. With my curiosity emboldening me, I trotted over to ask about it.

I did not know them, but knew they both worked for Mr. Hikomori. One looked at me and smiled. 'Heidi-san. I trust you are well?'

I nodded. 'I liked your—whatever it was you were doing. Has it a name?'

The other said, 'It is a Japanese martial art called Jujutsu. Well, that and a little other things thrown in for good measure.'

'What's it for?'

The two looked at one another. 'It is for defense, to focus the mind, and relax the body and soul. You yield to the force of your opponent's attack and use their energy to defeat them. We come here every evening to practice and to wind down after a day's work.'

'Ah. Yes, I see. Can you teach me?'

They looked taken aback, and I feared I had offended them. 'It is not custom for girls to learn this.'

'Oh, I don't mind if you don't. I mean, you can knock me on my ass, and I promise I'll work every bit as hard as a boy. I'm just as good as any boy. Back home, I used to fight and play with the boys, climb trees, swim in the creek. I did what they did and did so just as well. Sometimes better. See, I need something to defend myself and this looks—well—like just the thing I've been dreaming of.'

They looked at one another.

I gave them my best warrior look, knitting my brows and focusing my eyes. 'I'll be the perfect student.'

'Why do you need to defend yourself?'

I hesitated. 'Well—in the last year or so, men have attempted to rape me, and one more wanted to. It was only by good grace and luck that a man was there to help me. But one day I'll be alone, that's why.'

They looked at one another again. They shook their heads.

'My ma and pa won't mind. I need this.' I looked between them. 'Please. At least give me a chance to prove myself.'

And so it was. Every evening I joined Satoshi and Iori to practice Jujutsu. It empowered me and I learn fast. I had to. Of course, my combat lessons did not remain a secret and one evening Mayumi and Betty came to watch and I persuaded them to try. In the beginning, with their lack of my experiences to motivate them, they did not give it the gravity I did. But in time, as they gained the discipline and made progress, they appreciated the benefit. Betty, in particular, loved the physical side, and I don't know why it had never occurred to me, but I realized she was in love with me. How stupid I had been to not have seen it.

Within a month, we'd invited four other girls from the school to join, and the Monterey Girls Jujutsu Dojo came into being.

As time drifted by and I had room to settle and reflect, I knew for sure what was in my heart. After school, I would take Benjy so that Ella could get on with chores. Sometimes I'd sit in my room and do homework while he played and on others I'd meet up with Betty or Mayumi and mess about or just sit and gossip. But and on this particular day, I took Benjy and went to find Mayumi. We walked up to Johanna's point. While I was gone, Mayumi had kept tidy the small pile of stones that marked the spot I had buried ma's hair. We sat cross-legged, me with Benji on my lap, looking out to the ocean. There was a stiff, snug breeze blowing my long golden hair wildly about my face. I held Benji, his little hands wrapped around my index fingers, his keen sparkling eyes gripped by the vast vista, and I leaned my head against Mayumi's shoulder. She put her arm around me.

'I can't think of anything better than this, Mayumi. I have this little fella here, a ma and pa who love me, you my best friend, and lovely Betts.' I looked up at her and our eyes met. 'When I was back home, I realized I'm attracted to girls more than boys.'

She gazed out at the boundless ocean, her face passive. 'I wondered.'

'Our friendship is more important to me than anything else, but I know I am in love with you. It doesn't matter if you don't feel the same. I just want to be honest.'

She looked at me and smiled like a mother would to a child. 'I love you too, but I'm not sure in what way.'

I nodded. 'That's okay. For a long time, I didn't know either, but I do now. I'd love for us to be together, but it needs to be right for us both; I know that. So— it's okay if you just want to be my friend.'

She turned once more and looked out to the ocean, her delicate, silky black hair dancing about her exquisite face. 'I liked it that day on the beach we spent together. You were so tender and caring. After you left, I thought about it a lot. It was all new to me. I love being with you and I guess I'll only find out if I try, won't I? But we're young, and there's a beautiful world right out there just waiting for us. We can do anything, can't we? So, I guess we just take it as it comes.'

'One day at a time, eh?'

She looked into my eyes, leaned in and kissed me. She broke away and brushed my hair aside and held my face in her soft hands. 'What more could we ask for?'

I took a deep breath and closed my eyes. Though I think I knew what we'd always be to one another, I wanted, just this one last time, to let my heart rule my head.

— The End —

Read More

If you enjoyed this book and while you wait for the sequel, please leave me a review. They really help and I appreciate the feedback from readers. Join my mailing list to get news, special offers, and advanced notice of upcoming books. Also, I am sure you will enjoy my German Historical Crime Thrillers featuring Berlin detective, Max Becker, and his team. The books are available from Amazon.

Angel Avenger

A nation scarred by violence. Ugly signs of a serial killer. Is this homicide detective chasing a villain… or a victim vigilante?

Germany, 1960. Max Becker is haunted by his past. Once a Nazi soldier, the Berlin investigator works himself to the bone to make amends and bring his country some redemption. So when tortured and naked male bodies show up along with cryptic messages, he's determined to hunt down a cold-blooded criminal as the body count rises.

Driven to expose the truth when he discovers links to Russian soldiers responsible for unspeakable war crimes, Max fights a growing sympathy for the disturbed murderer. And now close to making an arrest, he's at risk of his emotions rejecting duty in favour of a dangerous choice.

Can he find the delicate balance between ensuring justice and permitting understandable vengeance?

Angel Avenger is the dark first book in the Max Becker historical crime thriller series. If you like edge-of-your-seat suspense, morally gray characters, and seamlessly accurate settings, then you'll love Tim Wickenden's hypnotic page-turner.

Buy Angel Avenger and spread the wings of justice today!

Take Back

A homicide detective investigates bizarre murders. And when children go missing a deadly game begins. But is it too late? Can the killer be stopped?

Berlin 1961. At a murder scene, veteran police Kommissar Max Becker comes under sniper fire. Further bizarre incidents each with an odd personal element perplex the conscientious detective. And as he wrestles with more murders, men posing as police abduct his children and turn his world upside down.

Hell bent on saving his family and with no clues as to his children's whereabouts, the anguished former ace tank commander, loved and respected for his leadership, and loyalty, employs every military and investigative tactic he knows, reaching out to old comrades and powerful contacts from his past.

With time running out, will Max rescue his children before it's too late?

Take Back is the electrifying second novel in the Max Becker historical crime thriller series. If you love intricate plots, high-stakes drama, and relentless action then Tim Wickenden's Take Back promises to keep you turning the pages long into the night.

Don't miss out. Join Max Becker in his perilous dance with death and buy Take Back today!

Join me at www.timwickenden.com

scan the QR code:

Author's Note
& Acknowledgments

I had always wanted to write an historical American novel. *That Girl in The Boxcar* first seeded in my mind during the long days at home during COVID lock-down when I researched the great depression. I came across a series of promotional photos taken at the time of ordinary folk living in one of America's darkest times. One photo titled *Damaged Child*, taken by Dorothea Lange, got me thinking. The depression years were a time of huge upheaval with millions on the move. I dug deeper and began researching America's great hobo culture. At the time, it was just a research project. Then I read *The Autobiography of a Super-Tramp* by Welshman W. H. Davies, and wondered about a story of an aging hobo meeting a damaged young girl.

A member of a creative writing group, it was serendipity that the writing task topic suggested by our tutor at one of out early meetings after lock-down was about a meeting on a train. And that was it: my damaged girl runs away and meets her hobo on a train. I fleshed out a short story and began writing. But some four thousand words in I saw I had an epic novel. But not just one, but three. I knew I had to begin my tale before the Great Depression, when times were good and the narrative could concentrate on introducing the main characters: Heidi Schlager, Joe Reisen (aka Bo Scribbler), and Ella Frank (aka Corbeau). The second book (still in planning) takes us into the depression years, with the third book moving us into and just beyond WW2. It is a family saga with a cast of rich characters living an adventure. It is a story of love, of companionship, of acceptance. It explores destiny and how a chance meeting between two people seemingly a million miles apart, can change so many lives. The main character—Heidi— is unconventional, a positive force, for the novels, though dealing with some dark topics, must for me strike a positive, uplifting note. It's important because we live in challenging times and so *That Girl in The Boxcar* is an uplifting adventure. Even in the sad parts, and when dangers consume our noble heroine and the reader thinks the tale will take them down a dark tunnel, I found ways to keep Heidi safe.

I am hugely indebted to my editor, Jess Lawrence, who helped hugely. Her suggestions made me rework parts of the novel and make it the best it could be. My thanks also to Dan Santos who read an early draft checking it from an American perspective, and having passed his scrutiny, he declared the story one of the most uplifting he has ever read.

Initially, I chose randomly Carmel-by-The-Sea but once it had my attention and I discovered the local newspaper, *The Carmel Pinecone*—which dates back to 1915—has an archive of back copies, it sold me on Carmel as a focus town. I began reading the Pinecone's archives from the mid-1920s, and several quotes from such copies appear in the book, as does a local paper (paying homage to the *Carmel Pinecone*) called the Cypress Courier run by William Reed whose daughter, Betty, befriends Heidi. I regularly receive my email copy of *The Carmel Pinecone* to keep abreast of this wonderful part of California. I discovered local historical characters, particularly local Japanese Abalone fisherman, Gennosuke Kodani, who inspired a family of Japanese characters, and the local library, and the Carmelite monastery, all appear in the book.

Though the story involves an element of hoboism, it is not a hobo tale specifically, but it does pay homage to hoboes, their way of life, the camaraderie, and spirit of acceptance. The annual hobo festival in Britt, Iowa mentioned in the book is a real festival held each year in August, and where you'll find the hobo museum.

If you're reading this, you've probably read the book and I thank you. Without readers, a writer's words have no wings.

Poem references:

Chapters 1 & 4: *From a Railway Carriage*—Robert Louis Stevenson
Chapter 1: *Hallelujah! I'm a Hobo*—The Author
Chapter 5: *On Delia (Bid Adieu, My Sad Heart)*—William Cowper
Chapter 13: *On First Looking into Chapman's Homer*—John Keats

About the Author

Tim was born in Zimbabwe. He spent his early childhood there and in Hong Kong, returning to the UK age eight to attend boarding school, which he describes as ten years of hell. He spent his school holidays in West Germany becoming interested in that country's turbulent history. A visit, age twelve, to the site of the former concentration camp inspired his article *A Brief History of Bergen Belsen*. Before moving into adult education, Tim worked in the IT sector. In 2005 he relocated to South West Wales, setting up a carpentry business, and began studying creative writing. He published his first historical novel *Angel Avenger* in 2019, with two more *Take Back* and *That Girl in The Boxcar* in 2024. His history article *A Tale of Two Boys* has been downloaded thousands of times and finally put an accurate date to a famous photograph of Hitler presenting awards to Hitler Youth boys. A passionate bookworm, Tim reads widely, and when he doesn't have his nose in a book, he can be found walking or paddle-boarding the coast near his home, which he shares with his wife and son.

Printed in Great Britain
by Amazon

47354472R00158

42 Rules for Applying Google Analytics

By Rob Sanders
Foreword by Michael B. Lehmann

E-mail: info@superstarpress.com
20660 Stevens Creek Blvd., Suite 210
Cupertino, CA 95014

Published by Super Star Press™, a Happy About® imprint
20660 Stevens Creek Blvd., Suite 210, Cupertino, CA 95014
http://42rules.com

First Printing: March 2012
Paperback ISBN: 978-1-60773-040-8 (1-60773-040-5)
eBook ISBN: 978-1-60773-041-5 (1-60773-041-3)
Place of Publication: Silicon Valley, California, USA
Library of Congress Number: 2011940278

Trademarks

Warning and Disclaimer

Praise For This Book!

"Rob Sanders has helped me to analyze and manage successful campaigns for clients from Fortune 500 companies to non-profits. In this book, he gives step by step, no-nonsense advice so you can do the same for your business, using Google Analytics. Read it and learn!"
Cathy Clifton, Brix Direct, E-Commerce Consulting

"Rob does an outstanding job of outlining the rules and methodology used by Google Analytics and presents a plausible plan for maximizing the marketing potential of this important tool."
Robert Wucher, Principle, Wucher & Associates

"*42 Rules for Applying Google Analytics* is a great resource for anyone interested in learning how to use, or make better use of, Google Analytics."
Seth Rosenberg, Senior Vice President, Sales & Marketing, Equity LifeStyle Properties

"Rob's 42 Rules are invaluable for gaining an understanding of all the moving pieces within Google Analytics. This is a must read for anyone who intends to tackle the task of growing their organization online. Even those who intend to use an SEO consultant will see value as they will be able to ask the right questions and "talk the talk" with their consultant."
Thomas Lyle, CEO, Frontdesk Anywhere Inc

Dedication

To my wife, Kathy, for showing me what patience and professionalism is all about.

To my employees at RSO Consulting for their support, assistance, feedback, and enthusiasm.

To my clientele that waited, waited, and waited some more for the book to finally be published after months of anticipation.

Finally, to my editor, Laura Lowell, who patiently worked with me throughout the entire process without giving up hope that I would indeed go to print.

Acknowledgments

A number of people contributed to this book. It would be impossible to list every name and acknowledge everyone I've worked with over the past few years. I am grateful for their time and energy, experiences, and insights as it has influenced my perceptions of Google Analytics.

I would like to thank the following people who provided support, feedback, ideas, quotes, and tidbits of information: Kiana Sharifi, Cathy Clifton, Thomas Lyle, Marina Quilez, Dew Chinsakchai, and John Little. Without their input, the book would not be what it is.

My mother said to me, "If you are a soldier, you will become a general. If you are a monk, you will become the Pope." Instead, I was a painter, and became Picasso.
Pablo Picasso

Contents

Contents

F i g u r e s

Foreword by Michael B. Lehmann

Let me introduce you to Rob Sanders' *42 Rules for Applying Google Analytics* by telling you why I read it.

I've taught economics for over 40 years at the University of San Francisco and I am the author of the best-selling *Irwin Guide to Using the Wall Street Journal*. The news media frequently seek my views on the business and investment climate. I also developed a successful seminar for corporate training. But when I decided to branch out into online education and develop my seminar *Be Your Own Economist* ® for Web distribution, I knew I needed help.

That's why I turned to Rob Sanders. Rob brings a wealth of knowledge and experience to the world of online marketing. He currently works with a diverse group of companies by providing creative and technical solutions for online growth, including overseeing their search-engine marketing, social networking, blogs, and video. Rob will help me market my course using Google Analytics and his wealth of online-marketing knowledge. Now you, too, can gain access to the world of online marketing by reading Rob's *42 Rules for Applying Google Analytics*.

Business is moving to the web, and any up-to-date business venture must have a web presence. But how can you make best use of the web to market your product, yourself, or your ideas? You just don't have the training and experience. That's where *42 Rules for Applying Google Analytics* comes in. It will share with you a visitor's experience when browsing through your site. You can begin to understand your site from a visitor's perspective.

How does a visitor react to the information and graphics you provide? To understand this you must leave the world of the amateur and enter the domain of the professional. *42 Rules for Applying Google Analytics* will show you how marketing professionals measure, collect, and analyze data from your site's performance. What sells and what doesn't sell? Once you have learned how to evaluate your results, you can begin to tailor your site to your customers' needs and preferences. That will mean more visits to your site, more sales, and better all around success. Your competitors are doing it, so should you.

Guesswork and flying by the seat of your pants no longer works in the modern world of web and mobile marketing. Metrics are key. Marketing requires measurement, not guesswork. Let this book be your gateway to tracking website behavior and website performance. Whether you are an advertiser, publisher, or business owner, this book will help you write better ads, strengthen your marketing initiatives, and create higher-conversion web pages.

I am confident you will enjoy and benefit from *42 Rules for Applying Google Analytics* as much as I did.

Michael B. Lehmann
Emeritus Professor of Economics
University of San Francisco

The objective of this book can be akin to my mission statement about Google Analytics. First, it is to educate "beginners" or those new to Google Analytics on how to best use the tool and its features. My other personal objective would be to have people use this book as a reference guide. Unfortunately, most of the books published on web analytics are big, thick, clunky, and really intimidating, especially for those recently introduced to Google Analytics. Do these books contain a lot of good, insightful information? Absolutely. Are they manageable in terms of reading and using the material being introduced? That's my point of contention.

I would also go as far as saying this book is a necessity for those novices given that it contains a lot of the same information in summarized form that is easily digestible. As a professional online marketer, I am always showing my clients things about Google Analytics that they would not otherwise have known. Over the past few years, this permeated into blog posts, webinars, speaking engagements, lectures, and then, a book deal.

1 Rules Are Meant to Be Broken

Rules are mostly made to be broken and are too often for the lazy to hide behind.
- General Douglas MacArthur

I've been using Google Analytics from almost day one. In fact, I was an avid user of the Urchin software until Google acquired the company in 2005.

Google Analytics has stayed true to what Urchin was. According to Google Analytics, that means creating a web site analytics solution used by web site owners and marketers to better understand their users' experiences, optimize content, and track marketing performance.

I use Google Analytics daily and depend on it for my business as an online marketing consultant. It's been a relationship that has grown organically stronger over the years. Interestingly, I don't have a personal relationship with anyone at Google. I feel it is not entirely necessary. They have built one of the best user-friendly web analytics products available and continue to improve on it. With that in mind, I know that I can count on reliable data that will allow me to effectively and easily communicate and train my clients, employees, and just about anyone with a website that is interested in knowing results.

Simply put, Google Analytics allows me to make informed decisions. In turn, I can paint a picture based on the data and provide suggestions, comments, recommendations, advice, examples, and a lot more. But all of this is from my perspective and the rules outlined in this book are mine, based on my experience. Some of these rules may work for some readers and others may not. It is all based on their business, strategy, and objectives.

The topics or "rules" in this book are geared towards non-techie types like marketers, business owners, data enthusiasts, consultants, and various stakeholders who don't have time or patience to master the ins-and-outs of Google Analytics. Instead, they rely on someone like me to provide a high-level overview and low-level details they seek. If you are comfortable with Google Analytics, or see yourself as an above average to expert user, then my hope is that you will still learn something or take away some tidbits of knowledge.

My rules cover the gamut of what Google Analytics has to offer in terms of everyday features. So, if you are one of those people that see time as a precious commodity, then giving you rules to abide by will arm you with a level of understanding that you can apply as you see fit.

What are the rules, you ask? Well, read the book and find out! But as you read each chapter, don't lose sight of the fact that these rules can be broken and applied as you see fit based on your needs. For example, if you have multiple websites or only one website then you may approach setting up profiles completely different than what I mention in Rule 31, "Profile Your Data". However, if you do agree with my recommendations then you will be on your way to benefiting from all that Google Analytics has to offer.

Part I
Preparation: What You Need to Know before You Begin

The content in this section is intended to prepare you for all the great features Google Analytics has to offer. Before embarking on more specific and challenging tasks, you have to begin with the right mindset. After reading this section, you'll have a better understanding of what lies ahead.

- Rule 2: Why Google Analytics?
- Rule 3: Learn to Read...the Data, That Is
- Rule 4: Understand the Language
- Rule 5: Keep It Simple, Silly
- Rule 6: Think like an End User
- Rule 7: Identify Key Metrics
- Rule 8: Identify Conversions
- Rule 9: Assign Monetary Values

2 Why Google Analytics?

Google Analytics is essential for understanding which marketing initiatives are working and [which] are not. It tells you how people find, navigate, and convert on your website so you can turn more visitors into buyers.
- Brett Crosby, Group Manager, Google Analytics

Why Google Analytics? The broad response is that Google Analytics provides all your web analytics data for your website or blog in one easy-to-use platform.

There are no limitations or requirements for using Google Analytics. You can be an entrepreneur or small business owner. You can work for a large corporation and manage a small or large team. Best of all, Google Analytics is absolutely free! Google Analytics is not a "get what you pay for" free product. It competes directly with other analytics programs that charge a rather substantial monthly fee. Installing it is simple and you can follow multiple websites using just one account.

What sets Google Analytics apart from its competitors is that it is aimed at marketing professionals. Marketing managers especially need the information about their marketing campaigns so they can see what works and what doesn't. For example, it would be important to know if a key web page associated with a particular marketing or promotional campaign was not receiving any visitors. The power of Google Analytics will provide that information in a timely manner via reporting or alerts (see Rule 13, "Use Your Intelligence").

The interface in Google Analytics is easy to use yet sophisticated enough for the advanced user. Most other analytics platforms are aimed at tech-types and webmasters who gave rise to the technology to begin with. With Google Analytics, you can set up automated, customized reporting and receive a multitude of reports. You can receive a summary of all data, or a specific report for a particular time span. The benefit is that Google Analytics reports will save you the time of having to go through each individual analytical section.

Furthermore, there is a lot of support from Google, third party vendors, "Google Analytics Authorized Consultants," forums, blogs, articles, and websites dedicated to assisting users (see Rule 41, "Know Where to Seek Help").

However, Google Analytics is not without its limitations. For example, reports are not generated in "real time" and users may have trouble browsing from mobile phones. I expect Google to rectify these issues over time. Regardless of the current issues, the benefits clearly outweigh the downsides for gathering web analytics data.

With Google Analytics enabled on your website you can track where traffic is coming from, from which referring website, to which landing page, and what search engine and keyword was used. It can also tell you about the visitor's location, how they found your site, their operating system, browser, and even monitor resolution! It gives you a snapshot of how much time the visitor spent on your site, the number of pages visited, the bounce rate (percentage of users who viewed only one page before leaving), along with the conversion rate. Oh, and if that is not enough, it gives you precise data on your past and current traffic. You get the point. Google Analytics has a lot to offer.

I foresee Google Analytics being the central focal point or "one-stop shop" for all data related to other Google products, including YouTube, Insights, Webmaster Tools, and more. For now, Google Analytics, on its own, is loaded with informative data that will tell you the "when," "why," "where," and "how" as it relates to your website.

3 Learn to Read...the Data, That Is

Data is a precious thing and will last longer than the systems themselves.
- Tim Berners-Lee, Inventor of the World Wide Web and Director of the World Wide Web Consortium (W3C)

Before web analytics, people with a product or service to sell online had to play a sort of poker game to win their customer; they hedged their bets, and hoped or prayed. Whether a visitor was just browsing your website, or a serious shopper was ready to make a purchase, gathering data to gain customer knowledge was like crossing the seven seas on a boat. It was a navigational nightmare. Now it is easier thanks to Google Analytics. Reading the data in Google Analytics gives you the power to know more about your customers and to differentiate the casual from the serious.

Data, in this context, means information related to a website's traffic. Website traffic is generated when a visitor directly types in the URL of your website in the web browser, clicks on a link in a search engine, or clicks on a link from another "referring" website.

Google Analytics collects and buckets the data into several categories. This categorization allows you to focus on visitors' behavioral patterns in order to better understand the type of people visiting and the nature of their visit.

Why and how is reading this data important for you, the website owner? Well, website traffic is the only aspect of your website that is monetized. Reading the data correctly will also increase the value of your website when the quality of the traffic gets better.

Here are some helpful hints to analyzing and measuring the data better:

- If you have an e-commerce site, then identify which traffic sources lead to revenue. Google Analytics has an overview section that allows you to see e-commerce by source, number of transactions, and the specific product sold (see Rule 32, "Measure e-Commerce Data").
- When analyzing your traffic, avoid focusing on just a single metric. For example, pageviews alone is not actionable because you don't know what the number really means. But, pageviews in the context of other metrics, like time on site, help you get a clearer picture.
- Use calculated metrics, such as return on investment (ROI), conversion rate, and cost per acquisition when performing "apple-to-apple" metric comparisons versus raw data, such as visits or pageviews.
- Use the graph mode whenever applicable to compare two metrics. Visualization always leads to a better understanding of the data.
- When in graph mode, focus on analyzing trends and identify any unique peaks or valleys in the data set. Google Analytics allows you to enter in a custom date range, compare that date range to the past, and view the data by day, week, or month.
- Ask yourself questions like, "Did visits increase or did each visitor look at more pages?"

Understanding how to read the data will move you closer to understanding your customers. More importantly, reading the data correctly will enable you with the knowledge to know when, why, where, to what extent, and which of your products and/or services meet your customer needs.

4 Understand the Language

The greatest obstacle to international understanding is the barrier of language.
- Christopher Dawson, English Scholar

In order to get the most out of your Google Analytics account, you need to understand the language of analytics. Without that knowledge, increasing the performance of your website will be difficult.

Understanding the language of Google Analytics will give you the answers you need to improve and refine the content and layout of your website. The benefits will allow you to drive more traffic and convert more business. But like any foreign language, it can be difficult for a non-native speaker. This is especially so in the online marketing world where buzzwords come and go and tech-related verbiage is an everyday part of the language. There are also A LOT of acronyms, including, but not limited to, CPA (cost per action), CPC (cost per click), CTR (click through rate), PPC (pay per click), and SEM (search engine marketing). Don't worry; I will cover most of these acronyms in later chapters. You can also refer to the Appendix A: Glossary for definitions.

Take the Chinese language, for example. It has thousands of separate characters and a vast vocabulary. Google Analytics is similar, in that the degree of information is endless. Some of the data can be easily understood without additional analysis. Other data may have multiple meanings or be difficult to comprehend, especially when combined with other metrics. For example, if someone told you that approximately 80 percent of your clicks came from natural results you need to know that "natural" is synonymous with "organic" and "SEO." You also need to know that when it comes to organic search, "clicks" really mean "visits."

Another common mistake usually made in the language of Google Analytics is the use of the word, "search engine marketing" (SEM). SEM encompasses all of the activities undertaken to promote a product or service via a search engine. This means search engine optimization (SEO) and/or pay per click (PPC). I find that most people improperly refer to SEM as just PPC, when in fact PPC is a part of SEM. Another example would be the misuse of "hit" in web analytics to mean visitors or page views. A "hit" is a request for a file from a server, regardless of what type of file, and are in no way a measure of the number of visitors that view a site.

As you can see, understanding the language isn't so clear-cut. For example, visits and clicks may seem similar but are defined differently and almost always show different numbers. This is because some visitors may have clicked on an advertisement and then later, during a different session, returned directly to the site through a bookmark. I found that this discrepancy happens most often with e-commerce related sites that offer coupons or deals. Savvy users will bookmark a product page or coupon download page in their browser as a shortcut. Understanding the difference between clicks and visitors will certainly come in handy.

Could you really make significant improvements to the performance of your website if you had this data? Not likely...if you do not really know what it means. Knowing the acronyms, common terms, and definitions will help you to get started in learning the language. (Definitions of key terms are included in Appendix A.)

Starting with the basic terms and expanding your grasp of the "analytics language" over time is the best approach. In addition, learn the acronyms first. Not knowing what CPC means could have a financial impact. Understanding the lingo of Google Analytics may take time, but it is not difficult. You will find that you will be conversing in a language you never thought possible.

5 Keep It Simple, Silly

Things should be made as simple as possible, but not any simpler.
- Albert Einstein

Let's face it, any program or tool can be difficult to master even for the most experienced among us. Google Analytics is no different. It can be complex, intricate, and at times intractable. Worst of all, it can inundate us with too much data and choices. The trick is to "KISS" all that it has to offer—that is, Keep It Simple, Silly. Whether you are the most experienced user or know next to nothing about Google Analytics, you can use a few simple tips to help KISS better in order to maximize your efforts.

Know the Basics

This may seem obvious to some, but to others, especially those viewing Google Analytics for the first time, the jargon may be a bit foreign. If you focus on these basic but important areas, you will be off to a good start in understanding most of what is reported.

- **Arrival method:** How are people finding you? Google Analytics breaks traffic down into three areas: Direct Traffic (visitors coming directly to your URL), Search Engines (visitors coming to your website via a search engine) and Referring Sites (i.e. Twitter, Facebook, etc.). For search engines, Google Analytics even breaks down the data between organic search and paid search. Understand why traffic is being driven or not being driven via one of these areas.

- **Bounce rate:** this is the percentage of visitors who went to one page only and left your site. The higher this number, the more people are leaving immediately. You need to ask yourself, "Why?" and then use the data you have available to find out.
- **Content:** What pages do people spend the most time on? Are your products/services pages attracting any visits? What about your blog?
- **Keywords:** What keywords are people finding your site with? Are the keywords relevant and converting?
- **Location:** Where is the traffic coming from? If you are local and receiving national attention then you might review your geo-targeting, or expand your business.

Create the Dashboard

Dashboards help you visualize and track trends on every level of your business. They also help to align activities with key goals while keeping you on top of vital statistics and key performance indicators (KPIs). In simpler terms, dashboards are there to communicate the performance of one or more metrics (starting with the metrics mentioned above). With colored bars and nice graphs trending over time, dashboards can be easy to look at and help you gauge your website's overall performance. (See Rule 17, "Customize Your Dashboard," for more information.)

Set up Reporting

You are probably very busy just trying to keep your head above water. But if you have taken the time to understand a few metrics and have gone as far as setting up a dashboard then you might as well take that final plunge and set up automated reports. It's the old saying in business, "You cannot manage what you cannot measure." Therefore, automated reports delivered to your email inbox weekly or monthly will establish a good habit of viewing your Google Analytics data.

Keeping these three tips in mind will help you keep it simple. Otherwise, you can easily fall prey to the mountain of data that Google Analytics has to offer and not know where to begin.

6 Think like an End User

Customers buy for their reasons, not yours.
- Henry Ford

It is important to remember that most of your site's visitors have very little patience, and can be easily distracted by all the jazz in your website that leads to nowhere. Functionality, relevance, and immediacy are key touch points in all sites.

Successful, revenue generating websites are gauged by traffic (to a degree) and by meeting website goals, not by buzz. To reach the pinnacle of success with your website, it is imperative that you think like an end user, not a site owner. Below are some ideas that can help you with your transition from seeing things like a site owner to seeing things like an end-user, along with a means of measuring your work.

Have a Clear Message

Make your website message loud and clear. If you are selling French perfumes online, say that right up front. Make sure the call to action is at the forefront of the site rather than flashy images that do not call for measurable and tangible action (like buying your perfume). Avoid masking your message with design. In Google Analytics, the measurement of success will be a decrease in bounce rate (e.g. viewing more than one page) and an increase in the amount of time visitors spend on your site.

Make It Easy to Navigate

The navigation of your website is the single most important element in creating an accessible and usable website. Therefore, a visitor should not feel challenged when using your site. Users should be able to go where they want on your site, quickly and easily. Period. The measurement of success in Google Analytics will be an increase in pageviews.

Remember the Shopping Cart

If you are selling something online, consider your credibility and your customers' peace of mind when deciding on a shopping cart. Default shopping carts are best avoided; always go for a branded shopping cart to lend credibility. Choose a shopping cart that includes features such as cross-sell, multiple add-to-cart, and other direct call to actions. You cannot be too careful when it involves your customers' money! The measurement of success in Google Analytics will be an increase in transactions and revenue.

You've Got Mail

Have you ever visited a website that looked impressive, professionally designed, and well written, but were unable to find the phone number? Don't make the mistake of sending prospects hunting for your contact information. Put your phone number/contact details in a prominent position. The best practice would be at the top of each page in the same, consistent location. The measurement of success in Google Analytics would be an increase in conversions (e.g. recorded calls and contact submissions).

Applying these best practices may just translate into better website performance metrics in Google Analytics.

At the very least, taking action on your website will help you better understand how your visitors are behaving by measuring the success. You can use Google Analytics to continue to improve upon the work you have already put into your website.

7 Identify Key Metrics

Within the language of analytics, there are several essential acronyms you need to understand in order to analyze the data in Google Analytics. Among the long list of acronyms in Google Analytics there are three that stand out among the rest because they are directly tied to results (mainly e-commerce results). Those three metrics are: conversion rate (CR), cost per action (CPA) and return on investment (ROI).

Conversion Rates (CR)

In the world of online marketing, a conversion rate is the ratio of visitors who "convert" a visit into a desired action such as email opt-ins, product sales, white paper downloads, and subscription signups. The calculation is simply the number of conversions divided by the number of visits or clicks if you are measuring pay per click performance. For example, if you had 100 visitors to your website on a given day and five of those visitors subscribed to your e-newsletter, then your conversion rate would be five percent.

Cost per Action (CPA)

A cost per action, also known as cost per order, cost per lead, or cost per conversion, is the advertising cost you pay for one completed action/order/lead/conversion. CPA is calculated by dividing the total advertising cost by total completed actions. For example, if last month you spent $1,000 on advertising to generate

2,000 visitors and 20 of them subscribed to your newsletter, your cost per action for a newsletter subscription is $50, or $1000 divided by 20.

Ideally, you want the lowest cost per action possible. In other words, the less amount of money you pay for a lead or conversion, the better. Of course, you may not mind paying a higher CPA, depending on the number of purchases a visitor made over time and their lifetime value. But in most cases, a low CPA is desired.

Return on Investment (ROI)

Return on investment is the most common profitability ratio for an online business. ROI is simply a comparison of how much you spent versus how much you made. Measuring ROI for online campaigns is a huge advantage over offline advertising, such as newspapers, magazines, radio or television, where this level of ROI is difficult to measure.

To calculate ROI, subtract the ad cost from the revenue generated. For example, if you spent $500 on an advertising campaign and sold $1,500 worth of product as a result, then the ad profit is $1,000. Then divide the ad profit by the ad cost. In this case, your ad profit is $1,000 and your ad cost is $500, so your ROI would be 100 percent.

CR, CPA, and ROI have a purpose and cannot be understated. They help you pinpoint the success of each marketing initiative and how much of your budget is allocated to each. What's great is that Google Analytics automatically measures the goal conversion rate and return on investment for you so you don't have to worry about the calculations.

8 Identify Conversions

A conversion can have multiple definitions, depending on the objective of the website or business. For example, it can be turning a website visitor into a prospect or lead if you are selling a service. It could also be converting a prospective visitor into a customer if you are selling a product. Conversion types come in many forms so there is no excuse not to identify at least one. Google Analytics is a handy tool that every website owner should use in order to assist in identifying conversions. Would a carpenter work without a ruler? Would a doctor work without a stethoscope? Would an accountant work without a calculator? Obviously not. So why would you, the website owner, work without your most important tool?

Here are some types of conversion activities that you could consider:

- Email opt-ins
- Newsletter signups
- Form submissions
- Product sales
- Coupon downloads
- White paper downloads
- Case study downloads
- Videos watched
- Forwards to friends
- Sharing of articles via social media websites
- Blog comments
- "Follows" on Twitter
- "Likes" on Facebook
- Phone calls

Most of the above desired actions are measurable in Google Analytics. They can also be applicable to anything, including social media. For example, suppose you are using Twitter to drive sales because your product requires a level of engagement with prospects. Therefore, the conversion could take the form of a specific number of tweets, re-tweets, and/or follows.

Still not sure you have identified one or all of your conversions? Then take the following into account.

- Review your organization's mission statement to better understand the business goals and objectives
- Maintain focus on what your website does and why
- For large organizations, collaborate with differing internal departments
- Identify your marketing objectives
- Eliminate competing objectives, create a hierarchy, and then sequence objectives
- Review historical data
- Identify short-term (six months to a year) and long-term (a year or more) conversions
- Consider your visitor's background, knowledge, language, etc.

Identifying conversions is a process that can include your customers, colleagues, and stakeholders. Conversions need to be an integral part of your organization. Achieving success is a team effort and company-wide initiative. Suppose you are a startup company or marketing a new product. Then it is important to indentify whom your "conversions" are in order to build visibility for the company or product.

Even if you are a marketing manager for a big brand and create a lot of chatter across the web then you will have to identify multiple conversions. Your efforts should be focused on finding what drives the most results for your business. This single objective of choosing conversions, regardless of how big or small your business is, will have a long-term impact and contribute the highest revenue potential over all other objectives.

The bottom line is that it is never too late to identify a conversion for your website. Conversions are your best friend in Google Analytics—they help you understand and identify the successes and failures of your website, which, in turn, will allow you to reach marketing goals faster.

9 Assign Monetary Values

Money was never a big motivation for me, except as a way to keep score. The real excitement is playing the game.
- Donald Trump, *Trump: The Art of the Deal* (1989)

When working with Google Analytics, you will want to assign a monetary value to any conversion you define. This is the most effective way to evaluate the true value of a visitor who converts on a desired action. Failing to do so could result in omission of critical data. You may also find it difficult to measure key metrics, such as ROI or CPA.

Most business websites measure incoming revenue based on the number of conversions, so assigning monetary values help keep tabs on your revenue stream. It also helps you to showcase the monetary value of your site to the website's stakeholders. There's no value in saying, "Our site has 355 newsletter signups, 260 comments, 20 leads generated from submissions, 900 social shares, 76 RSS subscriptions, and 286 account registrations." The true value is in adding the all-important rider: "...This represents $50,000 in value to our business, up 20 percent from last month."

You can assign a monetary value to a conversion by following these best practices:

First, specify a name that you will recognize when viewing the goals within each set of your reports. Example: "email signup," "newsletter signup," or "article download."

Second, identify pages in a defined "funnel" or the path that you expect visitors to take on their way to converting to the goal (see Rule 20, "Convert Your Visitors"). This will help you determine where visitors drop off during the conversion path.

Third, assign a monetary value for the goal. For example, if you are able to close 10 percent of your prospects/leads that are generated via your "contact us" page and your average transaction is $500, then you might assign $50 (10 percent of $500) as the value of your "contact us" goal. In contrast, if only one percent of mailing list signups result in a sale, you might only assign $5 (one percent of $500) to your "email signup" goal.

Monetary goal values give a holistic view of which traffic sources perform the best. Google Analytics uses an assigned goal value to calculate ROI, per visit goal value, and other important metrics. You can measure the real performance of traffic coming to your site by using the goal conversion rate, which treats all goals equally by adjusting the weight for each goal against the per visit goal value. You may discover that your email campaigns have a higher conversion rate compared to your PPC campaigns, but a lower per visit goal value.

When considering the monetary goal value for a conversion, don't focus solely on the absolute value. Take into account the relative value of each goal. For example, a blogger may find that a posted comment is a more valuable conversion than a "contact us" form submission.

In the case of PPC campaigns, goals with a monetary value can help you determine the true outcome for each active campaign. In other words, it can quickly tell you if you are making money or losing money. This is essential information for how to best optimize your PPC spending. You can go even further by comparing revenue per click against cost per click. You could be under spending on a PPC campaign that has a low average conversion rate but high revenue per click and vice versa. But you won't know unless you actually assign monetary goal values.

Finally, try to be as accurate as possible when assigning a monetary goal value. This will only lead to more accurate data and better decision making. However, with that said, monetary goal values can be changed at any time so don't fret. Just assigning a monetary value is an important step to effectively using Google Analytics.

Part II
Monitoring: What You Need to Focus on to Make Decisions

The content in this section is intended to help you maintain focus on some of the important aspects of working with Google Analytics. Some of those aspects include understanding your visitors and introducing best practices

- Rule 10: Understand Visitor Intent
- Rule 11: Understand Visitor Behavior
- Rule 12: Practice Kaizen
- Rule 13: Use Your Intelligence
- Rule 14: Benchmark Your Data
- Rule 15: Choose Keywords Wisely
- Rule 16: Do the Two-Step with Your Content

10 Understand Visitor Intent

If you do not know others and do not know yourself, you will be in danger in every single battle.
- Sun Tzu, The Art of War

What is your website worth? This million-dollar question depends on the number of visitors, pageviews, time on site, and visitor's intent. The last factor is not only the most intriguing but also arguably the most important.

The intent of a visitor is the primary reason they went to the website in the first place. Visitor intent could be information gathering, picture or video viewing, new product review, price comparison, or idle browsing.

Why Is Visitor Intent Important?

Whether you are selling to customers or directly to other businesses, information on visitor intent provides you with enough data to know exactly what your customer is looking for. You can then prepare and provide accordingly.

It also gives you insight into a visitor's interest. It will help to distinguish between value-add and non-value-add content and to understand what is missing. If a thousand visitors came to your site looking for product X and did not find it, there is an opportunity for you to add product X to the site.

How Do You Measure Visitor Intent?

Customer surveys and research reports are two traditional methods adopted by businesses to understand the needs and motivations of their end customers. Another method can be found right in Google Analytics. We have all seen the small search box on most websites where visitors can type in a keyword to specifically search for content. Imagine searching for something on Amazon.com without using a search box...that's how important a tool this is. Using the internal site search feature in Google Analytics will allow you to track how people use the search box on your site and what these visitors are actually looking for

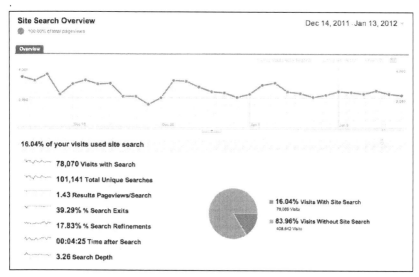

Figure 1: Site Search Overview

Using internal site search data, which is located under the "Content" section, shows how many visitors used this feature along with results per search request. Referencing this data is a very systematic approach to collecting visitor intent. The following is recommended in order to make the most of this feature.

- Figure out the percentage of visitors using site search by reviewing historical data (six months or longer).
- Note the search items in order of number of searches to prioritize addition of new content.
- Try to understand what the visitor was doing prior to the search—correlate that with the keyword query to help further understand the intent of the user.

Internal site search provides valuable insight into the visitor's intent by providing a list of keywords that were searched for. It also helps you understand what activities occurred, such as a purchase, a download, or a prolonged browsing session. The combination of the two provides a solution to produce content and retain visitors coming to a website looking for a particular topic.

11 Understand Visitor Behavior

In just a few years, Google Analytics has completely transformed how you measure your website's performance. No longer is measuring website performance just for developers and technology professionals, nor is it gauged solely on tracking hits. Using Google Analytics has now shifted to marketers, designers, small business owners, and business executives, all of whom seek answers to more complex questions about website behavior.

It is no longer about just getting visitors but rather turning those visitors into customers...and it all starts with understanding visitor behavior.

Whether you know it or not, the people who visit your website are doing you a favor by helping you improve site performance, telling you what's working or not working, and growing your business. That's why there is an entire section in Google Analytics dedicated to just visitors. To assist in understanding visitor behavior, you can adopt the following key performance indicators (KPI).

Bounce Rate: Google Analytics defines a bounce as any visit where the visitor views only one page on the site, and then does something else like clicking on a link to a page on a different website, closing an open window or tab, typing a new URL, clicking the "back" button to leave the site, or perhaps the user doesn't do anything and a session timeout occurs. A high bounce rate can indicate a poor site experience, irrelevant content, or confusion on the part of the visitor. On the contrary, you should expect high bounce rates for pay per click landing pages or sites with very minimal content.

Time on Site: this is calculated by generating time stamps on a visit to every page and then calculating the difference between the last and first time-stamp of a visitor session. In case of a bounce, time on site and time on page are both reported as 00:00 minutes. Keep in mind that a low time on site average is not perceived as negative. For example, if the average time on site is only 55 seconds, then your visitors could be landing on the appropriate page or finding exactly what they are looking for without having to navigate further.

Average Pageview: this is one of the most used key performance indicators as it is a quick understanding of website engagement. This is a ratio of the number of pageviews the average web visitor views per session—it is a ratio and not a metric. So, compare average pageviews between segments or different groups of people visiting your site, varying time frames, and across multiple sites or sub-domains (different sub-sites of your main site).

Funnel Visualization: funnels are custom paths that you want the visitors to take before they reach your designated goal (see Rule 20, "Convert Your Visitors"). This can be used for both e-commerce and lead generation websites. If your shopping cart abandonment rates are high, you can see what page visitors are most likely to drop off before making a transaction. Funnels allow you to take action by making adjustments to the page with the high drop off rate so that visitors are more likely to continue with their purchase.

You don't necessarily need experienced professionals to identify behavior patterns. Simply utilizing the above KPIs will help you identify and understand visitor behavior, which will, in turn, assist you in improving your website's overall performance.

Practice Kaizen

Web analytics, according to the infinite number of sources on the World Wide Web, is believed to do everything you want and more. So, you invest in Google Analytics and wait for it to work its magic. You wait and wait. However, you must realize that enabling Google Analytics is just the beginning. You can't stop at the installation and leave it at that.

Truth is, Google Analytics is a never-ending practice. You can be flying high in April and then be shot down in May. That's the nature of the website traffic. In order to cope with the inconsistencies and the highs and lows that go with it, practice what the Japanese call "kaizen," or continuous improvement.

To continually improve the performance of your website, use the following criteria to practice kaizen.

- **Data consistency and quality:** always make sure the data is accurate and consistent. Your goal is to compare apples with apples, not apples with oranges. The best way to compare data is using ratios. An example would be the conversion rate or click through rate of one marketing campaign against the conversion rate of another marketing campaign. Another example would be comparing the cost per action of two marketing initiatives.
- **Flexibility:** you have to deal with the reporting needs of various stakeholders, from global management to local/national marketers in a dynamic context where various content and technologies

coexist. Google Analytics can assist by allowing you to set up various reports for each stakeholder based on their needs (see Rule 39, "Share Your Data").

- **Organization and integration:** web analytics is a process you need to integrate into your organization AND your technical infrastructure. You need to define roles and responsibilities. You need to have methodologies. You need resources. Google Analytics can help by allowing you to grant "user" access or "administrative" access to others who may have an interest or can contribute to the success of your website.
- **Education and communication:** learn how to use the data, how to interpret it, and how to make it actionable. Not all websites are alike. You need to stick to it and give it time. Let everyone in the loop know the value of using Google Analytics and how kaizen practices are the way to go. Spread insights, knowledge, and data across departments, hierarchies, and the whole company. Otherwise, all those state-of-art detailed reports that Google Analytics generates will only end up in the shredder, destroying any possible incremental value to your business.

Continuous improvement. Continuous updates. Kaizen. It's what will make Google Analytics work for you. What use are those reports and data when no one has a clue about what to do with them?

Continuous improvement is not rocket science. With Google Analytics, and of course, patience, perseverance and kaizen, you will stop saying, "50 percent of our Marketing worked, we just aren't sure which 50 percent it was."

13

Use Your Intelligence

Intelligence is not to make no mistakes, but quickly to see how to make them good.
— Bertolt Brecht, German Poet and Playwright, 1898-1956

Google Analytics has gotten a lot smarter over the years. You can even go as far as saying they are more intelligent now, now that they have added an "Intelligence" feature. This feature acts as a virtual assistant by monitoring key information in your account and then alerting you to any irregular activity. For example, if your bounce rate suddenly jumps over the course of a week, then Google Analytics Intelligence creates an alert notifying you (daily, weekly, or monthly) via email or to your mobile phone via text message.

It also works with your AdWords account as long as the two are linked (see Rule 27, "Link AdWords with Analytics").

When you create a custom alert, you must input your parameters. You can also configure the settings that can apply to multiple profiles and include other email addresses.

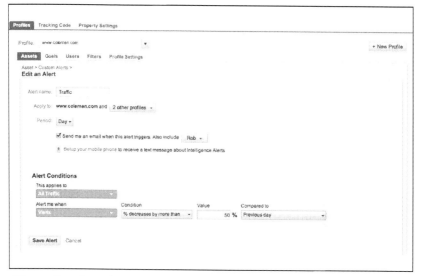

Figure 2: Creating an alert requires you to input your parameters

Google Analytics has added an insurance policy with its automatic alerts. Google Analytics Intelligence has already gone through your data and automatically posted alerts. How many and the type of alerts depends on your sensitivity to being alerted. A low sensitivity lets you view just the most significant reports, like dramatic changes in traffic. High sensitivity shows you all alerts created. It's up to you to set the scale based on your own preferences.

Intelligence is a great feature for understanding the following:

- Seasonality for specific products or categories over a period of time
- Percentage of organic or paid search results (if the number spikes or decreases) versus the average
- Impact of social media and whether traffic pattern increases due to your social marketing efforts
- Changes in conversion rates to your shopping cart or goals in order to take corrective action

It is comforting to know that Google Analytics Intelligence is constantly monitoring website behavior and noting and alerting significant changes. If something out of the ordinary happens (and trust me, something significant will eventually happen), you will be the first to know. Now that is intelligent!

14 Benchmark Your Data

All successful companies are constantly benchmarking their competition. They have to know what they have to match up with day-in and day-out if their company is going to be.
- James Dunn, Actor, 1901-1967

You may elect to share your Google Analytics data with other Google products, and Google will use the data to improve the products and services they provide you. Electing to share your data "anonymously with Google and others" allows you to use benchmarking. To provide benchmarking, Google removes all identifiable information about your website, then combines the data with hundreds of other anonymous sites in comparable industries and reports them in an aggregate form.

Please note that if you select "do not share my Google Analytics data," you will not be able to use the benchmarking feature.

How Does Benchmarking Work?

Benchmarking is a reporting mechanism that tells you where your site stands among the competition. Google Analytics is used by millions of websites. As such it has access to a lot of information traffic, visitors, average time visitors spend on a site, etc. Google buckets this information based on criteria, such as countries and verticals. It uses this information to rank the sites in each of these buckets. For example, Google can rank the sites by US visitor count in the technology vertical. You see a number of charts from sites of comparable traffic, so that you can find out if your visitors stay longer on pages than average, or if they visit more pages than average.

Information about where your website stands in terms of quantity and quality of traffic in comparison to your competition is vital to monetizing the traffic the website receives. It is about knowing where you stand in your industry and helps you identify the variance between average and good.

Remember, Google does not reveal any specific data about your website. Rather, it exposes your relative standing within your vertical. This is very different from other websites that release rankings of sites based on traffic volumes.

Why Is Benchmarking Useful?

There are primarily two broad uses to benchmarking: it helps website owners increase the value of the site and also helps them pitch the site to advertisers. Consider an example of a camera review site. If the benchmarking report says that the site ranks above benchmark with visits in its industry vertical but below the benchmark for pages per visit, then there is an opportunity to investigate further.

If you are interested in advertising and pitching to high-value advertisers, you can especially use the benchmarking report to your advantage if you have the high traffic volume compared to the benchmark in your industry.

Recently, Google removed the benchmarking report from the Google Analytics interface. They are now providing benchmarking data as an expanded report that will be emailed directly to Google Analytics users that are opted-in to anonymous data sharing.[1] According to Google, the benchmarking report will include broader trends, such as geographic and traffic source differences in visitor engagement.

You may not want to utilize the benchmarking numbers on a regular basis given that it does not compare your traffic against direct competitors. Rather, you may find it interesting and even inspirational to know how you stack up against other websites in your niche.

---

1. Phil Mui, "Evolution of Analytics Benchmarking Report, *Google Analytics* (blog), March 4, 2011 (3:39 p.m.), http://bit.ly/haML0s analytics.blogspot.com/2011/03/evolution-of-analytics-benchmarking.html.

15 Choose Keywords Wisely

Life is change. Growth is optional. Choose wisely.
- Karen Kaiser Clark, Inspirational & Motivational Speaker

All year long, without pause, Google is on a hunt to collect the data we need to in order to run a successful website. All that this high-powered engine requires is a few well-chosen words, or keywords, to produce results in nanoseconds. That's all there is to it. Or is it? It is actually the relevance of the keyword that draws in the qualified traffic to your website from the search engines. So in order to lure this highly qualified traffic, you need to develop an understanding of how to select the most effective keywords.

The task of choosing keywords can be very cumbersome given the infinite number of possibilities to choose from. Choosing the wrong keywords can be disastrous and set you back months while you are ramping up your search engine marketing efforts.

Below are a few considerations for choosing keywords that can help bring the most relevant, qualified traffic to your website.

- Say no to single words by using phrases or "long tail" keywords (a keyword phrase that has at least three words in the phrase). For example, choosing the keyword phrase "men's running shoes" will draw qualified traffic versus the singular keyword "shoes".
- Target highly searched terms that have as little competition as possible. However, do not use keywords that have less competition just for this reason alone.

Note that you can retrieve competition data by using Google's Keyword Tool (https://adwords.google.com/select/KeywordToolExternal).

- Choose keywords that are specific with a narrow focus, but avoid getting too specific so as to not lose traffic. For example, "Nike men's running shoes" might be specific enough versus something narrower like "Nike Air Pegasus men's running shoes".
- Localize your keywords by making use of your geographical location. For example, "shoe store in San Francisco" might yield better results by attracting local traffic to your website or storefront.

Of course, you may be tempted to focus your energy on the keywords that are driving the most traffic to your website. That's where Google Analytics comes into play. Take a look at a keywords report and see what is happening after a visitor arrives to your website. Your focus should shift to keywords that assist in achieving your website goals versus those with higher volumes that yield less revenue.

	Search Term	Visits ↓	Revenue	Transactions	Average Value	Ecommerce Conversion Rate	Per Visit Value
1.	lantern	549	$2,348.06	29	$80.87	5.28%	$4.27
2	tents	451	$654.58	5	$120.24	1.20%	$1.45
3.	canopy	439	$914.46	5	$187.97	1.24%	$2.08
4	instant tent	402	$212.26	3	$58.48	0.90%	$0.53
5.	lanterns	372	$1,274.18	21	$58.51	5.85%	$3.43
6.	cot	333	$654.61	7	$117.74	2.17%	$2.56
7.	cots	306	$29.02	1	$15.99	0.59%	$0.09
8.	tent	303	$1,295.78	10	$119.01	3.59%	$4.28
9.	canoe	270	$0.00	0	$0.00	0.00%	$0.00
10.	oven	261	$59.90	1	$33.01	0.69%	$0.23

Figure 3: Google Analytics displays what keywords visitors are using and which ones are converting

Furthermore, the average per visit value, or the value of a visit calculated as revenue divided by visits, may be a better indicator of keyword value as opposed to just total revenue. In looking at Figure 3, we can see that the search term "tent" (keyword 8) actually translated into a higher average per visit value at $4.28 compared to other keyword terms in the sample set including a similar keyword in "tents" (keyword 2), which yielded only $1.45 per visit value.

Regardless of how much traffic you get per month for a search term, even if you are generating very few visitors, the fact that you can drive a high conversion rate or a high per visit value from a keyword may suggest that it is a keeper! And while there are hundreds of ways to begin the keyword selection process, your best bet will be with Google Analytics.

16 Do the Two-Step with Your Content

Let's get right to the point: website content is the heart and soul of your website's success. The content you write can be informational, commercial, or a current event. Its purpose can be for entertainment, marketing, research, specific industries, online advertising, or search engines. It can be objective or subjective. Whatever the case, effectively using your content is a two-step process.

If you have ever taken dance lessons then you know that particular dances have several steps. For the uncoordinated amongst us, like myself, memorizing dance steps can be a difficult task. The dance number known as content is a mere two-step: leverage the content and measure it for success.

Leverage the Content

It is no longer a secret that search engines like content and feed off it to determine rankings. And it's not just content that gets search engines excited about crawling a site, it's "fresh" content that keeps the robots coming back for more. With the advent of "real-time content" in search listings, search engines (Google in particular) will seek out the best and most useful content on the Internet for any given keyword query. Updating your website content and blogging regularly will not only help fulfill the appetites of hungry search engines but also increase your chance of higher rankings and more traffic as a result.

Measure the Content for Success

Using Google Analytics, you can analyze the traffic that is reading unique, fresh, and relevant content and, as a result, moving seamlessly throughout your site. Below are a few reports that you can utilize in Google Analytics to interpret the flow of traffic.

Top Landing Pages

This report allows you to view the most popular pages that visitors first landed on. Compare your landing pages over time and check for consistencies and fluctuations. Give pages with strong content, but little traffic, more life with promotion on social media.

Navigation Summary

This report provides information on how visitors found your content and what page they went to next. Every time visitors click on a link within the copy and navigate to multiple pages they are giving you information about their content choices. Leverage this information in order to gain insight on visitor behavior. (See Figure 4.)

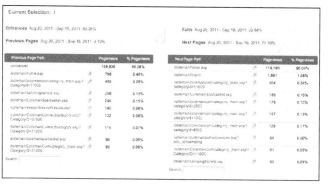

Figure 4: *The Navigation Summary Report illustrates the flow of traffic from one page to the next*

Entrance Paths/Keywords/Sources

These reports show the path, keywords, and sources visitors used to get to your content, what pages they viewed next, and the page they eventually ended on. If you add content frequently, then you should analyze the variation of keywords that are driving traffic.

Levering your content and then measuring it work in tandem. The results might be surprising and lead to better educated choices, such as the topics you choose to post.

Part III
Reporting: How to Get the Information You Need

The content in this section is intended to help you apply best practices in order to get the most accurate and precise information out of Google Analytics. Everything from filtering to tagging is included so that you can focus on what is important.

- Rule 17: Customize Your Dashboard
- Rule 18: Decide on Your Goal Type
- Rule 19: Measure Dollars, Not Design
- Rule 20: Convert Your Visitors
- Rule 21: Use Filters
- Rule 22: Tag Your URLs
- Rule 23: Differentiate Your Search Efforts
- Rule 24: Measure Page Value, Not Volume
- Rule 25: Measure Referring Traffic
- Rule 26: Monitor Your Social Media Efforts

17 Customize Your Dashboard

Similar to the dashboard of your car, Google Analytics gives you an overview of how your website is performing (see Rule 3, "Learn to Read...the Data, That Is") when running. Like the "check engine" light on your car dashboard, the Google Analytics dashboard can provide you with enough data to alert you when something doesn't look right. It probably won't give you everything you need to know to fix it, but it will alert you that something needs attention.

The Google Analytics dashboard is completely customizable for each profile you have in your Google Analytics account. You can add, remove, and reorganize any analytics module (a maximum of 12) for your website. Adding is as simple as hitting the "Add to Dashboard" button at the top of any report. Reorganizing the dashboard is as simple as dragging and dropping boxes into positions you prefer.

To make the most out of your dashboard, there are a few modules you should include as standard features on your dashboard. These items help you keep an eye on the leading indicators.

Content Overview

This module allows you to see what pages have the most pageviews. It's a great way to figure out which high-impact pages you should start testing and optimizing. As an alternative, you can add the "Top Content" module, which shows the most popular specific pages versus the content overview module.

Traffic Sources Overview

This module provides an overview of how much traffic you are receiving from direct traffic, search engines, and referring sites. The data is presented as a pie chart in order to visually see what is driving the trends.

Referring Sites

A subset of the Traffic Sources Overview, Referring Sites on the dashboard allows you to scan what external sites are generating, or "referring," the most traffic outside of search engines. This is especially helpful for tracking when your site is mentioned elsewhere on the web, like on blogs, social media sites, and directories.

Campaigns

A subset of the Traffic Sources Overview module, this particular module will report results from campaigns that you explicitly control, tagged with Urchin Traffic Monitor (UTM) tracking (see Rule 22, "Tag your URLs") and allow you to quickly determine the effectiveness of each.

Keywords

This module shows a list of the top five keywords that drive traffic. As a segment, you can also add the search engine associated with each keyword. You can also create two specific modules that displays paid search related keywords and organic search related keywords.

New versus Returning

This module displays the top five countries that are sending traffic to your website, the type of visitor coming from each country, and the number of visits.

There are hundreds of variations of modules that you can add to a dashboard. Again, what is important is that the dashboard is customized with key metrics so that you can easily flag data points that need further investigating. Just like on your car, this is something you do not want to ignore.

Decide on Your Goal Type

We create goals (in Analytics) because they have to be achieved. It does not matter how long they take because they serve us. The higher we set them, the higher we will go.
- Marina Quilez, Google Analytics Professional

Enabling a goal in order to track a conversion (see Rule 8, "Identify Conversions") is one of the best ways to assess how well your site meets its business objectives. The hardest task for most website owners always seems to be identifying what goal type to use. A goal can be any activity on your website that's important to the success of your business or that drives a certain type of behavior that is important to your business. An account signup or requests for a sales call are two examples of a goal. Goals are useful if you would like to understand how much time visitors stay or, more importantly, do not stay on a specific section of your website.

Every website should have at least one goal, especially now since Google Analytics allows for up to 20.[2] The following are different goal types available to choose from. Remember, select goals that help you achieve your defined business objectives.

Time-Based Goals

Time-based goals can be set if you would like to measure a specific amount of time a visitor has spent on your website. You are simply telling Google Analytics the hours, minutes, and seconds that you would like a visitor to spend on your site before a goal is counted. You can even track a time-based goal if a visitor does not reach

---

2. "How do I set up goals and funnels?" Analytics Help, accessed [May 31, 2010], http://bit.ly/aBiWqu www.google.com/support/analytics/bin/answer.py?answer=55515.

a certain period of time on your website. For example, you would use this goal if you added a video to your website and want to measure how long visitors stay as a result of adding the video.

Pageview Based Goals

This is similar to time-based goals except you are tracking goals when a visitor exceeds (or doesn't exceed) a certain number of pages. The same conditions apply as time-based goals, meaning you are telling Google Analytics the number of pageviews you would like to set up as a goal for each visitor. You could use this goal if you have a number of pages on your website (such as an e-commerce website) and want to establish a goal for the number of pageviews visitors reach with each visit.

URL Destination Goals

Identifying a specific URL destination has always been the traditional method of tracking goals in Google Analytics. To define a goal in Google Analytics, you specify the page that visitors see once they have completed the activity. For example, if you have a shopping cart on your website, then you would set the "Thank You" or confirmation page as the URL destination goal.

You can also assign a value to a goal in order to evaluate how often visitors become customers after reaching a goal on your website. For example, if you close 10 percent of the people who request to be con-tacted, and your average transaction is $500, you might assign $50 (i.e. 10 percent of $500) to your "Contact Me" goal. Or, if only five percent of mailing list signups result in a sale, you might only assign $25 to your "email signup" goal.

Setting goals is not a difficult process but it needs to be a thoughtful process. Keep the points below in mind and you will be on your way to successful tracking.

- Consider organizing goals by function (i.e. by time, download, etc.)
- A visitor can only convert each goal once per visit
- Consider consolidating all your goals into one profile
- Creating new goals will not modify your historical data, only future data

19 Measure Dollars, Not Design

A set definite objective must be established if we are to accomplish anything in a big way.
- John Macdonald, First Prime Minister of Canada

Despite the advances in web technology, availability of free, open source platforms, and all the social media buzz, the primary focus for website owners still appears to be on web design. True. Web design is important, especially when it comes to branding. However, if the design doesn't translate into dollars, then it isn't worth it.

Truth be told, the success of any website will depend on more than just design. Having a website isn't good enough anymore. If a business is spending money on a website then there must be some level of return on investment. There is no cookie cutter approach for this one. But, there are guidelines for establishing goals to measure the return on investment of your website.

Identify Your Objectives

Before you even start the design and development of your website, ask yourself what you want to accomplish for yourself and your visitors. For example, visitors want to be able to find information on your site quickly and easily, as mentioned in Rule 16, "Do the Two-Step with Your Content". That would equate to more pageviews and more time spent on site.

Also, describe what you want to accomplish with clarity and detail. If your goal is to provide information to the public or generate product brand awareness, write down exactly how you are going to provide information or generate product awareness. State exactly how and when you would evaluate your progress.

Make Them Obtainable

Break your website goal(s) into smaller, obtainable goals. For example, if you sell multiple products organized into multiple categories, then establish a goal for each category or each product web page. This will help identify areas of strengths and weaknesses on your way to evaluating your overall website goal.

Establish goals you know you are actually capable of obtaining. If the goal is to generate new leads, but you get very little site traffic, then set your sights low. Be realistic. It's better to reach your goal, regardless of how small, than to not reach it at all. This will allow you to better determine what works or doesn't work.

Make Them Time-Sensitive

Set goals by time and/or importance into specified target dates. For example, if you are trying to sell products for the holiday season or communicating the latest product or service information to customers, then make sure you note your start and completion dates. If your goal is to obtain new website visitors and customers, then your site should be centered on the relevant keywords that new customers would use to search for your site (see Rule 15, "Choose Keywords Wisely").

Whether it's increasing traffic, converting customers, or just simply sharing information, having clear, established goals and objectives will keep you focused and on the right path. And conversely, prevent you from performing unnecessary analysis. It will also help you better understand your website's successes and failures and allow you to fix and improve your website. Otherwise, you will never be satisfied with the results regardless of the design.

Convert Your Visitors

To convert somebody, go and take them by the hand and guide them.
- St. Thomas Aquinas, Scholastic Philosopher and Theologian, 1225-1274

A conversion funnel is a schematic representation of the different web pages in relation to the number of visitors each of these pages received. It visually displays the path taken by visitors navigating from the starting point (i.e. home page) to the ending point (i.e. conversion or goal page). It also shows visitor count at each page and the percentage of visitors who proceeded to the next step in the process.

Setting up a conversion funnel requires you to specify the various paths you would like to track as part of the URL Destination goal (see Rule 18, "Decide on Your Goal Type"). Google Analytics will then record the number of visitors on all the pages in each of these paths. The report generated will give a clear picture about the pages that help in conversion and the pages that have high abandonment rates.

Whenever the quality of a page falls, the bounce rate increases, and the website loses its visitor count. This is especially important for commercial sites that sell goods and/or services. Losing visitors before they convert means lost revenue.

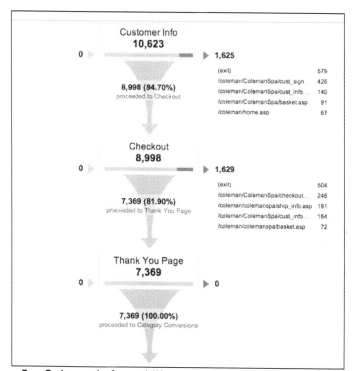

Customer Info
10,623

0 ▷ ▷ 1,625

(exit)	579
/coleman/ColemanSpa/cust_sign	428
/coleman/ColemanSpa/cust_info...	140
/coleman/ColemanSpa/basket.asp	91
/coleman/home.asp	67

8,998 (84.70%)
proceeded to Checkout

Checkout
8,998

0 ▷ ▷ 1,629

(exit)	504
/coleman/ColemanSpa/checkout...	248
/coleman/colemanspa/ship_info.asp	191
/coleman/ColemanSpa/cust_info...	164
/coleman/colemanspa/basket.asp	72

7,369 (81.90%)
proceeded to Thank You Page

Thank You Page
7,369

0 ▷ ▷ 0

7,369 (100.00%)
proceeded to Category Conversions

Figure 5: Coleman's funnel illustrates the success rate through a specific path

Consider Coleman.com, the website referenced in Figure 5. Coleman's website compares the features and prices for various categories and products. Ideally, the visitor will research the product of their interest, add one or multiple items to Coleman's shopping cart and then proceed toward securing the purchase. However, if there are too many steps in the check out process then the visitor will likely abandon, resulting in lost revenue.

Setting up a Google Analytics conversion funnel will help you identify the following:

- What causes visitors to abandon your conversion funnel
- Which behaviors lead to successful conversions
- Which web pages are negatively impacting the conversion process
- Where visitors go when they leave the funnel

Understanding conversion roadblocks via the funneling process will help you gain targeted insights into your visitors' conversion process and allow you to make the necessary corrections to avoid traffic loss and, more importantly, cart abandonment.

Use Filters

Most analytics applications (Google included) generate more information than can be easily processed or understood by the human mind. Few people realize that data that is not analyzed is data that is useless. The question becomes, how do we decipher all that data without missing anything? The quick and dirty answer is: filters. Filters allow you to modify data and customize reports so you can get the information you want in a useful, meaningful way. You can set up an infinite amount of filters.

So where do you begin? Well, before you create a filter in Google Analytics you want to first define the parameters and goal of the filter. Below are three examples of common filters that you can apply right away.

Lowercase/Uppercase

Lowercase and Uppercase filters are very useful for consolidating line items in a report. For example, if your reports contain multiple entries for a keyword or a URL, and the only difference between those entries is that the URL or keyword appears with a different combination of uppercase and lowercase letters, the Lowercase and Uppercase filters will consolidate these multiple entries into a single entry for easier data interpretation.

Exclude/Include

When you set up an Exclude filter, if the pattern matches, then the data is thrown away, or excluded from the report. Conversely, when you set up an Include filter, if the pattern matches, then the data is included in the report. An example of an Exclude filter would be to filter out all internal traffic by IP address to increase visitor traffic accuracy, meaning any visits by the website owner would be excluded from the report. An example of an Include filter would be to filter in traffic from a particular state or country.

Search and Replace

This "custom" filter can keep you sane when reading reports as the filter replaces category ID numbers and long URL strings with descriptive words that are easier to identify. A good example would be if you have a URL string containing http://www.domain.com/category.asp?catid=5. The Search and Replace filter will change this URL to something more recognizable, like the actual category name. So, the unrecognizable URL in Analytics "/category.asp?catid=5" would become "/cameras".

Below are a few important notes about filtering:

1. There are two types of filters in Google Analytics: pre-defined and custom.
2. Filters are executed sequentially in the order they are listed and may cancel each other out if not ordered properly.
3. Applying a filter to a profile only works with data going forward and will not apply to data already recorded in your Google Analytics profile.
4. You may need to use regular expressions[3] to create a filter pattern.[4]
5. You can apply a filter to a single profile or multiple profiles.

Knowing that filters are available, and applying one or multiple, will immediately pay dividends in terms of organizing and enhancing your data. It will also simplify the decision making process, improve your Google Analytics reading over time, and prevent you from pulling your hair out!

---

3. See glossary in Appendix A for definition.
4. "What are regular expressions?" Analytics Help, last updated March 8, 2008,
   http://www.google.com/support/analytics/bin/answer.py?answer=55582.

Tag Your URLs

Tracking, tracking, tracking, and more tracking. I can't say it enough. Tracking means knowing where your visitors came from so you know what is driving specific actions. This allows you to make better decisions and ultimately provide a better site experience to your visitors.

Tracking also means tagging your destination URLs in order to better understand the behavior of specific marketing campaigns. With Google Analytics, there are five such variables you can use when tagging URLs:

1. **Source:** use this to identify a search engine, newsletter name, or other source—the source of traffic or referral
2. **Medium:** use this to identify the type of medium, such as email, banner, or cost per click—the vehicle that communicated the message
3. **Campaign:** use this to identify a specific product promotion or strategic campaign
4. **Term:** use this to identify paid keywords
5. **Content:** use this to differentiate ads or links that point to the same URL within the same medium

Regardless of whether you are running display banners, email campaigns, or affiliate marketing, Google Analytics will allow you to properly identify, manage, and understand visitors who come from various multi-channel campaigns using their URL Builder tool (Figure 6). [5]

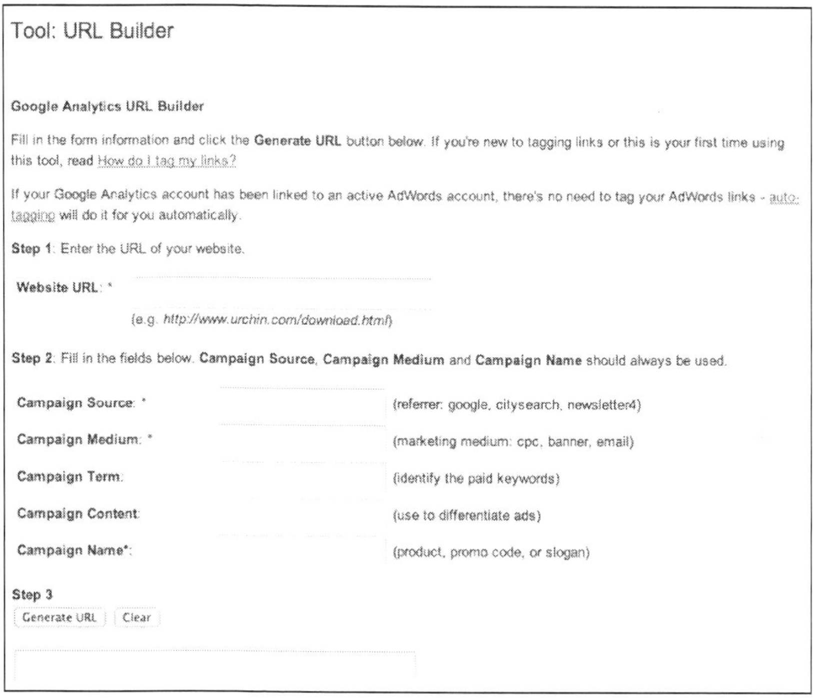
Tool: URL Builder

Google Analytics URL Builder

Fill in the form information and click the **Generate URL** button below. If you're new to tagging links or this is your first time using this tool, read How do I tag my links?

If your Google Analytics account has been linked to an active AdWords account, there's no need to tag your AdWords links - auto-tagging will do it for you automatically.

Step 1: Enter the URL of your website.

Website URL: *

(e.g. *http://www.urchin.com/download.html*)

Step 2: Fill in the fields below. **Campaign Source**, **Campaign Medium** and **Campaign Name** should always be used.

Campaign Source: * (referrer: google, citysearch, newsletter4)

Campaign Medium: * (marketing medium: cpc, banner, email)

Campaign Term: (identify the paid keywords)

Campaign Content: (use to differentiate ads)

Campaign Name*: (product, promo code, or slogan)

Step 3

Generate URL Clear

Figure 6: Google's URL builder is a simple three-step process that will produce a URL that Google Analytics can track

Stick to these best practices when tagging your advertising campaigns:

- Use consistent names and spellings for all your campaign values so that they are recorded consistently within your Google Analytics reports
- Use only the campaign variables you need—you should always use source, medium, and campaign name, but term and content are optional

If your Google Analytics account has been properly linked to your AdWords account (see Rule 27, "Link AdWords with Analytics"), you don't need to worry about tagging—Google Analytics will do it automatically! The beauty about tagging URLs is that it will allow you to measure which campaign was the most beneficial in terms of clicks, conversions, or revenue. Without this vital information, it will be hard to effectively measure the performance of each.

---

5. "Tool: URL Builder," Analytics Help, accessed [May 31, 2010], http://bit.ly/7dJR www.google.com/support/analytics/bin/answer.py?hl=en&answer=55578.

23 Differentiate Your Search Efforts

Google Analytics has a huge appetite for data. Among its most favorite is search engine traffic. This bodes well for Google Analytic's users as most websites generate most of their traffic from search engines. Google Analytics goes as far as breaking down search engine traffic into two buckets: paid search and organic search.

Paid search, also known as sponsored search, pay per click, or cost per click,[6] is traffic that originated from a sponsored listing that was paid for by the advertiser. Sponsored listings can be found in search engines (i.e. Google, Yahoo!, or Bing), websites that sell advertising space (i.e. WebMD.com), or social media sites like Facebook.

Organic search, also known as natural search or non-paid search, is traffic derived from natural listings found only in search engines. The cost is free when someone clicks on your listing in natural search results.

How Much Traffic and Revenue Are Search Engines Generating?

The "Search Engines" report (found under the "Traffic Sources Overview") provides data for both "non-paid" (organic) search and "paid" search. Clicking on "total" will display traffic for both organic and paid search. It is important to note that your paid search traffic will not

---

6. See glossary in Appendix A for specific definitions.

appear in Google Analytics if you do not properly tag your Destination URLs (see Rule 22, "Tag your URLs") nor enable the "Auto Tagging" feature in AdWords.

What Keywords Are Generating Revenue?

The "Keywords" report (found under the "Traffic Sources Overview") in Google Analytics will show the amount of traffic initiated by visitors who queried specific keyword phrases. It shows what keywords generated the most inbound traffic and highest revenue. For example, you may find that the broad keyword "cheap cameras" generated more traffic compared to the more specific keyword phrase "cheap cameras for sale". However, the more specific phrase may have generated more sales and yielded a higher return on investment.

Why Measure Paid Search Traffic against Organic Traffic?

Measuring paid traffic can help you determine the overall performance of your campaigns and keywords and whether you should invest more. Because you are paying per click for your paid search efforts, you want to make sure that your investment is justified.

You can also compare the quality of traffic between the two. Predefined search terms, specific keyword bids, ad copy and a specified landing page can influence the quality of paid traffic. Suppose you are selling products online. You would surely want to know whether your paid and/or organic search is a revenue model or a loss model. This can be accomplished by using goals (see Rule 18, "Decide on Your Goal Type") so you can compare how many visitors converted from paid search traffic versus how many people converted from organic traffic.

Organic and paid search each has its own advantages. Paid search is a short term or a seasonal strategy; it's a quick way to drive traffic from search engines. Organic search is a longer-term strategy, given the process, but the benefits of gaining organic search traffic are literally priceless. Regardless of which route you take the important part is to know how leverage the data in Google Analytics.

Measure Page Value, Not Volume

Most organizations, it seems, still put a lot of emphasis on measuring website performance in terms of volume. The focus is always on the total number of visits or pageviews. These "volume metrics" can be misleading. Yes, low traffic and low conversion numbers indicate that something is wrong with your website, but they do not tell the complete story.

Focus your efforts on attracting and converting your most valuable visitors and pages. That means identifying which visits and conversions are of high value. In other words, which visitors are the most profitable to acquire.

In Google Analytics, identifying high value is best seen in the "$ Index" value, or the average value of a page a user visited prior to landing on the goal page or completing an e-commerce transaction. The calculation for $ Index assigns the highest values to pages that are frequently viewed prior to high value conversions or transactions. In contrast, pages that aren't viewed prior to conversions or transactions will have the lowest $ Index values.

To calculate the $ Index for a page you would take the sum of the e-commerce revenue and goal value and divide by the number of unique pageviews for a given page per session prior to the conversion or transaction. Remember, unique pageviews means that a page is only counted once per visit, even if a person views the page multiple times before converting. In addition, only pageviews that precede the conversion or transaction is counted.

For example, let's say that there were four unique pageviews to your products page and two visits resulted in $100 in revenue. You also assigned a goal value of $20 to the products page. The $ Index value for your products page would be $55:

E-commerce Revenue ($200) + Total Goal Value ($20)
Number of Unique Pageviews for Products Page (4)

= $55 Index Value for Products Page

It just so happened that the two unique visitors who purchased also visited your "about us" page prior to purchasing. So, the $ Index value for your "about us" page, with a goal value of $20, would be $110 ($220 divided by two unique pageviews). Having the $ Index, for this example, is useful as a point of comparison or a ranking metric, not as a stand-alone number. It's designed to help you identify the pages on your site that are most valuable so you can put more emphasis into those pages that help convert, or pay more attention to those pages that are not assisting in the conversion process.

If you are not tracking e-commerce revenue in Google Analytics and you have not assigned values to your goals (see Rule 9, "Assign Monetary Values"), all of your $ Index values will be zero. The last time I checked, zero data added no value whatsoever, regardless of what level of reporting you are viewing. So what are you waiting for? Start calculating the value of your web pages!

Measure Referring Traffic

Have you ever considered where your visitors are coming from if they are not coming from the search engines? Probably the most overlooked area in Google Analytics is the Referrals section. Obtaining knowledge of "referring sites" is hugely beneficial especially given the advent and popularity of social media.

Truth be told, social networking is now a key channel for most online marketers. Not just because it creates an innovative marketing strategy or presents new business opportunities. Rather, social networks are such a major source of traffic for most websites that it is rivaling that of search engine traffic.

Looking at the referring traffic sources reports will reveal the website or social network your visitors came from prior to visiting your website. This can be extremely useful if you are running social media campaigns or other forms of advertising (such as banner ads) as it will help measure campaign success.

Leverage Repeat Visitors

Does a visitor make a repeat visit to your site? Like repeat customers, the volume of returning visitors you have are a more reliable indicator of your site's position, and are a vital part of your marketing strategies. Similarly, the data will reveal your site's usability, on-page popularity, relevance, quality of content, the proportion of images and their positioning, their contribution to drawing traffic, etc.

Find New Visitors

While loyal visitors are needed, you also need a consistent and regular flow of new, targeted traffic. The Internet is loaded with choices and loyalty is hard to come by. And when the loyalty factor is not working, the flow of new visitors will make up the difference in traffic volume.

Take the social media site, StumbleUpon.com. This site is known for its ability to generate massive amounts of referring traffic to a website that has been "stumbled." Therefore, if you just wrote a great article or created a website which offers creative and useful content then you'll want as many eyeballs on it as possible. Uploading to Stumble-Upon.com will give you the opportunity to generate rapid exposure, establish a reader base, and gain numerous backlinks (links from StumbleUpon.com visitors with websites).

Furthermore, if you are active on Facebook and Twitter, two of the more popular social media sites today, then you have a myriad of opportunities to place backlinks that point to your site.

Tracking referrers also gives you insights on several other factors, such as pageviews, time spent on page and site, referring sites, and bounce rate per referring site—all of which are highly useful for giving a qualitative edge to your numbers, again by leveraging the referring source to attract more traffic to your site.

According to the Google Webmaster Central Blog, "you can also understand overall trends in referral traffic volume by viewing your Google Analytics Referring Pages report directly from the links to your website page in Webmaster Tools."[7]

Just remember that analyzing referring traffic is not a one-time investment. Do not spot-check the referring traffic reports when you just launched a campaign. The result can only take you so far. Only a sustained and continual engagement with traffic referrers will yield hidden opportunities.

---

7. "Links to your site," Webmaster Tools Help, accessed [June 14, 2010], http://bit.ly/vozR2H
support.google.com/webmasters/bin/answer.py?hl=en&answer
=55281

26 Monitor Your Social Media Efforts

Marketing is no longer about the stuff that you make, but about the stories you tell.
- Seth Godin, Blogger [8]

Social media first started as a "gamey" kind of thing and was not taken very seriously by businesses. All that has changed. Social media, which is comprised of social networking (i.e. Facebook, MySpace), micro-blogging (i.e. Twitter), blogging, widgets, article submissions, and other forms of user-generated content, quickly became a platform for marketing and public relations.

Internationally known brands and products now embrace it to sell those would-be online networkers. Those very same companies started wondering how they would not only monitor social media, but also gauge the results. Unfortunately, gauging the results of social media is not as simple as looking at pageviews. It is much more involved. But fret not, Google Analytics is bridging the gap between what happens with social media and your website. For example, Google Analytics now has a report that shows you the value the Google +1 button (or Facebook "likes" and Twitter "follows") adds to your site traffic.

- **Social Engagement**—this report allows you to see site behavior for those that are "socially engaged" and are "not socially engaged" (visitors who do and don't interact socially on your website). These are visits that include clicks on +1 buttons or other social interaction buttons like Facebook "likes." Viewing this report, for example, will allow you to compare traffic

---

8. http://sethgodin.typepad.com/

behavior (time on site, pageviews, etc.) from those who +1 your page versus those who do not during a visit.

- **Social Actions**—this report lets you review the source and action (i.e. +1 clicks, follows, likes, shares, etc.) performed by a socially engaged visitor. You will be able to break down this report by looking at metrics like Unique Social Actions and Actions per Social Visit to help you analyze on-site performance by socially engaged visitors.
- **Social Pages**—this report allows you to compare the pages that have social actions. Since each social action is tied to a specific page, you can use this data to assign additional page value (see Rule 24, "Measure Page Value, Not Volume") for those pages that have a high number of social interactions, or focus on those pages that do not have a lot of social interactions.

Measuring social media in Google Analytics alone may not tell the whole story because the referrals from social media may compare unfavorably with a pay per click campaign. Besides, in social media, the action is elsewhere and may not be reflected in your website's performance. Also, social media is more about perception, engagement, and emotions, and less about numbers. This is why it is referred to as "monitoring social media" instead of "measuring social media" in Google Analytics.

Applying a filter is a good way to monitor your social media efforts (see Rule 21, "Use Filters"). This will allow you to compare visits from social media next to other mediums, such as paid search or email. Filtering allows for a quick comparison rather than having to drill down into each referrer.

There are many social media monitoring tools that tell us to what extent social media is informally providing the "touch and feel" of the product or brand you are pushing through to a larger audience. Tools like Radian6 (http://www.Radian6.com), for example, give you insights into your brand's performance on various social media channels, blogs, etc. with the help of detailed Google Analytics reports and charts that measure behavioral statistics and semantics.

Regardless of what social media tool you use, it is apparent that it needs to work in unison with Google Analytics. This means creating a specific profile in Google Analytics for your favorite or most popular social media channel (see Rule 31, "Profile Your Data"). Facebook even goes as far as allowing you to add Google Analytics to your Facebook page!

Part IV
Reading: Specific Action Steps to Help You Optimize the Data

The content in this section is intended to help you take the necessary steps toward optimizing the data found in Google Analytics. The result of the actions outlined in these chapters will help you narrow in on the data that is important to you.

- Rule 27: Link AdWords with Analytics
- Rule 28: Dial into Mobile Traffic
- Rule 29: Track Your Conversions
- Rule 30: Segment Your Audience
- Rule 31: Profile Your Data
- Rule 32: Measure e-Commerce Data
- Rule 33: Add in Event Tracking
- Rule 34: Practice the Art of Landing Pages

Link AdWords with Analytics

The relationship between Google AdWords and Google Analytics has taken another turn in the search engine soap opera. And, again, it's been for the better. Google, identifying the importance of goals and conversions in both programs, has made it possible to import goals and transactions from Google Analytics into AdWords. This is a significant step forward in the relationship.

In the past, AdWords users would have to click to and from Google Analytics to see which campaigns, ad groups, and keywords were performing on a website. Now, in typical Google fashion, they have made it as easy as 1-2-3 once you link Google AdWords and Analytics together. The result is an abundance of information. Here are a few more examples:

- Using Google Analytics data with other Google products, such as Website Optimizer
- Measuring what AdWords campaigns and keywords are converting into Google Analytics goals
- Reporting e-commerce data at the AdWords campaign and keyword level
- Comparing AdWords performance versus overall website performance
- Analyzing site performance (page views or time on site) for specific keywords
- Evaluating an AdWords campaign, ad group or keyword performance against other campaigns

Importing goals and transactions into AdWords from Google Analytics is arguably one of the biggest benefits.[9] This lets you track campaign ROI and optimize your account for conversions directly inside the AdWords interface. Previously, conversions were something you only measured in AdWords and enabling AdWords conversions required you to install separate tracking code. Now, all you need is to set up a goal in Google Analytics (see Rule 18, "Decide on your Goal Type") and then import those goals from Analytics into AdWords. Once that is done you can use these goals with AdWords features, like Conversion Optimizer, a bidding tool that helps manage campaigns against a pre-determined cost per acquisition.

If you are proficient in setting up profiles (see Rule 31, "Profile Your Data"), then you can even go as far as setting up a specific profile just for Google AdWords and/or other pay per click initiatives such as Bing. I consider setting up a specific profile for Google AdWords a best practice because it allows you to quickly understand the entire picture of visitor behavior generated from sponsored search, without having to take the extra step of segmenting out other data.

You can also link your Webmaster Tools verified site to an Analytics profile when they use the same Google account. Not only will your Analytics profiles be accessible within Webmaster Tools, but you will also be able to take advantage of new features.

Having another doorway into Google Analytics will offer a golden opportunity to look at more of your website traffic. Besides, logging more time in Google Analytics will help build your confidence level and expand your knowledge of your own website. You may also find yourself engaged in recently added mobile reports (see Rule 28, "Dial into Mobile Traffic") and social tracking (see Rule 26, "Monitor Your Social Media Efforts").

What are you waiting for? Take advantage of this ever-growing relationship now that your Google Analytics reporting is just one click away with other Google related products.

---

9. Sebastian Tonkin, "Import your Google Analytics Goals into AdWords," *Google Analytics* (blog), June 17, 2009 (6:26 p.m.), http://bit.ly/LZDEn analytics.blogspot.com/2009/06/import-your-google-analyt-ics-goals-into.html.

28

Dial into Mobile Traffic

To be happy in this world, first you need a cell phone and then you need an airplane. Then you're truly wireless.
- Ted Turner, Philanthropist, Founder, CNN

How important have mobile phones become in our daily lives? Ask yourself: Could you live one day without your mobile phone? They have changed our daily habits. The amount of money spent on mobile devices is increasing as some predict that smartphones and tablets are expected to outsell computers in 2011.[10] There are also significant increases in mobile application downloads. Text messaging is as popular as ever. In fact, most teens say they can even text message blindfolded.[11]

The globalization of mobile phones has given way to a number of opportunities in terms of content, ad format, apps, and overall interactivity of non-game applications in order to engage users. In many countries, the Internet is the mobile phone. For mobile marketers, that means opportunities. However, in order for you to better understand these opportunities and improve returns you should start with Google Analytics.

Just as you would with regular web-based traffic, you want to analyze your mobile traffic for trends. Google Analytics provides two reports in the "Mobile" section under "Visitors".

---

10. Kleiner Perkins Caufield & Byers, "Top 10 Mobile Internet Trends," *slideshare*, February 2011, http://slidesha.re/mwtBsP www.slideshare.net/kleinerper-kins/kpcb-top-10-mobile-trends-feb-2011/7.
11. "Interesting Statistics About Mobile Phones Usage," *iTech Buzz*, March 11, 2010, http://bit.ly/zNQeHQ itech-bb.com/831/obsessed-with-your-cell-phone/.

The overview report displays a breakdown of mobile traffic versus non-mobile traffic. The second mobile report, the Devices report, consists of three dimensions: Mobile Device Info, Mobile Device Branding, and Mobile Input Selector.

The Mobile Device dimension displays the actual hardware that a user used to visit your site. The cool feature with this dimension is that you can see a picture of any device by clicking on the camera icon next to any device. Mobile Device Branding provides the brand associated with the phone, such as the manufacturer (Apple) or carrier (Verizon). The Mobile Input Selector will show the primary input method for the device, such as a touch screen, click wheel, or stylus.

Given the amount of specific data Google Analytics provides, you may find traffic and revenue results to be quite interesting. For example, the iPad may be generating more revenue than the iPhone or even a PC/laptop. This is highly actionable in that you can optimize your site for the iPad and set up cross-promotional opportunities or create coupons.

You can even measure how Google AdWords or other pay per click campaigns are performing. If your results, for example, show that your mobile site is experiencing a high bounce rate and a low conversion rate, then like your web-based performance, you may want to review your landing page or ads.

There is more you can do to further analyze your mobile traffic including:

- Creating an advanced segment to align with the metrics that are relative to your business
- Setting up a separate profile (see Rule 31, "Profile your Data")
- Segmenting by medium or campaign (see Rule 30, "Segment your Audience")
- Scheduling an auto report to be sent to your email inbox daily, weekly, or monthly
- Generating a custom alert that is emailed to you when specific thresholds are met (see Rule 13, "Use Your Intelligence")

Whereas the web's ROI has proved rewarding, the possibilities in mobile have yet to be discovered. Knowing that more mobile users are surfing the web, taking part in social networks, and shopping should pique your interest. It is not too early to start taking the mobile market seriously, especially knowing that your data is just a few Google Analytics metrics away.

Track Your Conversions

There is little argument that measuring online advertising is easier and more accurate than traditional modes, such as radio and television. With the availability of web analytics, you, the advertiser, are privy to data related to your advertising efforts. For example, if you are advertising on Google, the AdWords interface will provide the number of ad views (i.e. impressions) and ad clicks, as well as a number of other metrics.

If you are not using Google Analytics goals to track conversions (see Rule 27, "Link AdWords with Analytics"), you have the AdWords conversion tracking feature as an alternative option. AdWords conversion tracking will allow you to categorize different actions by applying labels such as:

- **Purchases/Sales**—for tracking e-commerce related transactions of products or services
- **Leads**—for tracking how many users requested follow-up calls for more information
- **Signups**—for tracking subscriptions or newsletters
- **Views of a Key Page**—for tracking the number of visits to a particular page that you want visitors to view
- **Other**—for tracking a category unique to your service or business

AdWords conversion tracking involves adding tracking code to the appropriate page. Depending on your category/label, that could be the "Thank You" page after a sale or the confirmation page after a lead form is submitted.

In terms of tracking conversions, it's important to note that AdWords uses a 30-day cookie and ignores other marketing channels. In other words, Google AdWords will track a visitor's behavior on your website for a period of 30 days if they originally arrived from a sponsored search. In contrast, Google Analytics measures direct conversions regardless of any other marketing channel, such as banners or organic search. When it comes to tracking AdWords conversions, Analytics will still only credit conversions to AdWords clicks when there are no other traffic sources between the click and the conversion, such as organic search or referral from another site.

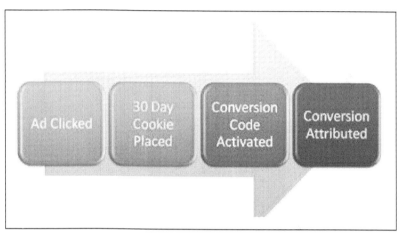

Figure 7:   The process of how AdWords conversion tracking works (source: Search Engine Journal)

Tracking conversions will dispel any notion of skepticism you may have when it comes to knowing what marketing channels are converting.

30 Segment Your Audience

When a visitor arrives at your website they could play the role of browser, casual visitor, first-time buyer, repeat customer, vendor, or wholesaler among others. Ask yourself how much more insightful it would be if you can further filter these consumer segments. Well, now you can by taking advantage of the advanced segments feature.

First, don't confuse the segmenting feature with filters. Filters parse out the data before it gets into the reports. For example, excluding internal traffic would be a reason to filter (see Rule 21, "Use Filters"). Segments, on the other hand, are specialized groups of defined customers based on their needs and wants and receive different attention and different levels of marketing. Focusing on referring traffic from social media would be a reason to use segments (see Rule 25, "Measure Referring Traffic").

Using advanced segments is an excellent way to understand what a specific audience type does on your site. A few examples:

- How frequently visitors from each segment use the search box on your site
- How many new visits versus returning visits came from each segment
- How many visits from each segment came from a specific region, state, or city

Segments can be demographic like city, region, country, or traffic sources like PPC (pay per click) campaign traffic, SEO traffic, email campaign traffic, or a segment where people clicked on a banner or landing page on the website. Comparing segments will allow you to easily compare key metrics like traffic and conversion rates from each.

For example, if you are advertising on Google AdWords then you can use the advanced segments feature to compare AdWords campaign traffic against:

- Bing or Yahoo! PPC traffic
- All site traffic
- A specific subset of AdWords traffic

Google Analytics allows you to segment data in different ways using the dimension pull-down menu. So, for example, if you want to see the traffic in your keywords report broken out by city or region then simply select the "city" or "region" option from the dimension pull-down menu. This can have a profound effect on which market you focus on for specific keywords.

Figure 8: Coleman can view visits by region for specific keywords by segmenting

Segmenting can be a powerful feature for making better decisions. It will also allow you to focus on marketing campaigns that are performing well or not so well. Bottom line: don't be in the segmented group that does not look at segments. The result will only leave you vulnerable to averages that can be misleading and prevent you from capitalizing on opportunities.

31 Profile Your Data

Google has made profiling one of the best kept secrets within Analytics. Google Analytics allows you to create multiple profiles under one account. When you first set up your Google Analytics account, you are, in effect, creating a profile under that account.

The following are some of the reasons and benefits for setting up multiple profiles under once account. You are able to:

- Control the flow of information about your website
- Separate out information about specific web properties, like your blog
- Track multiple independent web properties (i.e. http://www.domain1.com and http://www.domain2.com)
- Determine which data from your site appears in the reports
- Apply different rules and criteria for advanced analysis
- Restrict access for certain individuals
- Segment your visitors
- Set up reporting access for a variety of users
- Create custom reporting
- Track various, specific outcomes with goals
- Obtain information on internal search habits
- Establish a back-up for your main profile

Adding a profile is the easy part. The more challenging task is configuring your profile so that it is pulling in the appropriate data. There are a variety of options to make your account run more efficiently, so make sure you do the following:

- Specify the Default Page option
- Apply AdWords cost data
- Consider adding the Site Search option
- Set up at least one goal
- Filter your results to set up different properties that will affect your reports
- Add other users whom you want to have access to this profile only

Here are a few other important notes to keep in mind:

- The first profile for a property should be the "master" profile. A master profile should have no filters so that it contains ALL historical data since tracking began. Once this is set up, leave this profile alone!
- Once a profile is deleted, the profile data cannot be recovered (make a back-up of the master profile by clicking on "Add new profile" and selecting "Add a profile from an existing domain").
- Tracking for a profile begins as soon as the tracking code is installed on the website and a visitor's browser loads a page.
- When you add an additional profile from an existing website with its own profile, then the additional profile will **not** contain the historical data that you see in the first profile.

Setting up profiles rewards your effort with great customer insight. You can then leverage that insight to your advantage by developing better content or redesigning your page flow. The end result will help you market your product/service to your prospect-turned-customer.

So, in the end, for all the negativity that profiling in the "real world" receives, this is one area of your life where profiling actually does some good.

32 Measure e-Commerce Data

Money is not real. It is a conscious agreement on measuring value.
- John Ralston Saul, Canadian Author

Google Analytics not only tracks your website's data, but also your e-commerce transaction data. You get to know how, why, who, and what governs your customer's behavior to buy your product or service.

Before Google Analytics can report e-commerce activity, you must first enable e-commerce tracking on the profile settings page for your website and implement JavaScript in your shopping cart pages. Reference Google Analytics Help (http://bit.ly/zjbrd) [12] for specifics on what is involved with enabling e-commerce tracking.

After the e-commerce is enabled, you can use Google Analytics to your advantage by running specific reporting related to e-commerce. Below are two examples of the statistics Google Analytics provides.

Traffic Sources (Sorted by Most Revenue Generated)

So, where's the money coming from? From your email campaign? From SEO marketing? PPC advertising? Google Analytics tells you what is working or, more importantly, what is not working by giving you a list of the traffic sources that generate the most revenue (Figure 9).

---

12. http://bit.ly/zjbrd
    code.google.com/apis/analytics/docs/track-ing/gaTrackingEcommerce.html

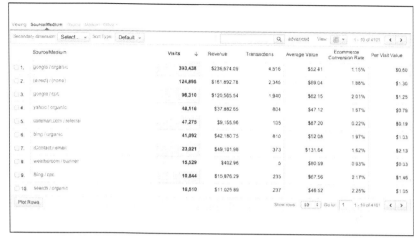

Figure 9:   Analytics report showing source and medium and the revenue each attributed for this profile

Keywords (Sorted by Most Revenue Generated)

The key to finding your website, from the customer point of view, is all in the keyword (see Rule 15, "Choose Keywords Wisely"). Google Analytics shows you what keyword phrase your visitors used to locate your website's product or service. Google Analytics then goes on to show you what keyword phrase contributed to a purchase or sale. Having historical data on what keywords converted is a big advantage that will help you convert future customers by allowing you to focus on the same keywords.

Google Analytics does make it possible for you to review the data and analyze it over time so that you are able to make better business decisions. Also, you now have a grip on your online marketing budget—by spending wisely and milking it to extract maximum dollar value.

Add in Event Tracking

There are no mistakes, no coincidences. All events are blessings given to us to learn from.
- Elisabeth Kubler-Ross, Swiss-American Psychiatrist and Author

The process of establishing website goals begins with identifying and then tracking specific events on your website. Thankfully, Google Analytics gives us the ability to track a wide variety of events, such as clicks on an image or the number of times the play button on a video is clicked.

Event tracking really depends on the specific goals and needs of your site, and what you want to track. So, you need to determine what event it is you need to track. You may want to know how many visitors are clicking on a product image, opting-in for your recurring e-newsletter, or downloading the latest e-newsletter in PDF format. Regardless, you should track some type of event because when a visitor interacts with a video player or game on your website, no pageview is generated, thus making it difficult to measure.

Here are some common tracked events that do not generate pageviews:

- Clicks on links that take the visitor to another site
- Clicks on an image or button (i.e. Facebook icon or "shop now" button)
- Banner ad clicks
- File downloads (i.e. PDF)
- Page widgets
- E-commerce activity/shopping cart purchases
- Member functions (i.e. tracking new member signups, log-ins, etc.)
- Flash, Ajax, and Javascript related content/play button on a video or audio

After you enable the tracking, it is just a matter of viewing the data in Analytics. For example, if you are tracking clicks on the "follow" Twitter icon/link on your website's home page then you can view the data by category, action, or label according to how you set up your event tracking. The "Overview" report under "Events" will show the top events and number of actions for each.

Figure 10: **The Event Tracking overview report shows the top events and number of actions for each**

Event tracking is there to help improve your overall online sales and marketing goals and allow you to have a better understanding of your visitors' actions.

34 Practice the Art of Landing Pages

People scan web pages like they would a book or magazine—from left to right, then diagonally across and down the page, and then finally back up to the top. That leaves precious seconds to grab the visitor's attention, communicate the purpose, and encourage them to act on your call to action. Sounds difficult, but it's not impossible.

A landing page is a single web page that appears in response to a visitor clicking on an advertisement. The landing page is an extension of the advertisement and is generally used with email campaigns or pay per click campaigns. Landing pages can be more effective than linking to your home page as they generally enhance the effectiveness of the advertisements.

Creating an effective landing page can be a difficult task but not an impossible one. Below are best practices you can apply.

Headline

This should be clear, direct, and an attention grabber. You want to make sure the headline is situated across the top of the page and that it tells visitors what they want to know. It should also contain a keyword to improve your PPC quality score and/or organic search efforts.

---

13. Scott Brinker, "The Top 5 Best (and Top 5 Worst) Things About Landing Pages," *MarketingProfs*, June 26, 2007, http://bit.ly/qzKGU0 www.marketingprofs.com/articles/2007/2401/the-top-5-best-and-top-5-worst-things-about-landing-pages.

Copy

Ideally, the copy on a landing page should be promotion-based with one appealing message while at the same time consistent with the brand message. Not an easy task. It should also be uncluttered with plenty of whitespace. Use bullet points to explain the benefits and include sub-heads to break up the text. Finally, write in plain English and refrain from using jargon.

Design

This is the trickiest of all the landing page elements as most people want to over emphasize design. Remember, a visitor is going to stay on a page for no more than five seconds so keep the design simple by avoiding overbearing colors (i.e. white font on a black background) and sticking with easy to read fonts. Don't be afraid to use images but use them in a way that balances out the copy, helps tell the story, sells the product, and portrays the biggest benefit.

Call to Action

I recommend placing the call to action at the top AND bottom of the page so that it is always visible (assuming not everything on the page is above the fold like it should be). Try to keep the call to action "soft." For example, use "Try it now" versus something stronger like "Buy Now". Remember, a visitor may not be ready to commit to your product or service yet, but are still interested. I also find that buttons tend to be better than text as they stand out more.

Conversions

The purpose of a landing page is to get the visitor to understand the product/service quickly and then have them act on it. The "acting" part can be accomplished by including the following:

- Phone number (preferably a 1-800 number)
- Form submission (limit the required fields)
- Value proposition (white paper, coupon, contest entry)
- Video (this is your best selling tool, it's interactive and will keep the visitor on the page longer)

Of course, all of the above is trackable. You can help the conversion effort by including a trust/security icon and a testimonial or two to provide credibility and give confidence to the visitor.

Finally, testing variations with a different message, image, layout, and/or color to find the right combination will help you improve your conversion rate.

Part V
What Now? What to Do with the Data Now That You Have It

Okay. You applied all the best practices mentioned in previous chapters. You analyzed all your marketing campaigns and pulled together all the appropriate reports. You feel good about the situation. But this is not quite where It ends. Some may argue this is just the beginning. This section will assist you in taking the next big step into applying Google Analytics beyond the numbers.

- Rule 35: Make a Decision
- Rule 36: Avoid the Dangers of Averaging
- Rule 37: Analyze Trends
- Rule 38: Use the Data to Take Action
- Rule 39: Share Your Data
- Rule 40: View In Page Analytics
- Rule 41: Know Where to Seek Help

35 Make a Decision

You have Google Analytics. Great start. You run weekly traffic reports on your website. Wonderful. Let's just say you are even crunching the numbers. Okay. But are you making the right decisions as a result? Or are you passing the buck to the so-called "experts" and allowing them to decide for you? More often than not the latter produces nothing but PowerPoint decks and not decisions. Lesson: you decide. And to decide right, you ought to know right.

First, don't get caught up in the geeky, overused jargon. Look at what Google Analytics is revealing and make a decision based what the data is telling you. If you can't quite make heads or tails of what Google Analytics is really trying to say about your website, then try telling a story out of the numbers. For example, "Our website received 100 visitors over seven days and 75 viewed more than five pages. Almost half of those visitors even purchased our product!" Creating a story out of your numbers may actually help simplify the process of trying to make a decision.

Spending as little as an hour or two a month to understand and monitor Google Analytics reports can make a big difference on the bottom line. Focus your attention to the behavior of your most important pages, such as the "contact us" page. If Google Analytics tells you visitors are exiting your home page at a high rate then it may be because the page looks more like a tax return versus a simple form fill. Evaluate the marketing campaigns and determine which ones are bringing in value and which are draining your budget. Your end goal is to make a decision and act on it.

What you decide now will pay off in real time with long-term results. Speed, however, can be a double-edged sword and one has to be careful in exercising it while making decisions. For example, your Google Analytics reports show that your marketing campaign has not yielded a single conversion in the last four hours. Does that mean you shut down the campaign? The answer is emphatically no. Avoid jumping to conclusions.

Consider various related factors, such as multiple metrics, and dig deeper into the numbers. Metrics are not proxies for performance, and they tend to cast a spell on us. When is the data interesting, and when is it actionable? This needs to be addressed carefully before making decisions on your data. But once you do, decision making will be that much easier.

In theory, applying best practices should empower you to make the decisions with the data. Remember to try to keep it as simple as possible (see Rule 5, "Keep It Simple, Silly"). If it still feels overwhelming, then seek help (see Rule 41, "Know Where to Seek Help").

Remember, web analytics is a developing language and one that is being taught to and learned by a growing population. With the rapid development of e-commerce coupled with the ever-expanding international information exchange and collaboration, the need to understand the data and make decisions becomes more and more essential to being successful on the web.

36 Avoid the Dangers of Averaging

I abhor averages. I like the individual case. A man may have six meals one day and none the next, making an average of three meals per day, but that is not a good way to live.
- Louis D. Brandeis, United States Supreme Court Justice (1916-1939)

A colleague once told me, "Metrics are not proxies for performance." In other words, avoid getting trapped in the dangers of averaging that can be easy to calculate and convey. I have heeded this advice ever since I heard it.

Averages are guilty of under-leveraging Google Analytics and do not offer fresh insights. And therein lies the problem. Yet, most of us are prone to using averages as a default metric in our analysis. But why do we love averages while number crunching? Perhaps because it is a commonly accepted feed for any metric cycle and it is an easy way to aggregate the numbers or analysis or data.

Here are two scenarios:

1. Average time spent by visitors on your site is 60 seconds. This can be on par with the previous year's results. What does this really tell you? That your site is not slipping up on its performance, popularity, and buzz value. Are you sure?
2. You have segmented the data from Google Analytics (see Rule 30, "Segment your Audience). And this is what it shows (additionally):
   a. Average time on site (all visitors): 60 seconds
   b. Visitors from social media: 35 seconds
   c. From search engines: 38 seconds
   d. Not from search engines: 75 seconds

Scenario 2 appears to offer more insight. You know the social media and search engine traffic are not staying very long and likely to be unqualified traffic. You also know where to focus your efforts so that you are able, empowered, and competent to act on this insight. Proof enough that you should not bet all your cards on averages.

When you take the averages route in Analytics, you may be led astray. In some cases, it may not have a strong bearing on your decision making arising out of such analysis. But in quite a few instances, it will perilously give you the wrong outcome.

Most marketing managers involved in various online marketing channels and campaigns will probably want to avoid averages in order to better compare the performance. Besides, your stakeholders and supervisors may not be interested in simple averages, especially when the focus is on revenue or ROI.

Google Analytics tells you that 60 percent of your website's visitors remain for zero to 10 seconds. But nearly 40 percent of your visitors stay for three to 10 minutes! These averages tell you that a majority of your site traffic is exiting very fast. Dig deeper, and with a small directed, focused dose of insight from Google Analytics, you may come to find out that your website is far from underperforming. Find out why the 40 percent of your visitors are interested. The answer will then allow you to invest, leverage, and convert the remaining disinterested 60 percent of your visitors so that you can add significant, tangible value to your site.

Analyze Trends

The key to using Google Analytics is to get important information that will help you measure results. However, reading Google Analytics data is not just absolute traffic numbers. Yes, it gives you a plethora of information, but will it allow you to make decisions or act on the data? Not necessarily.

Segmenting (see Rule 30, "Segment Your Audience") is a nice way to break up the data. But once you have the data you still need to take that next step. That is where trend analysis comes into play.

Traders on the stock market continually apply this method of analysis to predict the future movement of a stock based on past data. The idea behind trend analysis is that what has happened in the past gives you an idea of what will happen in the future.

Naturally, looking at trends is one of the most common activities upon first reviewing data. Google Analytics allows you to accomplish this with its myriad of graphs under each report, which visually display results over a period of time. When you notice a spike, you can drill down, look at the sources individually, and attribute the impact based on an individual graph. Google Analytics also has functionality built in that will allow you to click any of the data plots to quickly gain additional valuable insight. The figure below is an example of how Google Analytics helps visualize trends and comparing one time period against another.

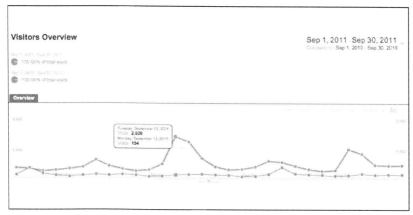

Figure 11: Identifying trends is an important part of analyzing the data

Some of the benefits of trend analysis include:

- Predetermining transactions that are most likely to be fraudulent
- Analyzing common characteristics of a consumer base
- Plotting aggregated response data over time
- Applying data for cost/benefit analysis
- Gauging customer response to changes in business
- Providing early warning indicators of probable issues
- Viewing strategies from a long-term perspective
- Safeguarding against costly errors

There is no doubt that practicing trend analysis will enable you to make analytical decisions about your business and products/services that will help you maximize revenue.

38 Use the Data to Take Action

Let's face it: every website is faced with a problem (or two). It may be related to an internal process or a customer, or both. As discussed throughout this book, Google Analytics provides you with the intelligence to understand and address the problem. Yet the data can be overwhelming, to say the least. This is especially true if you are a small business owner or new to the business of tracking website visitor behavior.

One look at Google Analytics data and you can come away feeling lost or anxious to get answers. Ah, but therein lies the key: intelligently interpreting, disseminating, and utilizing the data to arrive at conclusions and decisions. Otherwise, the information becomes useless. Here are some suggestions on how to properly use your data.

Invest in the Analysis, Not the Technology

Surround yourself with people, colleagues, friends, and the like who have analytical minds that will be able to interpret, disseminate, and manage the mounds of data. Google Analytics is sufficient for the needs of most businesses so there's no need to fret over the technology. However, you should try to avoid using two analytics programs. Experience has taught me that you get more questions than answers when dealing with multiple sets of data. Not everyone may agree but let's not forget that the primary goal and a better use of your time should be on the analysis and drawing conclusions, not on the technology.

Establish Goals

Ask yourself, "What is the desired result?" or "What am I trying to accomplish?" for a particular web page. Whether it's increasing traffic or converting customers, having clear, established goals and objectives will prevent you from performing unnecessary analysis. It will also keep your website on the right track to achieving its goals. Google Analytics allows you create up to 20 conversion goals per profile. So, there is no excuse for adding such simple goals, such as length of time on site and number of pages per visit.

Test and Tweak, Then Test Some More

Once you establish goals (see Rule 18, "Decide on your Goal Type") it is time to put the data to the test. Literally. Because what do bounce rates really mean if the data is not coupled with the testing of a message, design, layout, or call to action? The results will show how users react to changes. So, if your goal is to decrease the bounce rate, then did the test show the visitor staying on the website longer, or leaving quicker? You want to keep tweaking and testing until you reach the desired result. Without testing, how can you really make a sound, logical decision pertaining to your website? There are no excuses for not testing. Google has a free tool called "Website Optimizer" (http://www.google.com/websiteoptimizer) to achieve the desired test data you seek.

Patience Is a Virtue

It is generally not a good idea to make changes on the basis of a few days worth of data. Before you delete or pause a keyword or ad (either temporarily or permanently), ask yourself if you have "statistical significance" or statistically enough data to make a sound decision. A longer date range translates into statistical significance, which then translates into easier decisions. Shorter time frames offer misleading data, which lead to miscalculated decisions. Take into account returning customers or those who return to your website a second time at a later date to make a purchase. You may miss out on important conversion data if you react too quickly due to a small date range of data. Also, depending on your goal, it may take days or even months for many of your visitors to convert to customers. So, be patient and set a date range that will last as long as your expected sales cycle or that will return statistically significant data.

Share Your Data

Often, we are too slow to recognize how much and in what ways we can assist each other through sharing such expertise and knowledge.
- Owen Arthur, 5th Prime Minister of Barbados

Google Analytics is to help you understand how your site is performing so you can optimize it to accomplish your goals. Yet, there are lots of twists and turns to analyzing the data that Google Analytics provides. Understanding visitor behavior, trends in traffic, conversion and e-commerce reporting, and site navigation paths employed by the visitors can be a lot to ask of one person. Why not try sharing the load with others as an effective way for you, the website owner, to truly know if your website is performing at an optimal level?

Who are these "others" I refer to that might find this information useful? Well, for starters, these people are your partners, teammates, colleagues, and subordinates, not to mention the people you report to. Let's take a look at a short list of recipients of Google Analytics reporting.

You

First and foremost, make sure you are set up to receive reporting on, preferably, a weekly basis. Customizing your Google Analytics dashboard (see Rule 17, "Customize your Dashboard") is a good starter as it contains an overview of everything going on with your website. Besides, the dashboard should be tailored to meet your needs as someone who is responsible for multiple facets of the website.

Advertisers

In the context of online advertising, the advertiser has one goal in mind: maximizing ad revenue. Advertisers want to know and have a right to know how their ads are performing on your site. Rightly so, advertisers are particular about the quality of traffic they receive and how much they pay for that traffic. Therefore, sharing pertinent data would add a lot of credibility to the validity of your claims as a website owner. Keep the advertiser informed, and most importantly, provide them with a reason to spend more advertising dollars due to your website's performance.

Search Agencies

A website's worth lies in its visitors: quality and quantity. One of the ways of increasing visitor count is to ensure that the site appears in the top results in a search engine. Agencies that specialize in search engine optimization or pay per click advertising could use the reports to check the effectiveness of their efforts and make the necessary changes to correct any anomalies.

Website Designers/Developers

The aim of a website designer, in the context of a commercial website, is to make the site conversion as "user friendly" as possible. Information collected through conversion funneling reports, for example, could help the website designer pinpoint roadblocks resulting in low or no conversions caused primarily because of poor web design. Access to these reports could help a web designer continuously improve the website design to maximize conversions.

Stakeholders

The expression "There are many ways to skin a cat" in website terms really means that there are many ways to monetize a site. And those with a stake in the website want to know how it is performing monetarily. Details about which campaign or keyword performed well are not necessary at this level. The bottom line is overall site performance, and a high-level overview of e-commerce or conversions will keep your stakeholders informed.

The data that Google Analytics reports is as good as gold and should not be shared without discretion. A non-disclosure agreement might be in order before providing access to that all-important data. However, once you have multiple sets of eyeballs scanning the allotted data plots and providing feedback, then your decision to share the data may prove to be the best decision you've yet made.

View In Page Analytics

Ever notice the video surveillance camera in your neighborhood corner store? Well, Google Analytics has a feature called "In Page Analytics" that behaves in a similar fashion and is immensely valuable as it helps you understand how visitors interact and navigate your site.

In Page Analytics is a nice upgrade to the old "Site Overlay" feature that even Google will admit has not worked as well as it could have. In Page Analytics works as an overlay to a website allowing users to see data superimposed right over different products or design elements. The goal of this feature is to help you better correlate between site elements and traffic metrics, understand how your visitors interact with various pages, and allow you to make educated design and navigation choices.

In Page Analytics is good for determining the effectiveness of your content, navigation, page layout, and call to action.

Equally important, it will also help you answer which of the clicks have the highest value, conversion, transactions, and revenue. For example, when you can identify the widely used exit points of your website, you can display some of your most popular posts and other important content there. This could persuade the casual visitor to act on your desired goals. In addition, you get to know about your visitor's interest and focus.

In Page Analytics is a wonderful way for designers, marketers, analysts, and website publishers/owners in general, to get a virtual firsthand look at the nature and frequency of interaction between the visitors and all page elements on the site. In Page Analytics visualizes prospective changes with regards to layout, design, and positioning.

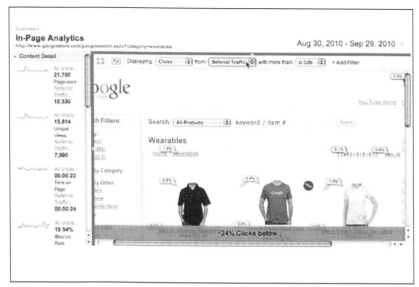

Figure 12: In Page Analytics visualizes prospective changes with regards to layout, design, and positioning. (Image Source: Google Analytics)

From my experience, people tend to be more visual, so translating raw data into something more illustrative and meaningful is valuable to both you and your visitors.

Know Where to Seek Help

You are not alone in the confusing world of interpreting Google Analytics. There are plenty of resources available online as well as offline to get answers to all your questions. Since Google Analytics does not offer direct support, I recommend the following solutions.

Google Analytics Help

The Official Google Analytics Help Center is probably the first place to start as they provide articles, tips, tutorials, and answers to frequently asked questions, as well as a forum. You can find a "Help" link in the upper right corner of any Google Analytics web page.

Books

There appear to be very few books written exclusively on Google Analytics. The books that are written on the subject are very informative. Two of the more popular and recommended readings are *Advanced Web Metrics with Google Analytics* by Brian Clifton (2008) and *Web Analytics: An Hour a Day* by Avinash Kaushik (2007). Both authors are experts in Google Analytics and have dedicated websites to Google Analytics.

Google Analytics Authorized Consultants (GAAC)

If you are looking for quick consultation, training, detailed help, or long term support with your Google Analytics account then you can turn to an authorized consultant. Companies that become Google authorized consultants have demonstrated a level of expertise and have met rigorous requirements. GAACs are rewarded with a Google Analytics Certified Partners logo so that they are more easily identifiable. Google Analytics lists all certified partners at http://www.google.com/analytics/partners.html.

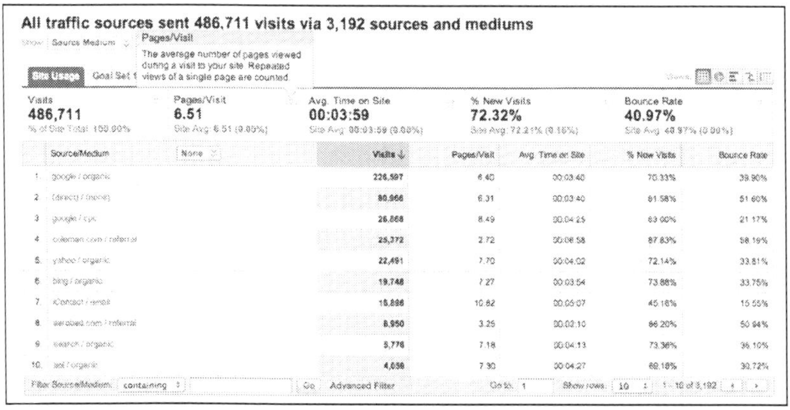

Figure 13:   Clicking on the small question mark next to each metric will provide a brief description—available in the "older" version of Analytics only

Blogs

Blogs are a great source of information. Of course, where else would you go but to the *Google Analytics* blog (http://analytics.blogspot.com)? *Occam's Razor* by Avinash Kaushik (http://www.kaushik.net/avinash/) and *Measuring Success* (http://www.advanced-web-metrics.com/blog/), the official blog for the aforementioned book, *Advanced Web Metrics with Google Analytics* by Brian Clifton, are two informative blogs on the subject of Google Analytics (see Appendix B: Resources).

Other Sources

Take part in the Google community and start a discussion that you are curious about. An example can be found at online community website, Get Satisfaction http://bit.ly/obbiTR. [14]
You can also subscribe to a feed of *Analytics Market*, a blog about Google Analytics, by going to http://feeds.feedburner.com/AnalyticsMarket.

---

14. http://bit.ly/obbiTR
   getsatisfaction.com/google/products/google_google_analytics

These Are My Rules. What Are Yours?

Congratulations! If you are reading this chapter then you clearly understand that Google Analytics is one of the most important aspects to marketing online and measuring your website's success. And you should know by now that what you can't or don't measure cannot be changed or improved. So, segmenting your audience, adding filters, enabling e-commerce, or using In Page Analytics and all the other features mentioned in this book should now be of serious interest.

Without it, there will be a lot of uncertainty, ineffectiveness, and unnecessary spending in the long run. That's how essential Google Analytics is to any business, website owner, or marketing manager. It also builds confidence. You will be able to make proactive decisions, address areas of improvement, plan ahead, and eventually meet your objectives. Overall, it will help you plan for maximum success by serving as a solid foundation for a stable website.

Analytics is impossibly hard to ignore. Everyone is talking about it, writing and jumping on the analytics bandwagon. Social media conglomerates, Facebook and Twitter, have even joined in the fun. Yet, there is even more fun to be had. What was covered in this book is merely a list of best practices and features that may be helpful to improving your website's success. My goal was to give the beginning user some basic understanding into:

- Preparing you for what you need to know about Google Analytics

- Focusing on areas of interest in order to make decisions
- Identifying specific reports so you get the information you need
- Taking specific action steps to help you optimize the data
- Knowing what to do with the data

There are a lot of features that were not even covered in this book. For example, there's the site speed report that will allow you to see how quickly your content was loaded for visitors. Or, there is the plot rows feature that allows you to mark off rows on a data table and see those segments displayed in your timeline for a quicker way into gaining insight into the performance of your traffic. The point being is that the potential for new features in Google Analytics is endless as time goes on.

According to Google, the future challenge for improving Google Analytics is not necessarily the lack of data, but the ability of tools to create actionable insights from that data. This makes me think that Google is still putting the end user at the forefront. They even seem to be aiming for a better control for multiple users to include more user levels, easier implementation, multiple dashboards, and easier sharing across users.

What the future holds remains a mystery. Though, I am optimistic and enthusiastic. For now, the rules outlined in this book showcase a number of common features that will help you prepare for online success.

If I missed anything obvious to some then I apologize in advance. However, I would invite you to share your ideas on my blog at http://rso-consulting.com/blog.php. I would also be curious to know how you have applied my rules, or others, to your advantage. So, let's keep the conversation going. What rules and best practices would you like to share?

Glossary

- **Auto tagging**—a feature in AdWords that automatically tags each of your ad destination URLs with tracking URLs in order to display the AdWords keywords and cost details in Google Analytics

- **Backlinks**—also known as external links, a backlink represents a link from an external website to your website

- **Bounce rate**—the percentage of single-page visits, or visits in which the person left your site from the entrance (landing) page

- **Click paths**— the sequence of hyperlinks one or more website visitors follow on a given site

- **Click through rate (CTR)**—calculated by dividing the number of users who clicked on an ad on a web page by the number of times the ad was delivered (impressions)

- **Clicks**—the number of clicks for which you paid and which your ads received

- **Conversion**—getting a visitor to take a desired action on your website, such as opting in to an email newsletter, purchasing a product, or downloading a white paper

- **Conversion rate (CR)**—the ratio of visitors who convert casual content views or website visits into desired actions

- **Cost per conversion**—also known as cost per lead or cost per application; cost per conversion allows you to measure how much you spent on marketing to obtain a lead, application, or conversion—it is calculated by taking the ad spend and dividing by the number of conversions

- **Direct traffic**—traffic that came to a web site via bookmarks or by directly typing in the URL

- **Funnel**—represents the path that you expect visitors to take on their way to converting to the goal

- **Hits**—a request for a file from a server—whether it is an HTML file, an image, a CSS file, or a JavaScript file—and are in no way a measure of the number of visitors that view a site

- **Impressions**—the number of times your ads were displayed

- **Key performance indicator (KPI)**—pre-determined metrics that help you define and measure progress toward organizational goals

- **Pageviews**—a request for a file that is defined as a page

- **Pay per click (PPC)**—an advertising payment model that requires the advertiser to pay when a user clicks on a sponsored advertisement appearing in the search engine results

- **Referring site**—the website that a visitor comes from

- **Regular expression**—also known as regex; provides a way for matching strings of text, such as particular characters, words, or patterns of characters

- **Return on investment (ROI)**—also known as invested capital; ROI is calculated by taking the total capital of the investment (gain minus cost of investment) and dividing by the cost of investment

- **Returning visitor**—a visitor that has made at least one previous visit to a website

- **Search engine marketing (SEM)**—includes all activities, such as SEO, PPC, or a combination of the two, that undertake to promote a product or service through search engines

- **Search engine optimization (SEO)**—activities undertaken to generate traffic to a website through the natural or organic results in a search engine

- **Unique visitor**—an individual who visits a website during a given period of time, and does not take into account, multiple visits made by the same individual

- **Visit**—a series of requests from the same uniquely identified client within a given time period often 30 minutes

B | Resources

- Google
  - *Google Analytics* blog
    http://analytics.blogspot.com
  - Google's Keyword Tool
    http://bit.ly/2c0iJz [15]
  - Help Forum
    http://bit.ly/11qr1Q [16]
  - Trends
    http://www.google.com/trends
  - URL Builder
    http://bit.ly/7dJR [17]

- *Measuring Success*, official blog for the book, *Advanced Web Metrics with Google Analytics* by Brian Clifton
  http://www.advanced-web-metrics.com/blog
- LunaMetrics, Google Analytics Certified Partner
  http://www.lunametrics.com/
- Market Terms.com,
  http://www.marketingterms.com/
- *Occam's Razor*, a blog by Avinash Kaushik
  http://www.kaushik.net/avinash
- e-nor blog
  http://www.e-nor.com/blog/

---

15. http://bit.ly/2c0iJz
    adwords.google.com/select/KeywordToolExternal
16. http://bit.ly/11qr1Q
    www.google.com/support/forum/p/Google+
    Analytics?hl=en
17. http://bit.ly/7dJR
    www.google.com/support/analytics/bin/answer.
    py?hl=en&answer=55578

About the Author

As founder of RSO Consulting, Rob Sanders brings a wealth of knowledge and experience to the world of online marketing. He and his team provide creative and technical solutions across many verticals, including healthcare, e-commerce, technology, law, and finance. RSO Consulting's core competencies include search engine marketing (pay per click management and search engine optimization), social media optimization, and web analytics consulting.

Prior to moving to San Francisco, Rob was an Interactive Project Manager chosen to lead multi-million dollar online initiatives for Ford Motor Company in Detroit, Michigan. Rob started his online career as a Web Producer for USA Today Online in 1994 before moving to Philadelphia to help launch an online media service at The Sports Network.

Rob was honorably discharged from the U.S. military after serving four years abroad. He volunteers for a number of non-profit organizations and splits his time between his homes in San Francisco and Murica, Spain, with his wife, Kathy, and two dogs, Pepe and Paco.

Write Your Own Rules

You can write your own 42 Rules book, and we can help you do it—from initial concept, to writing and editing, to publishing and marketing. If you have a great idea for a 42 Rules book, then we want to hear from you.

As you know, the books in the 42 Rules series are practical guidebooks that focus on a single topic. The books are written in an easy-to-read format that condenses the fundamental elements of the topic into 42 Rules. They use realistic examples to make their point and are fun to read.

Two Kinds of 42 Rules Books

42 Rules books are published in two formats: the single-author book and the contributed-author book. The single-author book is a traditional book written by one author. The contributed-author book (like *42 Rules for Working Moms*) is a compilation of Rules, each written by a different contributor, which support the main topic. If you want to be the sole author of a book or one of its contributors, we can help you succeed!

42 Rules Program

A lot of people would like to write a book, but only a few actually do. Finding a publisher, and distributing and marketing the book are challenges that prevent even the most ambitious of authors to ever get started.

At 42 Rules, we help you focus on and be successful in the writing of your book. Our program concentrates on the following tasks so you don't have to.

- **Publishing:** You receive expert advice and guidance from the Executive Editor, copy editors, technical editors, and cover and layout designers to help you create your book.

- **Distribution:** We distribute your book through the major book distribution channels, like Baker and Taylor and Ingram, Amazon.com, Barnes and Noble, Borders Books, etc.

- **Marketing:** 42 Rules has a full-service marketing program that includes a customized Web page for you and your book, email registrations and campaigns, blogs, webcasts, media kits and more.

Whether you are writing a single-authored book or a contributed-author book, you will receive editorial support from 42 Rules Executive Editor, Laura Lowell, author of *42 Rules of Marketing*, which was rated Top 5 in Business Humor and Top 25 in Business Marketing on Amazon.com (December 2007), and author and Executive Editor of *42 Rules for Working Moms*.

Accepting Submissions

If you want to be a successful author, we'll provide you the tools to help make it happen. Start today by answering the following questions and visit our website at http://superstarpress.com/ for more information on submitting your 42 Rules book idea.

Super Star Press is now accepting submissions for books in the 42 Rules book series. For more information, email info@superstarpress.com or call 408-257-3000.

Other Happy About Books

42 Rules for a Web Presence That Wins

This book was created for business owners, executives and managers, associations and nonprofit organizations who want to understand what it takes to create and sustain a successful web presence.

Paperback: $19.95
eBook: $14.95

PHILIPPA GAMSE, CMC
FOREWORD BY JIM BLASINGAME

42 Rules of Social Media for Small Business

This book is the modern survival guide to effective social media communications and the answer to the question, "what do I do with social media?"

Paperback: $19.95
eBook: $14.95

JENNIFER L. JACOBSON
FOREWORD BY JORY DES JARDINS

42 Rules for Successful Collaboration

The book filled with high-tech nuggets of wisdom for programmers and IT professionals. But it also has practical rules that apply to anyone who works with others.

Paperback: $19.95
eBook: $11.95

DAVID COLEMAN

I've Got A Domain Name—Now What???

JEAN BEDORD

This book is your guide to the many technology tools that can be utilized to build your web presence. Stages from registering a domain name to creating a website and utilizing your domain for email and internet marketing are outlined.

Paperback: $19.95
eBook: $14.95

Purchase these books at Happy About
http://happyabout.com/
or at other online and physical bookstores.

A Message From Super Star Press™

Thank you for your purchase of this 42 Rules Series book. It is available online at:
http://happyabout.info/42rules/applying-google-analytics.php or at other online and physical bookstores. To learn more about contributing to books in the 42 Rules series, check out
http://superstarpress.com.

Please contact us for quantity discounts at
sales@superstarpress.com.

If you want to be informed by email of upcoming books, please email
bookupdate@superstarpress.com.

15363057R00068

Printed in Great Britain
by Amazon